LOST TO WITCHCRAFT

A Story of Hecate and Aeëtes

MOLLY TULLIS

The Bibliophile Blonde LLC

For the witches and the necromancers.

A NOTE FROM THE AUTHOR

The beauty of mythology is how it transforms as it is retold, from generation to generation. *"Lost to Witchcraft"* tells the story of Hecate, a goddess who has very few stories written about her. This story includes original plot lines and mythological references that do not follow existing accounts to the letter.

"Lost to Witchcraft" is a Greek mythological retelling that contains graphic violence, swearing, and sex scenes.

Dear Reader, before you ask — I do not know where to find an Aeëtes. I couldn't find one, so I wrote one.

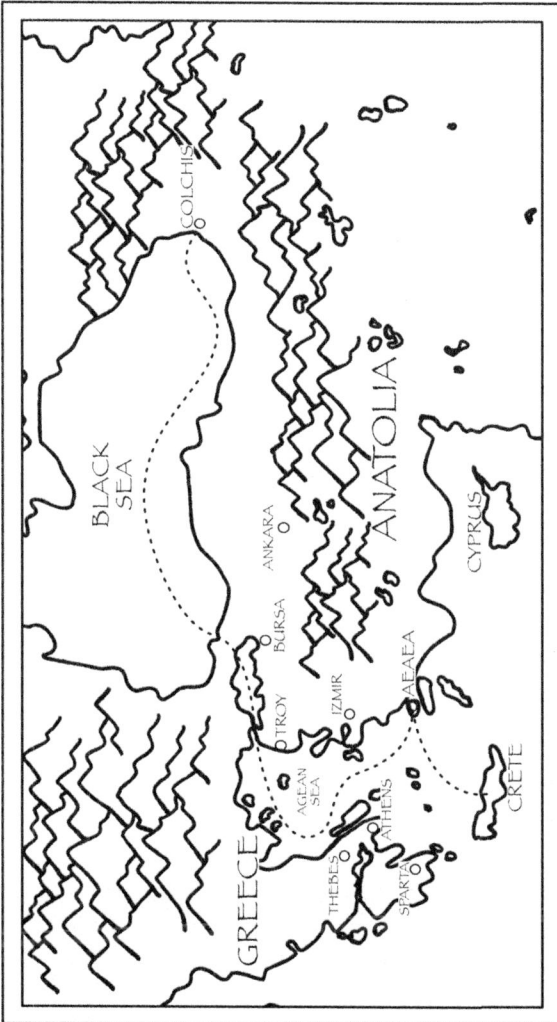

BLACK SEA

COLCHIS

ANATOLIA

ANKARA

CYPRUS

BURSA

AEAEA

TROY

IZMIR

GREECE

AGEAN SEA

CRETE

THEBES

ATHENS

SPARTA

PROLOGUE

"Sweeping tides, our love is sweeping tides. I am on the shore, I am out at sea, lost in our sweeping tides." Malialani Dullanty

S pell work was tricky. There was no magic that required the same amount of precision, no power that could be so easily miscalculated. In order to create the perfect spell, the right amount of intuition, knowledge, and raw ability were essential. When a good spell was cast, everything came together in a flash of alchemy, bending time and space to its will. That kind of magic took something from you every time, as it only worked if a part of you went with it. That precision chained you to it—everything became a composition or an equation. There were rules.

Hecate kept her heart bound in a spell all its own—where there was no space for freedom.

☩ ☩ ☩

THE WAR between gods and titans was over. The mortal world believed that Zeus reigned on Mt. Olympus, but only the immortals knew the truth. In the last great conflict with Kronos, it was Erebus and Nyx who had delivered the deciding blows. Nyx had developed the pantheon and cursed Zeus, imprisoning him on the mountain before returning to Tartarus with Erebus. The acolytes of Zeus and Hera, embarrassed by the defeat, set out in numbers to change the perception of the battle. It was through their efforts—encouraged by the king and queen of Heaven themselves—that the intervention of Nyx and Erebus had been erased from man's histories.

It happened swiftly, before even a year had passed since Kronos's defeat. The primordials were content with the limitations that they had placed on Zeus, and more importantly, that they were left alone.

The titan wars had been the first time in a hundred years that Hecate had returned to the world. She was a devoted goddess, one of the most stringent when it came to listening to the prayers of her disciples. No other god paid as close attention to their devotees as Hecate did. Ironically, this kept her in the Underworld where her power was the strongest: doling out remedies, answers, and even vengeance when needed.

Hecate had never seen Nyx as downtrodden as she had been during her feud with Erebus, which had nearly split the world in two. That had been the real threat, not the mere titans. It had put a new sense of respect and fear in Hecate's caged heart; she had heard the prayers and the cries of nearly every woman alive. The weeping voices of broken promises and abandoned lovers had crept their way into every crack in Hecate's chest, sealing it into a foundation that was as strong as stone. As Hecate watched Nyx cry out for a man—cry out for Erebus—she painted over the stones with tar, sealing her heart away for good. If even a love as ancient and elemental as

Nyx and Erebus's could go so wretchedly wrong, there was no need for her to stray there.

Not that Hecate would. Or could. Or had even been tempted to. There had been other gods, mortal men, a titan or two over the centuries...but no one who could dissuade her from her beliefs. Hecate's priestesses and devotees had come to respect that about the goddess—she was not a virgin goddess like Artemis, Athena, or Hestia, but she took no king consort, no husband, no god as her partner. This was a balance that was rare and one that was respected by everyone who took to their knees to bless her name.

There was only one problem with the caged-off architecture of Hecate's heart. The evidence by which she had built it, the plans that she had used, were incomplete. No one ever prayed to Hecate when they fell *in love* or when they woke up in the arms of a lover. No one lit incense in Hecate's honor when they realized how deeply they respected and trusted their partner. No one worshipped Hecate at the end of their days when they realized they had loved and they had not lost.

No, they prayed to Hecate when they had been wronged. They lit incense to Hecate when they had been abandoned or abused. They worshipped Hecate when they had been swindled and broken.

Even Nyx, the Goddess of darkness, didn't take up Hecate's ear after the battle when she was reunited with darkness once more. Hecate had not seen the love, adoration, the *freedom* written on Nyx's expression when she and Erebus had come together again.

No, Hecate had built a wall around her heart—a spell of the most intricate and wicked proportions—based on one half of the story. The other half was about to be told.

PART I

❧ I ❧

Hecate moved around the kitchen like it was muscle memory; she could dance her way through it with her eyes closed. There was a fire going in the hearth, and her worktable was piled high with herbs and fresh jars. A pot hung above the open flame, something warm and smoky bubbling inside it. Two dogs were spread out in front of the fireplace, dozing peacefully and unbothered by the organized chaos around them.

After the war on the titans—during which several incidents had caused her to need to rebuild her kitchen—Hecate was desperately looking for some time off. The Underworld had gotten nosier, crowded with more souls, and its keepers were busier than ever, too. She hadn't seen Nyx and Erebus since they departed Mt. Olympus although she could see their joint efforts turning the daylight to dark every night. The thought of her friend blissfully reunited with Erebus brought Hecate peace but not joy; she wouldn't ever be able to truly forget the pain that Erebus had caused Nyx. She had never seen Nyx that heartbroken before. Now, all that remained of that argument was an ongoing inability for the couple to separate from one another.

Hecate was carrying half of a heartbreak that wasn't hers and didn't know how to cleanse herself of it. The events of the past year had found a way into her soul. Her hardened heart remained, but her own inability to move past the idea of Erebus's betrayal, while Nyx had forgiven him, had put a glaring light on Hecate's bitterness.

Might as well call it what it is. Hecate pushed the thought from her mind and tossed a couple of sprigs of rosemary into a small mortar. *There must be something wrong with me. Maybe I've been doing this too long... What's missing?*

She had been working on behalf of the souls of women as long as time, staying in the Underworld where her powers were the strongest. She dropped a couple more herbs into the basin and mottled them all together, stepping closer to the fire. Hecate gracefully dropped to her knees in front of the hearth, closing her eyes and inhaling deeply. The heads of the virgin and the crone appeared on her left and right shoulders, flickering with power as it ran over her body. Her eyes started to glow as the mortar she was holding began to smoke, red sparks glimmering up and down Hecate's arms.

She resigned herself over to her power, the dogs getting up quickly and trotting to the other side of the kitchen with their tails between their legs. Hecate tossed the bowl into the pot, causing smoke to start pouring out of the top and billowing all around the floor. As soon as the ingredients mixed, the prayers of Hecate's acolytes began flooding the room. Hecate heard them all, each individual voice, and answered in kind. Sometimes that meant throwing a different concoction in the fire or sending her dogs to do her bidding. During the most difficult of times, it meant that Hecate could do nothing at all and only time would heal the wound.

"Come to us, Mother..." one voice in particular called out, and Hecate recognized it immediately as one of her priestesses in Crete.

"Come to us, Virgin..."

"Come to us, Crone..." The priestess's many devotees also cried out, making Hecate pause. She moved her fingers through the air, and the words materialized against the stones of her mantle. There was no desperation in their cries and no fear. There was only respect and longing. The prayers of her temple, bashful requests for Hecate's presence among them. It had been a long time since Hecate had left the Underworld and a very long time since someone had asked her to. Her devotees were often pleased with Hecate's dedication to her work in the Underworld; she didn't make nearly as many appearances as, say, Dionysus.

Hecate waved her hands once more, and the words faded away as she lost herself in thought. She was tired—tired of cleaning up the messes of the Underworld, tired of trying and failing to understand her own discontent. There was no reason for her sadness, for the sudden onslaught of this empty, confused feeling. It was as though she was now conscious of the ache that had been building in her for ages, something that she had never noticed before.

She was ripped from her thoughts when a loud crashing sound came from her courtyard, and Hecate sat up straighter and rolled her eyes.

"Hermes," she called out towards the door, "if you broke anything *again*, fix it before I come out there."

There was a beat of silence before Hermes stepped into the kitchen, as if he belonged there, grinning like a fool as he pushed golden curls off his forehead.

"Hecate, O Mother of manslaughter, Virgin of vengeance..." He leaned down and pressed a kiss to her forehead before she could swat him away. "Have I ever left your home in anything less than the condition I found it in?" Hermes straightened and sauntered over to the counter, hopping up on it and swinging his feet back and forth. Hecate couldn't help but shake her head at his juvenile mannerisms.

"You forgot 'Crone of chaos'," Hecate quipped, standing up

and dusting the edges of her tunic. Hermes clutched at his chest like he had been shot with an arrow.

"My memory betrays me. How could I ever forget each of your prestigious titles, dearest?" He only laughed, picking up a random leaf off the table and beginning to fidget with it.

"I'm not sure. You're the one who gave me those." Hecate deadpanned, sitting at her worktable while her eyes never left the god. "Now, what brings you here? I highly doubt that you're here for a social visit."

"Aren't we sharp-tongued today? Maybe I just wanted to come by and have a chat."

"Did you?" Hecate pushed him with a raise of her brow. She was surprised to see a flicker of severity in Hermes's eyes, something that she was not used to seeing.

"I did, actually," he said softly. There was something in his tone that Hecate couldn't quite place as she studied him. "It seems that everyone has stayed rather busy as of late. Hades running the Underworld, Nyx and Erebus…making up for lost time." Hermes grimaced at the last bit, giving a dramatic shudder at the implication.

"So? Good for them." Hecate shrugged, still unsure as to what that had to do with her or why the messenger was still sitting in her kitchen. Hermes cocked his head to the side and studied Hecate, the corner of his mouth twitching up into a small smile.

"Good for them, indeed…"

"Oh, stop it!" Hecate snapped, rolling her eyes and tossing her pestle at Hermes, who dodged it with a cackling laugh as he fell off the counter. "You did not show up here for *that.*"

"We had fun! You know, that one time." Hermes was now hiding behind her counter as his voice rang out through the kitchen. "I figured if you were the only one hanging out in the Underworld, bored…"

"Hermes," Hecate grunted, sitting up straighter and beginning to tidy up the mess on the table in front of her. She knew that there was nothing between her and Hermes. It had been one *very* drunk night at Dionysus's. There was something that twisted her heart about Hermes's offer, however, and it didn't have anything to do with him. Hecate began to drift off once more as she tried to place all of the emotions that had been warring within her for weeks. Hermes seemed to sense the shift in her mood as he poked his head up, noting that she was unarmed before he slid onto the bench across from her.

"What's going on in your head, hmm?" Hermes asked as genuinely as possible for the trickster. Hecate, against her better judgement, answered him.

"I think I need to get away for a little while." Her voice was inquisitive, questioning, as if she said it out loud to see how it would feel. Hermes said nothing, encouraging her to go on. "I've been in the Underworld a long time. Things are somewhat settled now," Hecate rolled her eyes, "and I haven't visited one of my temples in years."

Hermes nodded encouragingly. "It might be good for you to...get some air." His words felt loaded, and Hecate snapped her gaze to his.

"What is that supposed to mean?"

It was Hermes's turn to roll his eyes. "Hades may be the God of the unseen, but you don't get around like I do without picking up a thing or two."

"I know very well the kinds of things that you have picked up, and I already told you, I'm not interested."

Hermes blushed. "Hey! Now, that's not what I meant, and you know that if you gave it a chance... Never mind." He huffed and shook his head, staring at Hecate with a look of wonderment. "You figure it out for yourself. Go to the mortal world for a while. Relish in it."

"Why do I get the feeling that there's something that you're not telling me?" Hecate asked, skepticism written all over her face. Hermes held up his hands like he had been caught stealing.

"I think that you've been cooped up for too long, that's all. You've been particularly sulky ever since everyone came back from Mt. Olympus."

"I don't know what you mean," Hecate snapped quickly, grabbing another handful of dried berries and putting them in the closest empty jar. Hermes shook his head, wondering how the Goddess of women couldn't see what was in front of her. He decided that that was a conversation for another day, and presumably, a conversation that she shouldn't have with him.

"Where to first?" Hermes changed the subject.

"Crete, I think." Hecate nodded, releasing a long breath.

"Beautiful." Hermes kicked his feet out with a flourish. "Enjoy the sun, a little sand, maybe a sailor or two. See if you can't get out of this fog that you're in." He waved in Hecate's general direction while she scoffed.

"That sounds like *your* idea of a holiday, not mine."

Hermes stood, shrugging with a smile on his face a mile wide. "We'll see. Take the trip. Get out of here for a while." He started walking towards the door. "But you know, if you find that you still can't scratch whatever itch it is you've got…"

"*Goodbye*, Hermes." Hecate waved, her face unamused. Hermes ducked out of the door and disappeared down the hall, leaving only the echo of his laughter. Hecate shook her head and looked around the kitchen, her gaze finally landing on her dogs.

"You two don't think you could take care of yourselves for a while, do you?"

⚜ 2 ⚜

"**S**ister!" Lachesis's voice cut through the halls as she looked for the other Fates.

The Fates were devastatingly beautiful, a fact that they often hid from other gods. There was nothing that the Fates couldn't see, but one of the things that shone the brightest was the temper tantrums thrown by insecure immortals. It was easier for everyone if they appeared as the aged spinsters, only revealing their true selves to those who ruled the Underworld—Nyx, Erebus, and Hades. Occasionally Hecate, by extension.

Lachesis knew that they were not expecting a visit from one of those privileged few.

"Sister!" Clotho called back, sounding equally melodic.

"Did you hear—"

"Yes, I heard!"

"That it's Hera—"

"—who is coming!" Atropos chimed in at the end, all of the sisters' voices harmonizing with one another and finishing each other's sentences. Each of the Fates took a deep breath, rolling their shoulders or shaking out their wrists as they began to transform. Their shiny, waist-length white hair turned brittle and short. Clotho appeared almost entirely bald. Their backs became bent and their skin mottled and wrinkled, as if their flesh was two sizes too small and stretched over bones. Even their clothing lost its luster, the gleaming gowns turning into threadbare tunics.

It was the last stage of the transition that each of the Fates hated. Their teeth cracked and browned, and their eyes shriveled up and disappeared until only one remained.

"I've got it—"

"You got it—"

"She got it—"

Each of the sisters teased one another as Lachesis blinked twice, having kept the one good eye between them. The Fates moved quickly into the receiving hall, sensing Hera's presence as she approached the large estate. The sisters didn't live in a cave or in the deepest pit of hell, but rather in a large home of stone that was settled in between Elysium and Tartarus.

The Fates filed into a straight line facing the door as soon as it swung open, in perfect time. Their faces were devoid of any expression as they stared forward, Clotho and Atropos's empty faces unmoving. Lachesis didn't make a sound as the eye settled on the queen of the gods.

Hera stormed forward, a gust of wind trailing at her feet. She was hardly the picture of regality that she so often portrayed. Her brow was furrowed, and her lip was upturned in a grimace. A braid whipped down her back, as if it had a mind of its own, her eyes blazing in anger and frustration. Hera was increasingly frustrated with the fallouts of the Titanomachy and had come to the Fates with one question— her own honor be damned.

"What do I have to do to win back the favor of the gods?" Hera's voice sounded like a pit viper, cutting and venomous. She walked as close to the Fates as she dared, throwing a finger in Lachesis's face. The sisters showed no reaction, but their thoughts began flying wildly.

"How dare she —"

"—threaten us —"

"—in our own home —"

"Answer me!" Hera snapped again, breaking through the Fate's thoughts. It was Clotho who responded, making a withered, ancient sound that still echoed through the hall. "You make demands of those who do not take them, Hera." It was a warning. If Hera noticed, she ignored it. Her expression contorted once more, and the sisters studied the torn edges around her garments. She looked like a half-burnt candle, fuming with rage and melted, without the fire power to relight herself. The embers of her fury flickered like wicks in her eyes. It would have been a dangerous sight to anyone other than the Fates, a trick that likely always got Hera far outside of the Underworld.

"What must happen for me to win back the favor of the gods?" she hissed, taking one step back and surveying the three sisters.

"You have the—"

"You have the—"

"—favor of the gods."

Hera rolled her eyes, as if she was about to explain something again to an inattentive audience. "I have the favor of *men.* Zeus is believed to be king of the gods and I, his queen. But we have no respect. The other gods know what happened. They remember Nyx and Erebus." Hera spat out their names like they were bitter, her hands finding her hips as she stared the sisters down.

"Do you think —"

"I was thinking —"

"I thought it, too." The sister's inaudible conversation continued, Hera growing bored and beginning to look around the hall.

"Do you have an answer for me or not?" She readjusted a bracelet on her wrist and examined her nails in a series of actions that portrayed the illusion of aloofness while her anger still bubbled just under the surface. It was Atropos who broke the silence, a grin covering her aged face.

"We have an answer for you, queen of the gods. What will you do to hear it?"

"I'll give you anything." Hera's face contorted and filled with desperation as she dropped down to her knees, her fury evaporating. She was weak-minded and easy to manipulate. The sisters enjoyed toying with her as the great *queen of the gods* had no idea that she was the mouse. Hera's face was suddenly open and pleading, her hands going from her hips to wrap around her waist, as if she wanted to hold herself together.

"You will take this answer from us and never seek us again." Atropos grinned and Lachesis followed suit. She reached up a long, yellow nail, and Hera bit back a scream as she plucked out her eye, handing it rather unceremoniously to Clotho. The sister smirked, unable to hide her amusement at Hera's nauseated expression, and popped it in while blinking rapidly. The sisters looked at one another, unimpeded by the fact that only one of them had an eye, and turned back to face Hera.

"Yes!" Hera cried.

The wind picked up in the hall, beginning to spin around in a vortex that pulled Hera's hair from her braid and forced her down on the ground. She covered her head with her hands and felt the cool sting of the mosaicked floor cutting into her cheek, leaving the barest flecks of golden ichor on the stones. The sisters started to levitate, coming a few feet off the ground as their voices drowned out the sound of the hollowing wind.

"Listen now, Hera, Wife of Zeus,
If it is the god's respect that you seek,
The best place to find it is in a sheep.
One that is a god, either young or old,
A single, sacrificial ram—made of gold."

Hera tried to look up, blinking against the vortex as she

propped herself on one hand. The sisters remained in the air, staring straight ahead and ignoring her entirely. Hera ran over their words in her mind, repeating them to herself, trying to understand what they meant.

"That's all I have to do?" she shouted up at the spectral forms of the sisters, and her eyes widened in panic as they began to fade.

"Stop!" Hera screamed out again, coming back up to her knees and raising her hands above her head, as if she could catch them. "Answer me. What good is this riddle? Is that all I have to do?"

The Fates's forms stopped fading for a moment, and the wind died down. Hera stood, wobbling, her movements hesitant as if she was standing on a ship. She thought that she might get an answer, and her heart leapt. When the Fates opened their mouths again, one voice ringing out, it sent shivers down Hera's spine. Their empty faces began shining brighter than the sun, causing Hera to fall back to the floor and shield her eyes with her hands.

"Listen now, Hera, Wife of Zeus,
If it is the god's respect that you seek,
The best place to find it is in a sheep.
One that is a god, either young or old,
A single, sacrificial ram—made of gold."

They repeated the same prophecy, the same answer, with not even a change in inflection to decipher any additional meaning. The wind picked up once more, spinning around the room, and nearly ripping the fabric from Hera's body—until it suddenly stopped. The noise died down, and the atmosphere became still. Hera was afraid to move for a few moments, the queen of the gods reduced to a shriveling and shivering mess on the floor. After she realized that she was alone in the hall, Hera slowly stood up.

The Fates were gone. The hall was empty, and there was not a single thing misplaced. There were still sticks of incense that were burning in one corner, remarkably not blown out by the wind. Hera looked around and felt her face burning in shame, grateful that no one else had been around to witness her outburst and fear.

Hera spent a few minutes smoothing out her peplos, readjusting the drape across her shoulder, and re-pinning a garish pin. She tied her braid and adjusted her sandals before turning on her heel and walking quickly out of the Fates' estate. There was a heaviness in the air around her, but she was careful to walk slowly, with her shoulders tossed back and her head held high. There would be nothing out of place in her appearance to betray the fear that had been painted across her face mere moments earlier.

The front doors swung open for her, and she took a step back in surprise before regaining her false confidence and striding away. Hera held her composure until the estate was out of sight, and then she dissolved on the wind. Hera whisked up and out of the Underworld as quickly as she could, hurrying her way back to Mt. Olympus as her thoughts ran rampant.

A golden ram? A god? Is that all it would take? I have to sacrifice a golden ram…but where… I've never even heard of such a thing.

Hera was consumed as she wound her way up the mountainside, embracing the warm feeling of the sunlight. She was never comfortable in the Underworld. Everything about it made her skin crawl. However, only the Fates could answer her question and possibly help her find a salve for the sting of defeat that Nyx and Erebus had left behind. It sounded easy enough…if all she had to do was sacrifice a golden ram.

But where do they expect me to find one?

Hera landed at the top of Mt. Olympus, walking towards her husband's throne room as a deadly plan took shape in her mind. It was easy to find a god. The earth was full of them now… and if she didn't know where to find a golden ram—she could always make one.

Aeëtes was hot. While the sun was warm in Colchis, it was nothing compared to the heat of the beaches of Heraklion. This was what he had been craving—his feet in the sand, hair wild with wind and sea salt, and eyes squinted against the blistering rays of the sun. He supposed, as Helios's son, it was the most natural thing in the world to seek its warmth. So Aeëtes always returned to the shores of Heraklion, nestled in Crete, as soon as he could get away from the stilted court of Colchis. He blamed it on his parentage, telling himself that he was born with a wanderlust for the sun and sea —the only thing given to him directly by his parents, Helios, the sun God, and an oceanid, whose name Aeëtes never learned.

Once Aeëtes had been born, he had been given to the king and queen of Colchis to raise as their own. As a boon for taking in a demigod, the royal couple were granted immortality as well, something they now shared with Aeëtes. As soon as he was old enough to pick up a sword, however, he was sent to Crete to be raised amongst their court. It was a standard practice of the time, an easy way for young princes to start making friends and alliances, maybe even find a fiancée. But sending

Aeëtes to the island had been his adoptive parents' greatest mistake—for there he fell in love with the ocean, with the sun, and something in him was set ablaze.

He had no interest in court politics or defensive tactics. Aeëtes, though he was forced to learn how to be proficient with a weapon, failed miserably at combat. He had no heart for it. Whenever he was put to the test, he would simply run his opponent ragged with simple defensive maneuvers, never once striking on the offensive.

Aeëtes had lost track of how old he was. He didn't look any older than a man in his thirties, but he knew he was at least eighty years old by mortal standards. He had no particular gifts, no great strength, power, or healing abilities of any kind. He had no god form and could not breach Mt. Olympus.

Aeëtes was simply immortal, with a love for the water and a desire to spend all his countless days exploring every known corner of the world. His adoptive parents were growing tired of his antics and refusal to return home to Colchis. Aeëtes dug his heels further into the sand as he thought about his father's parting words to him.

"Everyone dies, Aeëtes—even immortals. It's time you seriously considered taking the throne. I don't care how long I live. I won't wait forever."

It had become clear on his last visit home that his patience had run out. The king and queen now threatened to call on Helios if Aeëtes didn't return home within a year to take the throne.

Now it was time to do what Helios had always done best… It was time to run away. The ability to run away from responsibility was a privilege almost exclusively limited to immortals and crown princes. Aeëtes was lucky enough to be both.

So there he sat, fresh off the boat from Colchis and nearly buried in the sand on the beaches of Heraklion. He had no idea where he was going to go next, and that didn't bother him the slightest. There was an ache in him, a longing, to be a part of something bigger and grander than himself. Not as the king of a country, no, but something that belonged to the rest of the world. It was out there for him, Aeëtes knew it, waiting beyond the horizon and nestled somewhere where the sun met the water—where his mother and father stayed tangled in a permanent embrace. That was where Aeëtes was headed.

He stood up, not bothering to dust the sand off his chiton and slowly began the walk back to the center of the city. He was too far away from the palace to go back, and he didn't want to spend the night cooped up in the trappings of royalty. It was too real, too symbolic of the entrapment that he faced. No, tonight, Aeëtes would sleep under the stars. He made his way through the streets, which had finally started to clear out as the sun began to set behind them. He was always more comfortable in the chaos, amidst wagons and stalls and the noise of the marketplace, even when it had quieted down for the evening. It brought him a sense of obscurity that he could never have when he was in the palace, in Colchis or Crete, where he was always the *Crown Prince Aeëtes*.

Even without the title, he could never completely blend in. He was a head taller than most men, with a wide chest and dark skin from a life mainly spent on boats. Aeëtes never bothered to shave, except to occasionally trim his beard when it got too unruly, and always walked around barefoot. He looked slightly wild when he stood next to mortal men like there was something undomesticated about him.

He loved his adoptive parents, and he cared deeply for those who had raised him, but nothing would keep him tethered—no force on earth could. Aeëtes shook his head clear of his melancholy as he approached a two-story stone house, just past the market.

"Pelias!" Aeëtes's face lit up in a smile, clapping his hands together as he called out to his friend. Pelias was a merchant and a sailor, who had frequently crewed the boats that took Aeëtes home to Colchis. Once they had been headed into a storm, and Pelias responded by breaking out the wine and declaring that he would never die sober. Aeëtes had liked him instantly.

"Your *Highness*," Pelias stepped out from the doorway, wiping his hands on a cloth and matching Aeëtes's infectious grin. He knew how much Aeëtes hated it when he referred to him with royal titles.

"Knock it off." Aeëtes rolled his eyes, walking up to Pelias and embracing him. "Or I'll finally seal the deal with your sister."

"Ha! You've never met my sister."

"I don't need to. I could win her over, and you know it." Aeëtes winked playfully, stepping inside of the dwelling and immediately settling down at the kitchen table. It was only partially a lie.

Aeëtes was charming—and he knew it. While immortality may have been his only gift from the gods, genetic material from Helios and an oceanid wasn't exactly common. Aeëtes ran a hand through thick, dark hair, parts of it bleached by the sun, and pulled out the cord that secured it. It fell to his shoulders in permanently salt-kissed waves, complemented by the wildness in his green eyes. As he leaned back and helped himself to a glass of wine on the table, Pelias shook his head in mock disbelief.

He was used to Aeëtes and his general familiarity everywhere he went and made no comment as he returned to the dinner that he had been preparing. Pelias, living the life of a sailor, had never married and lived alone, creating the perfect place for Aeëtes to retreat to.

"Are you staying the night then, I presume?" Pelias prepared a second plate and placed it rather unceremoniously in front of Aeëtes. He dug into the hot food and avoided his friend's question for a few moments. Pelias didn't push, knowing that Aeëtes was a free spirit. It was better to give him space. If he felt forced into anything, he'd resist, but once he decided that he wanted something, there was no stopping him. After Aeëtes had sated his initial hunger, he leaned back once more, sighing deeply. He nodded slowly as his head tilted to look out the window.

"If you don't mind." Pelias nearly startled, having forgotten his initial question in the silence. He nodded. "The usual place?"

Aeëtes stood, chewing on his lip. "Yeah, that would be best."

"It's easier than making up a space for you inside." Pelias sounded nonchalant, almost uncaring, but Aeëtes knew that there was no one else that he trusted more. Aeëtes said nothing in response and slipped away, ducking out of the doorway and almost disappearing up the stone steps before Pelias called out to him.

"Aeëtes." The crown prince poked his head back into the kitchen, and Pelias studied him. "What of the king of Colchis's mandate?" A grin covered Aeëtes's face, and Pelias's heart sank like a stone. He had hoped to see that his friend would take this somewhat seriously, but it looked like he had hoped for too much.

"Oh, you know Father," Aeëtes shrugged, turning on his heel and jogging up the steps before Pelias could continue the conversation. His response echoed down the stairs. "He would have to catch me first!"

Oh, Aeëtes, Pelias sighed. *If you don't find somewhere to land, the world will anchor you the first place it can.* He went back to his tasks, as if it was perfectly normal to have the crown prince of Colchis crashing at his house.

As soon as Aeëtes stepped out onto the roof, he felt like he could breathe again. There was a thatched awning and several worn cushions underneath it, but most importantly, it was open to the sky and sea. Aeëtes stepped as close as he dared to the edge, taking in a deep breath and extending his arms out in a stretch. He smelled the salt on the night breeze and watched as the torches at the docks bobbed on the water. The moon was bright that night, casting light on the rippling sea that would make the sun envious. *Do you ever get jealous of the moon, Father?* Aeëtes took a few steps back and settled down, getting comfortable under the stars. *I think it would be perfectly natural if you did. I certainly wouldn't judge you for it.* Aeëtes found himself staring up at the constellations, barely visible with such a bright sky. This was where he was most at peace, not in a palace or on a gilded throne. The lines around his face softened as he felt the tension of the past few weeks fade away, the sounds of the ocean nearly lulling him to sleep.

Aeëtes blinked his eyes open a few more times, unable to look away from the full moon. *Oh, Selene. If the sun gets too angry with me, you'll speak to him...won't you?*

He was asleep before he knew if his prayers were answered.

✝ ✝ ✝

HERA CURSED THE MOON. She moved through the night sky, unencumbered, but grew frustrated with the night that was as bright as day. There was no time to waste. If the Fates demanded a golden ram be sacrificed to win back her favor, then a golden ram they would get. All she needed to do was to find a god and curse him then lead him to her acolytes to finish the job properly.

She moved over all of Greece, beginning to send waves of power out through the ether to find flickers of divinity. Her power would respond to anyone who was immortal. As soon as her influence spread out into the night sky, Hera recoiled with a sharp hiss, as if she had been burned.

"*Nyx,*" Hera growled, futilely attempting to toss her strength around in the dark heavens, but it wasn't her territory. "*Stay out of this.*"

"*I'd love to take credit.*" Nyx's voice came flooding into Hera's mind. "*But that was Hecate. It's her full moon tonight.*"

To anyone watching from the mortal realm, it looked like two storm fronts rolling into one another in the sky—the odd flash of lightning or shooting star punctuating the clouds.

"*I don't care how you leeches get on —*" Hera nearly yelped, her own power shooting traitorously up her arms and threatening to strangle her. She tried to choke out a scream but found herself spitting black smoke and sparks.

"*That was me.*" Nyx's voice lowered. "*Keep your ire on me, Hera, and understand the respect every woman owes Hecate. Even you.*"

"*You can't —*"

There was a heavy roll of thunder that caused even the earth to shake beneath it. If Hera had been in a corporeal form, she would've fallen over.

"*She can, and she will,*" Erebus's voice boomed through the night sky, causing the moonlight to briefly go out.

"*You creatures of the Underworld.*" Hera's voice oozed with a slick, patronizing tone. "*One day you'll have to answer for...*"

"*Out of my skies, Hera.*" Nyx's command was swift and her power absolute. Hera fell out of the sky like she had been dropped. She quickly regained her composure and landed on her own two feet, dropping into her human body just as she hit the ground. She only took a moment to gather her senses as she looked around, taking in her surroundings. She was standing on a beach, not too far away from a harbor and a market. Hera readjusted her peplos, muttering to herself.

"Crete, of all places." She took a few steps and stopped, pausing to re-tie her hair into a braid. "Well, let's give this a try."

Now that she was out of the sky, Hera sent her power rippling over the ground, waiting for it to reveal the closest immortal. She relaxed as she felt it working, moving through houses and over sleeping mortals. It didn't take long for her power to come bounding back to her like a lost dog, clueing her in to the location of a god—asleep nearby on an open roof.

"Terribly sorry." Hera's face lit up with a wicked grin as she began whispering, walking towards the unsuspecting deity. "But whoever you are… your time is up."

❦ 4 ❧

In the end, Hecate had slipped away from the Underworld without much fanfare. There had been no reason to alarm anyone, and it was not like the gods couldn't find one another when they wanted to. Hecate simply released her dogs, sealed up her kitchen with a wave of her hand, and set wards around her courtyard to prevent any of Hermes's crash landings. It felt strange, walking out of the Underworld. She found herself fighting the urge to keep looking back over her shoulder, as if she was doing something illicit.

Maybe I have been in the Underworld for too long. Hecate shook her head, as if she could physically rid herself of her misplaced feeling, slipping into the mortal realm easily. It took her a few seconds to get used to the sunlight, which reflected off the sea like polished glass.

Hecate had materialized a few miles away from the edge of Heraklion, wanting to give herself some space to get used to the world as she walked into the busy town. The road there was well-maintained, but luckily not busy, and Hecate found herself inexplicably relaxing with each step that she took. She never would have dreamed that there would be comforts to be found outside of her precious Underworld, but something about the air loosened up the tightness in her chest.

A couple of travelers approached her on a cart, loaded with woven baskets, which they clearly intended to sell in Heraklion. Hecate tensed as she felt their presence coming up behind her, able to sense that it was two men—and they were already leering. Her magic began flickering between her fingers on instinct, nearly *begging* the strangers to speak to her. Hecate knew that her mortal form was pleasing. She hadn't been to the human world in a long time, but she hadn't received any complaints from the few lovers she had once entertained. She had long, auburn hair that now looked much redder in the bright sun, and a figure like an amphora swathed in the purple folds of her himation.

The cart caught up to her quickly, sending up a cloud of dirt as it came to an abrupt stop. Hecate had to cover her mouth to keep from inhaling it too deeply, waving her other hand around her face to clear her vision. She blinked rapidly as the dust cleared, the two men nearly falling off the bench to grin at her.

"Do you want a ride to town?" one of them asked, his eyes nearly bugging out of his head as the left corner of his mouth tilted up into a vile smirk. Hecate felt her blood beginning to boil, thrumming underneath her skin. She didn't need to read their minds to know what they were thinking about; it was written unabashedly on their faces. Hecate knew that she had the ability to take them both on, but mortal women didn't.

Men never think about how carefree their lives are. Hecate's thoughts morphed into something poisonous, something slithering in vengeance.

"Do you speak?" the second man asked, almost angrily, as if he was insulted that Hecate hadn't tripped over herself to answer them fast enough. Hecate tampered her magic for just a moment, taking one step forward and plastering a coquettish smile on her face.

The countenance of the two merchants changed immediately, one of them standing and nearly tripping over his friend to jump down from the cart. He walked towards Hecate and stopped all too close to her, looking at her like he was appraising goods.

"Did you want that ride then?" His smile was full of charm, but there was something dangerous in his eyes, something that let Hecate know that he acted without fear of retribution. It was a look that said, 'Play nice, and we'll pretend like I wouldn't be violent otherwise.' The expression was one that Hecate had seen on the faces of men since the dawn of time, one that she had seen through the eyes of all her acolytes. It didn't matter their age, their looks, their marital status...every woman knew that look.

It took all of Hecate's strength to keep her anger bottled and keep smiling. She tilted her head to one side and batted her eyelashes, an unoriginal, but well-practiced maneuver that tripped men up every time.

"A ride?" Hecate repeated it back to him. She had learned a long time ago that the stupider you acted, the more these types of men would respond.

"You aren't a quick one, are you?" The man laughed, flashing a look back to his companion. Something exchanged between them that they likely thought Hecate wouldn't understand, but she did. They were finalizing amongst themselves how far they thought they could go with an unaccompanied, apparently dim-witted woman. He looked back to Hecate. "Yes, a ride. You look like a pot of honey, gorgeous. Something like you shouldn't be walking to town all by yourself."

Something. Not someone. Hecate's patience pulled impossibly tighter. The second man spoke up, seemingly agitated once more.

"Come on, we've got to get to town before midday. Just grab her—" Hecate heard him, and her patience snapped. She whipped her gaze to the man sitting in the cart, raising one hand in the air. Immediately, dark, red sparks began flickering all over her skin. She tightened her fingers, and the man began clawing at his own throat, as if he was being choked, sputtering as he tried to breathe. Power was flying off Hecate in waves, sending ripples through the dirt road like it was the surface of water. Her eyes flickered purple and red, her full lips turned up in a sneer.

"Whoa, what the hell?" The man standing next to her raised his hands up in surprise, taking a few steps back. His eyes got wide as he tried to comprehend what he was seeing. "Stop that!"

He made a lunge for Hecate, as if he could throw her off balance, but she threw her other hand up in his direction. As soon as she did, he fell to his knees and began fighting for air like his companion.

"How many women have you accosted on your travels?" Hecate spit the words out, her gaze snapping back and forth between the two offenders. They writhed in the dirt and on the cart's bench. The horses were shockingly calm, as if they knew Hecate's magic would bring them no harm. The men did not answer.

"How many?" she growled the words, twisting her wrists and sending both of the men to their knees. The one in the cart tumbled off the bench, landing face down in the dirt. The second tried to answer but couldn't, only mottled attempts at words sputtering out. Hecate hissed.

"Too many, I'm sure." She dropped her hands and the men gasped, sucking air into their lungs and shakily attempting to stand. Hecate shook her head, undulating her fingers and they fell back to the dirt. Her lips barely moved, but her power rippled through the atmosphere. It circled the men's bodies and wrapped around them like ropes, tightening slowly in dark, red bands. Their expressions were frozen in looks of horror as they realized that they couldn't move.

"If you're so insistent that women should not walk into town, then you shouldn't walk either."

Hecate's words were final as she waved a hand through the air, her magic dissolving over the men's bodies. When the clouds of dirt and red power faded, there were only two snakes in their wake. Hecate smiled, a deep sense of satisfaction spreading over her as she picked up the edge of her himation and stepped over them.

She walked over and ran her hands over the horses, slowly removing them of their trappings and letting them run off. They would either go wild or find their way back home, both of which were likely preferable to spending another day as beasts of burden for such wretched men. Hecate turned around and saw the snakes sliding off the road and into the grass, hissing at one another, as if they were arguing whose fault it was.

I can't say that I've missed the mortal world too terribly, but I'll be damned if I don't get to have a little bit of fun. Hecate picked up her pace and began walking once more towards Heraklion, the sun approaching midday. While there was always some joy in vengeance the way that she executed it, that slow burning hole in her chest was still there. Witchcraft and healing was something that Hecate was known for, and she realized as she approached the city that she was embarrassed. There was a pain—her pain, a woman's pain—that she couldn't heal. She couldn't even diagnose it.

✛ ✛ ✛

ONCE HECATE WAS in the city, it was a short walk to find her temple. She had seen it in her mind's eye many times before but had never visited personally. The streets got quieter the more she wove inward, ducking under archways and slipping behind corners. The doorway cried out to Hecate like a song, echoing remnants of her power back to her. When she finally landed on the same block, it was peaceful, but still busy. Unlike some of her Underworld counterparts, like Nyx, Hecate was popular in the pantheon, and her temples were well known.

The front door to the temple was open, and Hecate could smell cinnamon incense and hear a soft lyre coming from within. She took a few cautious steps inside, pausing at the doorframe as a spark of insecurity ran through her. It was rare, for her, to be concerned about the affections of others, but these were women, *her* women, and their support mattered. Their kinship mattered.

Hecate was only there for a moment until a priestess walked by, freezing on the spot and dropping a hood from her head. Her eyes got wide as she took in Hecate's form, her head beginning to shake back and forth in a gentle shock.

"Goddess!" she gasped, still unable to move. Hecate could only offer up a bashful smile, nodding her head and finally stepping all the way into the temple. The woman's exclamation got the attention of a few others, and within seconds, there was a small gathering in the front atrium. There were six women who lived at the temple, and all of them were now staring, their expressions ranging from shock to smiles as they ran out.

"Goddess!" another one repeated.

"Hecate!" a younger woman called her by her name, and one of the matrons threw her a disapproving look. Hecate caught it and shook her head.

"Let there be no formality between us," Hecate smiled and took another step forward, grabbing the hands of the young priestess. "What is your name, child?"

"Thekla." The girl could be no older than nineteen and barely able to contain her own excitement. Hecate pulled her into a hug, her arms tightening around the woman as she buried her head in Hecate's shoulder and cried. Every time someone touched Hecate, she could hear their prayers, each and every one, past, present, and future, ringing out in her mind. She could hear the struggles and their praises, and it helped to get a picture of the women who stood in front of her. As Thekla tossed her arms around Hecate, she heard the cries of a broken-hearted woman, still so young, who had been lied to. Hecate kissed the woman's brow and eased her mental anguish. They all lost track of time as Hecate went to each woman, taking their name and bringing them into her embrace. She began to cry, overwhelmed with the look of love and support in their eyes. There was something in the air that was rare, impossible to capture, and more valuable than any riches in the moral or immortal realm—women, without pretense, recognizing the warmth in each other and giving into the support. Sisterhood.

Hecate smiled as the women led her further into the temple, proud and excited to show the goddess her sacred space. *This.* Hecate's heart was warm, and her cheeks hurt from smiling. *This is all I could ever need.*

But she didn't think about what she might want.

Hecate had informed the priestesses that she would be spending some time with them at the temple. The women were overjoyed at the announcement, almost to the point of tears, and immediately began preparing space for her to stay. Hecate insisted that they not put themselves out too terribly, that it wasn't worth the trouble, but the women only scoffed.

"Goddess, you are in *your* temple. The very point is that it is a welcoming for you."

Hecate could only chuckle and acquiesce, allowing the women to make up one of the bedrooms in the dormitories attached. The rest of the night passed easily, with all of the women gathered around the hearth and enjoying each other's company until well into the morning. Hecate had flicked her wrist and supplied the wine and bread, regaling the group with stories of Dionysus. It was nearly dawn by the time that Hecate retired, making the priestesses promise that they would not wake up early for their prayers.

"You have made me happier than I have been in years, sisters," Hecate had smiled. "Respectfully, I will not even hear your prayers if you do them terribly early tomorrow."

The women laughed and everyone departed, filing off to their rooms and chambers to sleep off the wine.

The room that they had given to Hecate was beautifully put together, but sleep was far off for her. She didn't need sleep like the acolytes did and had mainly excused herself for their benefit. It was one of the happiest evenings that Hecate had had in years, but she wasn't entirely at peace. There was still an uneasy feeling in her chest that she hoped would settle. *Maybe I'm being unfair...* Hecate's thoughts were gentle. *I've hardly been away from the Underworld for a day.*

The sun was rising over the horizon, and Hecate absent-mindedly wiggled her fingers, red sparks of power dancing between them. She made up her mind and slid out, quietly excusing herself from the temple and slipping back into the city streets. Even at dawn, it was busy as merchants and shoppers and craftsmen started to take advantage of the light. Hecate dampened some of her appearance, ensuring that her power was quieted enough that it wouldn't startle passersby. Hecate found herself on her way to the sea, hoping to watch the sun rise over the water.

As she passed through the alleys and went past the various market stalls being set up for the day, there was a wave of power that pulled Hecate from her mindless walk. It tasted bitter in her mouth, something acrid, something that was full of hatred but wrapped in a sunny smile.

Hera.

Hecate immediately felt power running up and down her arms, and she dispelled it quickly. She whipped her head toward the place where the power was coming from and saw a glimmer of distorted light down a side street. There was a fleeting glance of sandaled feet, and Hecate was off. Whatever was happening, she had an innate distrust of Hera, and no one in the Underworld forgot the massacre she had ordered on Nyx's temples hundreds of years ago. If Hera was sniffing around the mortal realm again with her acolytes, then there was a reason to be concerned. Hecate's protective instincts flared up in her chest when she thought of the women who were sleeping back in her temple, the women who trusted her. Her plans abandoned, Hecate moved swiftly down the alley to catch up with the trail of power.

As soon as she was out of sight from the main road, she muttered a quiet incantation under her breath and disappeared completely. Hecate's goddess form was different from some of the other immortals; most of the time, she was contained in a body that could pass for mortal. But Hecate was the Goddess of ghosts and of necromancy. When she felt like it, she could dissipate like smoke on the wind, appearing as a specter or entirely invisible. She moved through the air entirely unseen and when she rounded the corner, she saw them.

Six priests were moving quickly away from her, all of them reeking of Hera's control. Hera liked to influence her acolytes, to persuade them, to remove their free will. Hecate knew immediately that those men were moving under that power, almost blind to anything other than their goddess's demands. It wasn't the men that enraged her, however... It was what they were carrying. They all held a wooden staff, and tied to it was a golden ram. Hecate had never seen such a creature.

It was suspended upside down, its hooves bound tightly to the rod as it bounced with the fast-walking gait of the priests. Its wool was shining in the early morning light, now just past dawn, sending flecks of light and rainbows on the earth and armor around it. It took a moment for Hecate to even realize what she was seeing, and only then did she *hear* it. The ram was making a horrendous, desperate bleating noise, almost as if it was talking—or screaming. It was suspended in the air, bouncing awfully to and fro, captured between the men's grips. Their eyes were vacant and dull, and she knew that they were not fully in control of themselves.

They turned quickly, Hecate dodging around the corners and under awnings as she followed then. The men were ineptly good at remaining out of sight. Each road or path that they took was less populated than the last. The acrid waves of Hera's power likely gave them a large breadth as humans tended to stay away from it unconsciously. *What doesn't she want them to see?* Hecate's mind was whirring, ever the strategist and the thinker. Her soul was sharp, and her wit was sharper. Weaker men had even called her conniving. There was nothing malicious in her heart like there was in Hera's, and whatever was happening in front of her reeked of treachery and deceit. She had never even seen a golden ram before and as she stared at it, she still had trouble reconciling what she was seeing.

Hecate's eyes hadn't left the ram as she pondered and watched, waiting for snippets of Hera's plan to become clear. She realized that she had followed the priests and the ram out of Heraklion entirely. They were up in the hills now, a good mile away from the city center where they had begun their journey. Either Hecate had been distracted for longer than she realized, or Hera's influence must have meant the acolytes were moving double-time with immortal influence.

She blinked as she emerged in the clearing they had stumbled upon, dotted with Cyprus trees. The men had stopped moving although they were still holding the ram between them. Hecate looked up and realized that there was a stone altar in the center of the clearing, stained and dark with the remnants of dried blood.

It was impossible to deny what Hera's acolytes were planning on doing here. Whatever restraint Hecate had left snapped. Hecate — among her many titles — was a lover and goddess of animals, and while she was partial to dogs and snakes, something was ignited inside of her. There was no reason good enough for anything to die for the gods; she knew these buffoons, the air-heads, the cunning, petty spirit that resided in Hera. What good would the loss of this ram's soul be? Hera wouldn't, and couldn't, do anything with that. It was simply out of spite that she demanded such things, that she would orchestrate such a monstrous display. Hecate went to war for those who could not. Whether it was women who had been put at a disadvantage by men, a position that, contrary to man's tales, was not innate, or innocent souls like the one before her, subject to the whims of the powerful.

Hecate lived in a world where tenderness was ostracized and capitalized upon, where it was pulled like teeth from the bleeding mouths of gentler souls. That tenderness had long calcified in Hecate's chest, but it was that sharp, wicked loss that turned her into who she was. The Goddess of ghosts. Necromancy. Women. *Witchcraft*. Where not a soul would be lost or sacrificed to the vain and powerful, lest she hear about it.

There was a great swirling in the skies above the priests. Dark, red clouds began to gather in a vortex directly above the altar. It was enough of a shock to shake them from their stupor and pull them from the hypnosis of Hera. They shouted in confusion when they saw the ram hung between them, dropping it to the ground. The animal bleated, startled, and attempted to scramble to its feet but could not, still tied tightly to the staff. The priests began shouting, pointing at the red clouds and crying out in confusion all while they stepped away. The clouds began spinning faster and faster, descending down to the earth in a spiral…until Hecate appeared, in full form, standing on the altar.

Her eyes glowed as red as her hair, matching the magic that ran over her skin like water. Hecate's power began to take shape, turning into the bodies of twin snakes—sparkling, red snakes that wrapped around her arms and hissed, fangs out. The heads of the maiden and the crone appeared on her right and left shoulders, causing the priests to scream and fall to their knees. Some of them attempted to crawl backwards out of the clearing but were frozen to the spot; others covered their eyes to block the wicked vision.

"Be gone," Hecate said simply. Her voice took on its echo

effect that happened when she was in full expression of her power, making it sound like there were three people talking at once: the maiden, the mother, and the crone. Each of her mouths moved in synchronicity. The priests stumbled over one another but couldn't look away from Hecate's three heads. It was the curse of being a creature of such magic and divinity, wrapped up in the folds of a woman—men stared in fear but couldn't look away.

"Be gone!" she demanded it this time, taking one step off the altar and landing on the earth. It sent a shockwave through the ground, shaking the trees. The acolytes wasted no time. They ripped themselves from staring at the goddess and ran. This time, not a single one looked back.

Hecate shook herself free of the trappings of her power in a second—the heads of the maiden and the crone disappeared as well as the snakes of red magic that covered her arms. Her eyes dimmed to their ruby color, no longer glowing in fury. She moved quickly over to the ram, her hands flying over the bindings and releasing it from its bondage. The ram jumped up to its feet in a panic, fighting with the last of the ropes as Hecate freed it. She expected the ram to turn and run, to disappear back into the wilderness. Instead, it simply turned around and stared right at Hecate.

She turned her head in surprise, studying the creature. Surely, this was some sort of gift or boon since it did truly seem that the ram had a fleece of gold. What she didn't expect was how utterly human its gaze looked as it stared back at her, almost as if it was thanking her. What Hecate *really* didn't expect was that when she took a few steps back and sat down on a nearby boulder, the ram followed.

It stood next to her for a few moments, making Hecate pause, but when it showed no sign of running, she leaned forward and buried her hand in its fleece. It was still soft as wool. It didn't feel wiry or abrasive like metal, but it was undoubtedly gold. The ram didn't flinch or flee, and Hecate began stroking its back easily, her thoughts turning to Hera. She sat there for an unknown amount of time, waiting to see what would happen when Hera got wind that her sacrifice had been disrupted.

Hecate hardly noticed the ram nuzzling up against her legs, almost as if it was embracing her in return.

❧ 6 ❦

Hecate was too preoccupied with the thought of a furious Hera to go back to Heraklion. She had seen what Hera would do, or rather, what Hera was unafraid to do to temples and priestesses. She had done it to Nyx centuries ago even if Nyx's retribution had been fair and swift. At the same time, she didn't want the women at the temple to think that she had left them without saying goodbye —something they might interpret as a slight or a sign that she had been displeased with them.

While the sun was just past midday, Hecate turned and busied herself with grabbing firewood from the sticks and underbrush of the surrounding sparse wood. The whole time, the ram kept at her ankles, never straying more than a few feet from her. As she unloaded an armful of twigs into the clearing, she looked down at the creature.

It had huge, green eyes that seemed to soften when they looked at her. *Well, now you're just imagining things.* Hecate broke the silence of the clearing with a chuckle. *If you start talking to this animal, then you will be the crazy witch they say you are.*

As soon as she thought it, she found herself turning and

staring at the animal. "You think that the priestesses will have a fire going in the middle of the day?"

Shit. Hecate's lips pressed into a thin line as she shook her head and wiped her hands on her himation. *There goes the last of my sanity.* Her eyes widened in surprise when the ram gave a short bleat in response, moving its head almost in an affirmative.

"Careful," Hecate abandoned any concerns of lunacy—a talent she had picked up after eons of being known as the mother of witches—and spoke out loud to the ram as she began building a fire pit. "I'm not exactly going to do anything for my reputation by now avoiding my own temples and talking to a golden sheep." The ram made another bleating sound. "My apologies, a ram."

Hecate stopped, rolling her eyes at herself before tossing the last of the firewood into the pit. She closed her eyes, hummed a few things under her breath, and snapped her fingers. The flame was lit instantly, immediately built up to a roaring fire. The ram screamed, taking a few steps in surprise, causing Hecate to stifle a laugh.

"I'm terribly sorry." She grinned. "Goddess of witchcraft and all. It comes with the territory, but I don't suppose you know that. Strange though. Most animals do." Hecate paused for a second, staring at the ram for another fleeting moment before it came back up to her side. She ran her hand through its fleece again before sitting down and closing her eyes, losing herself nearly immediately in a trance. She sent a message to her temple that she would be back the following day, that pressing matters had come up, but she did not intend to leave without saying goodbye. As soon as she was satisfied that the message had been received, signaled by the smoke turning red, she waved her hand, and the fire went out.

Hecate leaned back against a boulder... and started to wait. There was a chance that Hera didn't care at all or was already onto the next scheme, but she couldn't risk drawing her out in the city. She would have to spend the night here in case she had drawn out the queen of the gods.

"Queen of the gods, what a joke," Hecate muttered, resigning herself to voicing her entire inner monologue now. "Did you know she was the first person to call herself that?" Hecate looked over at the ram, who made what sounded like a noise of assent. "I know. Terribly crude of her."

The rest of the afternoon passed pleasantly enough. Hecate had never minded nature, and she didn't remember the last time that she had an afternoon off. She didn't mind her work, but a full day to herself in the sun wasn't the worst outcome. The sun was beginning to set when Hecate stirred, not realizing that she had dozed in the hazy warmth of the afternoon.

There was a hot breath close to her face, shocking the goddess awake, when she sat up with a start. She panicked for a moment, thinking that Hera was poised above her and ready to strike. Her magic flared up, and she blinked her eyes open, only to realize that she was face to face with the ram...who had a length of her hair in its mouth.

"Oh, stop that!" she chided, detangling herself free from the ram and standing up, brushing her hair behind her shoulders. She sighed and shook her head. "I guess I can't fault you for doing...whatever it is sheep do, I guess." There was another noise from the creature. "Yes, yes, a *ram*, not a sheep. Goodness. You're touchy."

Hecate moved towards the still-warm fire pit as the sun began to set, preparing to relight it for the evening. She would be able to ascertain the prayers sent to her through the smoke and was planning on getting some work done through the night; the reputation that she was one of the most responsive of the gods was fairly earned.

As the sun began to set, a golden sheen began to cover everything in the clearing. It started pouring out from the rocks and the trees, suddenly everywhere at once, as if the heavens itself was weeping gold.

"What the…" Hecate stood up and looked around when she noticed the flames of her fire turned to gold, casting up sparks of gold leaf in lieu of smoke. She looked around the clearing in a panic, trying to ascertain what was happening, but only seeing everything encased in a golden sheen. The magic in the clearing wasn't ominous, but it was vague — something that Hecate knew from witchcraft was just as bad. *The ram!* Her heart stopped, suddenly filled with concern for the creature that she had risked Hera's wrath to save when she saw it. Except, she couldn't see it.

The ram was surrounded by a ball of golden light, so bright that Hecate brought her hand to her brow to shield herself from it. She couldn't make sense of the ram's frame hidden within it but watched as the ball began to grow…and grow… and grow…until finally, it exploded, sending cascades of raining, golden sparks all over the clearing. Hecate ducked to shield herself on instinct, covering her face with both of her hands. Hecate waited.

One minute.

Then two.

After three minutes of silence, she slowly straightened her back and stood up.

There were only three times in Hecate's immortal life when she had been surprised by a man. The first was when, during their inaugural meeting, Zeus assumed she would sleep with him. The second was when Hermes proved able to back up his own talk. But neither scenario compared to the very one that Hecate found herself in at this exact moment. In lieu of a golden ram in the center of the clearing, Hecate was now staring at a man. A very, very naked man.

She didn't move, and she certainly didn't look away. The sun was now setting rapidly behind them, but the waning light did nothing to distract from the man now looking back at Hecate. He seemed slightly bewildered, as if he wasn't sure how he'd gotten to the clearing, but Hecate couldn't think fast enough. In reality, it had only been a few seconds, yet it had felt like an eternity before Hecate cursed.

"Well...fuck." She had seen her fair share of chaos before, especially in spell work and necromancy, but those things were usually...dead. This man was undoubtedly alive. He was tall, taller than any mortal man she had ever known, with shoulder-length curling hair and a wide chest with a strong frame. Her thoughts raced.

A wide chest which you are not *staring at... No, no, yes you are. You're staring at his* chest. *No! His eyes. Yes. Eyes. Better.... That's better.*

As if he could read her thoughts, the man laughed. The sound nearly shocked Hecate more than his sudden transformation—and nakedness—and pulled her back to the scenario at hand. He was laughing, nearly tossing his head back as his shoulders shook with it. It was a truly joyful sound. Too often, Hecate had grown used to the laughter of man as mockery, as cruelty. This was a far cry from those sounds, and she couldn't process how it made her feel; there was enough to process in that moment.

"You were a sheep!" Hecate finally blurted, daring to take one step closer to the stranger. He only smiled again, nodding as if this was a very casual occurrence.

"Technically, a ram. As you can well see." He referenced his own nakedness without shame, and Hecate fought the urge to roll her eyes. She paused for a second before her brow furrowed.

"You tried to *eat* my hair!"

"Oh, yes, I suppose I did." The man chewed on his lip for a second, nodding as if he was in a great debate. "Well, that was the ram's fault."

"So...the ram is...its own...person?"

"I don't know!" He tossed his hands in the air and chuckled, as if he was endlessly amused by the whole situation. "Have you ever been a sheep before?"

"No, but I thought it was a ram." Hecate deadpanned but the stranger only seemed to find it funnier.

"Ha! Exactly. Who's to say? It's rather confusing being turned into an animal. One minute, you're sleeping on your friend's roof, and the next, an angry goddess makes you a golden ram."

Hecate's eyes got wide as she got over the shock of the moment, remembering what had made her wait out in the woods in the first place. Her voice was hurried, "The goddess! Do you know who it was?"

"The goddess who turned me into a sheep?"

Hecate buried her head in her hands and shook her head, making herself breathe deeply twice before responding. "No. The goddess who took your virginity. *Yes*, the goddess who turned you into a sheep!"

"A ram. I can't say I've had the pleasure of sleeping with an immortal." The man raised an eyebrow and tossed Hecate a devilishly charming grin. "I'd be more than willing to submit myself to the mercy of the experience, however."

Hecate stopped and stared at him, shaking her head slowly in utter disbelief. "You are unbelievable." Her tone was dry and exasperated, but he continued as if she hadn't spoken.

"Although," he laughed to himself, "I suppose whenever I've taken matters into my own hands, I've cavorted with divinity." Hecate opened her mouth to respond as she cycled through the meaning of his words.

"*You're* immortal?" she nearly shrieked, flickers of power running up and down her arms as her temper rose.

"You're utterly bewitching when you're mad. Ha! Bewitching." The man was an endless array of smirks, chuckling to himself at nearly everything he said. "I suppose that's fitting for Hecate."

"How do you know who I am?" The goddess tossed a stare at the stranger that had been known to melt men…but no part of him seemed frozen to begin with. He shrugged.

"You told me when I was the ram. I do suppose that puts me at an unfair advantage though. I'm Aeëtes," he made a sweeping bow, "Crown Prince of Colchis, allegedly," he rolled his eyes, "and son of Helios. Confirmed." If she had ever doubted him and his claims of immortality, his accompanying smile was so full of sunshine that Hecate didn't doubt he was Helios's son.

"Well." Hecate let out a long breath. "This has been…an experience. Do you remember who cursed you?"

"Yes!" Aeëtes clapped his hands. "It was Hera. That much I remember." Hecate nodded, having the proof that she needed that Hera was up to something—something that had led her to curse an immortal, one with important ties to the human realm, and that was enough to get the other gods involved. She sighed, straightening her back and lifting her chin in the direction of Aeëtes. Her cool demeanor had returned, and Aeëtes felt himself slipping further into her presence like she had her own tide, and he was dreadfully caught up in it.

"Thank you. Now, you may go. I highly suggest that you go seek refuge in Colchis or with your father. Perhaps, find some clothes first." She vaguely waved her hand in his direction, "I'll deal with Hera." Hecate said it like a command, intending for Aeëtes to feel thoroughly dismissed.

Hecate felt a cold sensation run down her spine when he shrugged, taking a few steps closer to her and settling down against another boulder. He put his hands behind his head and leaned back, closing his eyes while a lazy smile crossed his face.

"I don't think so, witch. It seems rather serendipitous that I've stumbled across your path. You see, I was looking for a new adventure—and I've just found it."

7

Hecate stared at Aeëtes, fighting to keep her jaw from dropping open. There was an easy expression on his face as he relaxed against the rock. He seemed entirely unbothered by the fact that he had been cursed by one goddess and was now sleeping naked in a field next to another. "This isn't the place for you, Aeëtes. I'm sure that you're not used to being denied anything, but you are not coming with me." He only shrugged in response, not even bothering to open his eyes. Hecate shook her head in ongoing disbelief. She had dealt with men and their attitudes before. Normally, all it took was one swift kick to their ego, and they would shatter. But he seemed entirely unfazed.

"Do you think that you've gotten far in life by simply ignoring what's happening around you?" The words came tumbling out of her before she could stop them.

There was something about the shocking arrogance of Aeëtes that reminded her of every man she had ever met—men who had lived their lives without any disregard for those they left behind them and the women who paid the price.

No one ever stops to think what would happen if a woman acted in such self-interest, the disdain they would pile upon her.

Aeëtes cracked open an eye, a puzzling look crossing his face that Hecate couldn't quite place. "I've gotten where I am in life because I'm not afraid to go where I'm not wanted. Do you only go where you're called?"

"Yes," Hecate answered easily, not afraid of Aeëtes's challenging tone.

"How obedient of you." He shrugged, as if her answer disappointed him.

"Why would I waste time where I'm not wanted?"

"Does that give anyone a chance to meet you?"

"You presume I want to meet new people."

Hecate's voice was clipped, but that feeling in her chest started to churn. His wording was specific. He hadn't asked if she had the chance to meet other people. Aeëtes had asked if other people had the chance to meet *her.* He tilted his head to the side and sat up a little straighter, Hecate looking away from him as she was faced with his nakedness once more.

"That's a terribly sad way to live."

"You'll get to a point in your long, immortal life where you realize that you've met every person already. They will all bring you the same joys, the same heartbreaks. Everything with cease to surprise you." Hecate sighed quietly, sitting down in front of the fire. "If your stupidity doesn't kill you first, which is where I'd bet my coin." Her voice lightened, as if she realized she had been too honest and needed to deflect. If Aeëtes caught onto it, he said nothing.

Hecate stared into the fire, and a shockingly easy silence fell between them. It annoyed her. This man, who was so brazen, so...unbothered was going to end up getting in the way. There was a bigger picture at hand — Hera and the fact that she had cursed an immortal. It wasn't a rare occurrence; the gods seemed to survive off curses as much as they did nectar and ambrosia. Those curses, however, were normally reserved for mortals. When the gods cursed each other, alliances got called into play.

Everyone was related to someone, and it got tricky quickly.

Zeus had passed a moratorium that the gods should attempt to remain somewhat civil to one another, but he had thrown a chalice at Hermes in the same sentence. Which might have been deserved but was beside the point. It might have been a very thin rule, but it was one. Hecate wasn't above admitting that she would take any reason to legitimately go for Hera. Even if it was a stretch.

The sun had set entirely now, and Hecate watched the smoke from the campfire wind up towards the heavens, knowing that it wouldn't be long until Hera had caught wind of her interference. Aeëtes had fallen asleep, utterly unconcerned with his nudity, and Hecate struggled to keep her eyes on the fire—something she was above admitting.

There was a sudden rush of wind in the clearing, and Hecate sat straight up, wiping sleep from her eyes as she realized that she must have passed out at some point. She had been slouched over to one side, and she rolled her shoulders to shake off the stiff feeling.

"Hecate?" Aeëtes called out to her, slightly wary, but not quite afraid. Hecate's gaze snapped over to him and saw that he was looking past her, towards the edge of the woods. She whipped her head around and followed his line of sight, releasing a long breath and shaking her head when she saw it.

The wind had picked up and had not slowed down, beginning to swirl around the edges of the clearing like it would trap them both in the center of a hurricane. The quicker it moved, the more Hecate felt the edges of her himation whip around her ankles as her hair obscured her vision. The fire initially jumped higher with the onslaught of oxygen but quickly died out, leaving them under just the light of the moon as the wind picked up speed.

"What's happening?" Aeëtes yelled over the sound of the

roaring wind, taking a few paces toward her and nearly falling over. Hecate's lips pulled into a thin line as her rich, dark power began to consume her. Flares of red magic erupted from her skin like she was a living volcano, rippling over her like heat waves. The heads of the maiden and the crone appeared, her power undulating as it morphed into the snakes that wrapped around her arms once more. Her eyes went red as her hair began to stand on its end, sticking out around her shadows like a halo. Hecate's magic was rising, and she was on the cusp of her immortal form.

"Stand back, Aeëtes," Hecate demanded, her voice taking on its triple echo and dropping an octave. Aeëtes listened, to Hecate's surprise, and looked over to the tree line.

At the very edge of the vortex, the wind began to twist and shape, spinning until Aeëtes could barely make out the body of a woman. The air around her took on a pinkish hue but not in the way that flowers and fruit are pink. No, this almost looked diseased, as if it had green undertones and was in the early stages of decay. The wind changed directions, and Aeëtes nearly gagged; the scent on the air smelled like rotted fruit.

"Oh my god…" Aeëtes watched on in horror, his eyes going wide, as he saw the body of air begin to solidify. The color became more opaque when suddenly, Hera stepped out of it. The queen of the gods had a look on her face that could only be described as feral, her power in its putrid shade flickering up and down her arms. It covered her hands in balls of pink light, crackling like she was holding onto the lit end of a torch. Her long, brunette hair was tied up in a braid around her head like she had forgotten her crown and did whatever she could to put one there. Aeëtes supposed that to some men, maybe in certain lighting…she would be beautiful, but the rotting smell that her power carried went straight through to her soul.

"Hecate," she spat, her voice sounding like daggers. "I should have known that you'd be here. Always sticking your nose where it doesn't belong," Hera sneered, tilting her chin up and raising an eyebrow.

Hecate said nothing, taking a few steps closer to Hera and closing the gap between them until they were only six feet apart. The wind died down now that Hera had descended, leaving the three of them in the open clearing. Hera looked over to Aeëtes, her face contorting into a nasty grin.

"I guess the ram's wool didn't really leave you with anything to cover up with, did it?" She mocked him, but Aeëtes said nothing, leveling his stare back at her. Whatever Aeëtes lacked in true god's power, he made up for in bravery, and Hera flinched ever so slightly when he stood taller, pushing his shoulders back, and looked her in the eye. Hera was obsessed with power and titles for the same reason as most people—she was a coward. No matter how *weak* Aeëtes may be in comparison, the fact that he seemingly met her challenge knocked her off balance.

"Eyes on me, Hera," Hecate hissed, her voice echoing throughout the clearing. The red veins of magic dripped down Hecate's arms and off her fingers, pooling at her feet. Aeëtes watched in utter fascination as it spread around her, and Hecate stood in a deep puddle of her own power, moving around like it was sentient.

"What?" Hera took another step towards Hecate. "Don't tell me that *you* of all people have fallen for him? And so quickly, too." Her tone was saccharine, as if she was taunting a child. "Surely, the great Goddess of witchcraft and women hasn't forgotten so quickly what a mistake it is for her to love."

Aeëtes's ears perked up at that as he turned his head towards Hera. He didn't understand the context, but whatever Hera had said was said with bite. It was intended to maim. He could hear it from the way she chewed on the words as she said them, like she was savoring their flavor. Hecate didn't react; her face didn't shift in the slightest. She didn't even blink. Hera's brow furrowed as she studied

Hecate's face for any reaction, sneering when she didn't find one.

A surge of power rippled up through Hera's arms, and almost immediately, she expanded. Her body twisted until she shot straight up, standing now almost ten feet tall and towering over Hecate.

"You have no use for this child-god, Hecate," Hera demanded it, every word sounding like it was a decree. "Hand him over to me and then there shall be no unpleasantness between us."

Aeëtes watched as the power around Hecate began to move, spiraling upwards, defying gravity, and crawling up over itself. His mouth dropped open as the red, umber power crackled into the shape of two dogs. One now stood on either side of Hecate, snapping and growling, pulling against invisible restraints. A chill ran up his spine as he studied the picture in front of him. He had known of Hecate, every Greek did...but how many people had *seen* Hecate?

This display wasn't even all of her power; Aeëtes knew enough about immortals to sense when they were at their full strength. She was a sight. The heads of the mother, maiden, and crone were expressionless. They weren't expressionless like someone afraid or frozen in fear, no... They were void. There was nothing but fathomless depths in those eyes, glowing bright red as red snakes of magic wrapped around her arms and dogs of power barked at her sides. When she spoke, the barrier between worlds shook.

"On my honor, Hera, his life debt is mine." Her words were finite, and Hera recoiled, nearly hissing.

"You wouldn't claim his life debt!" Hera shrieked, her braid falling loose and whipping around her shoulders like a scorpion's tail. "You don't know this man. I'm supposed to believe the protector of women would claim a life debt for a *man?*"

Hecate stood as resolute as marble. She nodded once. "Yes.

I saved him when he was in the body of a ram, stealing him away from your priests. That puts him under my protection. Now that I see you still mean him harm, I claim the life debt." Her voice was soothing, as if she was reading poems to accompany Apollo's lyre. It was a vast contrast to her body, writhing with snakes and accompanied by beasts tethered only to her will.

Hera shrieked, an awful sound that echoed over the woods and had Aeëtes dropping to his knees and covering his ears. Hecate didn't blink.

"You claim honor!" Hera screamed, her voice cracking as the clearing lit up in pink flames, tinged with wickedness and the same putrid, rotting smell.

Aeëtes could hardly see, his vision obscured by the perverted power of Hera. It was everything that was supposed to be feminine and beautiful, pink and flowers, but it was foul and corrupted. The only thing he could focus on was Hecate, the lines of her power and the essence of her magic combatting Hera's with true feminine essence. It wasn't weakness; it was boundless strength. Creation and death.

"You have none," Hecate quipped, the slightest bit of disgust entering her voice. "I take on the crown prince's life debt, following custom. If you come against us, then you break the laws of Olympus…" There was a quiet pause, and Aeëtes swore that he saw Hecate's lip twist up in the slightest bit of a smirk. "…I will have the support of the gods to destroy you." Hecate's smirk had turned into a full grin at the end, one brow arched gracefully as she taunted Hera.

Hera bared her teeth and growled, an animalistic and all unbecoming sound, as her flames licked higher up the trees around them. Aeëtes didn't see Hera's power sliding over the grass behind him, letting out a sharp cry as he fell forward when it licked over his heels. The face of the maiden whipped around, her eyes growing wide when she saw him.

Hecate flicked her fingers, as if she was dropping something, and the two dogs at her side burst forward. They expanded in size as they launched towards Hera, until they were nearly as tall as she was, their gaping maws foaming with flecks of Hecate's death magic. Hera screamed in fear and frustration, and as the dogs leapt for her, she vanished. In the blink of an eye, Hera and her power evaporated from the clearing, as if they were never there.

Aeëtes slowly got back up to his knees, looking around in confusion. His brain tried to catch up with what he was seeing, the clearing now looking entirely undisturbed. Hecate was still rippling with magic; the snakes wrapped around her arms moved their heads back and forth, but her dogs were gone. Aeëtes opened his mouth to say something when he was cut off, the booming voice of Hera chilling him to the bone. His body seemed to vibrate with the echoes as her voice flooded the air around them.

"So... it is to be war on you both."

8

Hera's threat boomed in the air around them, slowly fading away and hanging in the atmosphere. Aeëtes looked over to Hecate, almost afraid to breathe. Hera's reputation was no secret, but he had never seen the goddess before, and he had definitely never been on the end of her threats.

"Wait." Aeëtes turned and looked at Hecate. "You accepted the life claim over me." A small smile crossed his face as he tilted his head to the side, looking smug. The last of the bright, red glow left Hecate's eyes, and she turned to face him. She took a few steps towards the fire, muttering something and causing it to spring back to life, ignoring his statement.

"You will need to find some clothes," she waved in his general direction without looking directly at him, "and some-place safe to stay in Heraklion while I sort this mess out."

Aeëtes's smile widened as he sat down across the fire from her, peering over the top of the flames.

"I don't think so."

"That's final. It's not up for debate, and I don't remember asking you for your opinion." Hecate still wasn't looking at him.

"I'm coming with you." Aeëtes was very slow to anger, but he was annoyed. Hecate was still being dismissive of him, and he would take anything from her over dismissive. The goddess finally snapped her eyes to him, nearly growling. "Your capacity for persuasion truly astounds me. No." There was a viciousness in her tone that sent a spark down Aeëtes's spine. Something within her had captured his attention from the minute he laid eyes on her, and he had a feeling that the fact she had rescued him from being a sacrifice didn't even matter. It most certainly did, but Aeëtes knew that he wasn't unfairly projecting. He could have run into Hecate on a crowded street, and he would have been equally consumed by this woman.

She's not a woman. Aeëtes chastised himself. *This is a goddess... The Goddess of all women. Who are you to even assume that she wants to spend time with you and insist that she does?*

A dark voice of insecurity appeared from the corners of Aeëtes's mind, the same voice that came out when he would only learn defensive maneuvers when he trained as a child. It was the same voice that threatened to block out the sun when the king of Colchis threatened him, and when he wondered why he never even got to learn his mother's name. A voice that was loudest when he thought of Helios, who had sent him away, leaving him to be raised outside of the world of immortals.

It was an oppressive, cold feeling that threatened to pull Aeëtes under and drown him every time it appeared. He was an immortal with no real power, annoying to the gods and unable to relate to humans. The only way that Aeëtes was able to throttle the voice was to overpower it with such a confidence, such an easy bravado, that no one would guess what was happening in his head.

Yet, when Hecate looked at him with a deathly cold face and an unimpressed scowl, his only thought was to curl up next to her until they both had chased away their demons with sunlight. He wanted that for her, even if she couldn't spend another minute in his presence. It had been enamoring to watch her as she faced off against Hera, giving him a glimpse of gods and the world that he only half-belonged to for the first time.

He wanted her to be his next adventure. If that meant that he called on the life debt and forced their time together, he'd make her smile. If that was his adventure, he'd do it—no matter how insane it sounded, even if he hadn't known her for a full day.

Aeëtes swallowed thickly but hid it with a smile.

"I've been told that I can be incredibly persuasive."

"I will feed you to my dogs," Hecate sneered, "And I've yet to see it." Hecate's quip in return was quick, not missing a beat. Aeëtes continued to study her through the flames. She was sitting neatly, her hands in her lap, hardly moving except for a fidgeting of her fingers.

"It remains," Aeëtes tilted his head to the side, softening his tone, "You claimed a life debt. You claimed a life debt in front of Hera…and took it from Hera. I was hers."

"You are no one's." Hecate surprised even herself with the strength of her voice. She paused, coughing slightly and attempting to clarify. "You do not belong to Hera. She cannot grab people and immortals and do whatever she wishes."

"She did, though, and you held your ground. You took on my life debt, Hecate. I'm not a god, but I am immortal. I know what that means."

"I only did it to get back at Hera," Hecate growled, power flickering over her arms as her eyes burned red. The accusation that Hera had flung at her had found its target in the deep recesses of her heart, and she was still reeling from it. Aeëtes felt the heat coming off her words.

"You did it though," he pushed again, unperturbed. Hecate sighed, shaking her head as she looked up towards the heavens.

"I am not changing my mind on this, Aeëtes. This is not some wrestling match that you can jump into last minute. The games of gods don't stop until someone is dead."

"Good thing I'm immortal."

"You love to remind me of this." Hecate rolled her eyes. "You have no power, Aeëtes. I couldn't care less on a personal level, but it does mean that you're just as vulnerable to me as a human."

"But you do think of me on a personal level?" Aeëtes's face lit up, and Hecate could see it through the fire, his wide smile only illuminated by the crackling flames. "You do realize as soon as you turn your back or leave me in Heraklion, then you'd leave me defenseless?"

Hecate opened her mouth and closed it quickly, chewing on her lip as she found herself caught in a trap of her own making. If she was worried about the life debt and Hera's false claim on Aeëtes, then he was right. He would be even more exposed the minute that she left.

Aeëtes saw the moment that he had won written all over Hecate's face, and he had to keep from laughing out loud. It was getting closer to dawn, and the atmosphere seemed to lighten around them with the encroaching sun.

"What's the plan then?" He waggled his eyebrows at her, and he could've sworn he saw Hecate's magical snakes flicker across her arms. She sighed deeply and hung her head back, shaking it slowly before she responded.

"Hera didn't remove the curse. You'll probably turn back into a ram at dawn," Hecate delighted slightly in the shock on Aeëtes's face. "The fact that you turned back into a man at all was probably a loophole since she didn't intend for you to live past nightfall."

"Pleasant." Aeëtes clicked his tongue and suddenly felt a little more disdain for his father and the rising sun. Hecate continued without acknowledging him.

"I know of a spell that will probably work to undo the

curse. But we'll need to return to Colchis to do it." Hecate's words fell down on Aeëtes like heavy stones, slowing crushing him under their weight. She watched in slight concern as a grimace ate up Aeëtes's smile for the first time.

"Is there..." Aeëtes coughed awkwardly. "Is there any way that we can avoid that?"

Hecate eyed him warily, her curiosity spiked as to why a crown prince would have concerns about returning to their birthright. She shook her head.

"No. The spell needs the soil of your birth and the blood of your mother to work."

"Then we really shouldn't go to Colchis."

"Why not? You're the son of Helios, but you were born in Colchis, were you not?" Hecate assumed that Helios had slept with a mortal woman of the royal family, resulting in an immortal prince. Aeëtes shook his head, shifting uncomfortably as the discussion of his parentage, and his vulnerability and insecurities around it, seemed magnified by his nakedness. He was suddenly ashamed that he wasn't clothed.

"Helios left me in Colchis to be raised by the king and queen. You won't find the blood of my mother there." Aeëtes looked down at his feet and thanked the other gods that Hecate didn't push the topic of his mother. The silence stretched between them for a few more moments, and when he looked up, Aeëtes could see that she was deep in thought. Finally, she shook her head and sighed.

"We'll have to try. We'll have better luck summoning an audience with Helios if the king and queen help."

"That's a long way to go on a guess." Aeëtes's forehead wrinkled as he mulled over their options.

"It's the only chance that we have."

"Why?" Aeëtes felt himself getting a little angrier, and it unsettled him, but he did not want to return to Colchis if he could avoid it. Hecate bristled, equally unamused now that her expertise was being questioned.

"Because I wrote Hera's curse," Hecate growled, the heads on her shoulders flickering to life once more. "Every curse, spell, and incantation in existence came through me. Even when Hera uses her own power to cast curses, it is my essence that she calls upon to do it."

Aeëtes's eyes got wide. "So you let her curse me?" Hecate jumped to her feet, and her heads all screeched.

"I don't *let* anyone do anything. I said that she calls upon my essence. It is my spirit. I am a part of every single piece of magic and witchcraft in this world, Aeëtes, but it does not answer to me. It is mine, but it is bigger than even one goddess can contain." Her words were laced with her power, and Aeëtes felt it crawling across his skin as he only stared up at her in awe.

Hecate recoiled, slightly shocked as he looked on. Every time that she had stepped into her power and the faces of the maiden and the crone appeared, men fled. Most women wept, even if in gratitude. She had never, ever seen a man look at her in her power and seem... awestruck. He nodded, his telltale grin covering up his expression once more, encouraging her.

"To Colchis, then."

9

"To Colchis." Hecate nodded once, trying to understand the man in front of her. He was brash, not easily frightened, and hadn't shied away from her when power overtook her. He was staring at the flames again, looking shockingly calm for someone who had been cursed by Hera and now had to journey to Colchis to reverse it. Even her own presence should've been somewhat unnerving.

He is an immortal and *a crown prince.* Hecate's bitter thoughts stepped in, loud and dissenting. *Those are some of the worst men that you've met, and he's managed to hold both titles.*

Hecate stood, adjusting her hair as she stared at the path out of the clearing. "We should head out then. Your curse will probably take over again before long, and you'll be a distraction as a golden ram. Did you understand me when you were turned?" She looked over at Aeëtes, who nodded.

"I did. I may have been in the body of a ram, but I still had my thoughts."

"Good. That makes things somewhat easier." Hecate started walking towards the woods, pausing when she didn't hear Aeëtes stand and follow her. She tossed a raised brow over her shoulder.

"Did you want to come with me or stay here and wait for Hera?"

Aeëtes scoffed, standing slowly as his hands went to his waist. "I'm fairly certain that walking into town naked will be a distraction, too, Hecate."

She paused, a bit of color coming into her cheeks as she tried—and failed—to ignore Aeëtes's nudity. He had a point, though, and walking into town with Aeëtes as a golden ram *or* a naked man would cause unwanted attention. Hecate felt herself swallow thickly, and something heated up in her body that she had repressed for years. The thought of people, other women, seeing and staring at Aeëtes as he proudly walked through the streets, confident as ever... Hecate buried even the idea of jealously and leveled her gaze at him. She reached up, grabbing a shawl that had been tucked in the folds of her himation, and tossed it at him.

"There you go. You can cover up with that."

Aeëtes grabbed it and looked at her with a dumbstruck expression.

"You mean you've been wearing this the whole time?"

Hecate shrugged. "Well, now you're looking a little cold."

She turned on her heel and walked off into the woods, biting her lip to keep from smiling as she heard Aeëtes's guffaw in dispute.

He quickly caught up to her, and they made the trek back into Heraklion, Aeëtes growing more and more uncomfortable as the atmosphere lightened around them. They didn't know when his curse would revert once more, which created the feeling of waiting on an ambush. The sun hadn't cleared the horizon as they stepped into the busy streets, already abuzz with people but not nearly as crowded as they would be in an hour.

"This way," Hecate murmured quietly as she leaned closer to Aeëtes. It was the closest that he had been to the goddess. The scent of rosemary and cinnamon in her hair had him reeling, and he had to keep himself from tripping over his own feet. There was something about her that was threatening to drown his senses alive; he was completely captivated by everything about Hecate, and it only got worse the more time he spent with the goddess. She was immortal in a way that he would never be, with a purpose, with magic…with people who respected her for what she *did*, not only what she was.

Aeëtes nodded his head, not trusting his own voice, and followed Hecate as she slid through the back streets. He knew Heraklion almost as well as he knew Colchis. No, he knew it better than Colchis, but he had to admit that he had no idea where Hecate was taking them. It wasn't until the first notes of dawn, right before sunrise, that they arrived at an open doorway. Aeëtes paused, waiting to see if he should knock before stepping in, but Hecate breezed through without hesitation.

The wind shifted, and that scent of cinnamon caught Aeëtes's attention, and it dawned on him. They were at Hecate's temple, which was why she treated it like she lived there and why he had never seen it. Men didn't pray to Hecate. *Fuck, I'm about to.*

Aeëtes cursed his own thoughts, a bit of shame making his face flush as his brain quickly rifled through all the ways that he would worship Hecate if given half the chance.

Not here. He snapped at himself, almost violently. He knew that Hecate's temples were safe spaces for women, and her priestesses didn't always pledge to her temples when they were young. Some of them only came to her after great hardship — and he'd be damned if he followed her inside thinking about her like that. No matter how enchanted he was.

"Aeëtes," Hecate poked her head out of the door, a smirk crossing over her features, "we don't bite." There was a playfulness to her words that Aeëtes was still unused to hearing from her, as if being in her own temple pulled some of the weight off her shoulders. When Aeëtes stepped inside, he could see why.

The temple was beautiful, but he was immediately struck with the expressions of the acolytes, who had gathered around Hecate. They stared up at her with warm glances, their faces peaceful and content, with real admiration and affection glowing off them. Aeëtes had never gotten the chance to be around gods before. He was clearly overwhelmed in the presence of Hecate alone, but he knew that most of them didn't inspire devotion like that.

"Goddess," one of the women nodded towards Aeëtes, "who is he?"

There was no animosity in her voice, but she was curious all the same. Aeëtes noticed that there was a glimmer of panic that crossed Hecate's face, as if she hadn't thought about how to explain the situation to her devotees. The fear died in her eyes quickly. He had a feeling that she was relatively unaware of the sensation, but she made no move to speak. He bowed his head slightly in the most nonthreatening way he could to show his respects to the women around him.

"Priestess," he answered in response, his tone respectful and almost formal in nature, "it seems Hecate has done me a great favor, and I am in her debt." He left out the fact that she had taken responsibility for his life, putting the burden on himself instead. There was something that softened in Hecate's eyes although he couldn't be entirely sure what it was.

The priestess seemed to accept the answer, her expression utterly neutral as she raked her gaze over Aeëtes. Her voice was cold when she spoke, as if she had changed her mind and didn't like what she saw.

"The goddess does you a great favor in allowing you to stay on with her and fulfill your debt."

"She does," Aeëtes agreed easily, and the priestess seemed surprised, as if she had expected a more combative attitude from him. Hecate watched on, her expression unreadable as Aeëtes poured on the charm and bowed once more to the priestess. "I shall always be indebted to her for that alone, but now, I am at least able to work off the bulk of my transgressions."

The acolytes seemed content with his answer and went back to discussing amongst themselves, bringing Hecate into the fold of the conversation. She kept her eyes subtly on Aeëtes, watching as he waited calmly by the door. This mild acceptance of him was the most that any man would get out of her devotees, and it was an impressive feat all its own.

The thing that is dangerous about Aeëtes, Hecate mused, *is that his charm extends beyond being a smooth talker. He knows the best approach to win anyone over, it seems.*

"Sisters," Hecate turned her attention to the room. "I'm afraid that I must depart sooner than I had intended." She paused and gave the women space for their reactions. Some of them were moved to tears instantly at the idea of losing the physical presence of the goddess so soon. Aeëtes watched on, ever waiting, leaning up against the doorway with a steady gaze.

"I know," Hecate began again, and there was genuine sorrow in her eyes. "Now you know, like you always have known, that when you pray, I hear you. What happens behind this door, between these walls..." Hecate raised her hands slightly and looked at the temple around them. "I know of it. Be not of sad heart that I take my leave. You see me in your sisters, your friends, in one another. I am always with you."

Hecate waited patiently and bid each woman farewell, most of them stepping away from her with tears in their eyes. Aeëtes felt himself beginning to twitch, something stirring deep within him that he didn't want to acknowledge. Once Hecate was nearly halfway through her goodbyes, he took a few steps outside to wait for her there.

Aeëtes took in a deep, slow breath, tasting the salt on the wind. He looked up at the sky, knowing they only had a few more minutes until the sun would rise. *It looks like Hera takes dawn very literally.* Aeëtes pondered the curse. *I wonder if she knew* exactly *who my father was...and added that in as a little treat. Although, I suppose she never intended for it to last more than a day.* His thoughts were moving too quickly for him to keep up. He needed some air. He had only known Hecate for a matter of hours, and now here they were, on their way to Colchis, and she had taken on his life debt. She had taken on his life debt *from Hera.* He knew that the utter fascination and pull that he felt towards her had nothing to do with the fact that she was one of the first immortals he had truly seen. Well, it had something to do with that, but not enough to explain the intensity of his feelings. So Aeëtes did what every man had been known to do when faced with a challenge of the heart—he buried it until it would grow to the size of something that he would try to fight with his bare hands.

By the time that Hecate stepped out of the temple, she was brushing away a few tears herself. She opened her mouth to say something but sucked in a harsh gasp instead. Aeëtes turned to her, and as soon as he did, he felt it. There was a warm, almost liquid-like sensation running over his limbs as his vision began to flicker like a flame. He desperately tried to keep his eyes on Hecate, to anchor himself on the image of her face, as he felt his grip on his own mortal body disintegrating. It wasn't painful, but it was an entirely unpleasant process to be transformed from your own body into one that you were never meant to possess. There was a shining, burst of golden light, and Aeëtes felt like he was tossed into a stone wall. One burst of impact... then nothing.

He blinked his eyes open a few times, finding himself eye-level now with Hecate's waist.

Ah, so it is to be a ram again. Aeëtes sighed, praying that it didn't come out as a bleating noise.

"We knew this would happen." Hecate's voice echoed in his head, and Aeëtes huffed in confusion, stomping a hoof on the ground. She leaned down and picked up her shawl, draping it across his chest and tying it into her himation again.

"How are you doing that? Are you in my head?"

Hecate nodded. *"I have an affinity for animals, Aeëtes. I can't speak to all animals this way, but it seems that I can hear you still, quite clearly, as a ram."*

"Great." Aeëtes was suddenly nervous at the idea of Hecate hearing all his thoughts.

"Why would you be nervous about that?" Hecate's voice echoed between his ears, sharp and cunning, matching the devilish grin that she now gave him.

"This spell of yours better work."

Hecate turned towards the street and began walking in the direction of the pier, Aeëtes following close to her.

"It will, but we're going to make a stop first to confirm my suspicions. I also know someone who might be able to put a temporary stay on your curse, so you don't turn every morning."

"Really?" Aeëtes scoffed mentally. *"And who might that be?"*

Hecate stopped suddenly and looked down at him, one brow raised in a threat. The lightest sheen of red magic danced across her arms, and Aeëtes swallowed thickly. When she answered him, she did so aloud, with the maiden and the virgin creeping into her voice.

"We're going to consult with Circe."

10

I f Aeëtes were capable of expressing shock while in the body of a ram, he would've. He knew who Circe was— everyone in Greece did—but he was still a little surprised to hear that Hecate would consult her niece for help.

"She has even more of a kinship with animals than I do, if you can believe it," Hecate answered him in his head, and once more, Aeëtes found himself lucky that he couldn't emote. His face would've surely blushed crimson at his thoughts be heard out loud once again.

"That couldn't have anything to do with the fact that she only lives with animals, could it?" Aeëtes's filter, while thin, would've likely caught that before he blurted it aloud, but Hecate caught it, pinning her sharp gaze on him once more.

"You seem to have a very tricky relationship with the concept of respect." Her words slithered out of her like a spell. "I'd suggest you work on that before you find yourself made man again, or you'll be turning back into a gelding by nightfall."

Hecate's magic flared up once again, leaving that telltale shimmer of red sparking over her skin. She walked a few paces ahead of him, leading them through the most vacant streets that she could find while Aeëtes was turned. The market was almost at full swing now, the sun in full force, which caused distracting fractals of light to bounce off Aeëtes's gold wool. He watched her as he trailed a few paces behind, wanting to give her some space as he tried to get his head on straight. He didn't mean any disrespect to Circe. He didn't know Circe. He barely knew Hecate, but he had seen her work, and he was shocked that she needed council from *anyone*.

Hecate didn't seem to be responding to him as they moved through the alleys and under passageways, dodging heavy carts and the now fully crowded market, so he assumed that his thoughts were somewhat safe.

There was a resoluteness to Hecate that he had never experienced before. Aeëtes had very little experience with the gods, but the few encounters that he had made him generally pleased that he was *only* immortal. He admired it in her. It was no small feat to be unapologetically powerful and graceful. In fact, it was a quality that Aeëtes had never seen before. He was nearly drunk on it. Yet, there was a sorrow in her—that much he could tell—and there was something to the insults that Hera had thrown at Hecate. It didn't matter to him if he seemed foolish, there was more to the Goddess of witchcraft than even she let on, and she was pleased to be shrouded in mystery. But when she had tossed him her shawl, goading him, and when he had seen her at the temple...there were pieces to Hecate, joy and laughter, that should be existing on her surface, that shouldn't be rare occurrences.

Aeëtes leapt over pieces of broken amphora on the street and dodged around a corner, still following Hecate, and set his mind to one, highly specific goal. He'd bring that joy to her surface or would die trying; there was no reason for her to keep it so locked away. She wasn't just entitled to respect. Hecate was entitled to joy, too. To laughter. To warmth. She was capable of it, but something had locked it away, entrenched it deep within her, likely hidden behind a curse of its own.

Aeëtes was starting to realize he wasn't sure that Hecate thought she deserved those things. She knew that she deserved respect; she demanded it of him, but she did not demand joy. Aeëtes ducked under a moving cart and watched as the reddish ends of Hecate's hair disappeared down another street.

I love nothing more than an adventure, Goddess... Aeëtes mused to himself, trotting after the fleeting figure of Hecate. *If that means I have to follow you around until you reveal your secrets, so be it. I'll stay cursed if I have to.*

Aeëtes looked up and skidded to a stop, nearly crashing into Hecate. He could tell immediately that her countenance was off, having gone from determined to cautious. He watched as power sparked over her skin, and in the rays of the sun, he could see the light catching the faintest outlines of the maiden and the crone.

"*Aeëtes,*" Hecate's voice had dropped an octave, even in his head, "*Do not move.*"

"*What do you—*" Aeëtes's thoughts were interrupted as a massive barrage of shouts broke through the general din of the market. He looked up and saw four men, dressed as merchants, pummeling through the crowd to cross the street towards them. Aeëtes nearly bolted, but Hecate's command froze him to the spot. He fidgeted, stomping his hooves on the ground behind her and letting out a desperate bleat.

"*Those are...*"

"*Merchants, I know.*" Hecate's magic was flaring up all around her, and Aeëtes didn't know how the rest of the crowd couldn't see it. They were on a busy street, in between a fish stall and a stack of wine barrels, but no one reacted to their presence. Even the shouting merchants, who were now angrily wielding knives and kopis, didn't attract the attention of those standing right next to them.

"*How are they...*"

"It's a glamour." Hecate's words were clipped as her eyes started scanning the streets as if she were strategizing, looking the part of every general that Aeëtes had ever seen. *"It's Hera's doing. Everyone is oblivious to us and those merchants."*

The merchants were now pushing past carts, only a few stalls away, and getting closer with every second.

"Hecate, let's run while we can!"

The goddess shook her head, and Aeëtes could see the edges of her eyes start to glow that bright ruby red.

"They'll follow us. They're charmed to do it until they die or Hera releases them. They'll cut through civilians on their way to us. I won't let it happen."

Aeëtes looked around the street and saw it through Hecate's eyes—the street was filled with women, teenage girls helping their mothers sell baskets, even pregnant mothers carrying baskets of lemons and pitchers of water. She was right; if the merchants had been possessed, then they would cut through everything in their way to get to the two of them. Aeëtes had never felt as useless as he did in that moment, fidgeting back and forth on agitated legs.

He looked up at Hecate once more and saw her mouth begin to move although he could hear no sound coming out. Everything else began to happen so quickly that Aeëtes wasn't sure if they had died. The heads of the maiden and the crone solidified on her shoulders, and that red power began slowly dripping from her hair. It was sluicing off her body, running over her curves and staining her himation red until the entire garment was dyed the color of blood.

Aeëtes assumed that people saw that color and only saw death and terror, but he could see vitality and life. The color kept running, the magic pooling at her feet again, and Aeëtes knew to take a few steps back.

Hecate's dogs rose up at her sides, standing from the magic, and her power continued to spread until it was running down the streets. It was even going up the walls, slowly pouring over every fish in the market and dipping every piece of produce in its hue. The crowd moved around them like none of it was happening, like they weren't all standing in a sea of spells, coloring their entire world in the shade of both life and death. Hecate was both—she was the Goddess of witchcraft, of women and their life-giving forces, and the Goddess of necromancy, of ghosts. Hecate raised her arms and held them out at her waist, and her voice picked up, the tremors of it sending chills down Aeëtes's spine. It was a bone-chilling feeling that caused people to turn from her, and it only made him want to nuzzle closer to her like one of her dogs.

There was a loud shout, and the merchants had finally pushed past the last cart in their way. They charged forward, their blades held high as they shouted out misplaced battle cries, sounds that they had clearly never made before and would never make again. As the mismatched, bewitched group got closer, Aeëtes stepped back again until he was pressed up against the wall. He would've run, would've charged forward to distract them, but he remembered Hecate's command. Nothing would move him from that spot.

He did, however, feel his anxiety begin to rise as the wicked knives got closer...and closer still... Even Hecate's dogs were calm. The furor that they had possessed when he had seen them in the clearing was gone. They were downright stoic, as if they were made of marble and not pulsing witchcraft. Hecate, by comparison, was a live wire. Her arms were now covered in writing, Greek spells appearing all over her skin and pulsing with light. Her concentration was set on the merchants, her gaze unwavering, and not even a drop of sweat had broken out on her brow.

As soon as the leader of the ragtag group got close enough to strike Hecate, he leapt up in the air, kopi gleaming in the sunlight as he brought it down towards the goddess. Hecate let out a massive shout and threw her arms up in the air, clapping them together around the blade as it made to strike her. There was a sudden, bright burst of light and a shockwave that rippled through all of Heraklion out towards the sea. It nearly blinded Aeëtes as he fell down to the ground, shaking his head and knocking his horns against the wall. He could hear Hecate's voice for only a brief second, clear as crystal and shouting out something in a dialect that he didn't understand, words with power.

He blinked his eyes open as quickly as he could, jumping to his feet...and everything was as it had been before.

The streets were not bathed in red.

There were no merchants.

Hecate's power had sunk beneath the surface of her calm, cool exterior.

Her skin no longer glittered with written spells. Her eyes had lost their glow. Even her dress had returned to its original color, and her dogs had gone. The heads of the maiden and the crone were not visible, and there wasn't a single scratch on her hands where she had caught the blade.

Aeëtes stared up at her for a few more seconds before Hecate looked down at him with a pleased grin.

"What...what in the name of the gods was that?"

"You saw me battle Hera." Hecate shrugged as if nothing of consequence had happened, beckoning for Aeëtes to follow her as they slipped away from the street.

"It certainly didn't look like that."

"Ah," Hecate's eyes were no longer alight with her power, but they sparkled with a mischief of something else entirely. "What you saw then was the power of the gods, simple tricks. Things that most immortals can do."

"What just happened?" Aeëtes made another frustrated bleating sound, trotting to keep up with her long strides as they slipped out of the city walls.

"That...that was witchcraft."

The pair didn't speak as they moved away from the center of the town. Hecate was desperate to get them away from any crowds as long as Aeëtes was in his ram form. Hera had proved there was no boundary she was unwilling to cross. It put Hecate even more on edge than usual. She was worried that every person they passed was about to fall victim to Hera's possession. There was a bit of a walk down from the market towards the docks, where Hecate hoped that they would be able to find passage to Colchis. She assumed that Aeëtes would have some knowledge of where they could get a crew or a ship, but they hadn't even had enough time to discuss how they were getting to Colchis.

Hecate let her gaze drift over to Aeëtes every few seconds, checking that he was still walking alongside her. She wasn't overly nervous about him, not at all. It was simply a matter of honor and responsibility.

That's all it is. Hecate repeated to herself, careful to make sure that she wasn't projecting her thoughts to Aeëtes. *It's about honor and making sure that Hera doesn't cause any more havoc, not only to one man, but to all mortals in whatever self-appointed quest she's on.* She stamped down whatever else was lurking in her mind and in her chest and doubled her pace without thinking.

The road down to the water was well-traveled and busy; there was no way around that. Heraklion was a port, and it was popular. Everything in the market likely touched the sea in some way. Every person that they passed made Hecate anxious, and whenever she found a quiet moment in her thoughts, she found that her brain betrayed her, and she would immediately begin assessing for threats once more. Her eyes were sharp, and every time someone walked a little too close, her power flared up around the hem of her skirts.

Aeëtes was trotting alongside her, finding himself somewhat rather content in the body of a ram. It wasn't a permanent decision that he would make for himself, and he prayed that whatever attempt at a spell that they were going to try in Colchis would work. But it wasn't half bad. No one recognized him. He wasn't worried about a messenger or a sailor running up to him, demanding something or needing him to respond to a summons from his parents...and there was always a summons. The sun was bright, and the weather was warm. Aeëtes was, dare he say it, enjoying the walk. He glanced up at Hecate when he realized that they had gone several minutes without speaking, and felt his good mood dampen slightly.

She was watching. She was watching *everything.*

It immediately made Aeëtes's stomach go sour when he saw the tight expression on her face. He was relatively carefree by nature, especially now, but seeing the anxiety written across her brow felt like a punch to the gut. He had been so concerned minutes ago about her joy, finding happiness in her life, something for her to smile about, and here he was, shamelessly enjoying a walk to the piers without any consideration for what that meant for her.

The gods have cursed me indeed, Aeëtes shook his head a little bit in a display of a ram's indignation. *I'm not sure how much help*

I'd be at anything, anyway… but she's on the lookout, and I'm thinking about lunch.

"Hecate." Aeëtes wasn't entirely sure how he could get his thoughts to her, but he tried sending them to her with intention, and that seemed to work. She turned to look at him, nodding once to acknowledge that she had heard him, and immediately began to scan the road ahead of them. It was getting closer to noon. Everyone was either in the market or at the docks, likely eating or taking a break. The traffic wouldn't pick up again until mid-afternoon.

"It's going to be fine," Aeëtes repeated to her, nudging at her leg with his head until she stopped. Hecate whipped her head around and stared down at Aeëtes.

"How can you say that? You saw what Hera did back there. Don't be so foolish."

"Don't look for trouble!" Aeëtes countered, feeling a little smug when he saw Hecate's surprised face. *"How many times have you beaten Hera in the past…what, twelve hours?"*

Hecate didn't respond, her lips growing into a thin line as she looked away from him. Aeëtes could've sworn he saw her fight the temptation to cross her arms over her chest, and he couldn't help but shake his head in satisfaction. His expressive abilities were rather limited as a ram.

"How many?" Aeëtes asked again, and Hecate sighed, making a bit of a grunt as she refused to look down at him.

"Twice."

"Twice! You're magnificent." If a ram could have been beaming up at the goddess, Aeëtes would have been. Hecate could feel it in his tone of voice, and it made something in her melt. Something that she didn't want to acknowledge as she mentally brushed off the praise and stiffened her spine. Aeëtes continued.

"So if Hera shows up again, what will you do?"

There was a beat of silence, and Hecate started walking off.

Aeëtes could hear her murmuring under her breath. He chuckled to himself and followed after her.

"*What will you do?*" he repeated, gazing up at her with an expression that did look more like that of a puppy than a ram's. Hecate refused to turn towards him but kept her back ramrod straight and her head held high as she responded.

"*I'd beat her again.*"

"*I love to hear it,*" Aeëtes bleated in satisfaction, doubly proud of himself when Hecate suddenly had to stifle a laugh at the noise. Her hand came up quickly and covered her mouth, but the crack in that facade was there. He saw it. "*So relax a little. Don't look for trouble. You don't always have to be watching, waiting, all the time.*"

"*You don't know what I'm like all the time,*" Hecate quipped back, still playful but the edge had returned to her voice. Aeëtes wasn't really mad about either version of the goddess.

"*I know that look. It's seasoned. I've seen it on sailors, princes, and soldiers, Goddess. That's the look of someone who is evaluating a threat.*"

Hecate turned at that sharply and stared down at him with that emblazoned look in her eyes — now directed at him.

"*Is it?*" Her eyes glowed, the edges of her irises lighting up in a red ring. "*What do you think I see when I look at you, Aeëtes?*" It was a threat.

Aeëtes didn't take the bait.

"*Obviously, the most handsome ram that you've ever seen. You're worried you're attracted to a sheep. It's okay. I won't tell.*"

"*I thought it was a ram.*"

"*It can be whatever you want.*"

"*You are the most utterly insufferable person I have ever met. You aren't even talking for the god's sake…*"

"*If you took on the life debt for someone insufferable, I can't imagine what happens when you meet someone you actually like.*"

There was a beat of silence between them that went on for longer than Aeëtes's liking before Hecate responded. Her voice had gone cold, like one of her ghosts had taken her place.

"It's been a long time."

They fell into silence, and Aeëtes didn't push. He knew better. There was a fine line between goading Hecate into something more frivolous and distracting and knowing when he had struck a nerve. It had only been a few more paces when there was a shift in the wind...and Aeëtes smelled it. Rotting flowers.

He turned around as he tried to locate the source of the scent, but Hecate was way ahead of him. He felt her power ripple through the earth beneath them, as if she was pulling it up from the Underworld itself. That red, sparkling current was running in waves over her body. This time, when the heads of the maiden and the crone appeared, a circlet with the triple moon appeared on each of Hecate's three heads. Her crown. A crown fit for a queen. As if she was making a statement— a very purposeful statement—while she was waiting to square off with the queen of the gods.

Aeëtes couldn't help but feel that *maybe* he had a little bit to do with that.

There was a cracking sound, and they turned to the road's edge. A sharp wind burst through the trees that framed the path as trees began snapping left and right, as if invisible hands were breaking them in half. It got closer and closer, and Hecate's power flared up, the dogs appearing at her sides and the snakes winding around her arms.

There was a very primal part of Aeëtes's brain that suddenly wanted to run from the dogs—he rightfully assumed that this was the sheep's brain—but he greeted them like old friends. Hecate's magic smelled like rosemary, cinnamon, and death, and it made Aeëtes feel rooted. Grounded. He would no sooner run from her magic than he would run towards Hera's.

Aeëtes watched as Hecate moved her hands slowly in a circle, her gaze so focused that it almost looked vacant. Yet, ever so still, her lips moved, and so did those of the maiden and the crone. He could feel her magic pulse every time she uttered another word in a language that even he didn't understand — something that likely only the primordials would even recognize. Hecate's power moved like an element, cresting and crashing in front of her like water. It was enthralling to watch, and no matter how terrifying that cloying scent of flowers was, Aeëtes was not afraid.

The snapping sound got closer, and the last of the trees in front of them tumbled to the ground. Hecate threw her hands up in the air with a great shout. There was another torrent of wind all around them, and it began moving in a rapid vortex. Hecate's hair and the ends of her himation whipped around her, and she screamed — not out of fear or terror, but vengeance and anger. Aeëtes didn't know what she was saying, but it didn't matter.

She was illuminated in the center of the dangerous winds, her face obscured by her hair, but her eyes aflame and overcome with a blood red glow. Each of her heads was twisted into an expression of deadly terror, and Aeëtes saw it. This was the face of Hecate the Necromancer, Hecate the Goddess of ghosts, Hecate who lived in the Underworld...

Aeëtes didn't even realize that his heart had been on an edge, then suddenly, he fell off it. In his most foolish, reckless, and premature adventure yet, he fell in love.

He was unable to rip himself away from staring at Hecate, from looking up at her dark magic, the waves of power that undulated off of her. He was losing himself in it; it wrapped up around him like it circled Hera, both of them having very different experiences.

Because that was the essence of witchcraft.

It would meet every person, every soul, exactly where they were — and would return their sentiments back to them. It never interfered, never touched free will. Those who saw death and horror in Hecate's magic where the ones who were only ever the most terrified of themselves.

The world seemed to stop on its axis around them as the goddesses' magic collided into one another, causing the broken trees on the ground to shake. Hera was unseen, in the atmosphere around them, choking on the taste of Hecate's magic. Aeëtes was crippled at her feet, drinking willingly, and praying that the moment would never end.

Only a few moments had passed, but suddenly, the conflicting forces were gone.

Hera had vanished. Hecate dropped her hands and fell to her knees. She tried to catch her breath as her hand went up to her chest, her other arm holding her up. Her power slowly flickered out, and she breathed deeply, as if she was gently coaxing her magic to retreat. There was a soft sheen of sweat on her brow, and flickers of magic still existed in the shapes of snakes on her arms.

Aeëtes immediately moved over to her, tucking his head up under her chin, standing there, saying nothing…until she buried her head in the wool and leaned her weight against him.

Hera was gone.

There wasn't a word spoken between them.

❧ 1 2 ❧

"We should stay here." Hecate finally broke the silence between them, lifting her head and pulling herself away from Aeëtes. She leaned back against one of the broken Cyprus trees, closing her eyes. "It's too much of a risk when you're turned. Hera must be able to track you when you're under her curse."

Hecate quieted as her thoughts trailed off, her eyes popping back open. She straightened up, and Aeëtes turned his head to the side as he waited for her to continue.

"...and me. Of course. How could I be so ignorant? Hera can sense any god using their power. All immortals can."

Aeëtes made a noise in protest, and Hecate raised a hand in acknowledgement.

"Sorry. Most of the gods can, not every immortal." Hecate let out a long breath and leaned back against the tree, shaking her head and pinching the bridge of her nose. "We'll have to be more careful. No traveling while you're a ram, and I can't use large amounts of power. She'll be trying to find us that way."

"Will you be okay? Not...not using your power?" Aeëtes let the question slip before he had the good sense to bite his tongue, asking presumptuous questions about gods and their power. As

soon as he said it, however, he found that he didn't really care. He had never exactly been known for his restraint, but what little pieces he did have, he lost around Hecate. The goddess startled, looking at Aeëtes with a quizzical expression formed into her brow. She was careful to not let her thoughts be known, but Hecate chewed over the question, not remembering the last time that someone had asked her that.

"*What do you mean, will I be okay not using my power?*" In lieu of a shrug, Aeëtes shook his head a little once more.

"*I haven't been around the gods but it seems...personal when you use your power. More than I've heard of any other god. It feels like it might be, frustrating, if you have to...bottle it up.*"

"*You shouldn't be concerned with what I keep bottled up.*" Hecate's response was defensive, her eyes narrowing at him. There was mirth in Aeëtes's eyes that was unmistakable, and Hecate found herself wanting to turn him into mutton for it.

"*What can I say? I'm a giver. If you think that you need to release a little...pressure...*"

"*I will hunt you for sport,*" Hecate nearly growled, picking up a small twig and throwing it at him. "*Shoo. Go wait over there and don't cause any trouble until you're a man again.*"

"*You'll let me cause you a little trouble when I'm a man then?*"

"Aeëtes!" Hecate snapped, and he trotted a few paces away from her, making a noise that she swore sounded a lot like human laughter. She took a deep breath and closed her eyes, content to nap off the afternoon until it was time for them to finally depart for the harbor.

✛ ✛ ✛

THE UNLIKELY PAIR waited in the tree line, just out of sight from the road, until dusk. Hecate blinked her eyes open and held up her hand against a soft, warm glow of golden light that expanded until it covered her vision. Once it had faded away, she stood up without looking over at Aeëtes, pulling the shawl from her shoulders and tossing it in his direction.

"Don't tell me that you're suddenly shy?" Aeëtes's voice was so full of life, sometimes it made Hecate's shoulders tense. She had never met someone who was so full of it—both life and the capacity to drive her insane.

"Is it terribly hard for you to encounter a woman who has no interest in seeing you naked all the time?" Hecate rolled her eyes and looked over at Aeëtes, who filed in behind her as they headed back towards the main road.

"Is it terribly hard? If you'd look, you'd know." The chuckle was apparent in his voice, and Hecate turned around, shocked to find him so close to her. She had forgotten how...*big* he was. Everything about him was just large, even for an immortal, and it matched his personality in such a way that she wanted to send her dogs after him. It pushed and grated against memories that she wanted to bury and never resurrect. She took a step back and shook her head, pointing a finger at him.

"We are going to have to work together for some time to figure this whole mess out. If I can't use my magic without Hera finding us even quicker than she probably already will, it'll take even longer. Can you please attempt to be civil?"

Aeëtes scratched his jaw, rubbing his fingers over the overgrown stubble there as he appeared pensive.

"Don't hurt yourself too hard thinking," Hecate quipped, turning on her heel and storming off down the road towards the docks. Aeëtes, once again, only laughed in response, jogging up to her...and it took far too much of her own strength not to stare. He had wrapped her shawl around him and tied it in the style of chlamys, but without a chiton underneath, his entire side was exposed—including his thigh.

"Don't hurt yourself too hard staring," he grinned in

return, reaching her side and tossing an arm around her shoulders in a way that was entirely too casual. Hecate nearly froze. "What are you doing?" she hissed, moving away from him. Aeëtes's expression changed immediately as he stared at his arm and looked at her. His face contorted until there was an expression there that was equally challenging and playful.

"If you want me to let go," he said and when he spoke, his voice was low, as if he was speaking to a frightened animal, "all you have to do is say the word."

He was genuine, and Hecate felt the blood drain from her face. He was looking at her like she was injured, like she was something to be pitied, and it infuriated her. What she couldn't understand was that the pain in his eyes was duly out of respect, out of an admiration for her that he had betrayed, even innocently with his easygoing nature. After eons of dealing with men with malignant intentions, she didn't know how to process the genuine apology written on his face.

"I, oh… I didn't… I was just surprised." She swallowed thickly, the kindness in his face making something entirely different well up in her. "That, it…it was fine. I have no problem with," she waved her hand generally in his direction, "you know."

The smile returned to Aeëtes's face nearly immediately, his entire countenance brightening again. He raised a brow, and his grin turned nearly devilish.

"I thought that might be the case." He hugged her a little bit tighter to him, and she let out a strangled shriek of frustration.

"You insufferable prince!" she seethed, but Aeëtes dropped his arm from her and burst out into laughter, a sound that was getting increasingly on Hecate's nerves. He waved in the direction of the port, clearly looking at the sea with unbridled happiness.

"Shall we?" He stepped to the side and made a grand show of bowing towards her, his arm still extended in the direction they were headed. Hecate rolled her eyes as she sauntered past him, her head now held high, and an attempt at contempt flashed across her face. Aeëtes didn't believe it for a second.

He couldn't help himself as she walked down the sloping road, his eyes falling to the way her waist dipped and her ass moved as she walked. The drapery of the fabric clung to her in such a way that Aeëtes found himself jealous of a piece of cotton. He shook his head once to bring himself to reality and trailed after her, both of them falling into an easy silence as they neared the pier.

"Do you know anyone who might be able to take us to Colchis?" Hecate asked as they approached the first dock.

The docks at Heraklion were some of the busiest in all of Crete. It was the closest harbor to the palace and the seat of the royal family, as well as one of the biggest markets on the island. It was a popular spot for ships as they came from Greece and Anatolia, intersecting here before going on with their journeys. There were a few warships tied up, sleek and furious, painted with emblems and the symbols of Aries. It was the merchant ships that took up the majority of the docks, constantly loading and unloading with all sorts of goods. There were spices coming from Byzantium and even further East, fish from the Mediterranean, and bolts of cloth and gold coming from North Africa.

Hecate found herself slightly overwhelmed by the sights — everything here was a flood for the senses, vastly different from the calm of the Underworld. She found her steps faltering slightly, nearly slipping on the wet wood, until a large, warm set of hands went around her waist. It was just for a brief moment, but Aeëtes steadied her until she stood upright. He dropped away from her a moment later, a gentle smile on his face as if he didn't want to intrude upon her pride, and motioned in the direction of the far end of the pier.

"Trust me, there's always a ship ready to take me to Colchis, whether I like it or not." Hecate thought that there was a note of sadness in his voice for one second, but it faltered, and he gave her a quick wink and lead her through the crowd. She trailed after him, walking in the natural space that his body cut through all the people, trying not to think about the warmth on her skin where he had touched her.

There was a magnificent merchant ship at the farthest end of the dock. It was three levels deep, Hecate could see from the depth of its hull, with two large sails. There was an extended gangplank going from the pier up to the deck of the ship, being loaded and unloaded by a crew of men. Aeëtes was peering through the merchants, seemingly looking for someone in particular. She was about to ask who he was looking for when he yelled out something reminiscent of a battle cry.

"Aeëtes!" she chided, her hand going up to cover her ear as she scoffed and shied away from him. He tossed her a quick, bashful shrug but looked towards the ship, where someone was now hanging over the side.

"Pelias! My dear friend." Aeëtes smiled, running over towards the edge of the dock. "You wouldn't happen to be heading east, would you?"

Hecate found herself holding her breath, waiting for the answer, always waiting to see if they would need a new plan. Pelias laughed and shook his head, looking at Aeëtes in confused surprise.

"I've been waiting ten years for you to *ask* me to take you to Colchis. You spend one night at my house, disappear before sunrise, and now…you want to go home. Should I be concerned?"

Aeëtes winked at his friend and turned around, taking in the chaos around the pier. "When are you set to depart?" Hecate noticed that he didn't answer his friend's questions, assuming Aeëtes had been with Pelias when Hera had cursed him.

"The sun is setting," Pelias mused, looking out towards the horizon. "We'd like to clear the harbor by nightfall. We're a little behind schedule. If you want to come, there's always room."

"That's because it's my parents' ship, you fool," Aeëtes laughed. Pelias was unaffected, and he waved them on.

"Are you going to introduce me to your lovely friend, Aeëtes?" Pelias peered behind Aeëtes and looked at Hecate, a warm expression crossing his face that Hecate noticed was kindly devoid of any lechery. "Better yet, she seems like she can introduce herself."

I like you. Hecate decided as she evaluated the merchant, immediately approving of his countenance and how he had deferred to her. She opened her mouth to speak, but Aeëtes interrupted her quickly, taking a step in front of her.

"We'll get on board, and once we're out of the harbor, we'll fill you in."

Pelias looked slightly confused but nodded, moving away from the railing and disappearing out of sight on the ship. Hecate opened her mouth to chastise him, but Aeëtes turned to her, pressing a finger to his lips.

"I trust this crew, but I wouldn't trust just anyone you meet on the docks. Once we're aboard with Pelias, then we'll be safer. I would rather this crowd not know you're a goddess." He gave her an appraising look, noting the glamour she wore to dampen her magic.

"Why is that?" Hecate scoffed. "Do you not think I could handle myself?"

"I know that you could." Aeëtes's eyebrows shot up. "But once you take out every man on this dock who has a grudge against you because their girlfriend left them, Hera will catch a whiff of that magic."

Hecate opened her mouth to dispute him but shut it and nodded. "Fair enough."

"Let's go," Aeëtes said gently, steering her towards the gangplank. Hecate took a careful step up on the sharp bridge, and Aeëtes's hands went to her hips once more, steadying her.

"Watch your step there." His voice was hardly a whisper in her ear, his body pressed up against hers as he waited for her to catch her footing.

Hecate felt a chill go down her spine as he righted her for the second time since they stepped onto the docks. She hoped that he didn't hear the catch in her breath as she almost hoped he wouldn't move away. Hecate fought a sudden urge to lean into his warmth, to drop her head on his shoulder. She had never felt such an overcharge of emotions from the smallest of embraces.

Aeëtes cleared his throat, pulling away from her as he misread her sudden silence for disgust.

"Right up towards the deck, there you go," he said encouragingly enough, but Hecate felt her mood sour. She had never liked taking instruction.

"I know how to walk, Aeëtes," she snapped, turning around and storming up the rest of the way until she disappeared. She walked past Pelias, who took a few steps down the gangplank and looked at Aeëtes.

"What have you gotten yourself into?"

Aeëtes only smiled, licking his teeth as he watched Hecate walk away. "An adventure, Pelias…an adventure."

PART II

❧ 13 ❧

Hecate waited at the edge of the ship, keeping her eyes on the coast of Heraklion as the ship bustled with activity around her. She had been on a boat before, but it had been a long time ago…long before boats were ever this large, before they had fit so many people.

There was only the slightest bit of sunlight left. She watched Helios begin to drive his horses over the horizon, shaking her head at him and wondering if he knew anything about the mess that Hera had put his son in. He had never mentioned a son at all, now that she thought about it.

To be fair, I haven't exactly kept up with my correspondence to the Olympus squabbles. She rolled her eyes even if no one was there to see it. Hecate was the first to admit that she had no patience for the newly formed pantheon; she thought they had been annoying before the uprising against Kronos, and she thought they were annoying now. Still, she knew most everyone. Aeëtes had been a…surprise.

Yes, that's what we're calling it. Hecate was almost annoyed with herself as she mused over their first meeting.

There was a massive heave, and the ship tipped to one side, causing Hecate to grab onto the rail and dig her fingers into the wood with a hiss. She looked over the edge until she saw the anchor being hauled up from the sea floor, signaling that they were getting ready to depart. It was going to take awhile until she found her sea legs, if she did at all. She was comfortable in the Underworld, and there was nothing more solid than earth to her; spending this much time on water was going to make her uneasy for the entire voyage.

Aeëtes watched her from the opposite side of the deck, his arms crossed over his chest as he leaned against the railing in nonchalance. Pelias stood next to him, shaking his head in utter disbelief. The chaos around them picked up as soon the gangplank was pulled away from the edge, the boat pushing off. Once they were out of hearing range from anyone on the deck, Pelias turned to Aeëtes.

"You want to tell me how you disappeared from my roof and a day later, you ask to go to Colchis for the first time in your life...traveling with a *goddess?*" He said the last word in a whisper, pressing in closer to his friend and jamming a finger into his chest. "And half naked, for the god's sake!"

"She's not half naked," Aeëtes murmured, sounding almost disappointed, while Pelias looked ready to smack him.

"I'm aware. I'm also disturbingly aware of the fact that *you're* the one half-naked."

"Oh, that." Aeëtes adjusted the chlamys slightly. "I'll grab some clothes from my cabin."

"That would be lovely." Pelias rolled his eyes. "You also ignored my other question."

Aeëtes nodded, not paying attention to a single thing that his friend said, still staring at Hecate as she absentmindedly braided her hair in the rising moonlight. "Yes, I'll get the clothes—ow!"

Pelias smacked him upside the head and rolled his eyes. Aeëtes shook to attention and turned to him, a petulant look on his face like a child who had just stolen sweets.

"How did you end up bringing *Hecate* onto my ship?" Pelias asked again, his voice a little louder this time.

"It is probably more appropriate to say that I brought Aeëtes to you," Hecate's smooth voice cut in between the two men as they both turned to look at her.

Now that she had Aeëtes's promise that he trusted his crew and they were safely away from Heraklion, she had let her glamour begin to slip. She looked like she was floating as she crossed the deck of the ship, her eyes glittering with moonlight as it played off her skin and hair. Aeëtes could swear that when she moved, he could see the spells written into her skin by flakes of the moon itself. Even her diadem, in the shape of the triple crown, appeared when she turned her head a certain way. She was transforming by the second into the Goddess of the Moon, and Aeëtes stared at her with the look of a starving man.

Pelias gave him a sharp elbow to the side, causing him to straighten up. "You've got your heart written across your face, friend."

Aeëtes only shrugged as Hecate stepped closer to them, "Might as well. There's no point keeping anything from a goddess anyway."

"That's true," Hecate agreed with him, although he could tell by her attitude that she hadn't heard Pelias's remark.

"So what brings you aboard and on your way to Colchis? I'm sure the royal family will lay out all the tribute you'd desire for bringing their son back to them so soon," Pelias chuckled at the mention of the royal family, but Aeëtes remarkably didn't.

"Isn't it obvious?" Aeëtes looked from Hecate to Pelias. "She fell in love with me as soon as she saw me." Both Hecate and Pelias made a groan, stopping and giving each other a nod of camaraderie when they realized they both had the same low tolerance for Aeëtes at times.

"Wrong place, wrong time," Hecate quipped. "That's probably a better way to put it. In short, you need to know that I've taken on a life debt for Aeëtes, and he's been cursed by Hera. We need to go to Colchis to try and break the spell, but we'll need you to change course and take us to Aeaea first. Can you do that?" Hecate said everything to Pelias in a rather mundane tone, as if she was letting him know what the weather had been like on their journey. Aeëtes couldn't help but let out a squawk of laughter at the look on Pelias's face as he processed it.

"So…life debt, Hera, curse, Aeaea. Yeah. That's…normal." Pelias choked out the words before he looked over at Aeëtes, waiting a minute before bursting out into laughter. Hecate recoiled slightly, confused at his merriment, but watched as both men nearly sunk to their knees in mirth.

"Is something about that funny to you?" she asked rather genuinely. She had never seen a mortal man with such a trivial response to getting caught up in the whims of the gods. It was often fatal to man.

Pelias wiped a tear from his eye as he stood up, clapping a hand over his belly. "Aeëtes always said that no force on earth would get him to go to Colchis willingly." He gave Hecate a slight bow. "It looks like it took a force from the Underworld, after all. Now, if you will excuse me, we've got a new heading, and there is no way that I am going to be handling all of this sober."

He sauntered past them, disappearing below decks, presumably straight to the galley.

"He's…something." Hecate noted without any malice in her voice.

"He is." Aeëtes grinned, leaning back on his elbows against the railing. "We've been friends since we were kids. He comes from a well-known merchant family, so he trained a little at the palace. Since then, he's been hired by my parents."

"To do what?" Hecate raised a brow.

"Essentially, make sure I get back on the boat every time I need to go to Colchis."

"You really don't want to go back, do you?" Hecate studied

him, her head turning ever so slightly to one side. Aeëtes looked at her, feeling his heart tumble around in his chest as she met his gaze. He felt everything that had ever tied him to the mortal world begin to snap, bit by bit, as he realized that he would chase the moon itself for the chance to keep looking at Hecate.

"No, I don't want to go back," Aeëtes said quietly, the words hanging in the air between them before he stood up straighter and cracked his knuckles. "But what can you do?" His impervious smirk was back, grinning at Hecate like he had a secret.

She rolled her eyes, crossing her arms over her chest. "Has anyone ever told you that there are dogs more mature than you?"

Aeëtes's smile only got wider. "That's because you're the Goddess of dogs, Hecate."

"Well, they listen to me when I tell them to sit down and bark."

"I would, too." Aeëtes winked at her and stood straighter, pushing himself off the railing. As he passed Hecate, he leaned down until his lips barely brushed the shell of her ear. "I could be a very good boy."

She turned around as her face flushed red, ready to throw him overboard, but he was already laughing, disappearing down into the galley after Pelias.

"Ridiculous man." Hecate pressed a hand to her chest, trying to ignore the heat that had curled up at the base of her spine. She walked over to the edge of the deck, peering out over the moonlight on the water as the ship began to slowly change course for Aeaea.

✝ ✝ ✝

Aeaea was not far from Crete. It was a small island, walkable from one side to the other in about a day, and hardly ever attracted any visitors. That was due in part to Circe.

There were very few people who could be mentioned in the same breath as Hecate when it came to magic, but Circe could stand her ground. She was more well-versed in potions, and on some levels, her affinity with animals was even stronger. She had once been Hecate's greatest devotee, but since she was born immortal, she transitioned into a deity in her own right after years of study. There was a deep respect and a love between the two women that was shared through mutual pain as well as joy; each woman knew that there were parts of themselves that no one would quite ever understand like the other.

The night had passed rather uneventfully with Hecate staying on deck to try and keep her sea legs under her. Pelias and Aeëtes had disappeared to the galley, and judging by the amount of noise, Hecate rightfully assumed that meant getting drunk for the better portion of the night. As soon as it was nearing sunrise, the coast of Aeaea was finally coming into view.

Hecate peered over the railing as she looked at it, getting as close to a sense of homecoming as she could get outside of the Underworld. Aeaea was only ever visible to those who were allowed to visit — Hecate being one of them — and that visitor's list was subject to Circe's whims. As the glimmering sands came into view, her heart swelled. She hadn't realized how many things had been weighing on her since leaving the Underworld, and she was desperate to get to talk to Circe alone…if only just to beg for her help. And she would likely have to beg.

"I'm surprised you never stepped down for a drink!" Pelias's voice carried over the deck, and Hecate turned to face him. He was ruddy-cheeked and wild-haired, looking — but thankfully, not smelling — like he hadn't bathed in weeks. He had warm, gray eyes that matched his graying hair. It was her first good look at Pelias, and he was obviously very warm-natured, with a million small things hanging off his person, from sea-faring instruments to small wine jars.

"I figured it was best to let you two catch up." Hecate smiled gracefully, nodding in the direction of the galley. "I assume that Aeëtes is still..."

"Drunk off his ass?"

"Weighed down from last night's engagements." Hecate chuckled, unable to help herself around such a disarming personality.

"He'll be up soon enough. I know he's eager to speak with you before the sheep thing happens again."

"Ah, the sheep thing." Hecate raised her eyebrows and looked out over the horizon, seeing it begin to glow with the promise of Helios's journey. "Did he tell you anything else about the night that Hera cursed him?"

"No. You know Aeëtes."

"I'm rather afraid I don't," Hecate said quietly, her eyes flickering down to the floorboards. She desperately tried to hide the curiosity in her eyes.

"Ah." If Pelias caught onto what Hecate wasn't saying, he didn't mention it. He merely clapped his hands together loudly, letting them come to rest on his waist. "He's a good lad."

"You say that as if you were older than him."

"Well, I suppose I am, in a way. We grew up together, but he stopped aging around a certain point, damn immortality." He winked at Hecate to convey that there were no hard feelings in between the men for this. "I suppose he's...taken a bit more time to mature since he's got the time. However, know this—"

"If it isn't my two most favorite people!" Aeëtes swaggered towards them, throwing the door to the galley wide open as he sauntered over to the two of them, his arms held out. Whatever Pelias was going to say died on his tongue, and he held a finger to his mouth to silence Hecate on the topic. Aeëtes approached them, throwing an arm around Pelias and openly staring at Hecate as if she'd hung the stars.

"Good morning, Goddess," he grinned wildly.

Hecate shook her head, looking out over the water and nodding in the direction of the rising sun.

"You're awfully good-natured for someone about to turn into a ram," she warned, raising one eyebrow at him and refusing to acknowledge what his sunny disposition was starting to do to her.

"That's Aeaea, no?" Aeëtes gestured, pointing in its direction and skillfully deflecting.

"Yes," Hecate turned her head around to him, her expression sobering. "Listen, Aeëtes, when we get there, do not do anything to upset Circe."

Aeëtes looked slightly offended. "I realize I'm not your favorite person, *allegedly* —" He started to defend himself when Hecate held up a hand.

"I'm serious. Listen to me, do not do anything to upset her. You'll be turned, but just let me do the talking and do not throw a…sheep fit, or something."

"A sheep fit." Aeëtes cocked his head to the side, unimpressed. "Sure, I won't throw a fit, no matter what you say to Circe. Might I ask why you think I'm such a threat to our little adventure here?"

"As opposed to all the usual reasons?" Pelias chimed in, and Hecate had to quickly stifle her amusement. The sun was coming up over the horizon and that familiar, strange glow began to emanate from Aeëtes.

"Yes, I'll tell you, as soon as you've turned."

"As soon as I've turned?" Aeëtes squawked, now realizing that she didn't want him to be able to react properly to whatever she had to say.

"In a second…" Hecate trailed off, watching as he transformed again with the rising sun back into the body of a golden ram. She held her breath and waited until the transfiguration was complete, and he made another bleating sound in frustration. Hecate sighed deeply and looked from Pelias to Aeëtes.

"The reason you need to keep your mouth shut while we're on Aeaea…" Hecate bit her lip, and Aeëtes saw a glimpse of an insecure Hecate for the first time.

"…is because Circe is your sister."

🎕 14 🎕

Hecate winced slightly at the shriek that came out of Aeëtes, wondering if she had ever even heard an animal make a noise like that before. "I know," she sighed, running a hand through her long hair. "I will explain everything. Circe knows, however, so this won't be a surprise to her. The fact that we're here asking for help regarding you *will* be a surprise."

"We're not... um," Pelias fumbled over his words, anxiously looking around, "We're not in danger going on land to Aeaea, are we?"

Hecate's eyes flashed red for a brief second as she turned to Pelias. "Absolutely not. The rumors about Circe are just that. They're rumors. I won't bring a trembling, suspicious crew to her front door, so you better tell the men to cut that thinking out right now." She got louder as she spoke, another wave of red magic rolling over her skin as she finished.

Pelias nodded once and bowed his head, dismissing himself and going to prepare the crew to drop anchor and ready boats for going ashore.

"Do you want to enlighten me as to why I have a sister that no one told me about?" Aeëtes's voice was loud in her head, and

Hecate sighed. She looked down at him, taking pity on him for once.

"I'm sorry. I wasn't aware that you didn't know when I mentioned Circe. You didn't react at all... I realized you had never been told."

"She's...she's a daughter of Helios?"

Hecate sighed, tenderness bleeding into her expression as she nodded her head once. Maybe it would have been better to have this conversation with Aeëtes as a man.

"A daughter of Helios," Hecate confirmed, her breath catching, *"and the daughter of an oceanid, whose name Circe never learned."*

If Aeëtes could have fallen to the ground, he would've. He merely stumbled, before falling back onto his hindquarters, rather ungracefully. If Hecate had been having any other conversation with him, she would've burst out into laughter at the sight.

"She's...my full sister, then. She never knew our mother...?"

"She did not. Honestly. I've known Circe for many years, and I've never heard her speak of her mother. I didn't know that you were her brother when we met. When you said you were the son of Helios and an oceanid, I merely thought you knew about Circe. It didn't feel appropriate to bring it up."

Aeëtes knew that Hecate was being genuine, which somehow made it hurt even more. The gods' families and their family trees got messy, and quickly, so immortals weren't in the habit of commenting on them. There was a beat of silence between them, and Hecate could sense that a wall had gone back up around Aeëtes's thoughts. She waited patiently, resting against the railing as she heard the boats being prepared, the ship coming to a gentle stop off the shore.

"She knows of me, though?"

"She's much older than you, so, yes."

"Why...wouldn't she want to help me?" There was something in Aeëtes's voice, even in her mind, that sounded small. She knew that there was a part of Aeëtes that was asking why his family didn't seem to want *him,* and it ripped away a part of the barri-

cade around her heart. Hecate was overwhelmed with the urgency to put that goofy smile back on his face, to see that ridiculous, never-ending cheer come spilling out of him.

"It's not you that she has a problem. It's Helios. If she doesn't want to help, it'll be because she doesn't want to do anything to benefit him. Don't worry. I'll talk to her."

Aeëtes didn't respond at first, but when he did, it was with his normal vigor. *"Well, I can't have a bad day when my fate rests in your hands, can I, Goddess?"*

"Aeëtes…" Hecate groaned, fighting the urge to roll her eyes as her sympathy for him vanished as quickly as his cockiness reappeared. She was continually dumbfounded by his ability to rebound from virtually any scenario and remain unfazed.

"But I'd be happy if I could get any part of me in your hands, sweetness."

"It's truly shocking to me that another god hasn't killed you for the shit that comes out of your mouth." Hecate heard the call for the boats and walked off, Aeëtes trailing behind her.

"I can do much more wicked things with it, I promise."

"Pelias!" Hecate yelled out to the captain as she pointed at Aeëtes. "You come get Aeëtes, or I will cast a spell to castrate him before we even reach Aeaea."

☩ ☩ ☩

IN THE END, only Pelias, Hecate, and Aeëtes went ashore. Hecate was true to her word about not wanting to take anyone who might be disrespectful, and to their credit, the crew was honest about their hesitancies. As much as she didn't like it, she appreciated that they were forthcoming enough to admit their prejudices.

"It does seem a bit silly to be so bent out of shape over, what? A woman and her witchcraft?" Aeëtes pondered their skeleton crew as Pelias rowed them ashore.

"You'd be surprised," Hecate answered in a way that almost made Aeëtes angry, with a tone that said she had experienced too much of it firsthand. When their small boat finally moored on the shore, Aeëtes hopped out, and Hecate helped Pelias drag it further inland to avoid being swept out by the tide. They were on a small beach, only a stone's throw from a small hill that obscured their view of the rest of the island. It was dotted with Cyprus and lemon trees, and there was something different in the air.

Everything on the island seemed to be...alive. Aeëtes could almost smell it, from the sand to the trees, it was as if everything on the island was breathing in sync.

"The island is imbued with Circe's magic," Hecate explained, knowing that it was a bit of a shock the first time that someone visited Aeaea. "It breathes as she does. It responds to her."

"It's a little bit uncanny," Pelias's eyes hadn't stopped moving around, as if he was searching for a threat.

"You'll get used to it." Hecate refused to give into any more fear mongering around her Circe. She went a few more steps inland until she found a large piece of driftwood, promptly sitting down on it. Aeëtes watched as she rearranged her skirts, tightened her braid, and leaned back as if she was sunning herself.

"Are we going to...you know... find Circe?" Aeëtes trotted over to where Hecate was sitting, lying down at her feet. Pelias joined them, sitting on the other side of the log, giving Hecate ample room.

"You don't find Circe; she finds you." Hecate shrugged simply. "She knows that we're here. She'll show herself when she pleases." Hecate could easily locate Circe on the island, but the last thing that she wanted to do was cross her boundaries.

Circe had gone through enough in her life as it was, and
Hecate knew that she always liked to greet guests on her own
terms. The trio said nothing and settled in for the wait.

They didn't have to wait long.

Aeëtes found himself drifting off. As soon as his eyelids
began to droop, he sensed a fresh wave of magic go through
the topsoil. He could tell immediately that it wasn't Hecate's
magic, which he'd recognize anywhere, as if his system was
primed for it. This was similar, but different. While Hecate's
magic was like rosemary and cinnamon, death and rebirth, this
was…different. There was a sharpness to it that was unlike the
duality of Hecate's balancing act. This magic, while maybe not
as strong as Hecate, was equally potent.

It reminded him of citrus and vinegar, strong and astrin-
gent, utterly unapologetic. It wasn't unkind, but he immediately jumped to his feet and began looking for the source of it.
Pelias must have noticed the same thing, too, because his hand
was at the sword on his belt. Only Hecate stood slowly, a smile
crossing her face as she breathed in deeply, welcoming in the
scent and feel of Circe's pulsing magic.

There was a glimmer through the trees, and rather
suddenly, out stepped Circe.

She was strikingly tall, not taller than Aeëtes, but standing
taller than Hecate and Pelias. Her face was wide, with a sharp
chin and sharper cheekbones, with equally piercing eyes.
While she might not have ever been described as pretty, she
was an undoubtedly striking and handsome woman. She had
hair that went down to her waist, a curtain of thick brown hair
that had a few pieces tied in braids throughout. She wore a
white chiton, but she tied it only at one shoulder and wore it
without a belt; leaving both of her sides and one breast
exposed. As she walked towards them, her chiton began
stitching itself together; her hair braided itself, and sandals
appeared on her feet.

There was a wildness to her, something that Aeëtes had

sensed before in Hecate. Circe had not spent the millennia learning to control it, like Hecate had…and Aeëtes's only thought was to wonder what it looked like when Hecate *really* lost control. He was so lost in his own fantasies that he had completely forgotten Circe as she approached them—only until he was nearly face-to-face with the lioness at her side.

"*Hecate!*" Aeëtes yelled, coming out as a sharp bleating sound, which made both of the women laugh as they pulled away from hugging one another. They were already engaged in conversation, and he had been too distracted to hear it. Pelias looked on with wide eyes, wise enough to keep his mouth closed as he tried to absorb everything happening around him. Circe had tampered some of her own wildness, effectively putting a glamour over herself to not frighten them, now dressed like any other woman.

"Aeëtes," Hecate chided, looking down at him and then towards Circe. "She already told you that no harm would come to you."

"Aeëtes?" Circe's head snapped back to Hecate. "You mean…?" Hecate held her ground, nodding her head once, before reaching out and gently grabbing hold of Circe's wrist in a loving gesture.

"Yes. Please believe me when I say that I mean you no harm by bringing him here. You must know this. We need your help, and only you can help us. I hadn't realized you two had never met until we were already on the way here."

There was a thrumming of magic all around them, as if the air came alive in response. Aeëtes couldn't explain it, but he could feel it in the sand and in the trees, as if the whole island responded when Circe didn't. The lioness at her side remained still but kept looking at Aeëtes with eyes that were far too comprehensive for a normal animal—and he would know. It felt like everyone held their breath until Circe spoke.

"Of course. I trust you, Hecate." The relief between the group was palpable, so palpable that it made Circe chuckle.

She threaded her arm through Hecate's, and the two began walking off towards the hill, Pelias and Aeëtes following behind them.

"Were you so worried that I wouldn't help you, sister?" Circe said with a grin, partially pleased that her fearsome reputation had managed to slightly affect even Hecate herself.

"I knew that you would." Hecate smiled, looking over her shoulder at Aeëtes before turning back to Circe. "I just didn't know how much convincing I would have to do."

The two witches lost themselves in conversation as they walked over the hill, threading down a gently used path until a small house came into view. There was nothing overly grand about it, but it was thoroughly made with stone, as opposed to wood, mud, or straw. A modest but fine dwelling. It reverberated magic, and both women seemed to come a little more alive when they caught sight of it.

"You should stay for a while and recharge," Circe noted, seeing some of the visible relief that flooded Hecate's face. "You know that Aeaea always does you good."

"I would be a fool to deny it," Hecate shrugged, "but we are hurried. I'll tell you everything once we're inside. The longer we stay, however, the greater danger that you're in."

"Ah," Circe sighed, making a small *tsk* noise. "It's like that?"

Hecate only answered with a nod.

The four of them made it down the hill and were welcomed into Circe's home, a feat that was rare enough as it was. It was nearly identical, if not smaller in size, to Hecate's home in the Underworld. There was a large, wooden kitchen table, a counter nearby, and a roaring hearth. The counter was overflowing with empty jars, half-filled amphoras, and herbs of every variety. Even Pelias, who had seen most every spice and plant in the known world throughout his time as a sailor, couldn't identify a few.

Aeëtes settled himself in front of the fire, acting a little bit more like a dog than a ram, his golden wool casting rainbows of light all over the kitchen. He figured it was as good a time as any for a nap. Pelias joined him, sitting down at the table and leaning against the wall. Hecate and Circe went around and stood at the kitchen counter, Hecate easily identifying what Circe was working on and beginning to help. The two women moved in silent tandem for a few minutes, basking in the familiarity of being next to someone with whom you didn't need to explain yourself.

Hecate helped Circe make quick work of the potions that she had in progress before Circe poured them both cups of wine as they moved to the other end of the kitchen. Circe flicked two fingers up in the air, and Hecate recognized the gesture. She had blocked their voices from traveling towards Pelias and Aeëtes, effectively giving them privacy.

"Tell me then, what's happening?" Circe finally asked, taking a long sip. Hecate did the same, nearly downing all of her wine before she began. She managed to tell Circe everything, from how she felt like she needed to leave the Underworld, to Hera's life debt, and the spell that she thought would break the curse.

"The blood of the mother, hmm?" Circe pursed her lips and tapped a finger at her chin, looking over to Aeëtes. "I don't suppose you think that's in Colchis."

Hecate shrugged. "We'll have to try and get an audience with Helios there. You don't…you never learned her name, did you?" Hecate was gentle, hating that she had to ask the question at all. Circe went still, as if she wasn't even breathing, and shook her head.

"I hope that's not what you needed my help for. I will be of no assistance to you. Helios dropped me in Colchis, too, and never told me our mother's name."

"No, no." Hecate took another sip from her cup. "I came for your talents, sister."

"Where do you need me?" Circe interrupted her at that part. "It sounds like you can carry out that spell in your sleep."

"I can." Hecate nodded. "He still turns into a ram every day. He transforms back at night. It's getting increasingly dangerous for us to travel while he's…"

"A solid gold ram?"

"Noticeable, isn't it?" Hecate deadpanned, both women looking over to where Aeëtes was nearly sparkling in front of the fireplace. "You're better with animal transfiguration than I am. Is there any way you can put a temporary stop to it? At least until the curse is lifted."

Circe took another sip of her wine, seemingly mulling it over before she nodded. "I think that it'll work. I should be able to turn him into a man, and it'll hold for…well, I can't be sure how long. It will hold until Hera's curse wears through my spell, but that could be tomorrow, or it could be in two weeks."

"I certainly think that you're a better spell caster than *Hera*, Circe." There was a lift to Hecate's voice, and she smiled over the rim of her cup, knowing that she was goading Circe slightly. She always performed better magic when she was angry, and sure enough, she let out a low hiss.

"I'll make it hold. It should last until you get to Colchis."

"I knew you could do it." Hecate grinned. "Do you need anything in particular?"

"No." Circe waved Hecate off and topped off both of their cups. "I'll do what I always do. I could do it backwards. Now…" There was a change in her tone that was downright conspiratorial. "Tell me more about you and Aeëtes."

Hecate choked on her wine, spitting some of it out and staining the front of her himation. "Circe!"

"Oh, stop." Circe waved her hand once, and the stain vanished. She wiggled her eyebrows. "Be honest with me now. You don't get to show up here with my long-lost brother, cursed by Hera, and don't tell me the fun bits."

"There's nothing to tell." Hecate pursed her lips, refusing to meet Circe's gaze.

"Uh-huh." Circe was wholly unconvinced. "Then why does he look at you like you're the sun? Which is an impressive look to pull off as a sheep. Why did you take on a life debt for a mortal man that you didn't know?"

"It was the right thing to do. I couldn't let Hera win."

"Sure," Circe conceded, acknowledging that that was valid. "That's not the only reason, though."

"I assure you, it very much is. He is the worst kind of man, utterly spoilt and always walking around with that stupid grin on his face. Do you know that he always has a retort for *everything?* The things he says, my god, another goddess would've struck him down, and he's so... He's ridiculously tall."

"You haven't said a single thing to convince me that you aren't into him," Circe interrupted her, turning her head to the side as she encouraged Hecate to go on.

"Now, that's not fair. I'm only involved with him because of..."

"Yes, I know." Circe smiled, not believing Hecate in the slightest. "The life debt. It's just an observation." She took another sip of her wine, clearly pleased with herself as Hecate let out a puff of air.

"He loves his freedom. He ran from your adoptive parents in Colchis. He's always on the run..." Hecate's voice trailed off. "Men will always choose their freedom, Circe, remember that."

"I live on an island with a lion."

"Fair point."

"Come on now," Circe smiled, grabbing both of their cups and putting them down on the counter. "Let's go turn your prince back into a man."

"He is *not...*" Hecate started to defend herself, but Circe waved her fingers again, breaking the privacy wards that she had put up around them. It effectively cut Hecate off, who merely scowled at Circe. The latter was laughing into her hand as she walked over to where Pelias and Aeëtes were having their midday nap.

"Alright, let's get this underway, so you can be on with your journey." Circe cleared her throat, stirring both men to attention. "Are you ready to be a man again, Aeëtes? Or should I say, *brother?*"

✢ 15 ✢

Aeëtes made what Hecate assumed to be a cheerful noise, standing up on four legs. Pelias stretched his arms out behind him, looking rather well rested, smiling at Circe as though she was the most magical thing that he had ever seen. Which was also true. Circe merely looked him over once, stopping where his feet were propped up on the bench and raising an eyebrow.

"Feet on the floor," she said sharply. "My home is not a ship." Hecate liked Pelias but had to stifle her own bout of laughter at the mortified look on his face. He scrambled to get his feet off the bench so quickly that he nearly tumbled off it entirely. Circe was unamused, turning her attention back to Aeëtes, who was fidgeting back and forth on his hooves.

Hecate did not admit to herself that it was rather cute.

She did not.

Circe stepped closer to Aeëtes, holding her hands out gently with her palms facing down.

"Stay still, Aeëtes," Hecate said aloud, looking at him with a stern glance.

"Is this going to hurt?" He turned his head over to her and nodded in Circe's direction, looking up at her hands.

"Are you a child? No, it's not going to hurt." Hecate's mouth settled into a thin line as she stared down at him, looking utterly unamused. Circe turned back to face Hecate with a little shrug. "Well, I couldn't tell you to be honest. It might." She cringed slightly and turned back around to Aeëtes, rubbing her hands together as if they were cold.

"*Hecate!*" Aeëtes's bleated loudly, the sound echoing in Hecate's head so loudly that she held a hand up to her ear and sat down. "Stop screaming!" she snapped. "Goodness. Men always love to talk about their bravado, but the threat of a bit of pain, and you're no worse than a babe."

"It will be fine," Circe reassured Aeëtes. "This might be the first time I've changed an animal to a man, though." She paused, tilting her head as if she was running through an internal list. "Yes, yes, I think it is. I've really only ever changed men to animals, not the other way around."

"Let's get on with it," Hecate sighed, reaching back over the counter and grabbing the wine. "The sooner this is over, the sooner we can get to Colchis, and then...the sooner this can be over."

"*You certainly don't want to be rid of me that quickly, do you, witch?*" Aeëtes's voice was warm inside her head, almost coaxing. Hecate topped off her cup and took another large sip, refusing to answer.

Circe straightened her shoulders and rubbed her palms together, standing taller. The simple motion changed the atmosphere of the home, and everyone turned their attention to her. Hecate watched carefully as Aeëtes stamped his feet a few times, as if mentally preparing himself, and stared up at Circe with wide eyes.

All at once, the oxygen seemed to be ripped from the room. The fire in the hearth went out, tendrils of smoke beginning to pour out from the embers. Pelias looked out the window, swearing that even the sun had dimmed slightly. Circe swayed on her feet, her eyes fluttering closed, but suddenly, they flew open. Her neck snapped back, now staring at the ceiling, while her arms extended out in front of her, and her palms faced down over Aeëtes. She began muttering something under her breath, similar to what Aeëtes had seen Hecate do when she practiced magic.

It was different with Circe, however. Not bad, just...different. There was no power that flickered over her skin; dogs and snakes did not conjure themselves out of thin air to join her. Rather, the atmosphere had gotten colder and thinner, and Circe looked as if the color had been drained out of her. Her hair began to fall out of its crown of braids until it was whipping around her shoulders, caught in some imaginary breeze. As she slowly lowered her head, her eyes were glowing entirely white, something utterly otherworldly in them. It sent a chill down Aeëtes's spine as he tried not to fidget too terribly.

The words that Circe was repeating started to get louder, and everything in the house began to vibrate. Small bowls and herbs began to rise into the air, shaking all the while, as the kitchen started to look as though gravity did not apply. Pelias let out a squawking noise as he, too, levitated slightly off the bench. Hecate was also suspended in midair, but she seemed utterly unfazed, not a hair out of place as she watched on.

The atmosphere around Aeëtes started to glow, and like each time that he had transformed before, he began to disappear in a ball of golden light. The tension seemed to thicken throughout the room as they waited—Hecate and Pelias watching on, Circe lost to her trance. The ball of light expanded until it obscured Aeëtes entirely, and nearly as quickly as it had started, the light exploded, covering the room in bright shards of iridescence. Hecate was temporarily blinded, sitting down at the counter and blinking her eyes to regain her vision.

"That was amazing!" She heard Pelias's enthusiastic cheer,

who was clapping his hands at the table like he was watching foot races. Hecate looked over and felt her breath catch in her throat.

There was Aeëtes–the man, standing in Circe's kitchen. She had never seen him in the full light of day, and he was...a sight that she knew she would, unfortunately, commit to memory. Circe's magic had worked beautifully, as Aeëtes stretched his arms and legs, shaking them out. Fortunately, the transfiguration spell had left him with a golden ram's fleece wrapped around his waist. Aeëtes looked down at it, seeing it for the first time, and let out a chuckle.

"Nice touch," he winked at Circe, who had regained her senses and no longer looked like a shade. She raised an eyebrow at him, crossing her arms over her chest as she let out puff of air in disbelief.

"I told you." Hecate caught Circe's reaction, taking another sip of her cup. "He has this effect on people."

Circe promptly ignored Hecate, studying Aeëtes's face. "Well, forgive me for not wanting to see my brother naked."

As soon as she said the word 'brother', the ever-present smile on Aeëtes's face faded. Hecate's eyes got wide as she found herself standing and was almost immediately repulsed by her instinct to go to Aeëtes's side at the first sign of emotional distress. She buried the feeling, keeping her face stoic and expressionless, not allowing anyone to see it warring within her. Circe had no malice in her tone, and she shrugged, turning around and stepping into the kitchen. She grabbed another amphora and held it out to Aeëtes, who shrugged and took a swig.

"I guess it's sister, then," he said with a small, warm smile on his face, handing the amphora back to her. Circe took a sip of her own, putting it down and nodding in his direction.

"I swore a long time ago that I would claim no family ties to Helios." Her voice was quiet, but there was a sincerity to her words that Aeëtes did not take for granted. "I would be happy to make an exception for you, Aeëtes."

He grinned again, the smile that looked like sunshine pouring over his face like Helios's dawn itself. Something about it made Hecate's heart hurt, and she busied herself with her own glass of wine.

"You don't…" Aeëtes's tone got somber as he took a step closer to Circe, "You never learned our mother's name, did you?" Circe sighed deeply, and Pelias and Hecate had the good sense to look away and give the siblings as private of a moment as they could. She shook her head.

"No. Helios gave me to the king and queen in Colchis, same as you. He never spoke of our mother."

Aeëtes's eyes got dark, and his brow furrowed, his mind reeling as he absorbed what Circe had said.

"Why did they never mention you?" His voice was sharp, and it was the closest to anger that Hecate had ever heard him. Circe shrugged again, taking a sip of her wine and looking out the window, waiting a moment before she gathered herself enough to respond.

"I angered Helios. I summoned him as soon as I was of age, and I think he was expecting a reunion."

"I'm assuming that's not what he got." Aeëtes bit his lip, nodding along with Circe, understanding her exact pain more than anyone else in the world.

"No. I berated him as soon as his chariot's wheels touched the ground. I demanded to know who our mother was and why he decided that I wasn't good enough to be raised among immortals." The pain that had made its way into Circe's eyes was unmistakable, and it drove stakes through Aeëtes's heart.

How many times I have asked the same question, sister. He dared not agree with her aloud, but he nodded, wanting to keep his own wounds close to his chest. She continued.

"He banished me without a thought. I could barely get my questions out before I found myself on Aeaea. Don't judge the king and queen too harshly." Circe took another sip of wine. "Helios played with their memories until they forgot me."

Aeëtes bit back an angry shout, suddenly fighting the urge to run outside and scream into the sun until Helios came down and addressed him. He had never had a direct problem with his father, per se; they'd only met once. Aeëtes certainly had questions for Helios. There were answers that he wanted, but now he found himself rolling over in fury on his sister's behalf.

"All because you asked him a question?" Aeëtes shook his head in shock. Circe didn't respond to him, her eyes going vacant. Hecate stood up from where she was sitting at the counter, grabbing the cups of wine from both Circe and Aeëtes.

"Helios is…complicated," Hecate offered as way of explanation, "It does not excuse him, but I have never heard of any of the gods have the same opinion of him. We'll need to summon him in—"

Suddenly, there was a roaring sound outside that cut Hecate off. The entire party turned to the window, Pelias nearly sticking his entire head out of it, trying to decipher what it was. At first, it had sounded like an animal, almost like a scream. The noise got louder and louder until it felt like it was right on top of them. It wasn't one noise, rather, several sounds joining together in a terrifying cry that was somehow both discordant and harmonious. There were snorts, heavy breaths, animalistic screams, and the sound of hooves. Massive, thunderous hooves.

"Oh, gods above us!" Pelias fell from the window, cursing, and the entire kitchen seemed to come to life at once. Hecate and Circe looked to one another, immediately releasing their power. The color began to fade from Circe once again as the triple heads appeared on Hecate. Aeëtes ran towards the window, grabbing his friend's shirt and pulling him away from it.

"Get back in here!" he hissed, pausing only momentarily to

look out himself. "Fuck!" Aeëtes then very nearly landed on top of Pelias, both men scrambling to get away from the open window.

"What is it?" Hecate snapped, both her and Circe moving towards the front door. Whatever it was, they weren't afraid to face it head on; they surely weren't afraid to face anything when there were two witches on hand. Aeëtes felt his chest tighten at the sight of Hecate heading outside, her own safety be damned. The rational part of Aeëtes's brain knew that she was a *goddess* and could handle herself, but Aeëtes had stopped listening to that inner voice as soon as he met Hecate. There was nothing rational about how he felt for her, so quickly, and he decided he would much rather bathe in his own lunacy than convince himself of anything different. So when he saw her walk straight out the door, he jumped to his feet.

There was a large vase next to the hearth, containing a myriad of different weapons. All of them were dusty and likely dull, but Aeëtes didn't know that they had all belonged to men who, at some point, had showed up to Aeaea to cause Circe harm. He reached into the vase and pulled out a short sword, nearly tripping over himself to follow Hecate and Circe. Pelias watched Aeëtes go, shaking his head as he stood up and sat down at the table.

"Absolutely not," he muttered. "These antics require immortality as a prerequisite, and I'd rather not tempt the god's fortune today." He poured himself a cup of wine and watched.

As soon as the witches stepped outside, Circe let out an impressive string of curses. Rapidly approaching the house, there was a pack of wild hogs with their tusks nearly scraping the ground and a murderous red glow to their eyes. These were no normal livestock, each one of them nearly coming up to the shoulder of a grown man. Their eyes betrayed an intelligence that let Circe and Hecate know that the animals were possessed.

"Do you think —"

"It's Hera," Hecate confirmed, raising her arms until the dogs appeared again, glittering in dark magic. Hecate flicked her fingers, and the two shadow hounds set off, baying and running straight into the center of the horde. Immediately, nearly a third of the hogs turned and ran, afraid. A few of them began to engage the dogs, who never tired and could never be wounded. Only a couple of the beasts remained, now charging full speed towards Hecate and Circe.

"Two for each of us," Circe grinned, her magic beginning to pour out of her fingers like smoke. "What do you think of those odds?"

"Not bad," Hecate winked, then both women threw their hands up as the wild hogs descended on them. Circe flipped both animals on their backs in a moment, wisps of magic binding their feet in invisible bonds. Hecate laughed wildly as she let her power unfurl. Waves of her magic rippled across the ground and caused the hogs to stumble. They waited for a second, watching…and then all animals jumped to their feet, as if nothing had happened to them.

Hecate cursed again, "They're being controlled by Hera." The women refocused as the animals charged again, and this time, the power was stronger. Circe and Hecate took turns sending blow after blow towards the creatures, watching as inevitably, each time they stood up. Magic was pouring through the valley as the land began to respond, and pulse after pulse of god's power threatened to heave the island in two. It had only been a few minutes, but the blows were incessant. No matter what each of the women did, the charging animals returned.

Finally, Hecate let out a strangled cry, motioning for Circe to cover her for a moment. The goddess hardly had a hair out of place, but it was obvious that Circe was beginning to tire. Hecate took a step back and closed her eyes, the snakes appearing around her arms and the wind picking up in a torrent around her. She breathed deeply, beginning a low, slow incantation, that caused her hair to stand more and more on edge with each verse.

Aeëtes, who had been standing in the doorway, sword drawn, watched in a state of all-encompassing awe. For him, there was no sight that could compare and no sensation that rivaled that of when he watched Hecate surrender entirely to the power within her. He had been watching both women, and he was smart enough to know that he would be a distraction to their delicate dance of power if he charged in, sword raised.

Hecate's voice lowered in pitch until it thundered throughout the entire island, the ominous triple echo of the maiden, the mother, and the crone ringing through the trees. She raised her hands for a brief second, and everything seemed to go still. The entire island almost stopped moving, down to the branches. Even Circe and the charging hogs paused. Everyone turned to look at Hecate as her arms dropped to her sides. As soon as that happened, her snakes went cascading from her side and launched themselves at the beasts. As they traveled through the air, they got larger and larger, meeting with their foes and swallowing them whole. No sooner did they devour them than they vanished—almost as quickly as they had come.

Hecate dropped to her knees, her eyes' red glow slowly diminishing as she breathed heavily, her hands resting on her thighs. She hadn't called on all her strength, but what she had used to defeat Hera's puppets had demanded a lot from her.

There was a sudden warm presence at her back, and without thinking, she leaned into it. Solid, strong arms went around her shoulders, and a large hand came to rest atop hers. She stayed there for a moment as she slowly came back to the present, the faces of the maiden and the crone flickering away. Hecate blinked her eyes open, letting out a sharp gasp at seeing Aeëtes's face so close to hers. He was sitting next to her, and that was his arm around her shoulder...*his* hand holding onto hers.

"Excuse me," Hecate quipped, standing up too quickly. She swayed as she stood, but Aeëtes was right there, jumping to his feet and his hand going to her back again for balance. The imprint of it nearly burned Hecate as she was brought back to the dock in Heraklion, the smallest of touches from him seemingly setting her on fire. She took a step back from him, grabbing his arm and removing it from her.

"I'm quite all right, thank you." Her eyes narrowed as she studied the ever-present grin on Aeëtes's face. "I don't know what you're smiling about."

"Your eyes do this thing when you're mad, did you know? They positively sparkle." Aeëtes leaned in closer as if he was trying to get a better look, and Hecate scoffed and nearly reeled backwards.

"Easy, you two." Circe's voice cut through the air, walking away from the bodies of the hogs, which were now lying immobile on the ground. She had a wicked smirk on her face, and Hecate knew that she would hear about it later.

"I don't know what you're—*Circe! Behind you!*" Hecate screamed as one of the hogs stood on shaky legs, preparing itself to charge at Circe's back.

"What?" Circe yelled back, unable to hear her over the thrum of magic echoing in her ears.

Hecate tried with a gasping breath to summon her power, but she could feel it inside of her, rebuilding. Circe stared at Hecate's stricken face and then turned around, nearly face-to-face with the gaping jaws of the possessed hog and only had time to throw her hands up to cover her face.

Circe fell to the ground and waited for impact, holding her breath as her body tensed up. There was a great shout and a sickening squelch, then…silence. One breath, then two.

"Oh my god…" Hecate's voice was muffled, but Circe blinked her eyes open.

There was Aeëtes, pulling a sword out from the head of the hog. In that moment, he was the picture of every hero, every subject painted on a vase, destined for a different kind of immortality. He finally freed the weapon with a sharp grunt, his torso and the Golden Fleece splattered with blood. Aeëtes dropped the sword, shaking out his wrist, before turning and helping Circe to her feet.

"Are you alright?" His voice was steady as he scanned her for injuries, but Circe could only nod. She nearly fell again as Hecate barreled into her side, pulling her into a tight embrace.

"Oh gods." Hecate's voice was thick, as if she was holding back tears. "I really thought for a second that beast was going to get you."

Circe said nothing, letting her tears soak the folds of Hecate's tunic. She took a few moments to compose herself and then stood, rolling her shoulders and giving Aeëtes a nod.

"Thank you, Brother." When Circe said it, she said it like it was a title of honor. Aeëtes supposed that it was.

Hecate turned and looked at Aeëtes, unable to keep up with her own racing heart. He stared back at her, something unspoken occurring between them. A small part of the walls around Hecate's heart fell away. She had been terrified that she was going to lose her sister in that moment…and then there had been Aeëtes. He had moved without hesitation, without any fear, not even knowing if a mortal blade could kill a bewitched creature. But that was his sister; it was someone Hecate loved, and that was enough to send him hurtling towards danger without a second thought.

"Well." Circe coughed, taking a step back. "I need a drink. I'm going to go…check on Pelias." She ducked out of Hecate's grasp and walked away, leaving Hecate and Aeëtes in silence. Hecate looked down, unable to stand the heat in Aeëtes's direct gaze for another minute, lest she do something incredibly stupid.

"Thank you." The words were soft when she spoke them, and they acted like a boon to Aeëtes's very soul. He smiled, once again, that damned smile that made Hecate feel like she could do anything when he grinned at her like that. But she did nothing.

"You're welcome." Aeëtes's nodded, his voice low, as if he knew that pressing the moment any further would spook her. "Now, I believe you wanted to get on our way to Colchis. We should get the target off Circe."

"Yes, yes." Hecate snapped back to reality, tucking some hair behind her ear. "Let's go fetch Pelias, and we'll be on our way."

Aeëtes only nodded in response, and the pair began walking back to Circe's home. Aeëtes looked down between them, wanting to crawl out of his skin, his fingers just grazing hers. It would be so easy to reach out and take her hand, to stroke his thumb across her palm and break this barrier between them.

Except there is something between us—and it's not entirely a wall.

Aeëtes stopped walking.

Hecate turned around, looking at him with a brow raised. "Aeëtes?" she asked gently, her voice missing its normal disdain for him. There was something in his eyes that Hecate couldn't place as Aeëtes stared at her. He let out a long breath and rubbed a hand over his eyes. The air around them shifted, alive with the magic of the island, and Hecate could have sworn she felt the breeze pick up, almost pushing them towards one another.

Aeëtes picked his head up and looked at her, the intensity in his gaze unmistakable. He looked half-mad, still covered in a bit of blood, only wearing the fleece around his waist.

"Aeëtes?" Hecate asked again, taking a step towards him. "Are you alright?" Her mind began to race as she studied him, wondering if there was some sort of Hera's magic affecting him.

"No," Aeëtes growled, his voice low. Hecate took a surprised step back, frustration etching itself onto her features.

"What is wrong with you?" she snarled at him.

"Fuck this." Aeëtes snapped his head up, stared at Hecate for a split second, and then all hell seemed to break loose. He crossed the short distance between them, grabbing Hecate's face with his hands. Aeëtes's grip was shockingly tender for such a large man with embers in his eyes. Hecate nearly whimpered, feeling herself lean into him entirely on instinct. She felt her magic reacting to him, coursing through her veins and making her go blind to anything except Aeëtes.

"Tell me now if you don't want this," he whispered, his breath warm on her face. Hecate said nothing, unable to think or rationalize anything other than the look in Aeëtes's eyes.

"Thank the gods," he grunted, and the next thing that Hecate knew was only heat. Aeëtes crushed his lips to hers, and everything around them dissolved entirely. His hand moved to cup her jaw, the other wrapping around her waist and pulling her even tighter to him. It was a tender, almost cautious embrace, and Hecate gasped at the feel of him. He took the opportunity, the kiss morphing into something desperate.

Everything in her body seemed to turn molten, her magic moving in waves. It danced from her to Aeëtes, making him moan as he felt it running over his skin. There was nothing else in the world that mattered in that moment, the taste of him, the way her body drifted towards him unconsciously.

Aeëtes pulled back slightly and bit at her lip, groaning her name against her own skin. Hecate sucked in a deep breath... and it was like the oxygen cleared her muddled brain. She lurched back from him suddenly, her hand flying up to cover her face. They were both silent for a second, trying to catch their breath.

"Hecate..." Aeëtes murmured, taking a step towards her. She held up a hand and stopped him, shaking her head.

"No." Her voice was shaky, and she couldn't look him in the eye. "This didn't happen, Aeëtes."

"Now, wait a minute —"

Hecate was already walking away, hurrying back to Circe's house. "This didn't happen," she bit the words out, hardly tossing him a glance over her shoulder. Aeëtes stood there, stunned and trying to understand Hecate's hot and cold attitude. He gave her space as she went towards the house.

Except it absolutely fucking did, little witch.

Circe was waiting for them as they approached the house, the lion having rejoined her side. She stroked its head lazily and took a sip from her cup, raising a subtle eyebrow at Hecate. Aeëtes ducked inside, going over to Pelias, and both men laughed about something that Hecate didn't hear.

"Don't say a word." She looked over at Circe, pausing in the door frame.

Circe shrugged. "I didn't open my mouth."

"You said it with your eyes." Hecate's lips pulled into a thin line.

"What would you rather me do?" Circe looked at Hecate with an expression that was downright conspiratorial.

"There's nothing to react to," Hecate clipped, cutting the conversation short as she stepped inside.

Circe followed, both women joining Aeëtes and Pelias in the kitchen. Pelias was laughing at something that Aeëtes had said, and Aeëtes turned his head as soon as he heard the women. Rather, as soon as he heard Hecate; it was as though he was a sail and Hecate was the wind. He was utterly attuned to her presence. His face morphed the moment he saw her, turning from something boisterous and joyful to something softer, but as always, still smiling. It did something to Hecate's insides, and she fought to keep it off her face.

"We'll head back to the shore." Hecate ignored him and nodded towards Pelias and Circe. "And we'll get out of your hair." Circe let out a small laugh, putting her cup down on the counter and walking over to Hecate. She pulled the other woman close to her, wrapping her up in a hug and squeezing. Pelias and Aeëtes took that as their cue to leave, stepping outside to give Hecate and Circe some space for their goodbyes.

"You know that you're hardly an inconvenience," she chastised. "I miss you when you aren't here." Hecate held on for a moment longer, relishing the feeling of closeness that she so rarely felt with others. She pulled away with a sigh.

"We shouldn't stay in one place too long with Hera on our tail," Hecate said wistfully, knowing that she would rather spend another few days on Aeaea if they could. "You know how much I love this place but..." she trailed off.

"I know." Circe nodded, all too aware of what was happening to Hecate, even if she had no clue. She found herself pulling Hecate close for one more hug, whispering gently in her ear.

"I would trust him if I were you," Circe said gently. "I can't say that about most men." Hecate froze before disentangling herself from Circe's grasp.

"Men and their freedom, Circe." Hecate shook her head, her voice barely above a whisper.

"Men love a lot of things," Circe offered by way of explanation, waving her hand in the air as if she was brushing off Hecate's concerns. The pair headed towards the door where the men were waiting outside. Hecate's mind was spinning. She had watched how quickly Aeëtes had moved in order to save Circe. He had acted without any regard to his own safety;

they didn't know if weapons would work on those cursed animals. What if they didn't? *Then he would have been dead in an instant...but Circe would have gotten away.* Hecate's thoughts were tumbling over themselves as she ran through all the possibilities. *Either way, Circe would've lived. It was lucky what Aeëtes did, but he didn't seem to mind those odds.* As if Circe seemed to sense Hecate's mental anguish, she stepped forward and pulled Aeëtes and Pelias into conversation. Hecate watched on as Aeëtes and Circe said their goodbyes. Her heart felt like it was about to burst forth from her chest, something building inside of her, and she took a deep breath as she tried to keep her walls from crumbling.

"It's not every day that I learn I have a sister." Aeëtes laughed, hugging Circe farewell. Her face lit up, and she chuckled, rolling her eyes in a way that only a big sister could.

"It's not every day that I meet my younger brother because he let Hera turn him into a sheep."

"It was a *ram!*" Aeëtes said exasperatedly, his head falling back in disbelief. Pelias snorted at that and gave Aeëtes a sharp elbow to the ribs, looking to Circe.

"He's very concerned about the perception others have of him as you can see."

"I'm sure he is," Circe said knowingly, in such a way that Hecate knew what she was referencing and prayed that neither Pelias or Aeëtes understood. She took that as her signal to break up the small party and stepped toward them, tying her hair off in a braid as she approached.

"Off we go. We'll want to make sure that we catch the tide back out to the ship."

There were general noises of assent amongst the group and another round of embraces exchanged. Circe thanked Aeëtes once more for saving her life, and Hecate pretended not to hear it.

I wonder if I can set wards around my own feelings. Hecate

distracted herself with the one thing that always got her attention—witchcraft—and began walking off towards the path to
the sea. Pelias trailed behind her, and Circe watched until
Hecate was out of earshot. As soon as she had stepped away,
Circe pulled Aeëtes close to her.

"Be careful with Hecate, okay?" she whispered, looking
genuinely worried. Aeëtes's brow furrowed as he turned on
impulse to look for Hecate.

"She's fine," Circe rolled her eyes, getting Aeëtes's attention
back. "Just…with her heart. Be careful with her heart."

Aeëtes's eyes got wide as he looked at Circe, understanding
the gravity of what she was saying. He got the feeling that this
was a rare admission coming from her, and he bowed his head,
expression solemn.

"I will."

Circe took a step back and appraised him before giving him
one final nod before she turned and walked back to her house.
Circe didn't look back once as she stepped inside and shut the
door. Hecate hadn't put off their departure or wasted any time,
either, knowing that quick exits were best for Circe. She didn't
take well to goodbyes, watching people walk away from her
and Aeaea. It was different with Hecate, whom Circe knew
loved her and would return, but the scars remained.

Aeëtes caught up to Pelias and Hecate in a few minutes,
slowing his pace as they walked towards the shore. They were
silent as they moved through the sparse trees, the ground
under their feet slowly becoming sandier. As they climbed up
to the top of the small hill that looked over the sea, they all
breathed a slight sigh of relief to see the small rowboat
waiting for them. Nothing would be past Hera at this point,
so every step that they took without interference was a
good one.

Pelias rolled his shoulders back as he took off down the hill
first, stretching his arms out as he prepared to row them back
to their ship. That ship, too, was luckily still sitting out in the

deep water, waiting for them. Aeëtes took in a deep breath, taking in the feel of magic in the air.

"Do you feel this all the time?" He turned and asked Hecate, referring to the atmosphere around them. "Does everything feel this…alive?"

His eyes were full of wonderment, and it sent another sharp, stabbing pain into Hecate's chest. She had never seen a man who was so attuned to magic, to *women's magic*, a man who was so welcoming of it. Hecate knew for a fact that it was this power in the air around them that made most men turn from the island, that made soldiers and heroes claim that the island was cursed. They could sense it from the air, that a woman lived here and practiced her magic here, unapologetically, and they called it cursed.

Not Aeëtes.

He looked like a child witnessing a rainbow or their first shooting star. There was a light to his eyes that was electric. He was smiling softly as he felt welcomed and encouraged by the power in the air around them.

Oh, Aeëtes. Hecate's thoughts betrayed her stoicism. *You don't realize how radical you are, do you?* She cleared her throat, hiding it with a cough, before she answered him.

"Yes," she gave him a small smile in return, "I always feel connected to this magic." Aeëtes's expression was one of pure glee as he shook his head in happy disbelief.

"That must be wonderful." His voice was full of awe as he looked out over the island again. Hecate hummed a noncommittal noise, picking up the folds of her himation as she began descending towards the rowboat.

"It's…" she paused, ready to negate him, but found herself simply nodding. "Yes, it's wonderful."

She turned back to him with a smile, and Aeëtes winked at her, jogging down the hill and passing her to help Pelias haul the boat to the water. It was a small moment, but something had passed between them. Hecate had not admonished him or disputed him; rather, she surrendered to him in the smallest of ways. Aeëtes had gently pushed her to acknowledge the wonderment and the gift that was her magic; he had gotten her to agree with him. It was small, but the repercussions spread through Hecate like she was falling into warm water.

What am I going to do with you? Hecate shook her head as she followed down the hill, wondering what part of her Aeëtes was going to chip away at next. Pelias and Aeëtes had got the boat to the water, and as Hecate approached the shoreline, Aeëtes extended a hand to her. She didn't hesitate in slipping her hand in his, his grip tightening ever so slightly as he helped guide her into the boat. As she stepped in, his other hand went around her waist, steadying her as the small vessel rocked back and forth.

Hecate sucked in a sharp breath at the feeling of his arm at her waist. She found herself fighting the sudden impulse to draw her body close to his, to surrender to that grip and feel his warmth flush against her. Aeëtes froze as soon as he heard her gasp, wondering if he had done something wrong. He didn't let go of Hecate, his eyes scanning hers for a sign of discomfort. When Hecate met his gaze, she found herself flushing, his eyes full of warmth and concern. He was so attuned to her, that every noise or movement she made, he followed.

They stood there for a moment, nearly paralyzed with the tension between them, until Pelias coughed twice. He had settled himself down on a bench, fiddling with the oars to make some noise to break the trance. Hecate shook her head and stood up taller, stepping away from Aeëtes and adjusting herself before sitting down.

"Excuse me," she offered lamely, "I just don't have my sea legs, is all."

Aeëtes nodded once, his body tense as he looked anywhere but at Hecate.

"It happens to all of us." His voice was soft for a moment

until a mischievous smirk lit up his face. "Except for me, of course—agh!"

He toppled over as Pelias dropped the oars in the water, surging them forward. The momentum caused him to fall, and Hecate let out a loud giggle before clamping her hand down over her mouth. Pelias began roaring with laughter as he watched Aeëtes sit up from the bottom of the boat and take a seat.

"Except for you!" Pelias could barely speak, "Hecate, you should know, the first time that I was ever on a ship with this man..."

"Don't you dare!" Aeëtes pointed at Pelias. "Or I will tell everyone what happened that time that we were in Athens!"

That immediately made Pelias go quiet, his face turning just as red as Aeëtes's.

Hecate merely smiled, looking back and forth between the two men as they rowed towards the ship. "Well, now I know what stories to get out of you both when you're drunk."

A s the rowboat approached the ship, everyone held on tightly as they prepared to be pulled up to deck. Once the small dinghy had been secured, Aeëtes hopped off first, turning around and extending his hand to help Hecate. She looked away awkwardly, pretending to fuss with her hem, letting Pelias climb out next. There were more crew members crowding around them, asking about their heading and helping secure the lines. It took everything in Hecate to reach for another man's hand.

She did her best to make it look purely coincidental, as if she wasn't avoiding Aeëtes, but both of them knew better. As soon as she felt the sailor touch her skin, it felt wrong.

Hecate quickly stepped on deck and walked past the crew, disappearing down the steps to her assigned cabin. With every step that she took, she could feel Aeëtes's eyes watching her. Hecate felt her heartbeat quickening, as if something was boiling beneath her skin, desperate to get out. It was all that she could do to make it to her cabin in one piece. She quickly threw the door open and stepped inside, taking precious seconds to lock it before sliding down to the ground. The cabin was small, but clean and well-furnished, with a table, a bed, and some barrels being stored in a corner.

"This isn't like you," she hissed, reprimanding herself out loud as she watched a few flickers of her magic ripple. "Get your head on straight! It takes more than a few paltry touches from a man to get you all weak in the knees."

Hecate took a harsh tone with herself, ignoring the other part of her brain that wanted to argue it was about more than a few, measly touches. It hadn't been, *technically*, but there had been a tension between them since the moment they met. It was approaching a dangerous boiling point.

On Aeaea, something had finally snapped between her and the crown prince. It was something small, and that was all that it took. Hecate was unable to deny that she was affected by Aeëtes. It didn't sound like much to admit, but that was a big admission for her. Even if she never said it aloud. Aeëtes was so encouraging of magic, and his response to the island had been drastically different from any man that she had ever known. Even Circe had told her to trust him, and she had turned more men to animals than Hecate cared to count.

"Circe, you traitor," Hecate grumbled half-heartedly, standing up and beginning to pace.

She had seen Aeëtes in a moment of crisis—those moments where all pretense was stripped away, and you must act so quickly, that your truest self was revealed.

What had Aeëtes done?

He had run *towards* death for Circe and Hecate. It was a far, far picture from the spoiled, annoyingly cheerful persona that she had constructed for Aeëtes. Hecate desperately wanted to believe that he was always smiling because he had no real problems in life. He was an immortal crown prince, with the best of both worlds. She knew it wasn't true.

"This will be over soon..." Hecate sat on the bed, burying her head in her hands. "Then you can go back to the Under—"

She was cut off by a sharp knock at the door. Without

thinking, Hecate stood up and threw the door open, barely holding in a gasp as she came face-to-face with Aeëtes.

"Aeëtes." Hecate's eyebrows shot up, clasping her hands in front of her as she tried to sound more composed than she felt. "What do you want?"

Aeëtes shook his head slowly, leaning against the door-frame as he chewed on his lower lip. Hecate fought the rush of heat that it sent through her, seeing how he filled up the entire space. His eyes zeroed in on her. She felt like prey...and didn't want to run away nearly as much as she should. Aeëtes chuckled softly, running a hand through his thick curls before crossing his arms over his chest.

"What do you want me to do for you, witch?" Aeëtes's voice was low, and it sent her blood on fire. The air between them seemed to solidify. Everything left unsaid was threatening to come bursting to the surface, everything that had been building from the moment they laid eyes on one another.

"I don't know what you mean." Hecate blushed, taking a few steps backward. Aeëtes took one step forward, ever cautious, still giving her space to deny him.

"You do, though."

"I most certainly don't." Hecate mentally chastised herself. She had *never* been so tongue-tied around a man. She was one of the few goddesses who was neither a lifelong virgin or hadn't taken a long-term consort. When it came to her interactions with men, they were straightforward. She had never allowed herself to feel anything for them.

Aeëtes looked at her like he could still hear her thoughts, his head turning to the side as a positively devilish smirk grew across his face.

"Come on now, Goddess. Do you really want me to insult your intelligence and spell it out for you?"

Hecate crossed her arms, squaring her shoulders and feeling herself breathe a sigh of relief at the challenge in his voice. She could do this—spar with him, argue. That was easy.

It didn't involve betraying herself by admitting she didn't know how to describe what she felt for him.

"I'm afraid you'll have to. I still don't have the slightest clue what you're going on about."

Aeëtes's smirk grew into a grin as he stepped further inside the cabin and shut the door behind him. He leaned back against it, where Hecate had been collecting herself moments before.

"Last chance," he warned her with a playful note to his voice that told Hecate that he was enjoying this far too much. She merely shrugged. He let out a low chuckle, rubbing his hand across the stubble on his jaw. Aeëtes ran his tongue over his lower lip slowly, never taking his eyes off Hecate as he spoke.

"Do you think I didn't notice how you haven't been able to keep your eyes off me?" He raised a brow. "How badly do you want to fuck me, Goddess?" Hecate's eyebrows shot up, and she felt another flush rise to her face as she heard the words out loud. Aeëtes studied her reaction and kept speaking. "You don't have to answer. I'm happy to admit that I want to fuck you...have wanted to since the moment I saw you."

Hecate nearly growled, "Do you often win women over with such poetry? I should tell Apollo, let him know he's been replaced."

She took a step towards him, red magic dancing between her fingers. Aeëtes was unfazed.

"No." He shook his head. "But you'd rather jump overboard than hear me tell you that I'm enamored with you. That I've been nearly driven to obsession over you since the second I saw you in that clearing. That every brief moment we've spent together, I have wanted to claw my own heart out and give it to you so you can dissect it and cure me of this wildness."

Aeëtes's cool demeanor shattered. He crossed the cabin

towards Hecate and grabbed her shoulders, pulling her to him until there was barely an inch between them.

Hecate was hardly breathing, unable to comprehend his words as she looked up at him.

"You would hate that," Aeëtes purred, leaning down until his lips were grazing Hecate's ear. "Isn't that right?"

"You would be a madman if that's how you felt." Hecate swallowed thickly, intoxicated by his towering presence over her. Aeëtes only laughed, the sound making Hecate's stomach flip.

"Sure." Hecate felt his arms slip to her waist, pulling her tight to him. He whispered again in her ear, coaxing her ever so slightly. "Which is why I'm *not* telling you how I feel. I'm simply telling you that I want—no, would be honored—to fuck you."

Hecate had to bite back a gasp at the sensation of his body pressed up against hers, her senses almost blinded to anything but the heat that was coming off him.

"You're very confident to believe I want that, too, Aeëtes." Hecate rose to his challenge. "What if I don't want you to?"

"Don't want me to...what?" Aeëtes's lips were now ghosting down her neck, so close that she could feel his breath tickling her skin. "I would hate to misinterpret you. Say it."

Hecate tilted her head on instinct, giving him more access to her. "What if I don't want you to fuck me?" Aeëtes let out an unabashed moan, leaning over so his forehead was now resting against her.

"Then I guess it's a good thing that there are still a million things I'd love to do to you, witch." He pressed a kiss to the junction of her neck and shoulder, the subtlest of touches sending magic flickering off Hecate. Red sparks danced across her skin like she was a jewel caught in sunlight. Aeëtes made another pleased noise, pulling away to watch as the magic faded.

"So responsive," he chuckled, moving to continue the

assault on her neck. "Are you always this responsive? Or is this just for me?"

"Aeëtes." Hecate's voice was breathy, unable now to contain her arousal. Her hips moved of their own accord, shifting and grinding up into his body. There were a few blissful moments where she could feel herself on the brink of surrender, so tantalizingly close to letting go and giving in. Her mind reeled with how *good* Aeëtes felt, how *right* his body felt pressed against hers.

He continued to whisper against her skin, small sentiments that she couldn't hear, and part of her knew that she couldn't handle them if she did. His hands were tight around her waist as they stood in the center of the cabin, their bodies both grinding against each other as Aeëtes's mouth drifted from her neck to her jaw to the dips of her collarbones.

He moved like a man starved, his grip nearly tight enough to hurt, but Hecate found herself reveling in the possessiveness of it. He held her like he was afraid of losing her.

It was that thought that pulled her out of her reverie, nearly dousing the flames that were threatening to burn her alive.

"Why are you here?" she nearly spat the words, pushing herself away from Aeëtes and untangling herself from his hold. Hecate took a few stumbling steps back.

Aeëtes looked up at her, panting heavily, rubbing a hand over his face as he shook his head a few times. Both of them were silent for a few seconds as they slowly came back to reality, Aeëtes looking at Hecate with an expression that she hadn't seen on him before — he was *angry.*

"Why am I here?" Aeëtes's voice was quiet, deadly. His dark eyes surveyed her like he was anticipating her next move.

"Yes." Hecate nodded as she attempted to stand up straight. "What do you *want* from me, Aeëtes?"

"What do I want from you?" He took a step closer to her,

his brow furrowing in anger before it melted into sheer disbelief.

"Stop repeating my questions!" Hecate snapped at him, moving to readjust the folds of her himation across her chest. Aeëtes scoffed, beginning to pace away from her as the tension between them started to build again. Hecate found herself moving back towards the wall until she hit one of the barrels.

Aeëtes turned and looked at her—really looked at her. He was standing in the opposite corner now. Both of them were poised like they were ready for a fight. Hecate felt her heart beating erratically in her chest, an ache growing between her legs that she hadn't felt in a century. It took all the magic she had left within her to keep her eyes on Aeëtes's and not let her gaze drift down to see if he was similarly affected.

When he spoke, it almost sounded like a command.

He spoke to her like a prince.

"I meant what I said earlier." Aeëtes stared at Hecate, his chest rising and falling. She could see the muscles in his arms and shoulders tense. "Ever since I've laid eyes on you, I've been unable to look away. I've stopped wondering how I've found myself here so quickly because I have."

Hecate felt her stomach begin to twist as she closed her eyes and shook her head rapidly.

"You don't mean that, Aeëtes. You're mad!"

"So then I'm mad!" He started laughing as he nearly pulled his own hair out. His voice got louder and louder, losing its princely authority, seeming almost enraged. "That would make the most logical sense. There's nothing rational about how I find myself drunk in your presence. How I find myself wondering if it's worth it to sleep, to even blink, when I'm around you—lest I miss you for a *second*."

"This is utter nonsense," Hecate hissed at him, her power flickering to life as her snakes wound themselves around her arms. Her mind was reeling with disbelief that he would insult her so gravely by pretending this was anything more than lust.

She took a step closer to him, her finger pointing at Aeëtes accusatorially. "I don't believe you for a second. Men will say anything if it gets them where they want to go!"

"I'll go anywhere you send me, Hecate." Aeëtes's voice almost chewed on the words. "You just need to say it."

"I'll ask you a final time." Hecate took a step backward, retreating to her corner. "What do you *want* from me, Aeëtes?"

Aeëtes paused. He stood up taller, taking a deep breath, as he leveled his stare at her. His gaze was piercing, and Hecate felt it nearly drown her as she fought to keep the intoxication off her face. The sun was setting outside, golden light now bathing the cabin, casting Aeëtes in rapturous glow. He truly looked like a son of Helios, and the sight of him made Hecate want him on his knees.

"I'll take whatever you give me, Goddess." Aeëtes looked at her, a brow raised in challenge. "But don't get it confused. I want it all. I'll take it all." Hecate felt shivers run down her spine at the resoluteness in his voice. The cheerful, happy-go-lucky sailor that she had become used to hadn't entered the cabin with her. This was Aeëtes, the Crown Prince of Colchis and the immortal son of the Sun God, and he was offering to lay down everything at her feet.

The thought of it alone fortified the barricades around Hecate's heart. In that moment, she pictured herself giving in to seeing where something would go beyond a night. She was so overcome with the meager idea of it, what that would feel like to have someone attuned to her needs, to take up life by her side that she locked down the notion before she broke her own heart.

She could play a man's game.

Hecate picked up her chin, looking every inch like the Goddess of witchcraft, and a cold, tricky smile grew on her face. She shrugged, bracing her hands on the lip of the barrel and hoisting herself up, seating herself on it.

"Just sex." Hecate looked at her nails distractedly. All the air seemed to vanish from the room.

"What?" Aeëtes's voice was quiet, almost hurt.

He had offered up his entire world to her, as irrational as it was, but she clearly saw him as something only fit to fuck. He felt a deep, sharp pang in his chest, one that felt awfully similar to how it felt when he wondered why Helios had abandoned him. His father had never taken him seriously—why would she? Aeëtes pulled himself out of his thoughts before they could spiral, ripping himself almost violently back to the present.

No. He shook his head, staring at Hecate from across the room. She looked flushed, and while her expression was calm, her eyes were wild. *You're just as overwhelmed with this as I am. Alright. I can give you time. You'll see.*

"I accept." Aeëtes grinned at her, his smile lighting up his face. Hecate's eyes got wide as she startled, looking over at Aeëtes in disbelief.

"What?"

Aeëtes crossed the room until he was in front of Hecate, bracing his arms on the barrel on either side of her legs. He leaned down until his lips were just barely brushing up against hers. Hecate bit back a whimper at the closeness, feeling that ache deep in her core beginning to pound at the proximity of him.

"I said I accept." Aeëtes shrugged, licking his lip slowly. "I'll take whatever you give me, and I mean it. If that means you want to pretend that you don't have any feelings for me for a while, that's fine."

"You're insufferable," Hecate snarled, raising her hands up to his chest. She had prepared to shove him off her, but his skin was hot under her palms, sending her down a path of wicked thoughts.

"I'm patient," Aeëtes corrected her, his hands moving to grip her legs. Hecate let out a small gasp at the contact, his palms nearly covering her thighs—and she did not have the body of a willowy nymph.

"I'm not," Hecate felt her hips canting up towards Aeëtes as her head dropped back and her eyes fluttered closed. "Put that mouth of yours to good use for once."

Aeëtes let out a dark chuckle, dropping to his knees in front of her. In one quick movement, he shoved her skirts up around her thighs and pulled her legs open wider. Aeëtes pressed his lips to the inside of Hecate's thigh, inhaling the scent of her and getting his first look at her arousal.

"Fuck the gods," he growled, the sound reverberating against Hecate's overheated skin, "I'll worship you alone for the rest of my life if you let me taste you."

Hecate had fallen backwards and was propped up on her elbows, her hips grinding against the air. Aeëtes had barely touched her, and she was ready to burst. Her magic was responding to him as she listened to him praise her, and her own powers were amplifying his seduction from the inside out. After what felt like an eternity, Aeëtes's hands moved to Hecate's ass, pulling her forward and licking a hot stripe up her core.

"Aeëtes!" Hecate shrieked, her back nearly bending in half at the sudden sensation of his mouth on her. As soon as he tasted her, Aeëtes didn't let up, immediately beginning to fuck her with his tongue. Hecate was unable to control herself, her whole body contorting. The stubble on his jaw chafed against her thighs in the most exquisite burn. His grip on her would leave bruises, but she didn't care. She cried out for him to hold her tighter. Every single one of her senses seemed to be over-loading at once, with Aeëtes at the center of it all. Hecate had never had such… *success* with a lover the first time, but Aeëtes was merciless. It was like he knew every button that she had, every swipe of his tongue sending her spiraling further into oblivion.

Hecate's hands flew to his hair, and she gripped the mess of dark curls, finally finding some purchase and using it to grind against his face. Her heels curled around and dug into his muscled back, their bodies nearly slipping against one another from sweat. Aeëtes only let out a dark laugh in response, the vibrations shooting up Hecate's spine and down to her feet. Her whole body felt like lightning as he nipped her thigh.

"Use me, Goddess," he encouraged Hecate, his hands now rubbing almost soft circles on her. "I told you I'd take whatever you had to give me. Ride my face until you only remember my name." His tone switched from playful to commanding, and he bit her thigh a little harder.

Hecate let out a wanton moan, feeling sweat drip down her back as she pushed Aeëtes back towards her center.

One of his hands released its grip, and as Hecate was about to cry out at the loss of it, Aeëtes sucked her clit into his mouth, rolling it between his tongue, and curved his fingers into her. Hecate released a shattering cry as he worked her over with a near deadly precision, his tongue and his fingers alternating so she didn't get a moment's reprieve, just a constant barrage of continuous sensation that worked her higher and higher.

"Fuck me!" Hecate screamed, the last of her inhibitions gone as she gripped Aeëtes's hair even tighter. He laughed again from between her thighs, picking up his pace.

"There we go," he sounded nearly chuffed about the onslaught of Hecate's hysteria. "That's it."

Aeëtes's voice was now like spiced honey, rough and smooth all at once, gently pushing her to the edge while he never stopped his perfect rhythm. Hecate was utterly incoherent now, her voice a mottled mess of consonants and sounds. She was unable to string together even a coherent groan between gasps.

"Let it all go." Aeëtes nodded, pulling away from her as his thumb replaced his tongue on her clit. "I want to watch you when you come, Hecate. I want to see you ruined for me."

"I—fffuu—Aeëtes!" Hecate cried out, nearly in pain with overwhelming need.

"That's perfect." Aeëtes grinned, unable to look away from her as she writhed from his touch, the infamous Goddess of witchcraft panting for *him*. "Don't stop now, let it happen. You're doing so well, my little witch…"

Hecate nearly screamed as he curled his fingers inside of her, grazing that one spot which only she had previously been able to find. Aeëtes picked up the pace as he drew circles around her clit and pumped his fingers, hitting it over and over again…but something was still there, tethering Hecate's control, and that just wouldn't do. A wicked thought crossed Aeëtes's mind, and as he leaned forward towards her center, he commanded her.

"Come for me, Hecate—*now*."

As soon as he said it, he pressed his lips to her clit and sucked, curling his fingers at the same time. Hecate's whole body spasmed as she nearly fell off the barrel, Aeëtes's hands going to her waist to keep her from falling. Her legs spasmed around him with the strength of her orgasm while Hecate started to scream so loudly that her voice cut off.

Aeëtes was transfixed, finding himself suddenly fighting his own release, too. She was so stunning when she lost control, bent over the back of a wine barrel in the bottom of a ship, no less; he nearly came from the sight alone. He didn't know how long he sat there, running his hands over her thighs and her belly as she came down. Her eyes stayed closed as her breathing slowly returned to normal.

"Hecate?" Acëtes whispered gently, standing up and wincing at his own nearly painful hard-on.

No response.

"Witch?" He leaned over her, a soft smile lighting up his face. Aeëtes realized that she had passed out, and was now sound asleep, with likely no chance of waking her. His whole chest was ready to burst with male satisfaction as he gently collected her into his arms. She stirred slightly, making a muffled sound of assent.

Aeëtes quickly and quietly rearranged Hecate on the bed, adjusting her himation so she wouldn't feel confused or self-conscious if she woke up half-naked. He stood and paused for a moment, feelings of inadequacy creeping in from the wings as he looked at her sleeping face. She was stunning, relaxed, and breathing deeply.

All Aeëtes wanted to do was to prove himself worthy of climbing in next to her.

Soon. He pushed away the most deprecating of his thoughts and refused to think of anything but how intoxicating Hecate tasted. *Soon.* He allowed himself one last look, and quietly saw himself out of her cabin, making sure the door locked from the inside behind him.

The next morning, Hecate stirred in her bed and blinked her eyes open. The bright, shining rays of Helios were already streaming through the porthole, letting her know that it was barely past sunrise.

I'm already cleaning up your messes, Helios. Hecate nearly snarled at the sun as if he could hear her. *The least you could do is let me sleep.* They were really in their current predicament because of Hera. This early in the morning, however, Hecate couldn't be blamed for shifting the source of her ire to the sun.

All at once, the memories of the night before came rushing back to her. Hecate stifled a gasp, rolling over and burying her head in the pillow as she shook her head.

Oh gods…what did we do? Hecate was never one to feel ashamed after a tryst and she wasn't going to start now…but this was larger than that. This wasn't about feeling embarrassed or cautious after crossing a line with someone or a one-night stand. This was *Aeëtes.* He had consumed her thoughts ever since that kiss on Aeaea.

Last night was…fuck. Hecate turned over and stared up at the ceiling, trying to straighten out her thoughts before she got out of bed. *It can't go any further. Even if it's just sex, I don't think I can have* just *sex with Aeëtes.* The thought alone made a sick feeling sink in the pit of her stomach, and that did fill her with shame. She would never forget the look on his face when she told him that she only wanted sex. He had laid everything out for her, and she denied him, claiming that the only thing she wanted him for was physical.

It's not like I didn't want him for that. Hecate continued to try and rationalize with herself, as if she could find an angle to look at the scenario that didn't make her feel terrible. There wasn't one. As she twisted around in the thin sheets, Hecate found herself on a delicate precise. On one hand, she had seen the hurt in Aeëtes's eyes when she told him that anything between them would be purely physical. On the other hand, there was simply...no way that she could believe he felt that way about her. She wanted to believe it—she had heard his voice when he told her, and he had backed off the topic of his feelings just as quickly. He knew this would be her response, but it was as though he needed to say it anyway, even if partially in jest or even if it would fall on deaf ears. Gods, how she wanted to believe it. As soon as she could see herself trusting him, accepting that that was truly how he felt, Hecate would feel her walls slam up around her.

It was as though there was some invisible tether that kept jerking her back, keeping her from believing it. No matter what she told her mind to do—and she tried as she tossed back and forth—she couldn't just...accept it.

Men are fickle. They only care about their freedom, and in the end...that won't mean you. Her thoughts were quick and sharp, her wounds always poised like arrows to hit the target of her deepest insecurities when she least expected it.

Finally, without any resolution, Hecate stood slowly. She readjusted her clothing and retied the braid in her hair, praying that she didn't look as discombobulated as she felt—and she felt like she had been taken apart and hastily put back together again.

Maybe Aphrodite has it all wrong. Hecate mused as she left the cabin. *Maybe it's Hephaestus that we should pray to when we are broken, when our hearts and minds are shattered with feelings of affection. Hearts are fickle things, and they must be put back together carefully... Maybe we need the craftsman to fix us when we splinter, not the Goddess of love.*

Hecate was deep in her thoughts as she stepped onto deck, expecting that it would be empty so close to sunrise. It would be busy enough soon. There was no time to waste, but this early, she was praying for a brief reprieve in the sea air.

She didn't get it.

As soon as she looked up, there he was. Aeëtes was standing across the deck from her, leaning against the railing. He was staring right at her, having turned when he heard the door from the galley open. Hecate paused as her heart got stuck in her throat, nearly choking on her own surprise. She quickly pushed her face back to stoicism, hoping that he hadn't seen the flicker of surprise on her face.

He had.

Aeëtes pushed himself off the railing and began walking towards her, slowly. Yet again, he reminded her of a predator, his gaze leveled at her with gentle eyes that still seemed lit from within. Hecate swallowed thickly and raised her chin slightly, hoping that she looked every bit composed. How this conversation played out would define how they related to one another after last night.

She took a few steps away from the door, positioning herself at the side of the boat, overlooking the water. Aeëtes quietly came up beside her, joining her and saying nothing. They both stared out at the endless horizon, getting lost in the clouds and the sea. Hecate could feel his body next to hers, and she knew that he didn't have magic, but she was questioning it these days. She could feel his presence like witchcraft, a heavy, heady feeling that consumed her senses when he was around her. Even though they weren't touching, just the presence of him so close to her was enough to trigger a barrage of memories of the night before.

It didn't help that he looked positively sinful in the early daylight, a true son of Helios. It was as if his father's favor meant that he looked desperately delicious in each turn of the light, dark curls brushing his shoulders, set free from their usual leather cord. Hecate might have felt a little bit better if she knew that he was equally unhinged by her presence—and Aeëtes's thoughts were possessed.

My gods. When he had watched her emerge from the galley, it took everything in him to not run towards her. *I've never seen a single thing that compares to her face in the morning.* He fought to keep his eyes on the horizon and not openly stare at the goddess next to him, who glittered with magic and power. He knew she could destroy him and barely lift a finger. He wanted to run his hands through her braid and let it loose, to watch how the salty winds would whip it around her face...what she would look like carefree. It was the one expression that he hadn't seen on Hecate's face yet. They had come close on Aeaea, he could tell, but something was holding her back.

If you tell me what it is...I'll slay it. Aeëtes found himself promising silently to Hecate's profile. *Whatever is keeping you from me and from this, whatever makes you deny whatever I feel is happening between us...tell me what it is. I'll destroy it.*

They sat there for a few more moments, neither person wanting to be the one who broke the silence. Aeëtes, as usual, had no problem playing the fool, so he did.

"Sleep well, Hecate?" He propped one elbow up on the railing and turned to look at her, angling his whole body towards hers. Hecate's lips curled up into a small smirk, even if she didn't turn to look at him, and he counted that as a win.

"I don't think there would be any point in denying that. Yes, I slept well."

Point one for Aeëtes. He couldn't keep the grin off his face as he mentally cheered himself.

"You were asleep before I even left," he noted, a playful tone in his voice. He knew better then to take it to a serious place too quickly. He had to be cautious with her; he'd seen the night before how she reacted to him admitting his feelings.

"I was," Hecate turned to face him, the slightest blush on her cheeks. "I do suppose that means I owe you."

Two points for Aeëtes! He nearly pumped his fist in the air but managed to give a slight shrug.

"Nonsense." He leaned in closer, an arm tentatively going to wrap around her waist. "If I ever have the pleasure of getting your lips, or any part of you, on me, little witch, it won't be because you *owe me.*" Aeëtes nearly purred the words in her ear, and Hecate found her hand tightening on the railing as she nearly melted into the floorboards. "It will be because you are begging to touch me, to feel me…as much as I needed to touch you."

Aeëtes pulled away, releasing his grip on her waist and giving her a small shrug. He leaned back against the side of the ship, bearing his weight on both of his elbows.

"You're awfully confident of that. Again," Hecate chided him, but they both knew that there was no heat in her voice. He merely shrugged, turning to look at her and winking. The silence settled back over them, but it was comfortable this time. Ironically, acknowledging the attraction between them had made it less awkward. At least they both knew that they were suffering.

Hecate reveled in the ease of his company for only a few moments until she could feel her treacherous mind working overtime again. Her thoughts drifted to her anxieties once more, always waiting in the wings, enforcing that he only wanted her for one thing. That Aeëtes couldn't possibly feel anything for her beyond the bounds of lust. It didn't matter what he said or did. She sat there for another few minutes, feeling suddenly like she was about to explode, her anxiety coming on quickly and building in her until she felt pressurized.

You'll see. Her brain was wicked. *Ask him. Ask him why he loves the sea, why he doesn't want to return to Colchis or be king.* She blurted it out before she could control herself.

"Why don't you want to be king?" She turned to look at him, and Aeëtes looked stunned. He recovered quickly, shrugging and running a hand through his hair.

"I don't know. I don't want to be...chained down, I guess. I have love for my adoptive parents, but it's hard. If I stay in Colchis and take up the crown after my father, then, well, that's who I am. It feels like doing that would erase part of me. The wild part. The immortal part. I don't know if I'm making any sense..."

"I get it," Hecate held up a hand gracefully, cutting him off. "It'll stifle you if you have to conform in any way. You'll have to deny parts of yourself if you were tied down, as you said, in any way."

Aeëtes snapped his fingers in response, looking at her with a smile.

"Yes! That's it. You understand."

"I understand perfectly." Hecate's smile didn't reach her eyes as all of her worst fears were confirmed. "If you'll excuse me." She stepped away from him quickly, disappearing back below deck, as Aeëtes watched her fleeting form in confusion. He shook his head, letting out a long, slow breath as he looked up towards the sky.

I don't know what it is that has you so spooked, little witch...but if you think I'm going to go anywhere, you're wrong.

❧ 19 ❧

A eëtes had been in turmoil ever since his earlier conversation with Hecate. He still fought with himself over the true nature of her feelings—going back and forth from believing she only wanted to sleep with him to believing that her eyes gave her away. Those eyes, blue as the sea and the sky he loved, that betrayed her conflicting feelings for him. She wanted him, wanted more, but something was holding her back. Every time he managed to convince himself of that, his insecurities would crash over his brain like a tidal wave, attempting to drown him in the idea that he was unworthy as both a man and a demi-god. He brushed those thoughts aside as best as he could, returning to the deck and his friends amongst the crew, joining them in their chores to distract himself from his mind.

It was midday by the time that Aeëtes saw Hecate again as the door to the galley was thrown open and out she stormed, her face contorted in annoyance. Aeëtes felt a chill go down his spine at the same time his stomach flipped. He was feeling an irrational amount of attraction towards Hecate, no matter her mood. He was standing near Pelias at the mast, talking about nothing of importance while the crew kept the ship on course to Colchis.

Aeëtes raised a brow as she walked towards them, her shoulders back and her head held high; she looked every bit the proud goddess that she was. Hecate, in turn, got an eyeful of Aeëtes, shirtless and sweaty from a morning's worth of labor on deck. She felt her body flush hot at the sight. She only allowed herself the slightest of distractions before the annoyance settled back on her face.

"Something bothering you?" Aeëtes couldn't help but bite back a grin at her expression, finding it equally endearing and terrifying.

"He's about to be," Hecate snapped, crossing her arms over her chest. Aeëtes's brow furrowed as he processed her words.

"What does that—"

"If it isn't my Venomous Virgin, the Mother of madness, the Crone of corruptness…"

Aeëtes's question was cut off by a loud voice that seemed to echo from everywhere around them. There was a flash, and before Aeëtes could blink, Hermes was standing in front of them. The god was dressed in a gleaming white tunic with golden curls hanging down his face and infamous gold sandals tied to his feet.

Pelias's eyes got wide, and the rest of the crew stopped what they were doing, staring at the god. Hermes glanced around and held his hands up in mock surrender, a smirk on his face.

"Alright, alright, back to your posts or your…ship duties. Whatever it is that you all do around here." He gave a little wave and most of the men scattered, not wanting to defy a god even in the slightest of ways. Hermes turned to Pelias, Aeëtes, and Hecate, the latter of whom was glaring at him.

"I should've known not to tell you where I was going," she deadpanned although there was the smallest glint of humor in her eyes. Aeëtes turned to look at her, noticing it and feeling something akin to jealously settle in his chest.

"You know that I could find you anywhere, regardless." Hermes shrugged, crossing the distance between them and pulling her into a tight hug.

Aeëtes braced himself for Hecate's inevitable rage, but only felt the ball of envy in his body begin to spin as she accepted the gesture. Pelias turned to look at Aeëtes, as if he could sense this, and tried to lighten the mood. Pelias did not know Hermes, and broadly, he wasn't very devout.

"Aeëtes," Pelias grinned, "do you want to tell me how I've ended up on a ship with both Hecate *and* Hermes?" Hermes overheard this and pulled away from Hecate, his face full of mischief. Aeëtes couldn't help but feel himself soften slightly towards the god. Anyone who always looked ready to cause a little bit of healthy chaos, as he called it, was inevitably a friend to him.

"You should be so lucky." Hermes winked, causing Pelias to pale slightly and nod his head rapidly. Hecate burst out into laughter—a sound that made Aeëtes want to bottle it up and drink it—as she shook her head in Hermes's direction.

"Don't you dare frighten this poor man. Pelias, listen to me, Hermes is about as dangerous as a flea. Annoying, yes, but hardly deadly."

"Ha!" Hermes tsked. "She only says that because I censor my stories. I wouldn't want a lady hearing about my great and terrible gruesomeness."

"You say that like you've ever treated me like a lady, Hermes." Hecate rolled her eyes. "Speaking of stories, however, you best tell us why you're here."

"Again, you wound me! How come you always assume that I have some sort of perilous update? A dreadful bulletin, a development of the cruelest—"

"You are the bloody messenger god," Hecate grit her teeth, "and you are getting on my nerves in record time."

Hermes only laughed in response. Aeëtes was transfixed by the dynamic between them. It wasn't flirty although everything that Hermes did or said could be perceived as flirting, but there was an underlying...*companionship* there, a familiarity. It made Aeëtes want to shove Hermes off the deck of the ship without his fancy sandals and see how fast he'd sink.

Whoa there. Aeëtes stopped his own thoughts. *That's a bit much. I'm not jealous. I just don't trust the gods. Anyone could be working for Hera. Yeah, that's it. He might be working for Hera.* Aeëtes shook his head to clear it and focused back on the conversation happening in front of him.

"Well," Hermes grinned, leaning towards the group with a conspiratorial look on his face, "no one is shocked, but word of Hera's skirmish with you has reached Mt. Olympus. She has asked for Zeus to take her side."

Pelias and Aeëtes paled at the news, thinking that this spelled certain doom.

"What does that mean?!" Pelias nearly yelped, but Hecate simply scoffed at the news.

"Ha! How did that go for Hera? Zeus doesn't want anything to do with her beyond distracting her from his affairs."

"Exactly." Hermes snapped his fingers. "Zeus is refusing to engage with her, claiming that she needs to stop her whining. I guess he's still licking his wounds a little bit and doesn't feel like getting involved in another god's businesses."

Hermes chuckled, and Hecate couldn't help but crack a small smile. Aeëtes and Pelias realized that there was a joke there that they didn't understand; they wouldn't have understood, the mortal realm only hearing stories of Zeus's victories over the titans, not of Nyx and Erebus's involvement.

"That won't last," Hecate noted. "He'll be back to his tricks soon enough, but at least that means it's only Hera after us for now."

"For now," Hermes agreed. "She's causing quite a racket, so who's to say who will join her cause simply to shut her up."

"What does Helios say about all of this?" Aeëtes blurted before he could stop himself, his face turning a slight shade of red as soon as he said it. Hermes stopped, turning his whole body to face Aeëtes, his eyes narrowing as he studied him.

"Ahh," he nodded slowly, appraisingly. "You're a son of Helios."

"How did you—"

"It's my job to know things." Hermes shrugged, sounding grandiose, but Hecate let out a squawk.

"Ha! He's nosy. He's incredibly nosy is what he means to say."

Hermes only brushed her off.

"Helios normally doesn't spend much time on Mt. Olympus, you know." He waved his hand around aimlessly. "He's pretty occupied during the day. If I see him, I'll tell him…"

"Don't," Aeëtes muttered, his eyes going downcast. "It would be best for now if I wasn't brought up."

Hermes fell silent before he nodded slowly, a rare and somber look crossing his face.

"Understood."

There was a beat of silence and a moment between them, Aeëtes acknowledging the god's restraint with a quiet nod. It would be easy for Hermes to get involved, to entertain his normal tricks, to stir up some more chaos about their journey. Yet, Aeëtes trusted him to keep to his word, and it seemed like Hecate liked him—that was enough for Aeëtes, as much as it made him want to throw Hermes back into the sky.

"One more thing, Hermes." Hecate held up a finger. "I don't want word of this getting to the Underworld. Have Nyx and Erebus heard about this?" Hermes shook his head.

"I would imagine that Hades knows. He keeps up with Poseidon quite regularly. Ever since that whole coup attempt."

"That *what?*" Pelias yelped, looking between the two gods.

Of course, this was news again to the mortal men, who had heard a very different story about what happened with the titans.

"Don't worry about it. It happens more often than you'd think." Hermes playfully rolled his eyes at Pelias.

"Hermes." Hecate got his attention again. "I'm serious. I want to make sure that Nyx and Erebus don't know."

"Why not? You know that Nyx would easily help end this." Hermes leaned against the mast, examining his fingernails as if they were the most interesting thing in the world. As soon as Aeëtes thought about their journey coming to an end, it made his chest ache. He knew that it would eventually, but he certainly didn't want it to end prematurely. Or at least, what he considered to be prematurely.

"She could," Hecate nodded, "but I will not be like Hera. She runs to Zeus and the other gods to cry foul instead of fighting her own battles. I will do this honorably, and I'll do it without dragging other people in to fight my fight." Her voice decreased in pitch until she was nearly growling at the end, which did something to Aeëtes's insides.

"Alright, your deviousness." Hermes only smiled as his eyes went from Hecate to Aeëtes and back to Hecate. "You know that I simply live to serve you." He gave her a little mock bow that had Hecate rolling her eyes and tossing a braid over her shoulder.

"All of the gods do, even if they don't know it. Now, play nice with the other boys, Hermes, and I want to see how close we are to landfall."

Hermes gave her a salute as she sauntered off to find the navigator, leaving Pelias and Aeëtes standing next to the god. Pelias looked at Hermes with a wide-eyed expression, still getting used to cavorting with the gods.

"Don't leave your mouth open, young man, it's hardly very becoming." Hermes pointed at Pelias playfully, who immediately let out a little sound of indignation.

"Young man! Why, I cannot believe you—"

"Everyone mortal is a 'young man' to me, Pelias. You can't take it personally." Hermes cut him off with a chuckle that made both Aeëtes and Pelias soften. Hermes collected himself and stood a little straighter, cocking an eyebrow as he leveled his gaze at Aeëtes.

"Now, you." He cocked his head to one side. "Do you want to tell me a little bit more about how in love you are with my darling Hecate?"

"*Your* Hecate!" Aeëtes felt his blood boil, and his face darkened as he looked at Hermes. "I'll believe that as soon as I hear it from Hecate herself." He stepped a little closer to Hermes, squaring his shoulders back and his hands tightening into fists. He stood about the same height as Hermes, and while they were both immortal, Aeëtes had no powers. Hermes had the full powers of an Olympian. Hermes's face darkened as he stepped towards Aeëtes in return, and for a moment, it looked like the immortals were about to brawl. After a few seconds of terse silence, Hermes broke the tension with a belly laugh.

"Oh, oh I was so curious if I was right..." He could barely speak through his own laughter, nearly bent over at the waist. "You proved my point so gloriously, Aeëtes!" He stood up and clapped the man on the back. "My goodness, you are smitten with her."

Aeëtes felt his face flush as he realized that he had been set up, and he glared at Hermes. A fresh wave of embarrassment washed over him. He chewed on his lip and said nothing, waiting for Hermes to finish. Pelias, next to him, tried to stifle his amusement as he saw how quickly Hermes had been able to push Aeëtes's buttons.

"Oh, don't be a bad sport about it," Hermes told Aeëtes, a devilish grin on his face. "C'mon, what did you expect from a trickster?"

He held his arms out as if he was offering himself up to

Aeëtes. He still said nothing, but he scoffed. It had a lot less anger behind it.

"It's complicated," Aeëtes admitted, running a hand through his hair, his expression turning sheepish. Hermes only smiled wider.

"I would assume so. Trust me, you'll get no competition from me in that department. Hecate is…"

"I won't hear a bad word about her, messenger," Aeëtes snapped, his mood turning foul again as he misread Hermes's tone. Which, of course, set Hermes off in another round of boisterous laughter.

"Oh, gods above and below! You are really gone for her, aren't you?"

"I've never seen him like this," Pelias tossed in with a grin, earning himself a glare from Aeëtes.

"Does she know how you feel?" Hermes pushed, moving closer to Aeëtes and Pelias, as if they were about to gossip around an amphora of wine.

"I think so." Aeëtes shrugged, abandoning any discernment and sighing deeply. "I didn't want to tell her outright. It would spook her."

Hermes only nodded, as if this was a dreadfully serious topic. "That was wise of you. It most certainly would've." Aeëtes and Pelias waited, but Hermes didn't elaborate.

"I'll take whatever I can get." Aeëtes's voice was wistful as his eyes began to scan the deck for Hecate, perpetually eager to have her in his sights. Hermes noticed this subtle action and knew beyond a shadow of a doubt that Aeëtes was ready to give his life for Hecate if it was required of him. He nodded in a quiet approval, appraising him.

"Walk with me, Aeëtes," Hermes said gently, motioning for them to move to the other side of the deck. He turned to Pelias with a nod. "It's been an honor, sailor. You make a swift god proud with your command of the seas."

Pelias fumbled and gave Hermes a quick bow, unsettled by

the praise, before he ran off to find something to attend to. He moved as if he was eager to prove himself worth of an immortal's compliment.

Aeëtes followed Hermes to the other end of the long ship, joining him at the railing as they both looked out over the water. Aeëtes's eyes still scanned the deck for Hecate. He only relaxed when he found her chatting aimlessly with the navigator at the opposite end.

"Listen," Hermes said gently in a tone that Aeëtes hadn't heard him use before. "I think you would be good for her." Aeëtes felt his heart expand so quickly at Hermes's approval, he thought it might kill him. "Be sure in your affections if you are to pursue her. You will be denied more than once in your course, but if you hold true…"

Hermes trailed off, as he, too, looked at Hecate's distant form. He smiled and let out a long sigh before turning back to Aeëtes.

"You will be denied more than once. Many a man, immortal or not, cannot face that kind of rejection. You must be surer of your love for her than of anything you've ever known if you are to prove it."

"For Hecate… For her, I would face it a million times over. I'd cross the rivers of Hades and back if that was what she demanded," Aeëtes interjected, his voice tinged with desperation, turning away to look out over the sea. Hermes nodded.

"You just might have to, Aeëtes… You just might have to," Hermes spoke in such a foreboding way that Aeëtes turned to ask him to clarify.

The god was gone.

Hecate wasn't bothered by Hermes's abrupt disappearance when Aeëtes told her.

"It's pretty common amongst immortals," she commented with a wave of her hand. "We can't be expected to constantly be giving formal hellos and goodbyes."

Aeëtes felt the sharp sting of rejection, embarrassed by the notion of what the immortals did and didn't do. It sent a surge of insecurity through him, that he was half of a man and half an immortal. His naïveté when it came to the way of the gods caused him to flush around Hecate more than anything. Well, almost more than anything.

They were standing together at the bow of the ship, watching other ships pass them in the distance. Hecate didn't notice the slightest dip in Aeëtes's behavior. It had turned out to be a clear day, the sun shining brightly down on the water without a cloud in the sky. Pelias had resumed his typical duties with the crew, and Aeëtes had sought out Hecate as soon as Hermes had disappeared. The messenger god's words were still ringing in Aeëtes's ears, wondering what Hermes meant when he said his affections would be tested.

When he looked at the goddess, however, relaxed against

the railing and her hair loose in the wind, he realized that there was nothing he wouldn't withstand for her. Even his own insecurities, which continued to echo in his brain that he could never be good enough for a woman like Hecate.

The same tune looped endlessly in Hecate's mind, too, as she tripped over the remnants of old wounds. She chewed on her lip absentmindedly as they both looked out at the water, the ship moving seamlessly through the waves. Aeëtes wore his heart on his sleeve for Hecate, willing to give her everything and afraid that it wasn't enough. She kept her heart hardened, afraid to accept anything he had to give her—not because it wasn't enough, but because it was too much. It would drown her, rip apart her battlements, and set her free.

Hecate told herself that Aeëtes would always choose his freedom. And her soul hadn't been set free in a long, long time.

"There we are," Hecate spoke in a singsong, pointing to a group of buildings along a not-so-distant skyline. "Byzantium."

"Byzantium?" Aeëtes nearly shouted, half-leaning over the ship to get a better look. "It should take us days more to get to Byzantium. Weeks, even, depending on the weather. How did we get here in *two* days?" He turned to look at the goddess, who had a small grin on her face.

"I can't use my powers without Hera finding us, but it seems we may have had a little bit of assistance."

"From whom?" Aeëtes's brow furrowed as he thought of any other god who might be clamoring for Hecate's good graces.

"Poseidon," Hecate answered simply. Aeëtes felt his chest constrict, fighting possessive and nearly overwhelming feelings of jealously.

"Should we be accepting favors from other gods?" Aeëtes's tone was cautious. Hecate turned to face him, her expression quizzical as she nodded.

"I wouldn't think you to be the mistrusting type all of a sudden. Did Hermes say something to you?" Hecate pressed, taking a step closer and looking Aeëtes over as if she could discern the answer. He managed to keep his face stoic, shaking his head.

"No, no, he didn't. Well, he said plenty but nothing of consequence." Aeëtes must have sounded convincing enough since Hecate scoffed and waved her hand in the air.

"That sounds like Hermes. It's tough to come by genuine trust amongst immortals, yes, I'll give you that. For now, we can trust Poseidon. The sooner that we can get to Colchis, the better."

"Yes," Aeëtes drawled, unable to keep some of the ire out of his voice. "The sooner that you get rid of me and this is all over, the better."

"Excuse me?" Hecate snapped, her temper flaring up at the accusatory tone in Aeëtes's statement. "What's that supposed to mean?"

"I think that you know perfectly well what it means."

"I most certainly do not!" Aeëtes took another step closer to Hecate so their bodies were almost touching as he shook his head slowly.

"You *really* like making me spell things out for you, don't you, little witch?" Hecate felt the heat rise to her cheeks as she made an irreverent sound, shaking her head but also unable to will her body to move away from him. She felt her heart beating faster as attraction and aggression warred with one another.

"Maybe it's just impossible to understand what you're saying! Always speaking in riddles."

"Riddles!" Aeëtes laughed loudly. "Ha! Only someone who constantly is hiding from themselves would think that someone being direct is speaking in riddles. I've been more honest with you than you'd like!"

"Now you just sound ridiculous," Hecate growled at Aeëtes, her magic sparking to life over her skin. She caught the way that Aeëtes's eyes glowed at it, how her magic seemed to spark something in him, too. She would be lying to herself if she said it didn't make her heart skip a beat. Her magic always had made man run away—always.

"You want this entire thing to be over as soon as possible, isn't that right?" Aeëtes accused her, his mouth pulled into a taut line as his body seemed to tense.

"Yes, I want to make sure that this is over as soon as possible!" Hecate nearly shrieked, causing a few sailors to turn their heads towards the commotion, only to quickly busy themselves with other errands. Aeëtes let out a noise halfway between a snort and a growl, running his hand through his hair and nearly ripping the leather cord out. He looked away to collect himself.

"Because you want to be rid of me that badly?"

"Because I want you safe!" Hecate screamed, magic bursting from her as soon as she said it. Glowing, red sparks rained down around her and Aeëtes as she caught her breath, her hand immediately going up and covering her mouth in shock. Aeëtes stood immobile, his brain moving too quickly to try and process what she had just said.

They stood there for a few, dreadfully long seconds, as Hecate's magic slowly diminished, and she released a long sigh. Hecate and Aeëtes started speaking at the same time.

"I didn't…"

"You did…"

They both stopped. Hecate leaned her head back and closed her eyes, and Aeëtes turned to watch the horizon in a semblance of giving her a private moment.

"I wouldn't want to see anyone come to harm under Hera." Hecate broke the silence, clarifying her outburst like it was an amendment. Aeëtes said nothing, watching her carefully, his eyes studying her so intensely that Hecate thought she might fall under his gaze.

You've never *felt this way when a man looked at you*, her traitorous brain reminded her, and Hecate nearly turned on her heel and went running for the galley. Her pride won out in the end, and she stared back at Aeëtes, her chin lifting in challenge in the slightest of ways. As soon as she did it, Aeëtes sighed, reaching up and tightening the cord around his hair.

"Of course. It's all about Hera."

"It is." Hecate nodded primly, and Aeëtes shrugged in response, as if he didn't believe her but was going to let her have her moment anyway. "Now," Hecate cleared her throat, "Let's see about going ashore." She smoothed the folds of her chiton and walked briskly away from Aeëtes, leaving him standing at the railing as he watched her leave. He couldn't help it as a small, hopeless smile etched its way onto his face as he thought about her reaction.

This might have started as something about Hera, but you and I both know that it's not just about her anymore.

He turned to look at the sea and felt at ease, watching and waiting as the ship moved nearly effortlessly closer to the docks of Byzantium.

✝ ✝ ✝

HECATE NEARLY RAN AWAY from Aeëtes, trying to calm her heart rate. She couldn't help her earlier outburst, as much as she was chastising herself for it now. She was growing increasingly anxious for them to get to Colchis, especially after Hermes's arrival. If it was becoming a topic of gossip on Mt. Olympus, it wouldn't be long before other gods did join the fray—no matter how much Hermes said that they didn't seem interested. At least it looked like Poseidon was on their side. Even Hecate had woken up that morning and was surprised to see how swiftly they had made it, but it seemed like Poseidon still had the creatures of the Underworld in his good will.

She saw Pelias on deck, chatting with one of the cabin boys, and turned towards his direction.

Get yourself together, Hecate. Hecate's thoughts were sharp, almost cruel. *A man has never affected you like this before, and this is not the time for firsts.* Her reaction to Aeëtes had angered her, made her feel weak. She was already concerned about the peril that she had put him in. If it came down to it, she could defend herself against Hera, but that didn't mean that Aeëtes wouldn't get in the way.

As she approached Pelias, the ship began slowing down, causing it to lurch and nearly toss Hecate into the sailor. He caught her and righted her quickly, laughing in a way that was not unkind, while all of the random compasses and bottles he held on his person jangled.

"Careful now, Goddess, sea legs are a bitch to come by. Once you've got them, do your best not to let them go." He spoke like any old man of the sea, constantly full of idioms that didn't always make sense.

"Thank you." Hecate's smile was genuine, and she stood straighter. "Can we go ashore in Byzantium?" She was desperate to get to Colchis, but she needed a few moments to herself on land. The tight quarters on the ship with Aeëtes was getting to her brain.

"Err," Pelias looked ashore, realizing that the waves were carrying them in towards the docks regardless. "I don't really have anything against it. We are rather ahead of schedule." He laughed at his own joke, slapping his belly as he did so.

"Thank you." Hecate breathed a sigh of relief, grabbing hold of Pelias's hands. "Thank you!" Pelias looked at her with a slightly bemused expression, and Hecate realized that her relief was questionable. She let go of his hands and smiled, a flush covering her cheeks that she couldn't quite get rid of.

"It seems that Poseidon wills it, so who am I to defy him? Or you, for that matter."

Hecate gave him a wink. "It's me that you should be more

scared of."

Pelias bowed low. "Of course, Goddess."

Hecate only laughed in response, a genuine, trilling sound that made Aeëtes turn and search for her from across the ship. The great ship came to a slower pace, the waves ebbing and flowing beneath it, as if guided by Poseidon's hand itself. The sails fluttered in the strong winds, pushing them towards the ever-busy port of Byzantium.

If the docks of Heraklion were busy, then this was something otherworldly. There were more ships behind them yet, all piling in and fighting for a spot amongst one another. Flags flew from all over the known world, and even a few that some of the men hadn't seen, all of them proclaiming different allegiances.

The air smelled of salt and spices, drifting off the bows of other merchant ships, while the cries of sailors and passengers alike mixed with one another like notes of a song. Stone and wood buildings were piled on top of one another, domes reaching up the highest of all, like soldiers in a row making up the skyline. Every different creed and religion with a boat eventually landed in Byzantium, where they all pledged allegiance to one god—coin. All skirmishes, political, interpersonal, and of the religious nature had to be put aside to not affect commerce—it was the one thing that everyone could agree on.

Hecate had not been to Byzantium since it had been given its new name, the first one lost to time, and even to her. She leaned up against the railing and took in a deep breath, closing her eyes as the mist from the waves came up and covered her face and hair. She was looking forward to slipping away and finding her temple; realigning herself with her acolytes would get her head on straight again. The ship approached an empty spot on one of the docks, coming up to it with a soft thud. Hecate moved to the side to accommodate the sailors preparing the gangplank, her mind beginning to spin.

If you really don't care about him, pick up a lover. Her thoughts returned, cruel as ever, goading her from within the walls of her wounds. Hecate prepared to argue with *herself* when a piercing shout broke her concentration.

"Hecate!" Aeëtes's voice thundered over the deck, getting her attention. She turned to look at him, her brow furrowing in confusion as she saw him racing towards her from the other end of the ship. He waved his hands in the air, shaking his head furiously. "Get down!"

Everything else seemed to happen in slow motion. She felt the threat before she saw it, her magic glowing to life as the snakes flickered across her arms. Hecate did the opposite that Aeëtes demanded, spinning around to look at the docks. The gangplank was half descended, where there was now an angry mob of men waiting for them. She didn't know how quickly they had gotten there, or how it had happened without any of them noticing, but she noticed the dull gleam in their eyes.

They were bewitched...entirely under Hera's control, the same as the wild hogs on Aeaea.

"Get *down!*" Aeëtes's voice was closer now, nearly halfway to her. She whipped back around to him, and even from a distance, she could tell that his eyes were wild. He looked like he was also possessed, racing towards her and nearly barreling into the sailors who couldn't get out of the way fast enough. He pulled a sword off one of the men as he ran, raising it as if he was prepared to strike.

"Aeëtes!" Hecate screamed, her magic flowing off her and moving over the deck towards him like water. "What are you doing?"

"Get! Down!" he huffed out the words again, yelling as he jumped over a railing and skidded past barrels to get to her. "Now!" There was an urgency in his voice that she couldn't ignore, and she would later regret remembering how the command in his tone did things to her insides. Hecate listened, for arguably the first time, and dropped down to the deck of the ship.

No sooner had she done that than a flaming arrow went hurtling through the sky above her—right where she had been standing. Aeëtes must have seen the archer hidden in the Hera-controlled mob before she did. A mortal arrow wouldn't kill her, but it would've hurt and taken her and her magic out of commission.

"Aeëtes!" Hecate yelled, realizing that he wasn't slowing down. He was running at full speed, his hair now fallen out of its cord, and he looked utterly deranged. His entire body was poised like a weapon, his teeth gritted together and his form wound tight. Hecate felt her heart rate skyrocket as he came running towards her, looking not like a sailor or even a prince, but a *god*. Sun beams seemed to be pouring out from his hair and his eyes, and Hecate couldn't determine whether it was a trick of the light, her own imagination, or the powers of a son of Helios.

"Stay down!" he commanded, hardly stopping as he ran past her. "Pelias!" he barked right as he paused at the gang-plank. "Get out to sea!"

Pelias shouted something in confirmation, but Hecate didn't hear it, her jaw dropping to the ground as Aeëtes turned and disappeared off the ship.

"Stop! What are you—" Hecate screamed, her voice full of terror as she realized that Aeëtes didn't know what he was up against. If those men were bewitched by Hera, it would take more than mortal strength to kill them—it would require magic.

She pulled herself up off the deck, feeling power beginning to surge through her, almost against her will. All she could see was Aeëtes. He tuned and managed to wink once at Hecate before taking off at a full run. Aeëtes launched himself off the gangplank, and time itself seemed to stop.

He seemed to fly through the air, his sword raised high

above his head as he let out an earth-shattering cry that rivaled Aries. When he landed on the dock, the whole ground seemed to shake, causing several of the men around him to fall to their knees. Aeëtes kept shouting, waving his sword and cutting through the first line of men with devastating skill. Hecate was almost frozen as she watched him, Pelias quickly coming up behind her.

"He'll be fine," Pelias's voice was soothing as he gently gripped her arm. "Don't use your magic. We don't want to call more attention to ourselves."

"But those men! If Hera already knows we're here —"

"Does she, though? Or do you think she might have just enchanted men at every port from here to Colchis?"

Hecate chewed on her lip, realizing that Pelias had a point. Hera was lazy. It would've been easy enough for her to set enchantments like a trap and wait. If Hecate released her powers, it would only be a bigger alarm bell for the goddess.

Hecate swore up and down, enough to make Pelias blush, and turned back to look at the dock. The boat was already speeding away, no doubt carried once more by enchanted waves, getting farther away from the chaos.

"Wait!" she shrieked, nearly throwing herself off the plank as the sailors hauled it up the rest of the way. She turned and flung herself at Pelias, pounding against his chest. "We can't leave him! That's suicide! How could you —"

Pelias waited until Hecate caught her breath, gently holding onto her arms like a father and an upset child.

"Trust in Aeëtes, Goddess. Trust. He wouldn't leave you too far out of his sight, would he?"

"How dare you all!" Hecate swore again, pushing herself off Pelias and moving back towards the railing. They were moving swiftly, and she could no longer see faces on the dock, only the moving crowds. The boat then came to a halt as quickly as it had started, and Hecate gripped the railing to keep herself from falling with the momentum.

She watched on, unable to pull her eyes from the docks when she saw him. A head taller than the rest of the men, moving through the crowd, Aeëtes suddenly appeared at the very edge of the pier. Without warning, he jumped into the sea.

Hecate let out a sharp cry as her hands came up to cover her mouth before she quickly was spurred into action. Hera might be on the lookout for Hecate's magic, but she likely wasn't paying attention to any of the other gods. Thin, nearly translucent spider webs of red magic danced across Hecate's skin, pouring off her, down the side of the ship, and disappearing into the water. She pulled her power back as quickly as she could, praying the short message wasn't enough to attract Hera's attention.

Please, Poseidon. I need a favor, she began muttering under her breath, pleading with the God of the sea to buoy Aeëtes's journey. It only took a moment before the sweet smell of citrus and sea air assaulted her senses, and she knew that Poseidon had heard her. Hecate watched on as a swift current appeared in the bay, undulating in a near-perfect line from the pier to the boat. It only took another second before two great horses, in the shape of waves, appeared on the very top of the water.

They made triumphant noises as their bodies were flecked with sea foam, and suddenly, a wild sound of laughter joined them. Hecate felt the anxiety in her chest release when she heard Aeëtes loudly laughing from the back of one of the horses as it hurtled him closer to the ship.

Thank you. She sent her prayers to the sea, knowing that they would be well-received.

"I'll collect another time." Poseidon's voice rang out in her head, but it was not said in a warning, but a rather playful tone. Hecate tried to put a damper on the joy that she felt rising up in her as the horses came to a halt and sank back into the sea, depositing Aeëtes right at the side of their ship. Pelias and another sailor hustled to toss a rope down towards him and began hauling him up on deck.

"You owe me, Pelias!" he shouted playfully from the waves. "I told you I'd make it out alive!"

Hecate stuck her head over the side of the boat as Aeëtes was dangling in mid-air, somehow now shirtless and soaking wet. He still managed to keep the sword at his side.

"You made a *bet* on your *life!*" Hecate hissed, staring at him like he was the stupidest man alive. Aeëtes only smiled, the grin lighting up his entire face and warming up the coldest parts of Hecate's heart. Even if she only scoffed in response.

They finally pulled Aeëtes up on deck, who landed in a tangle of limbs with as much grace as a dead fish. Hecate walked right over to him with hellfire in her eyes, shaking her head furiously at his idiocy to wager on his life.

Aeëtes stood up quickly, raising his hands in mock defeat. "Okay, look, I know that may have seemed stupid, but…"

Hecate crossed the distance between them and cut him off, grabbing his face and pulling him to her in a desperate kiss.

He stood there for a split second before his arms went around Hecate on instinct, leaning into the embrace. Her chiton was immediately soaked through, but she couldn't find herself to care as she wound one hand up into his hair. Everything about the embrace was frantic, as if she was convincing herself that he was alive, and Aeëtes was convincing himself that Hecate was real.

When she finally pulled away with a sharp intake of breath, Hecate slammed a hand into his chest and shoved him off her.

"Don't you *ever* do something that stupid again!" she hissed at him, the snakes around her arms echoing the sentiment, before she stormed off and disappeared to the galley.

Aeëtes stood there for a second, utterly dumbfounded and unable to move, but still with a gleaming smile on his face. He finally shook himself of his reverie and clapped his hands, shaking his hair out.

"Time to pay up, Pelias!"

Hecate slammed the door to her cabin shut with such force that it shook dust free from the floorboards above her. She froze, momentarily worried that she had broken something irreparable, but when there was no immediate, catastrophic consequence, she moved away from the door and nearly threw herself on the bed.

It's not like you to be so…so…so impressionable!

After the events on Aeaea, Hecate was already worried that she was too far gone for Aeëtes. This infuriating stranger, who managed to fall into Hera's path, get turned into a gold sheep, and cause her to claim a life debt. *A life debt.* Hecate, in her long, immortal years of existence, had never claimed a life debt; she had certainly never thought that when she did, it would be for a man. Yet, here she was, and now, it was much worse.

She tossed and turned so rapidly that she nearly fell off the bed, the small cabin moving on the waves as the ship hurtled towards Colchis. Hecate was paying better attention now and could feel soft touches of Poseidon's power all around the boat. The boat that had nearly gotten ransacked by a mob of men under Hera's control.

He leapt off a ship to make sure the crew and I could get away. Hecate could very nearly hear the difference between her head and her heart arguing. *And? Men do foolish things. That doesn't mean that you forget they'll always leave you in the end. They'll always choose freedom. Freedom, freedom, freedom!*

What was freedom if you locked yourself away from feeling? If your heart was solid as stone and barricaded from affection, were you safe or in a prison of your own design? Were you the architect of your own suffering if you refused to feel or love? Let yourself be loved?

Hecate let her own thoughts nearly drive her to madness, pulling one knee up to her chest and holding herself in her own embrace. A touch that was cold, one that she had become used to knowing. She curled up around the pillow and gripped it tight to her chest, letting her mind wander. For a few, brief minutes, it would be okay. It wouldn't hurt that badly if she let her thoughts go a little further, to imagine what it would be like if she allowed Aeëtes in.

If she let him give her everything that he was offering. She mused on the idea of waking up next to Aeëtes, of seeing his face in the morning sun of his father. What it would be like to fall asleep on his chest, to see his goofy smile every time that she looked up from her table...her table.

The thought of her life in the Underworld came crashing down on her like a burst of cold water. She nearly sat straight up in bed, the crushing reality threatening to drown her and her heart in the sea. Her warring emotions mixed within her, sending her careening down a hill with so much force, she didn't know if she would ever stop. Hecate ran her hand through her hair, absentmindedly braiding the long, auburn strands again, like she did whenever she was anxious. The front of her chiton was still wet from when she had nearly thrown herself at Aeëtes on deck. What it had felt like to be pressed up against him...

A quiet knock at her door shook her from her spiral.

Hecate stood up, smoothing and retying the drape of her garment, squaring her shoulders. It was her greatest witch-craft, how quickly she could repress her emotions, and it wasn't a skill she was proud of. She opened the door, expecting to find Aeëtes...and there stood Pelias.

"Oh!" Hecate couldn't keep some of the disappointment off her face, and Pelias only smiled.

"You were expecting someone else?" He had a wry smile, not unkind, but he raised an eyebrow.

"Maybe." Hecate blushed. For some reason, she felt calmer around Pelias and didn't rush to hide her emotions or keep her stoicism.

"Do you mind?" Pelias held up a jug of wine, motioning to the inside of her cabin. Hecate nodded and opened the door wider, letting Pelias step inside. He walked towards the barrels in the corner, pouring cups for the both of them. Hecate grabbed one and couldn't help but study Pelias a little more closely. He had a peculiar way of dressing, with a short chiton and a million things always hanging off him. She counted no less than three seafaring instruments and two other small satchels of what she assumed was wine.

"What can I do for you?" Hecate took a prim sip.

"Why do you think that Aeëtes doesn't mean what he says?" Pelias's voice was quiet and unassuming, but he cut straight to the quick. Hecate took another longer sip of wine.

"I don't know what you mean."

"I've known Aeëtes since we were boys. I've never seen him like this. He cares for you, Hecate, deeply."

"If you've never seen him like this, how do you know that this isn't some fleeting flight of fancy? Some trial of lust?"

Pelias shook his head.

"Nice try. I've seen him infatuated. I know what it looks like. This is nothing of the sort. He's offering you his entire heart on a plate, Hecate. If you don't like him, then it doesn't matter. But…I have a feeling that you feel the same. Which is the only reason I'm saying anything."

Hecate was quiet for a moment. Pelias didn't push her. He didn't goad. He simply waited, as if he had all the time in the world. Which was ironic, coming from the one mortal in the conversation. When Hecate finally spoke, her voice was quiet, as if she said her fears too loud, they would come true.

"He would never be happy in the Underworld, Pelias."

The sailor's eyes snapped to Hecate, studying her without judgement as he mulled over her words. He waited, his silence encouraging her to continue.

"I could never commit to living in Greece. I don't even commit to visiting the other gods on Mt. Olympus. I need to be in the Underworld. This trip was supposed to be a short break."

"You don't think that Aeëtes could learn to love the Underworld?"

"I'm sure that he would find the positives in it." Hecate playfully rolled her eyes. "As he always does, but time passes. Eventually, he would begin to resent it. Resent me. He would miss the sea…and his freedom."

"His freedom," Pelias repeated the words gently, nodding, one hand stroking his beard. "Would he be trapped?"

"Goodness, no." Hecate shook her head. "He could travel across realms with my help or another god's. He might be able to learn to do it himself if we ever discover the extent of his abilities as a demi-god." She took a sip of her wine while Pelias continued to nod.

"So…he wouldn't be trapped. That seems pretty free to me."

"It wouldn't be enough. It never is."

"Ah," Pelias let out a long sigh. "There it is. The resolution of someone who has had their heart broken." There was a sad smile on his face while Hecate looked stunned.

"Excuse me?"

It was Pelias's turn to take a long sip of wine.

"Only someone who has had their heart broken would speak in such depressing ultimatums. You may be a goddess, but even the gods grant men their free will. This sounds like a choice that you should give Aeëtes, yet you've made it for him."

"He's not a man. He's a demi-god."

"Semantics."

"I'm not letting him make that choice because I'm not going to give anyone the option to hurt me," Hecate growled softly, the holes that had been made in her walls beginning to patch themselves over. "I did that once before and it ended—badly."

"So no one can choose to love you, either?"

"No!" Hecate snapped, her voice growing more agitated. "What does that even mean?" she hissed, Pelias's words feeling like hot coals over her skin.

"You're only hurting yourself if you won't let love in, Hecate. If you won't let love in because of something that someone did to you in the past, you give them power to keep hurting you."

"I won't be made the fool."

"There is no one wiser than the fool." Pelias countered quickly. "No one who is more open, more sage, more genuine than the person who lets themselves be foolish. Life is short, then you die," Pelias chuckled to himself. "Well, some of us anyway. Alas. Let yourself be the fool for once, dear goddess, and you'd be surprised who will catch you."

Hecate said nothing. Pelias knew that he had struck a nerve somewhere deep, a part of the goddess that she kept hidden. The only reason he could even see this side of her was because of her affection towards Aeëtes. It was confusing her, throwing her off her game. The pair sat in silence, an old sailor and the Goddess of witchcraft sharing a lousy jar of wine. Everything about the scene should have made Pelias feel awkward and Hecate indifferent, but it didn't. She enjoyed his company. The ship moved gently and rocked them back and forth, and Hecate found her mind racing for any reason to deny Pelias.

She finally looked up at him with a smile that only looked sad.

"I would betray my acolytes."

Pelias studied her, his brow furrowing only slightly as he took another sip. He paused before grabbing one of the small satchels on his waist. He opened it and took a quick sniff, making a grimace that made Hecate laugh, and poured it into his cup.

"I'm going to need something stronger before you explain this."

Hecate rolled her eyes but indulged him, waiting until he tossed his cup back before she elaborated. "The women who pray to me... they've been hurt. They carry the cruelty of men like scars, and for some of them, that's very literal. The chaste pray to Artemis and Hestia. The married pray to Hera, and the youth pray to Aphrodite."

Pelias offered up a tension-breaking smirk. "If the married women are praying to Hera, no wonder there are so many unhappy couples."

Hecate couldn't help but bark out a sharp laugh before quickly trying to compose herself. She shook her head and tossed him a side-eyed glance in mock chastity before continuing.

"The women who pray to me, they respect my position in the pantheon. I am no vestal virgin, but I've taken no consort. I'm the only one in that position and to...to indulge this any further..." Hecate trailed off, and her voice started to break.

Everything that she had been suppressing was suddenly coming hurtling towards the surface like a bitter taste in the back of her throat. The underworld of her own broken heart was threatening to drench her daylights in darkness, to canni-balize her joy. Her hand went to her chest as if she could phys-

ically stop the pain in her soul. She bit back a gasp, afraid that
if she opened her mouth at all, she would cry out for Aeëtes —
call out for his eternal joy, that the son of the sun might warm
the depths of her mind.

Pelias reached out to her. He gently covered her palm with
his, and the gentle touch nearly broke the thin barrier of
Hecate's control.

"To indulge this any further," she continued with a heavy
voice, thick with buried tears, "would mean that I would
threaten the respect of my acolytes. You can understand that,
can't you, Pelias?" She looked at him with searching eyes,
desperate for the first time in her immortal life for someone to
affirm her decisions.

Pelias studied her carefully, his eyes warm and full of
caring, but there was an intensity to them. He had a way about
him that was soothing and harsh like the sharpest blade that
cut quickly to reduce your pain but went straight to the bone.

"You're lying to yourself, Hecate."

She swallowed thickly, fear now intermingling with the
anxiety and heartbreak in her veins, sending pulses of red
magic over her arms. She pulled away from Pelias and ran her
own hands over her arms like she was cold, as if she could
soothe the response away. She felt chastised although she was
looking for an insult that wasn't there. Pelias shrugged.

"Your acolytes, those women, they would want you to be
happy. No one says that you have to become Hera or some pillar to
the institution of marriage," Pelias deadpanned, taking another sip
before continuing. "You owe yourself happiness after heartbreak.
Isn't that what everyone wants to see after they bleed?" He shook
his head slowly, staring her down with such fire that she swore he
could've been a demi-god himself. "*That* is what your acolytes
deserve from you. The strength to continue after you have been
wounded, the courage to know that you deserve a greater love."

Hecate let out a strangled cry, her hand coming up and

covering her mouth quickly to stifle it. She felt like her pain was going to crawl out of her chest, like each heartbeat cracked her ribs. It took her a minute to compose herself and Pelias waited patiently, not offering another word. When Hecate picked up her head, her eyes were empty, and the tears were gone. There was a coldness to her expression that made Pelias feel like he was looking at a mere statue of the goddess. She shook her head once.

"It would never work between Aeëtes and I, Pelias. I don't deserve that."

He said nothing and Hecate stood, going towards the cabin door and opening it for him. She waited there, and it was clear that Pelias had been dismissed. He walked calmly to the door, sighing as he passed her.

"I certainly wish that you didn't believe that."

It was Hecate's turn to say nothing, her power flying up around her body like an invisible shield. Pelias shuffled out of the cabin, making his way to the deck.

He didn't notice Aeëtes, hidden behind the stairs, leaning back against the wall with his eyes screwed shut.

'I don't deserve that.' Aeëtes's thoughts were the cruelest of tormentors, barking at him like baying dogs—dogs that reminded him of the goddess. *That's what she thinks of being with you, Aeëtes.* His insecurities sneered, threatening to overtake his body with hot shame. *She doesn't* deserve *that kind of disappointment.*

And so, the ship moved on to Colchis throughout the night, and there was no sadder vessel on the seas. Even Eris, the Goddess of discord, looked down on their journey and spread her power out throughout their sails, soaking up their agony like nectar. She didn't even need to sow the seeds of dissonance, and yet she reaped and dined on their tears.

Hecate, sealing off the corners of her heart like a living tomb.

Aeëtes, believing that Hecate thought she didn't deserve the disappointment of his love.

And Pelias, who stared at the starry sky, watching Erebus and Nyx paint the cosmos with darkness. He offered up a silent prayer to the goddess, that she might blanket their agony with starlight and ease their pains in the tranquility of nightfall.

🐿 22 🐉

The next morning, the sunrise seemed earlier and brighter than ever. Aeëtes blinked his weary eyes open, cursing Helios—because god or mortal, no son could escape being woken up too early at the request of his father. They were close to Colchis—he recognized the horizon and the change in the terrain on shore—but even with Poseidon's help, they had at least another day or two of travel. Aeëtes had never been particularly good at naval navigation, and he wasn't in the mood to start now.

He had been up until the very edges of the stars had begun to bleed, slowly, one-by-one being recalled back into Nyx's bosom. Aeëtes reckoned that he had only been asleep for a few hours. He had fallen asleep in the galley, wedged between coils of moldy rope and barrels of water. The atmosphere around him was damp and still chilly in the early light, making his bones ache. He sat up and stretched, trying to shake the wine-addled thoughts from his mind. He had remained hidden below deck after overhearing Hecate and Pelias's conversation, unable to see the face of another god or mortal while he waited for his pain to shrink enough that it might be hidden. When he stood, a cup fell from somewhere hidden in his chiton, the clay shattering on the floorboards.

"Figures," Aeëtes mumbled, rubbing a hand over his unshaven face. He didn't need to catch his reflection in glass or water to know that he looked probably as well-put together as he felt. He stretched his arms out and yawned, hauling himself towards the steps to topside.

Aeëtes blinked in the glimmers of sunlight that were penetrating the galley from the gaps in the wood, hardly paying attention and eyes half-closed as he stumbled forward, crashing right into a soft, warm body. He knew before he even looked down or opened his eyes that it was Hecate. They both pulled back from each other in a rush, a mess of sleepy limbs, insecurities, and half-asleep minds. Both of them quickly readjusted themselves, straightening their hair and untangling their clothes. The tension between the two of them seemed to choke the air itself, chasing the chill away and replacing it with a current that they could feel under their skin.

"Excuse me," Hecate finally offered with a calm voice. She still looked the picture of stoicism, her head always held high without reproach, but Aeëtes could see the conflict hidden deep within her eyes. He felt clumsy next to her, stumbling from the depths of a ship, hungover, his hair half tied-up and unshaven.

No wonder she thinks that she deserves better. His inner critique was apparently not hungover and had reported to work with the sunrise. He wanted to blame his father. Aeëtes nodded, holding a hand out towards the steps, ushering her to go ahead of him. Hecate didn't move.

She had slept poorly, also finishing off the bottle of wine that Pelias had left in her chamber. It had taken a little more magic than she would've liked to admit to perk up her tired appearance. Her thoughts had been consumed with the words that Pelias had left with her. As the night turned and she felt Nyx and Erebus in the skies, high above them, her mind had drifted to the thought of Aeëtes. Of strong, obstinate Aeëtes, and what it would be like to have him in her bed on nights like this. She had to push the idea from her consciousness, almost violently, as his presence even in her dreams made the echo in her heart's chamber increase tenfold. As if his joy shined a light on how vast and empty parts of her felt.

When she had crashed into him moments ago, it had felt like a balm. Even a sudden, messy, passing touch of him ripped through her, and she had to claw back a sigh of relief. She studied him in the early morning light, sleep-mussed, and he looked…safe.

You would never deserve him. Hecate nearly felt tears spring to her eyes in response to her own inner voice, its biting words never far off.

Aeëtes's mind began to clear the longer that they stared at each other, the few brief seconds stretching into what felt like hours. Heat and anger growing in his stomach, wondering if she felt the same and refused to move. She simply stared at him, judging him, he falsely assumed. His heart twisted in his chest as he realized that it didn't dampen a single shred of affection he had for her. Finally, he could take it no more, and his voice was low when he spoke.

"Would you not prefer to go on deck with Pelias?" There was a slow-building anger in his voice that Hecate didn't know if she had ever heard. "Seeing as you don't deserve my company." Hecate recoiled as if she had been struck, feeling like his words were a stab to her gut.

"What?" She couldn't stop it now, and she cursed herself as a tear fell down her cheek. Her reaction froze Aeëtes on the spot; he was ready to maroon himself when he saw her cry. He realized in that moment that he had drastically misunderstood the conversation—and had just sounded like a pompous, arrogant ass.

"I-I heard you last night." Aeëtes held his hands out to her, just barely out of reach of her. His body language shifted as he leaned down to see her face more clearly, pleading. "You told Pelias that you don't deserve...this, that you deserve something better." He paused, not knowing what to call them. Hecate paled, an impressive feat for her already Underworld-approved complexion, and she shook her head vigorously.

"No!" She nearly yelled it, unable to suffer the pained expression on his face for another moment. "You've got it all wrong."

She paused, the explanation for her insecurities frozen on her tongue and stuck in her throat like she was choking. Aeëtes waited, his face gentled. Hecate took a deep breath, calling on every last piece of strength that she had; she turned her face from him as she spoke, unable to say it while looking at his eyes. When she started again, her voice was both shaky and resolute.

"I don't deserve *you*, Aeëtes." Hecate swallowed thickly, and Aeëtes's shock blanketed his face as he almost physically recoiled. "I can't stay in the mortal world forever, and you have responsibilities in Colchis—"

"I would burn Colchis if you asked me," Aeëtes cut her off, closing the gap between them and grabbing hold of her arms. His eyes were pleading, desperate, but Hecate screwed her eyes shut tighter and shook her head.

"That's the point! You would. I know you would, and I..." Hecate paused for a moment to keep her tears at bay. "I don't deserve that. You would never be happy in the Underworld—"

"I've never been, so that's impossible to say," Aeëtes negated, his grip tightening on her ever so slightly. He could never hurt her, and the touch felt so devastatingly safe that Hecate started to cry harder, her head falling back.

"No! You wouldn't be. Y-you love the sun, the sea, the things that are at odds with my very existence. It's dark, *I* am dark, my heart is—"

"Perfect," Aeëtes finished for her, and Hecate nearly flung herself out of his touch, but he pulled her closer to him, wrapping them together as his arms found their way around her body. Her hands fell limp at her sides, like the conversation was taking all of her strength and Aeëtes held her up.

"My acolytes…the women, Aeëtes, please try to understand. If I took a consort, if I loved again—"

"Again?" Aeëtes knew that there was something in Hecate's past, but she had never elaborated. She shook her head once, straightening up a little in his hold but not moving.

"It doesn't matter. You're not listening to me! I would lose the respect of all of those women, *every one of them in Greece* who prays to me. How can you not see what position that puts me in? I can't do this!" Aeëtes felt his own chest beginning to heave as he reeled against her statements.

"Then I'll be your lover, Hecate. Don't do this. I'll take anything that you can give me, and I'll give you everything. I don't need to marry you. I don't need to be a consort. I hate titles anyway." His attempt at humor was brief, cutting through the building electricity around them. Hecate only smiled sadly for one fleeting moment before he watched her sink back into her convictions.

"It's not that simple."

Aeëtes felt his temper rising again as he peered through the thin veil of excuses that she kept between them. "I don't believe you. I saw those women in Heraklion, the ones in your temple. They love you, and they would want you to be happy. Why do you think that you have to suffer to be loved? For fuck's sake, Hecate!" He let go of her and stepped away, huffing out a breath as he ran his hand violently through his hair, snagging his fingers on the leather cord.

He turned to face her, his eyes dark. "What's the point of keeping yourself from this? You only get one life. I don't care how long it is. Why won't you allow yourself *something*?"

"And that something is you?" she snapped back, her expression tensing as she was able to grapple with some of her indifference now that he wasn't touching her.

"It damn well could be! Even if it isn't me, do you see how you're only hurting yourself?"

"How privileged of you," Hecate sneered, standing up to her full height—still much shorter than Aeëtes but managing to look down on him all the same. "What a privileged take to have, to say that! Have you ever had your heart ripped out? To the point where you would do anything to stop the pain?" Hecate took a step towards him, spitting mad and sparks of red power dancing over her skin. "To the point that you would take a hot blade and cauterize yourself, if only to stop the bleeding?"

"You are my pain!" Aeëtes shattered, screaming back in response. His eyes were now wild, his hair mussed from his fidgeting. As he turned his body to her, he looked like a bull about to charge. "You are my wound and my cauterizing blade. The look in your eyes is my hurt and the smile on your face is my fix. Do you not *get that?*"

Hecate froze. They were only separated by only a few feet. Their expressions shifted between shock and untamed aggression and attraction, the chill of the early morning utterly wiped out by the full force of their passions. Chests were heaving as they looked at each other, shocked and disbelieving. Hecate spoke first, trying and failing to sound calm.

"You are not thinking clearly—"

"Fuck this," Aeëtes snapped, throwing his entire body at Hecate and cutting her off with a kiss. He moved with shocking dexterity for a man of his size, wrapping the goddess up in his arms and cradling her to his chest, as if her body was as fragile as her heart. He wrapped an arm around her waist and cupped her cheek in his hand, almost cushioning her against the intensity of the embrace.

There was nothing gentle about it as he took her mouth, all teeth and tongue and desperation. Hecate responded on instinct and immediately tangled her hands in his hair, not freezing for even a moment in surprise. The desire was building around them to a fever pitch. She gasped against the feel and heat of him, and he took the opportunity to deepen the kiss, as if he could coax her body to make peace with her mind. His hands slid down to her thighs, nearly bending him over as he tried to accommodate their height difference, lifting her up. Hecate wrapped her legs around his waist. The blood in her veins turned to liquid desire as she felt him, hard and ready beneath her.

Aeëtes walked them back into Hecate's cabin, deftly holding onto her without breaking the kiss while slamming the door shut behind them. Hecate pulled away from him with a gasp, both of them fighting their need for air and their need for each other. Aeëtes laid her down on the bed, Hecate letting out a soft moan into his mouth as she felt his weight settle down on top of her. There was something in her that soared, that was set free when she was pinned underneath him.

"Fuck, Hecate," Aeëtes murmured against her skin, both of them already short of breath as he broke away and placed kisses up her jaw. She was suddenly moving on her own accord, desire churning in her stomach, her hips rolling up to meet his.

"Please," she turned her head and bared her neck to him, and something utterly primal in Aeëtes growled at the ancient sign of submission. Her eyes fluttered closed as he nipped and bit at her neck, adding the right amount of pain to accompany the traitorous ecstasy coursing through her veins. A wave of power rolled over her, coating both her and Aeëtes in the tangible expression of her intoxication. Aeëtes drowned in it, tossing his head back and moaning wantonly in her ear. He lost some of his control and sank more of his weight on top of Hecate, but she only melted in response, as if she could surrender her doubts to his possession.

Aeëtes suddenly hauled himself off her and up onto his knees, straddling her waist, and Hecate let out a cry at the loss.

"What the hell?" she hissed at him, pushing sweaty hair off her forehead. "If you don't —"

"Tell me you want this," he growled, his voice turning into something gravelly and possessive. His hands dropped to her rib cage and held her there, his thumbs rubbing circles that had Hecate arching to get him to touch her. Every part of her felt like she was on fire, something otherworldly and intoxicating consuming her from the inside out.

"Aeëtes, *please*," Hecate only whined, grinding up against him. Aeëtes let out a sound that was somewhere in between a growl and a moan as he felt her heat through their clothes. He shook his head and tried to focus on anything other than how painfully hard he was, looking back down and staring at Hecate with an intensity that made her core turn molten.

"I need to hear you say it," Aeëtes gasped the words, his voice sounding like he was physically strained. He leaned back over her, his hands nearly covering her entire torso. Hecate bit her lip and felt another rush of arousal run through her as his hands moved and he cupped her breasts, running his thumbs over her nipples. He studied her, all curves and dips, with her long, auburn hair spread out around her like a halo. His hands nearly twitched with the decision of where to touch, what to grab, every bit of her looking like a perfect handful. Everything about her was refined, even when she looked debauched with want, and he felt like an animal on top of her — but he needed to hear it. He needed to hear the words come out of her mouth, that she wanted this, wanted him.

"Say it," he was pleading with her now, and he didn't care. "Or this all stops. I can't do it."

Hecate paused, swallowing thickly as she nodded once, then twice. Aeëtes shook his head slowly, pain creeping into the edges of his expression.

It's not enough. He wanted to cry, his heart — that eternally sunny place in his chest — was faltering. Aeëtes closed his eyes, ready to get out of the bed and leave when she began whispering.

"I don't just want it, Aeëtes." There was desperation in her voice, but he nearly ran out of the room before she could finish. "I need it. I need *you*. This will ruin me...but I have no intention of being saved."

"Oh, gods," Aeëtes cried, and in a flash, he was back on top of her, ripping at the folds of her himation until it came undone in his hands. He threw it off the bed and bent over her, his weight pressing Hecate into the mattress as she moaned in sweet surrender. "Tell me how you want it," he purred against her skin, his stubble leaving a gentle burn on her chest as he kissed across it. When Hecate didn't answer, he gave her breast a soft bite, and her hips immediately rocked up into him as she let out a groan.

Aeëtes chuckled against her overheated skin. "Like that then, I suppose, little witch?" All it took was her admission, and she had chased away his demons, his playful mood rebounding as it fought its way through the fog of lust they languished in. Hecate was nearly wild with it, every part of her body touching and rubbing up against some part of Aeëtes, her senses overloaded with heat, sweat, and *man*.

His hair had fallen down around his shoulders, and she relished in the feeling of his skin against hers. Where she was smooth, he was rough, and his beard, his chest hair, his calloused fingers caused delicious friction. It was as though every part of him was designed to tease and stimulate her, and she was going mad with it.

"I need you inside me," she gasped as he moved up and sucked on a sweet spot behind her ear, making her whole body twitch. "And I need you naked."

Aeëtes chuckled softly, the vibrations of it sending chills down her side.

"Anything the goddess demands."

Aeëtes sat up and tugged off his chiton, and Hecate bit her

tongue to not moan at the sight of him. He was a wall of muscle, not overly defined but every part of him solid, dark hair dusting over nearly every inch of olive skin. She felt a wave of arousal rush through her again at the sight of his cock —erect and thick to the point where she knew she'd feel him for days.

"If you keep looking at me like that," Aeëtes grinned, leaning down and kissing her gently, "this is going to be over before it's started."

Hecate smiled into the kiss, the soft moment breaking through their heady attraction.

"It's a good thing I know what you can do with that tongue then."

Aeëtes bit at her lip, sending another delicious jolt of pain *just* shy of too much through Hecate.

"Wait and see what I can do with the rest of my body, little witch."

His hands drifted down to her thighs as he guided Hecate to wrap her legs around him. She moaned at the feel of him, hot and ready at her entrance, and cried out as he lazily thrust his hips, teasing her as he ran himself through her folds. The head of his cock was grinding against her clit, and red magic sparked over Hecate's body.

Aeëtes nearly blacked out at the sensation, already soft and warm around him, and it took every bit of control he had not to immediately fuck her into the mattress. Hecate could see the restraint written across his brow and smiled, leaning up to kiss his brow.

"Fuck me, Aeëtes," she growled, her voice at odds with her tender actions, and the contradiction made Aeëtes impossibly harder. "Fuck me like you mean it."

That was all it took, and Aeëtes sat up on his knees and gripped her hips, finally moving himself inside of her. He moved wickedly slowly, languidly, and Hecate could feel every inch of him as he entered her. She felt like it went on forever, all heat and stretch as each neuron in her brain began to fire. She felt like she was being undone underneath him, and Aeëtes wasn't fairing much better.

His whole body was coiled tight, sweat breaking out across his chest as he rocked forward in a steady motion. Her body gripped him like a vice, and he had never felt more insane than he did in that moment. As he looked at her blissed out expression beneath him, every part of his brain and his soul chanted one thing: *Hecate, Hecate, Hecate.*

With a final roll of his hips, he settled into her to the hilt, letting out a garbled moan at the sensation. Hecate was panting underneath him, one hand in her hair as she tried to breathe, feeling like she was split in two but willing to die from the burn. There were no more words between them. In that moment, nothing else needed to be said. Aeëtes leaned down and wrapped one arm around her back, the other elbow holding his weight near her head. She looked up into his eyes and nearly cried at the sight of him, the warmth and intensity in his gaze as he looked at her.

Aeëtes was utterly lost—every part of himself, he now signed over to her. Any sovereignty that he had left in this world now belonged to the goddess. He stared at her flushed face, trying to say everything that had been bottled up inside of him. His affection for her, the way that he had been lost to her witchcraft as soon as he laid eyes on her, he poured it all out at her feet. Hecate had never let a lover take her like this before, on top of her, all around her, *looking* at her.

Really looking at her.

The vulnerability and acceptance in Aeëtes's eyes were a far cry from the lust and fear that she had always seen in a man's gaze. As he began to rock his hips against hers, each thrust created another crack in her walls. He started slowly, increasing his pace as Hecate felt the last of the tension in her body release. She surrendered to the delicious feeling of her body moving with his, rolling her hips up lazily to meet each thrust.

"Fuck, Aeëtes!" Hecate cried, her magic responding to him and running all over her body in waves. *Has it ever been like this for you?* she was really asking him.

"I know, I know." *No, it's never been like this for me with anyone,* he would've answered her.

Every part of them was open to the other. As they went hurtling towards the edge, they were terrified to realize that they had always been searching for this—for calm that could only be found in chaos, to the darkness that let the light rest, and the brightness that kept the night from being never-ending. Aeëtes reached down and gently rolled his thumb around Hecate's clit, and with a final thrust, pulled the release out of her. She arched her back as her face contorted in a silent scream, her entire body electric with pulsing, white-hot pleasure.

She spasmed around him, and Aeëtes's orgasm was ripped from his body, pulling his soul out with it. He collapsed forward and bit at Hecate's shoulder to keep himself from shouting until they both went limp with the aftershocks. Hecate's legs were shaking, and Aeëtes eased out of her, kissing her cheek softly when she whimpered at the sensitivity.

Neither of them said a word.

Aeëtes was careful as he rolled off her, taking in the sight of a thoroughly satisfied and flushed Hecate next to him. He pulled her to his side and gently laid her head on his chest, both of them falling fast asleep again in the bright light of morning.

☩ ☩ ☩

WHEN HECATE WOKE, it was mid-afternoon. Every part of her was sore, but it paled in comparison to the panic that had settled in her stomach. She had never felt anything like that before; had never seen a man look at her like that. Hecate had never spent the night with a man, either. Sleeping next to someone required too much vulnerability, too much intimacy. She could never relax enough to do it. But she had fallen asleep immediately with him…and had rested. Aeëtes's chest was rising and falling beneath her in a steady rhythm, and she breathed in the scent of him as if trying to commit it to memory.

The anxiety in her bones turned to leaden guilt, heavy and shameful, as she slowly untangled herself from the warmth and safety that she felt in his hold.

I'll be cursed for this. She knew that when she made it back to the Underworld, even the Fates would damn her for her decision.

Hecate quietly stood up and got out of bed, her feet feeling cold on the floor. She found her himation in the corner and wrapped it around herself quickly, moving towards the door in total silence. As soon as her hand touched the doorknob, Aeëtes's voice called to her from the bed, sounding rough and utterly wrecked.

"It's a good thing they call you the necromancer, because if you walk out that door…you've made me a dead man."

There was a perilously long beat of silence, and Hecate stepped out and didn't look back.

❧ 2 3 ☙

The crew was wise enough to give an angry woman space when they saw one, and when Hecate emerged on the deck of the ship, the men scattered. She hid behind an angry face and glimmers of red power, keeping her battle-bruised heart under lock and key.

A key that Hecate realized she had unwittingly given to Aeëtes, who was downstairs in her cabin.

There was a warm breeze, and Hecate moved towards the stern, sitting down on a small bench and looking out at the water. She let herself take a deep breath and close her eyes, sending her power out from her in waves. It sometimes did her good to release waves of it, to keep it all from bottling up inside her. There was enough contained inside her at that moment, multitudes of hurt and attraction, and she didn't know if she'd ever been in her mortal body this long. Her power might alert Hera but there was no intention behind these spells, rendering them weaker; she hoped it wouldn't betray their location.

Her power poured out from her like water, invisible except in the direct sunlight, a sheen of red sparks that coated the end of the ship. It almost had a mind of its own, carefully avoiding the crew that were milling about, trying to accomplish their chores before supper was served. She felt Poseidon's power still wrapped around the boat although she could tell that he was far off. Wherever he was, he was still doing them a favor, and she made a note to mention of his goodwill to Nyx.

As Hecate watched the waves in the wake of the boat, her heart felt heavy in her chest and her mind preoccupied. Even though every part of her soul and body cried out for Aeëtes, she couldn't let herself give in. She blamed her acolytes, but in the end, she knew better. It was the dull ache of wounds that should've been healed hundreds of years ago, but Hecate had decided that they were better left sealed up.

She could no longer deny it — Hecate was lonely. The kind of lonely that crawled its way into every crack and crevice of your body and stayed there. It was a kind of loneliness that morphed with you until you were no longer separate from it.

The kind that made you tired.

So, so tired.

Hecate put her hand to her chest, as if she could physically stop the ache there, and let a few tears fall. She stood slowly, her hair loose from its usual braid and flying in the wind, and moved towards the ship's edge. There was a small gap in the railing, where an additional ramp could be pushed out to dock, and she found herself standing in it. She held onto the banister with both hands, leaning forward until she was partially hanging over the water.

The wind whipped against her face, and she felt a rush of the sea air, and it soothed her. For a moment, she was wild — as wild as she had always been before the hurt and the heartbreak that caged a part of her. She was the weather — tumultuous and unpredictable, but always with its purpose. Hecate let out a quiet sob and released her tears to the sea, letting herself cry so she couldn't tell what were her tears and what was the ocean's spray. Her heart fluttered, and she knew why Aeëtes loved the sea.

She would not take him from it.

Hecate leaned out a hair's breadth further, taking in another deep, sweet breath when there was a shout, and strong arms suddenly wrapped around her body and yanked her back.

"Hecate!" Aeëtes screamed, his voice full of fear. Hecate slipped as he pulled her away from the edge, causing both of them to fall to the floor.

"What the hell!" Hecate snapped, ending up on top of Aeëtes in a way that made her insides clench. She quickly shoved herself off him, her legs getting tangled up in the skirt of her himation.

"What were you *doing*?" Aeëtes shook his head in disbelief, his tone furious. There was a deadly stoicism to it that made even Hecate shiver, knowing that this was Aeëtes at the most upset she had ever seen him. He climbed to his feet and re-tied the knot in his hair, kicking his foot into his sandal that had come off.

"I was just... It doesn't matter!" Hecate stood, fidgeting, feeling the snakes on her arms flicker to life with her anger. Their presence didn't even phase Aeëtes, who kept looking directly at her.

"It *matters* because you were hanging off the edge of a ship! A fast-moving ship, I might add," Aeëtes growled, taking a step towards Hecate. "If you had fallen, you would've hit the side of the boat, likely been knocked unconscious, and drowned."

Hecate made a tsk noise and shook her head. "I'm immortal, Aeëtes. It would've taken a lot more than that to kill me."

He floundered for a moment, as if he had forgotten that detail, and blushed slightly, speaking quickly as if to recover.

"It certainly wouldn't have been fun!" he shouted in response, his hands going to his hips as he stared at her, pointing an index finger in her direction. "Sure, maybe you wouldn't have died, but you would have been injured. I have an immortal's body, same as you." Hecate tried her best to not picture it naked, failing miserably.

"Not the same as me," she murmured under her breath, rolling her eyes because she knew that he had a point. Aeëtes let out a sigh and ran his hand through his hair, shaking his head and looking off into the distance. There was silence between them, one that was no longer comfortable, but empty.

Aching.

"All the same," Aeëtes finally responded, waving a hand in the air. "I'm sorry if I ruined your grand moment of contemplation." His voice lifted at the end, his face contorting into a smile. The smile that Hecate knew so well, and she couldn't help but return it.

"I was just...breathing," Hecate stuttered to find the right word, cursing herself again that she had been reduced to nearly monosyllabic conversations around him. She was never the type of woman to feel bad or awkward about a morning after, but this was something else entirely. There were—she now had to admit—feelings involved.

"Ah, breathing." Aeëtes nodded, leaning up against the ship's railing and crossing his arms over his chest. "Wonderful pastime, that." He couldn't help but toss a smirk in her direction. Hecate let out a scoff although there was no venom in it. She seated herself on the small bench, now across from Aeëtes.

"I needed a minute, that's all. And the sea felt..." Hecate trailed off, her eyes going past Aeëtes to the horizon. His expression was one of awe and understanding, and the smirk on his face didn't reach his eyes.

"I know." He turned and looked out at the water, understanding what she meant. They sat there for a few peaceful moments, the quiet between them becoming something a little more alive. There was a lot that still needed to be said, but the silence didn't feel as crushing as it had moments before.

Aeëtes had loved the sea for as long as he could remember. How many times had he hung off sails and riggings and the edge of ramps to get a taste of it? He knew that Hecate hadn't been about to jump or anything close to it. Yet, when he came

up on deck, the only thing he saw was her body hanging off
the side of the ship. It had chilled him to the bone, as if there
was a vortex in the pit of his stomach that absorbed all the heat
in him. He had moved entirely on instinct, with one goal—to
protect her.

It was that same intention, whether she believed him or
not, that inspired his next statement. He coughed once and
stood taller, as if he was preparing himself to strike an opponent with swords play, getting Hecate's attention. When he
spoke, his voice was quiet, barely intelligible over the sound of
the waves beneath them.

"You know, I'm not giving up."

Hecate froze in her seat. She didn't know what she had
been expecting from Aeëtes, but it wasn't this. Maybe she was
expecting anger, sorrow, or rejection—she did expect rejection,
which was why she had to reject him first—but she wasn't
prepared for this. Her mind reeled as she stared at him, the
first glimpses of golden hour light painting the side of his face.
He was the most beautiful man that she had ever seen and
there was no way that this was happening to her.

She must have fallen off the boat and knocked herself
unconscious after all. Any moment now, Pelias or someone
from the crew would haul her up from the icy cold depths, and
she would be revived. Aeëtes would not be in front of her,
telling her that he wasn't going to give up on her. That he
wasn't going to give up on them.

No one had ever told Hecate that they would fight for her.

Gods and men over the centuries had always asked Hecate
to fight for them. Women all over Greece asked her to fight
their battles for them. Even Nyx and Erebus had asked, in
their own way, for her to join the titan wars.

Aeëtes was like no one that she had ever met. When she
opened her mouth to speak, no sound came out. The deep cuts
of her past dug themselves in deeper, as if they were excavating
themselves to get to the center of her soul, to bury themselves

permanently. Her insecurities were wrapped up around her as if they held her tongue, and she found herself unable to say a word.

Aeëtes could see the shock on her face as her mouth opened and closed, and there was a sick realization that settled into his stomach. It wasn't that Hecate didn't want to respond; she didn't know *how* to respond. A horrible picture was painted for Aeëtes in that moment as he gleaned that no one had ever told Hecate that they wouldn't give up on her before. He took a step closer to her, and then another, his steps feeling shaky even though he was solid on his sea legs. When she didn't move, he took one more. He kept this up, always giving her the option to speak or move, until he was standing in front of her.

He got down on his knees, bringing them eye-to-eye. He held his hands out for her, refusing to touch her after their coupling until she initiated it. After a few perilous seconds, Hecate slid her hands into his. Her heart sang at the feel of him, and she had to fight to keep her pulse steady, knowing that Aeëtes might feel it in her wrists. His thumb ran soothing circles over the backs of her palms, and he looked at her with the gentlest eyes that Hecate had ever seen.

"I'll fight for you, Hecate." His voice was low, intended only for her, and her eyes fluttered shut when she heard it. She was rocked by a wave of emotion that was so powerful, she thought that it would overturn the ship itself. Another tear dropped down her cheek, and she opened her eyes, barely shaking her head as she looked at him.

"There's no one to fight." She gave him a small shrug, not fully understanding his meaning, thinking that he had no foes for her affections. But Aeëtes shook his head once, gripping her hands a little tighter.

"I'll fight your demons, little witch." His whole face was open to her, shining in such a way, she'd never question his parentage. Hecate let out a choked sob and looked down,

suddenly feeling as though she was drowning. Aeëtes continued. "I'll fight you for *you* if I have to."

Hecate let out a small giggle at that—the rarest of sounds
—and Aeëtes grinned. One of his hands let go of hers, and he
placed a finger underneath her chin, lifting her gaze to his.

"That doesn't make any sense." She let out a quiet sound of
discontent.

"Yes, it does." Aeëtes was still smiling, his cheerful resolve
pulling them together. "You've made up a million enemies in
your mind to keep us apart. But that's just it. They're all in
your mind. I'll fight your demons for your heart, Hecate, and
don't you think for one second that you've put me off course."

She let the tears fall freely now, her display of emotion
telling him all that he needed to know. Hecate nodded her head
once, a movement so subtle that anyone else would have
missed it.

Aeëtes didn't.

His expression turned joyful, nearly giddy, as she relented.
Hecate said nothing else, but she did not admonish him. Her
quiet movements echoing to him that they both knew she was
keeping them apart. If there was one enemy that Aeëtes was
prepared to take on, it was the idea that they shouldn't be
together. He would fight that battle a thousand times over, no
matter the outcome. Hecate slipped her hands from his and
wrapped her arms around his neck, pulling them closer as she
tucked her head into the crevice between his neck and shoulder. Aeëtes returned the embrace immediately, letting her cry
out a few more gentle tears on his shoulder.

They both knew that in a few hours, this conversation
never happened. Hecate would deny him. Aeëtes wouldn't
care.

"You're terribly obstinate," Hecate said as she pulled away
from him, her voice sounding clear and full of authority. A
switch had been flipped, but Aeëtes only laughed, all of his

movements full of gaiety as he stood up and clapped his hands together.

"You seem to forget that I'm an immortal, too, Hecate." He gave her a sly wink as he walked past her. "I've got just as many years ahead of me to play this game as you do," he leaned down and whispered in her ear, "and I've been bored for a very, very long time."

🦁 24 ♓

A eëtes's words made Hecate shudder as he walked away, leaving her sitting at the stern. She could hear him disappear down the steps towards the deck, calling out for Pelias and some of the other men. Her mind reeled with what had just happened. She had expected any outcome other than Aeëtes doubling down that he wanted them to be together. Especially after how she had left him, not even an hour prior.

Even her thoughts couldn't keep her down for too long as they were often prone to do, like some of Aeëtes's sunshine had infected her bones.

He isn't going anywhere. Hecate was in almost a pleasant state of shock. *Aeëtes said that he would fight for this, for us and…oh, gods below. Am I crazy? Only the Fates know the answer to that question.*

Hecate stood up from the bench, tightening the belt around her waist as she made her way towards the stairs. The sun was setting now, Helios coloring the sky in hues of pink and orange, colors so vibrant that Hecate almost forgot that he was part of their problem. It would be time for dinner shorty, and she really, really needed another glass of wine.

Maybe I can snag Pelias for another conversation. I need to work out some of my thoughts. Hecate nearly laughed out loud at the thought, her hand going to physically cover her mouth as she made her way down the stairs. *Yikes, poor Pelias. He has enough to worry about. Maybe I can summon Nyx for a chat. Ah. No. It's best that the rest of the gods stay as far out of this as possible.*

The last thing that Hecate wanted was to be answering questions about where she was and what they were doing; even about who Aeëtes was. She knew that once Nyx understood what was going on, it would be war. It would be well-intended, of course, but Hecate thought that for now, these things were best settled with a little witchcraft. She was musing over her thoughts when she was nearly thrown off balance by a massive crash. The entire boat seemed to sway dangerously to one side, nearly tipping over, causing Hecate to slip down the remaining stairs.

The crew was sliding down the upturned deck, nearly falling off it, before the ship righted itself with enough momentum to give Hecate whiplash. She grabbed her head and stood up, already shaky on sea legs, holding tight to the banister. Everyone was looking around wildly, sailors running across the span of the ship, tying down barrels and dropping the sails. There wasn't a person aboard who wasn't screaming some sort of command or response, and the cacophony began to suffocate Hecate's senses. Her power surged to life in response, the heads of the virgin and the crone appearing on her shoulders, her feet alighting with red power.

"Hecate!" She heard Aeëtes's voice call to her, and she sought it out, finding him standing near the mast with Pelias. Hecate grabbed a hold of her himation and ran to him, dodging other sailors and puddles of sea water on deck. As soon as she reached him, he grabbed ahold of her shoulders, giving her a once over. She placed a hand over his in response.

"Are you alright?" His eyes ran over her body as if he was doing a mental tally, and she nodded.

"Yes, yes, just shaken. You?" Aeëtes nodded. "And you?"

She turned to Pelias, who looked pale, but affirmed his
wellbeing.

"What was that?" Hecate looked around, trying to glance
at the surface of the water and see if she could determine the
cause of the crash.

"Whatever it was, it's probably coming back around."
Pelias's tone was grim, one that Hecate had never heard him
take before. She felt her stomach twist, another wave of power
rushing over her arms and pooling at her feet. She could feel
her immortal form pushing at the barriers of her skin, dying to
come out.

"Whatever *it* was?" Hecate snapped out of fear, not
unkindly.

"Yes." Aeëtes nodded, rubbing her shoulder before
releasing her. He unsheathed a sword that Hecate hadn't
noticed he had been carrying, and Pelias did the same. At the
sight of both men arming themselves, the entire crew followed.
The sound of twenty swords ringing through the air created a
sharp-pitched whine. "That wasn't a rock or a sand dune." He
turned to look at Hecate. "This isn't going to be pretty."

"What are you implying?" she hissed back at him, and
Aeëtes let out a grunt.

"Not that you aren't strong enough for whatever this is,
that's—" Aeëtes was cut off as the ship rocked from impact,
this time from the other side of the boat. It wasn't nearly as big
as the first crash, and the crew righted themselves shortly, but
the boat was now perilously rocking from side-to-side. A dull,
roaring sound had started to pick up on the winds, sounding
muffled as if it was coming from fifty yards beneath them in
the depths.

"You're not in the Underworld anymore, little witch,"
Aeëtes yelled as the sound got louder and louder. "Now would
be a good time for you to abandon your mortal pretenses!"

"Hera will—"

"Umm," Pelias cut Hecate off, "I think she knows where

we are." He pointed with a shaking finger over the side of the ship where the entire crew had gathered. As if it were happening in slow motion, Pelias, Hecate, and Aeëtes ran to the railing, peering over to see what was emerging from the blackness. The roaring sound was now loud enough that Hecate could barely hear either of the men beside her. A dark, churning mass was rapidly moving through the clear water up towards the bottom of their ship.

"You don't think…" Aeëtes started, but Hecate answered immediately.

"I do. It's Hera." She could sense the overly sweet and rotten magic in the water. She would know that scent anywhere, and it meant that whatever creature was coming after them had been sent by her. Sailors began running in all directions before the beast had even breached the water, some grabbing more weapons and others climbing up to the sails with bows and arrows.

"How did she find us?" Pelias yelled over the confusion, ripping another dagger from his belt.

"I had to release some of my magic. It must have alerted Hera," Hecate took a few steps back from the railing, red sparks erupting over her hands like flames. "I was just hoping that we'd already be in Colchis."

Aeëtes had somehow managed to find a second sword, too, and all three of them slowly moved backwards until they were at the mast. Without warning, the sea quieted, and the noise vanished, leaving the entire crew in still, utter silence.

"That's not good," Aeëtes muttered.

"Ssh," Hecate hissed at him as the entire crew began to slowly look around. Everyone was now armed to the teeth, moving only a few paces from side to side…waiting. Hecate could feel something in the water lurking below them, its power reeking of Hera and her control, but something about it was wrong. There was something she wasn't seeing.

"Whatever it is," Hecate turned to Aeëtes, her voice a

whisper as they waited in the terse silence, "it's controlled by
Hera; it's not in its right—"

A massive wave crested up over the side of the ship,
crashing down on the deck and knocking half of the crew off
their feet. The silence was broken by a horrendous screeching
sound like that of a bird of prey. As the wave washed over
them, a monstrous face emerged from the sea foam. It was the
face of a woman, mottled with green scales and bright red eyes,
her hair matted down to her skull. She opened her mouth and
let out another terrifying scream, her teeth filed down to
points, and the sailors began to scatter.

"Scylla!" One of them screamed, running to the other side
of the ship and jumping into the water.

"It's not supposed to be in these waters!"

"The Scylla!" The screams of men were drowned out by
the creature's terrible noises, echoing all around them as if they
were coming from inside their own heads. Six different heads
burst up abruptly from the side of the ship, each of them a
massive sea serpent.

The Scylla rose on the surface of the water, looking down
at the crew as if she was looking for someone, and she was.
Her eyes were not hers, her body manipulated by the equally
monstrous queen of the gods. The Scylla was as tall as the
mast, with a woman's head and torso that disappeared into the
body of a snake. The six additional heads of the sea serpent all
wound together at her waist, snapping with teeth the size of a
man's leg.

Aeëtes and Pelias wasted no time, quickly recovering from
their shock and rushing towards her with their swords held
high. They split up and went after different heads of the sea
monster, jumping in front of them and saving some of the
sailors who were too shell-shocked to move. With each of them
preoccupied with only two of the six different heads, Hecate
took a few steps back and felt her power consume her.

Hecate's body was drenched in undulating waves of thick,

red magic, covering the deck with the scent of cinnamon, rose-mary, and...death. She began to rise, the heads on her shoulders whispering, the low baritone voice echoing over the water and causing ripples across its surface. Hecate expanded as her eyes went red, matching the Scylla's, and the lower half of her body disappeared in maroon clouds. She kept growing until she was as tall as the mast herself, looking the Scylla in the face, and began speaking in the language of the dead.

The language of witches.

The language of women.

It caused some of the men on deck to drop to their knees and cover their ears as the heady, melodic chanting shook them to their bones. This was like no other god or goddess they had ever seen before; this was a goddess from the Underworld, whose gifts invoked life and death. Aeëtes only paused for a moment, looking up in utter awe of Hecate, before he narrowly missed getting swallowed whole by one of the serpent's heads.

The sailors engaged with the many-headed sea snakes below them, and Hecate and the Scylla squared off eye-to-eye thirty feet above them. Magic erupted from the clouds of Hecate's power, and red snakes poured from the fog at her feet, joining the sailors and hissing, snapping their jaws at the other faces of the creature.

Hecate's face remained impressively stoic as the ship began rocking beneath them, the Scylla throwing her weight against it. The ship wouldn't last more than a few minutes from the constant impact, and it would capsize.

"Hera." Hecate's mouth didn't move as she spoke, the other two faces on her shoulders spinning webs of spells and counter spells around them. The air was thick with magic as written incantations of protection appeared in shining red letters on the bodies of the men fighting below. *"Release this woman."* Hecate knew the legend of the Scylla, and her heart went out to her. She would not see another person destroyed by a man's folly or by Hera's wickedness towards women.

When the Scylla opened her mouth, her voice was not her own. *"I told you that all you had to do was hand Aeëtes over to me. If this woman suffers, it is because of you!"*

Hecate smiled, the faces of the virgin and the crone doing the same, creating an utterly eerie effect. She shook her head slowly, her hands rising as her fingers reached out for the Scylla. *"This is not my doing, Hera, nor is it yours. A jealous nymph turned Scylla, the maiden, into a monster. You've pulled her from hiding to act as your blade, and* that *makes this* my job." There was a nearly wicked gleam in Hecate's eye as she stretched her arms out, and snakes came tumbling from her fingers. They moved over the deck, flickering with magic, coming down from the sky like rain.

The sailors on the deck hollered in confusion, unable to tell if the creatures were friend or foe. Some of them began diverting their attention from the sea serpent heads and began fighting with the snakes as they landed at their feet.

"Stop it!" Aeëtes yelled at them, his voice hoarse. His body was drenched with sweat, his sword knocked out of his grip long ago, and he was currently holding open the jaws of a serpent with his bare hands. "They won't harm you!" Pelias turned at the sound of Aeëtes's voice and ran across the deck, tossing his sword in the eye of the serpent. It immediately let go of Aeëtes with a massive cry, slipping off the ship and disappearing into the dark waters.

"Next time you show up with a goddess," Pelias panted, leaning down to help Aeëtes to his feet as they grabbed their weapons, "you better bring me Aphrodite." Aeëtes laughed and both men grinned, wiping sweat from their brows and charging back into the fray.

In the sky above them, Hecate's power was winding around the body of the Scylla, murmuring in quiet, low tones that Hera fought to understand.

"What are you doing?" she shrieked, thrashing around and causing the Scylla's body to shake back and forth. The motion

caused another wave to crash over the side of the ship, sending another few men right off the other side and into the depths.

"You may control this body, Hera," Hecate's voice was now audible, sending ricochets of power through the air as the tri-voice spoke, "but this body was not always a monster."

The whirls of magic kept winding around the Scylla's body, whose eyes began to flicker like a flame, from red to black and back again. She let out another screeching cry, a couple of the sea serpent's heads retreating into the sea as she started to sink.

Hecate kept chanting, murmuring something beyond the realm of comprehension, words that were engraved on the veil between words. Her face flickered between the virgin, the maiden, and the crone, each one taking center stage as she reigned above them. There was another cry ripped from the mouth of the Scylla. This time it was Hera's voice, who began cursing Hecate as she felt her control beginning to fade. No power over a woman in trouble was greater than Hecate's, and hers ran over the Scylla like warm hands, bit by bit, as she chased away the remnants of Hera's influence.

The last remaining sea serpent slipped into the water until only the woman-half remained, slowly shrinking. Hecate's voice was now filled with dulcet tones, soft songs, almost like a lullaby. Her own body began to sway, and she shrank, too, until she was standing on the deck in her mortal form. The Scylla's eyes rolled back into her head as she collapsed backwards, crashing into the sea, now only the size of a horse.

The sailors began to cheer, but only Aeëtes and Pelias turned to look at Hecate. She was walking with a steady pace towards the edge of the ship, her eyes not disappearing off the spot where the Scylla had sunk. Her lips were still moving while the evidence of her immortal form slowly flickered out. When she reached the edge, she held a hand up over the water, repeating something that only she would recognize. The entire crew was now silent, their celebrations muted as they watched

Hecate's actions, something dawning on them that this was not over.

The deck was slick with blood and saliva, the open jaws of the sea serpent's still fresh in their minds. But still, they watched. There was no one more transfixed than Aeëtes, who felt himself pulled to Hecate like she was home. Hecate dropped her hand and stepped back. A sudden geyser shot up from the sea floor, taller than the sails. The spray drenched the ship but did not sink it as the sailors held up their hands over their eyes to protect themselves. The burst of water quickly lost its inertia and dropped back down towards sea level, and as it retreated, Aeëtes squinted against the setting sun. On the top of the sea foam, there was the unconscious body of a woman.

There wasn't a sound on deck as the water gently rocked against the boat and deposited the woman on its deck. She was a beautiful maiden, no older than twenty, with long, black hair that provided her modesty. Hecate turned to the closest soldier and snapped her fingers, and he immediately removed his shirt and handed it to her. She stepped towards the woman and knelt down. The heads of the virgin and the crone were gone, and only Hecate remained. Her eyes were no longer flickering red with power, but were their mortal blue, full of kindness.

She helped ease the woman into the shirt, both of them still drenched to the bone, but now at least covered. Hecate cradled her to her chest as if she was a babe.

Pelias jerked his head in the direction of the galley, wise enough to know a private moment when he saw one. The sailors moved slowly, begrudgingly, wanting to see what happened next but not stupid enough to cross Hecate after what they had just seen. Only Aeëtes remained on deck, watching respectfully from a few yards away.

"Sweet Scylla," Hecate sang, and the woman opened her eyes. She took in the face of the goddess and gasped, sitting up so quickly that she was woozy. "Ssh, easy. Don't move too fast. You haven't been in your human form for years."

Aeëtes's eyes got wide as he realized what had happened. Everyone knew the legend of Scylla, the dread sea monster, but her origin story was the true horror. Scylla had been, and was now again, a young maiden. She often worked near the sea and had been pledged to Triton, Poseidon's son and a demigod. A jealous nymph had turned her into the sea creature, and while Triton and Poseidon had put her to death for her crimes, they hadn't been able to figure out the spell by which the nymph had done it.

Hera must have controlled Scylla and brought her...straight to the one goddess who could reverse the spell. Aeëtes's felt a rush of warm pride go through him as he watched Hecate, gently answering all of Scylla's confused questions and helping her sit upright. Aeëtes sprang into action, fetching a satchel of fresh water and bringing it over to Hecate. He approached slowly, not wanting to threaten the frightened Scylla, and handed it to Hecate.

She accepted it warmly, with a surprised look in her eyes. While she was preoccupied at present, she couldn't help but feel a twinge in her heart when she saw how Aeëtes leapt to help her.

Men never did that in Hecate's line of work.

"Thank you." She nodded quietly before helping Scylla drink its contents. They were silent as Scylla rested, trying to comprehend what had happened to her, when there was a sudden burst of fresh air. The wind whipped around the mast, bringing with it the scent of salt and citrus, and Hecate sat up a little straighter.

"Poseidon," she called out, "I do believe that this young woman is eager to see you." Scylla sat up in Hecate's arms, scooting away from her, a smile etching its way across her face for the first time.

"Poseidon?" she echoed Hecate, Aeëtes hearing her speak

for the first time. There was a flash of light, and when it faded, there was Poseidon, standing on the deck of the ship.

Aeëtes's face flushed and his eyes got wide, trying to not react in the presence of one of the brothers. Poseidon was everything that a god of the sea would be, from his beard to his coral bracelets and his tunic that seemed to be made of water. He held a trident in one hand, but he dropped it upon seeing the face of Scylla.

"Sweet Scylla! My daughter!" He rushed forward, scooping the woman up to her feet and wrapping her in a hug like a father would with a lost child. Hecate got to her feet and walked towards Aeëtes, slotting herself into his side as his arm wrapped around her. They tried to give the pair a little privacy, but it was hard not to watch the moment unfurl.

"How is Triton?" Scylla finally asked when she pulled away, her face simultaneously full of hope and fear. Poseidon only smiled, pushing some of the wet hair off her forehead.

"He has waited for you every day. There will be great rejoicing in the chasms and currents of the sea when you are reunited—and shall be married, as soon as possible, to avoid any more...unpleasantness."

Scylla burst into tears again and buried her head in Poseidon's chest, as if she had been holding onto some fear that after so much time, the engagement would be off. The God of the sea held her for a precious minute longer before looking over her head at Hecate.

"Goddess." He bowed his head, and Aeëtes nearly squawked at seeing one of the brothers defer to Hecate. There was no end to the respect that she was owed—he believed that wholeheartedly—but he trusted no man or god to give it to her. Except himself.

Which he was trying to prove.

"Poseidon." Hecate smiled, looking at Scylla and the god. "Do tell me what is known of Hera and her pursuits?"

"Everyone wants to make sure that it doesn't turn into a

war." His voice was gruff, and he spoke like a strategist. "A few of the gods know what she did to Aeëtes, a son of Helios." Aeëtes felt a cold shiver go down his spine at the mention, but Poseidon carried on. "And a few more know that Hera struck against you. They are all slow to move because as soon as someone does, allegiances are called in..."

"Yes, yes," Hecate waved a hand in the air like she was bored. "Trust me, I am aware of your pantheon politics. I avoid them." Poseidon nodded in agreement.

"You are wise to do so. The gods are all afraid of another war so soon." Poseidon and Hecate exchanged a look that Aeëtes could not interpret.

"Sometimes I wish that during the titan wars..." Hecate trailed off, not wanting to say it out loud, but Poseidon knew the outcome that they had planned for. While Zeus and Hera had been defeated, they had not been stopped permanently.

"I know." Poseidon rolled his eyes. "I know."

"What news of the Underworld?"

"Hades is aware of your...adventure." Poseidon paused, his eyes roving over Aeëtes as if in judgement. "Hermes let us know of your desire to keep things from Nyx and Erebus."

"They *would not* hesitate to start a war," Hecate felt the need to clarify. "This must be sorted quickly and with honor, something Hera does not have, and I can handle it."

"You certainly can," Poseidon agreed, his voice firm when he said it. Aeëtes took note. Poseidon believed it when he said it. "I cannot do all that I would wish for you, Goddess, especially considering that you have returned the greatest gift of all to my household. I will do what I can and shall continue to bless your winds. You shall be in Colchis by nightfall." Water began moving in a small vortex around Scylla and Poseidon's feet, signaling their imminent departure.

"You bless us, Poseidon." Hecate tilted her head in farewell, and Aeëtes noticed once again that she did not bow.

"Be well, Hecate. Be well, son of Helios." Poseidon had

already partially disappeared as his words rang out through the air, vanishing with Scylla in a flash of light.

Hecate and Aeëtes stood on the deck for a minute in silence. Remarkably, Poseidon's magic had wiped the ship clean of any signs of a battle. Even their clothes were now dry. They could hear the crew murmuring about in the galley below, and the unmistakable sound of wine cups clattering against one another in toast. Hecate swayed, her eyelids fluttering closed with exhaustion from the exertion, and Aeëtes was in near total shock. When she wavered on her feet, however, he snapped out of it and grabbed her before she fell.

Hecate was fast asleep, her mortal form requiring rest as her immortal power recharged. Aeëtes scooped her up against his chest, carrying her like a bride back down to the cabin below. She murmured something in her sleep against his chest, causing Aeëtes to only squeeze her tighter. He looked down at her face, at peace in sleep, and tucked her in bed. As he went to untangle her arms from around his neck, Hecate's grip tightened.

"Stay." The word was quiet, barely audible, and was spoken from somewhere in between sleep and wakefulness. That was where Hecate lived, in the space between worlds, between life and death, and it was where her words were most honest. It went straight to Aeëtes's heart. He maneuvered her over to the side and slid in the bed next to her, pulling her to him.

Hecate's eyes flickered open in surprise, but she let out a long breath. He could see the sweet surrender on her face as she laid her head back on his chest, too tired to fight with herself over what she wanted.

"Don't worry," Aeëtes said with a soft smile. "We can pretend this didn't happen either."

25

A eëtes woke to a cool breeze. He sat up slowly, even conscious of Hecate next to him before he was fully awake. She barely stirred, and he gently untangled himself from her, taking extra care to make sure that she was comfortable. He could tell from the light that it was right before dawn. He told himself that it was wise to step away, to not test his limits. Even though Hecate had acknowledged that it was her fears keeping them apart and that she knew he would continue to pursue her, some things needed to go slowly. She had invited him to her bed after the draining events with Scylla and Poseidon, and after that, she didn't need to wake up and overthink his presence there.

Aeëtes let himself take one more long, lasting look at her—every part of her looking like the goddess she was—and pulled himself away. It took almost a physical effort to leave her cabin, knowing that the bed was soft, warm, and full of her.

He somehow managed it and wondered if it proved that he did have god-like strength. He was still in remarkably good spirits, having slept the night soundly, and took the stairs up to the deck double-time. His hair was still mussed from sleep, and he knew that somewhere in Colchis, his mother had a sixth sense for when his tunic was this dirty. He couldn't be bothered with it, feeling lighter than he had in years.

It was still dark as he emerged topside, seeing that it was vacant. Poseidon's power still guided the ship, so there were no rowers at work or navigators at the helm. It was a surprisingly peaceful moment on the ship, which was hard to come by. As Aeëtes made his way to the bow of the ship, the cold wind picked up again, making him shiver. It was unnaturally cold, too cold for where they were and what time of year it was. He stopped and turned around slowly, standing at the end of the ship as the breeze wrapped around him.

There was something about it that was soothing like a melody. It brought him a sense of peace and calm, and even in a relaxed state, Aeëtes knew to question that. The stars seemed to twinkle a little brighter, even as they prepared their way home to their mother, Nyx, and Aeëtes felt what he knew to be the unmistakable presence of a keeper of the Underworld. Aeëtes had grown accustomed to the feeling of Underworld gods from his time spent with Hecate. There was a sensation to their power that was different from any other gods. It was all-encompassing, quiet yet loud, full of contradictions like death and rebirth.

Aeëtes took a few steps backwards until he was leaning against the railing, putting the horizon behind him in his blind spot.

"If it would please you," Aeëtes spoke lowly, "show yourself. I know the presence of a messenger of the Underworld when I feel it. I will pay you respects if you demand it."

There was the smallest bit of fear in Aeëtes's voice, for no matter how soothing a god's presence was, no one was ever fully comfortable in the presence of the Underworld immortals. There was a soft laughter that echoed around Aeëtes, not cruel, but not entirely joyful. It was almost pitying.

"I demand no respects. Everyone pays their respects towards me in the end. All come my way." The voice seemed to require all of Aeëtes's senses to process it. It was the deepest voice that he had ever heard, sounding like it was carved from obsidian.

"Who..." Aeëtes started to ponder before his eyes got wide and he shut his mouth. The god laughed again, still unseen, this time from somewhere in front of him.

"It sounds like you have guessed who I am," the voice responded. Thick, dark clouds came down from the sky in a vortex, spinning slowly until they touched down on the ship. They picked up speed and began to spin faster, flickers of lightning flashing in the funnel, until they disappeared instantly. In their place, was one of the tallest gods that Aeëtes had ever seen in their mortal form—and these days, he was getting pretty familiar with immortals.

"Thanatos," Aeëtes breathed, feeling a mix of fear and respect. There was one god that everyone would bow to in the end, immortal or mortal, and it was Thanatos, the God of death.

Thanatos stood taller than Aeëtes, with hair that was so dark, it seemed to shine blue-black in the fading moonlight. His hair was shorter than most Greeks and immortals, and it seemed to stick up from all directions. He wore hoplite armor, without a sword and shield, and had a calm smile on his face.

"You guess correctly," Thanatos nodded his head once towards Aeëtes.

"I suppose you'll tell me if you're here for my soul?" Aeëtes cut straight to the quick, wanting to know why the god had showed up on their ship. Hecate had never mentioned him, like she had Hermes, so he didn't think that they had much of a relationship. Thanatos let out a low laugh that sounded like rocks falling.

"No." His smile widened. "I'm not here for your soul. However, I'm here because you were put on my list earlier today."

Aeëtes blanched at that, the blood draining from his face as he heard Thanatos. If he had been on Thanatos's list, that meant that at one point today during the battle with Scylla, the Fates had determined he was to die. Fate sometimes had several different ways of playing out, and it looked like his life had been saved. Still, it was no small feat to hear that you evaded death.

"You look pale." Thanatos tilted his head to one side.

"I bet you tell that to all the girls," Aeëtes scoffed, his humor overriding his shock. There was a beat of silence before Thanatos burst out laughing, clasping his hand over his stomach and nearly doubling over.

I certainly didn't think it was that *funny,* Aeëtes mused to himself as he watched the rather stoic god lose himself to borderline hysterics. *I guess he doesn't hear a lot of jokes from his traveling companions, seeing as they're dead).*

"Goodness, I am glad that I made the trip." Thanatos straightened and mimed wiping a tear away from his eye although Aeëtes didn't see it.

"You did feel the need to make the trip," Aeëtes pointed out, leaning back against the railing in a way that he hoped seemed casual. "Apparently, to see me."

"Yes." Thanatos didn't elaborate further. Aeëtes waited a few more moments before he shrugged, chewing on his lip. They were both standing on the bow of the ship in the fading moonlight, and it wouldn't be long before someone discovered that the God of death was their latest passenger.

"Was there...a reason for that?"

"Yes," Thanatos sighed, sidestepping to take a seat on one of the barrels nearby. He was much too tall to use it as a chair, and as a result, his knees were nearly bunched up to his chest. Aeëtes stifled his laughter since it felt improper to laugh at Thanatos, but he committed the sight to memory regardless. Thanatos rolled his shoulders back as if he was shaking them out or preparing to go for a run. When he turned and leveled his gaze on Aeëtes, it was solemn, and Aeëtes felt his blood run cold again.

"I get glimpses into people's fate lines when they end up on my list. That way, I know when and where to collect them. I saw your fate line briefly before your path changed today." Thanatos paused, as if he was waiting for Aeëtes to react, but he kept his face calm, and Thanatos continued. "Your line was wrapped around another one — the line of another immortal."

Aeëtes couldn't help himself as he jumped to attention, his eyes getting wider as he stared at Thanatos. He could feel his heartbeat increasing in his chest and his palms getting sweaty while his whole body seemed to flush.

Could he be saying…?

Thanatos studied Aeëtes and when he saw his reaction, a smirk slowly spread across his face. This was the response that he had been hoping for.

"I see. So you already have an immortal on your mind. Would you like to ask me whose line it was?" His expression was one of pure devilry that could've given Hermes a run for his money. Aeëtes felt himself blushing like a schoolboy, but there was no point in hiding anything from a god.

Aeëtes took a deep breath, feeling his entire universe condense down to a single point. He was almost too nervous to speak. "I don't know what you're talking about." The words tumbled out of him before he could recall them; he felt a sting of shame in his response, chastising himself for denying Hecate, even when she wasn't there. He had promised to pursue her, no matter the cost, and it seemed that he was already failing.

Thanatos sensed his inner anguish and extended a hand, a cool stream of dark, navy power undulating from his fingers. It wrapped itself around Aeëtes and squeezed, and he found himself immediately calmed. Thanatos's power was one of rest and ease, which was incredibly useful when it came to telling someone that it was their time to die.

"Would you like to ask me whose line it was?" Thanatos asked it again, his tone kinder, as he could sense Aeëtes's anguish. This time, Aeëtes did not falter.

"Was my life line intertwined with Hecate's?" His voice shook when he said it, but he needed to know. His heart was practically in his throat. Thanatos's face changed again, twisting into a wide smile, one that would almost seem cruel under different circumstances.

"Yes," Thanatos answered simply enough, but Aeëtes felt as though he had grown wings. He couldn't stop from laughing, a wholly joyful and undignified sound, as he clapped his hands together. He knew that anything could change—fate also had planned for him to die today—but there *was* a future for them. That was all that he needed to know. After he took a few seconds to collect himself, he turned to face Thanatos, his brow furrowing.

"Did you...did you come all the way here to tell me that?" He took a step closer to Thanatos, feeling like the tension between them had eased.

"I will admit, I came on my own volition." Thanatos looked almost bashful, as if a personal visit instead of a professional one was uncouth. Aeëtes had to admit that he did prefer the former given Thanatos's line of work.

"I wanted to know who this man was. The man who had his fate line wrapped around my aunty's."

Aeëtes raised his eyebrows slightly at that, surprised to hear the God of the dead speak so affectionately. The kinship between Nyx and Hecate was no secret. Logic would assume that it meant that Nyx's children and Hecate were also close. Aeëtes pursed his lips for a moment, waiting in silence as Thanatos continued to stare at him.

"So. Um." Aeëtes coughed awkwardly. "A coin for your thoughts? Am I up to measure?"

Thanatos grinned at that. "Taking coins is more my brother's thing. I couldn't possibly know just by looking at you. You are handsome, though."

"Thank you. You've seen...well, you've seen everyone. I guess you'd be a good judge of that. Except you do see people on their deathbeds, so maybe not."

Thanatos let out another small chuckle at that, rubbing a hand over his jaw. "I like you. I think you're good for her." The statement was short enough, but it made Aeëtes feel like he was shining so brightly, he could give his father a run for his money.

But Thanatos isn't the one to decide. Aeëtes's intrusive thoughts were waiting in the wings, ready to strike down at the first sign of optimism. It was another reason that his ongoing enthusiasm was such a testament to his strength. Thanatos sensed the shift in his mood.

"If you are pursuing her," Thanatos let out a heavy sigh, his voice getting even quieter as he beckoned for Aeëtes to come closer. "There is something that you should know." There was something in his tone that made the hair on the back of Aeëtes's neck stand up, and fear to begin churning in his gut.

"Tell me. I want to know," Aeëtes insisted, stepping closer to the god, so they were nearly head to head, looking positively conspiratorial. Thanatos let out a long breath and began, speaking slowly at first.

"Have you heard the story of how Hecate became a goddess?"

"Sure, all of the gods..." Aeëtes stopped, mulling it over in his mind. He realized that he didn't know the story although he had assumed it was a typical story of birth or creation by a primordial. "No. No, I don't think I've ever heard it."

"That's because it is not typical." Thanatos sighed, running a hand through his dark hair. "I'm one of the only gods who knows and that's because I was there."

Aeëtes's heart nearly stopped, and he held his breath, refusing to move as he waited for Thanatos to continue.

"Hecate was always talented when it came to witchcraft, even when she was a mortal." Aeëtes's couldn't keep the shock off his face at hearing that Hecate had once been mortal, but Thanatos continued. "She was a priestess at that time, working for Gaia, before Hera and the rest of the goddesses demanded tribute. She was well-skilled and became a refuge for many, a sign of hope. She was loved." There was a tone to Thanatos's voice that made Aeëtes's bones chill, indicating that the story was going to get worse before it got better. "And...she loved. She was in love with a mortal man, whose name I cannot say. It has been wiped from the Underworld. He loved her, too, but he could not match Hecate in passion."

Aeëtes couldn't help but smile, although there was a touch of sadness to it. "That sounds like her."

Thanatos made a noise of assent. "Another priestess grew jealous of Hecate's reputation and her great love affair. She had the man murdered in his sleep and left his body on the steps of the temple where Hecate worked." Thanatos stopped, his voice sounding pained, and Aeëtes couldn't help but let out a sharp gasp at the story.

"What happened to that woman?" Aeëtes growled. "Tell me that she was dealt with swiftly, Thanatos." Thanatos held up a hand for Aeëtes to be quiet and continued his story.

"She was dealt with, I assure you. Although, your outrage warms my heart. There have been too few people who have been pushed to anger on Hecate's behalf throughout the millennia. Unfortunately, the murder was seen as a bad omen, and Hecate's reputation was ripped from her, and she was cast out from her temple. She didn't mind; she knew that her witchcraft was sound, and she still had favor with the gods. Her heart, however, was shattered."

"I can imagine..." Aeëtes looked pained.

"Hecate was desperate to have her lover back again." Thanatos let his head fall back, looking up at the sky before he continued. He looked at Aeëtes with a serious expression. "You know that in addition to witchcraft, Hecate is the Goddess of necromancy?"

"Yes," Aeëtes nodded eagerly, his brow furrowed in confusion as to why this would be a point of concern. Thanatos seemed surprised.

"Most men do not know this about her, and they are terrified of her when they hear it." He waved a hand in front his face, brushing off the concern. "You do seem suited for her. Ah. I have lost my story. At the time, Hecate did not know anything about the practice. She spent ten years learning it, traveling to all corners of the country, even across the sea. There was nothing that would keep her from learning every secret she could about communing with the dead."

Aeëtes heart cracked a little further, and he wondered if she would ever come close to feeling that sort of devotion again. Thanatos noted the shift in his countenance but did not comment on it.

"At the end of those ten years, Hecate proved herself a skilled necromancer. The first person that she brought back from the Underworld was her lover. Of course, it had been a decade by the time she was able to commune with him."

"Fuck," Aeëtes groaned, a sick feeling settling in his stomach. "Did he drink from Lethe? Did he forget her?" *How someone could ever forget a woman like her, even when she was mortal, I could never know.*

"No," Thanatos's eyes flashed with anger. "Worse. He no longer cared. He was content with his life in the Underworld and had no desire to return to the land of the living. Hecate understood this, or so she said, saying she knew that there were risks in disturbing souls. She accepted it, but..."

"Oh, no." Aeëtes stopped, that dread growing in him as he sensed what was coming. Thanatos nodded.

"She asked if she could commune with him from time to time. She wanted his consent to bring his shade from the

Underworld to see her, talk to her, until she could join him. He refused."

"That piece of—"

"Your rage is admiral but unneeded." Thanatos raised a hand and silenced Aeëtes. "As you can imagine, this broke her heart. She had lost everything, and her lover didn't even want to speak to her anymore. Hecate was on my list a few days later, one of the few souls that I have ever come across who was truly dying from a broken heart."

Aeëtes buried his head in his hands, keeping tears at bay at the thought of Hecate, broken-hearted and alone.

"I had never seen a mortal soul who had given so much for others. I had never seen heartbreak like that before." Thanatos's tone was nearly reverent. "I took her to my mother. It didn't feel right for her to go and join the souls of the mortal dead, to be confronted in the fields of Asphodel with the man who had scorned her."

"What happened?" Aeëtes's eyes were wide. He had never heard this before and was hanging onto every word coming out of Thanatos's mouth.

"My mother made her immortal. She turned Hecate into the goddess of all the things that she loved—witchcraft, dogs, and necromancy. Even the moon, although Selene does the heavy lifting there these days."

"It's why she works with women, isn't it?"

"It's why Hecate works specifically with *scorned* women, Aeëtes. She has never truly healed; I don't think. There are parts of her that bleed fresh every time she enacts her justice. She sees herself and her lover in every stilted woman."

Aeëtes had no words. No wonder she was so afraid, so hesitant to believe that there could be a happy ending in store for her. She had spent her immortal life by reliving the same story over and over again, acting like her own confirmation bias. It was a wicked way to patch up over her heartbreak, but he couldn't blame her for it. His thoughts quickly turned violent again as he mulled it over in his mind.

"What happened to her lover?" Aeëtes growled the words, grinding his teeth together as he turned to look at Thanatos.

"Hades had his shade destroyed." Thanatos said it so casually that it reminded Aeëtes he was dealing with the God of death. Aeëtes's doubts crept in.

"Did Hades and Hecate…?"

"No," Thanatos laughed at that, which brought Aeëtes peace that the idea seemed preposterous to him. "Absolutely not. There is a deep respect there, and they are both creatures of the Underworld. Hecate did him a favor, and he responded in kind, although you'll have to ask him for that story."

Aeëtes felt his body shiver. "I'd really rather not."

Thanatos's tricky grin was back. "You'll meet him sooner or later. Especially if your fate stays intertwined with hers."

"May the Fates keep their course," Aeëtes muttered under his breath, saying a quick prayer to the sisters. The light was beginning to shift all around them, and the earliest rays of the sunrise were peeking through the stars. Thanatos looked up at the shifting night sky, able to discern the shape of his mother and father among the stars.

"I must be going. My work never ends."

"I would imagine—"

Thanatos cut him off, stepping forward and placing a hand on Aeëtes's shoulder. "Listen to me, son of Helios, prince of Colchis. I have seen your fate wrapped around Hecate's, and they glowed like the gifts of your father. You will not find that it is an easy path or a fast one. The only reason that I have told you this story here today is to remind you that Hecate's willingness to love is not centered on you. It is her own fears that hold her back. If you understand her…may you be prepared to face whatever obstacles come up between you."

Aeëtes was silent, the weight of Thanatos's words settling over him. The God of death was not one to trifle with, and there was a threat in his words, too. Aeëtes could only nod in response as the dark, blue clouds began swirling around them again, Thanatos beginning to fade into them.

"Remember, Aeëtes," his voice was disembodied and already being carried away on the wind, "what happens to the shades of men who break Hecate's heart."

26

Aeëtes watched until Thanatos faded away, the god's words ringing in his ear. He didn't care how many threats he faced; there was only one woman for him, and that was Hecate.

You really have lost your mind. Aeëtes rolled his eyes at no one in particular, looking around and noticing that the ship was still quiet. The sunrise was now in full-force, and he found himself looking at it with a particular level of indifference. He watched as the sun climbed higher, and with it, his distaste for his father grew. His thoughts drifted to Circe, whom Helios had admonished, and how he didn't seem to care what happened to his children after he abandoned them in Colchis.

Abandoned probably isn't a fair word, Aeëtes's chided himself. He did love his adoptive parents, but after learning about everything that happened with his sister, it sat with him differently.

There would still be an hour yet before the crew began springing to life, and Aeëtes found himself making his way back towards Hecate's cabin. The fact that he had a cabin of his own conveniently slipped his mind...as well as his resolve to give Hecate some space. Before knocking on her door, he slipped towards the storerooms, grabbing a couple of bundles he would use as a peace offering.

He knocked once and waited, wondering if it was impolite to knock again or if he should take a hint. As he was deciding, Hecate swung the door open with a surprised look on her face.

"What are you doing up so early?" she mumbled, running a hand over her face and disappearing back inside. "And why did you have to wake me up with you?"

Aeëtes followed her and shut the door with his foot, placing the satchels and wrapped pieces of cloth down on a barrel. He turned to look at her and found himself smiling, his stomach turning in playful knots as she sat down on the bed. Hecate's hair was loose from its braid and was mussed from sleep, her eyes blinking as she got used to the morning light. She looked *soft* and utterly touchable.

She shifted on the bed, crossing her legs as her stare turned more inquisitive. "Aeëtes?" Her voice was coaxing, still rough with sleep, and it brought all of him to attention. "Was there a reason you came to wake me up?"

She leaned back on her elbows, the movement pushing her breasts out ever so slightly. Aeëtes gaped openly, her seduction of him obvious. He took a step towards her and stopped, shaking his head and remembering that he had a plan. In that same instant, it dawned on him that she had misread his expression.

"I brought breakfast." He motioned towards the bundles. "I thought that you might want to eat with me."

Hecate's head tilted to one side, looking confused. "If you want to have sex, you don't need to bribe me." There was a playful look in her eyes, but there was more hidden in her tone.

"No." Aeëtes coughed, taking a step back. Hecate sat up quickly, a sharp sting of rejection quickly piercing her side. He saw it on her face and immediately began backtracking. "Not that I wouldn't — I would, you would...it was good when we... I mean." Aeëtes was now red with embarrassment, and Hecate bit her lip to stifle her laughter, realizing that it was not a question of desire. Aeëtes watched her and sighed, a dopey grin on his face, shrugging good-naturedly.

"You brought breakfast just to…" she trailed off, confused as to why he would've come back for anything else. Not that she was complaining, per se.

"Yes." Aeëtes nodded slowly, a certain hesitancy in his voice. He felt a sick realization wash over him, evaporating what was left of his good mood. "Hecate…have you never…" His voice trailed off. "Like, after a night with someone, just… had breakfast?"

Hecate felt her face heat up, and she wanted to drown in her embarrassment. She chewed on her cheek, struggling with the realization of how jaded she was. She wondered if he was judging her.

Aeëtes, who owed quite a bit of his emotional intelligence now to due to Thanatos's willingness for stories, was one step ahead. He got down on one knee in front of her, one of his hands encompassing both of hers. Hecate turned her face away so he wouldn't see how wet her eyes were.

"Hey." His voice was soft. "I meant what I said. I want everything, Hecate, and I know it's probably easier for you to pretend this is just sex…" Her eyes snapped back to his. "But it isn't for me. I don't want that. So yes." Aeëtes released her hands and stood, grabbing a few of the parcels and coming back to sit beside her on the mattress. He scooted backwards until he was sitting up against the wall, patting the space between his legs with his free hand.

Hecate froze.

Aeëtes realized that while their chemistry meant falling into bed was easy for them both, intimacy was going to be another story.

I will castrate any man who made the concept of affection so foreign to her. Aeëtes's thoughts raced violently while he waited patiently. There was no judgement on his face, only a tender eagerness, hoping that she would choose him for this, too.

She moved slowly, and Aeëtes found himself holding his breath like he would frighten her away. Hecate pushed herself backward until she was sitting between his legs, but she looked straight ahead and was stiff as a board. She was almost acting as if it were her first time, with anxious movements and an uncertainty about where anything might lead. Truth be told, in that moment, she felt like a virgin. Casual sex was one thing, but she couldn't remember the last time that she had intimate, physical affection with a man.

"Hecate," Aeëtes's lips were at her ear, and she shivered. "If you're really uncomfortable, then we don't—"

"No," she cut him off with a small shake of the head. "No, I want...this."

Aeëtes nodded, his smirk slowly growing as he wrapped an arm around her waist. He tugged her to him until her back was flush with his chest, comfortably nestled in between his legs.

"Look at that!" His voice was full of mirth, trying to cut the tension between them and make Hecate feel less self-conscious. "A perfect fit. Alright, little witch, bread or cheese?" He held up two of the fabric-wrapped blocks. Aeëtes felt her relax slightly as she smiled.

"I'll take the bread, thank you."

"A woman after my own heart." He winked, opening it up and ripping off a piece before holding it up to her lips. Hecate froze again, turning to look at Aeëtes's with an expression of near panic.

"It's okay." He reassured her again, ever patient. "I just want to sit with you, feed you breakfast. Eat some cheese. Tell me about the Underworld."

There was a genuine expression of interest and tenderness on his face. It almost pushed Hecate to tears again. She leaned forward slightly, accepted the bread, and found herself laying her head on his shoulder as she chewed. Aeëtes had an arm around her waist, his hands holding the food in front of her.

"You know, this one time, when we were younger men," Aeëtes ripped himself a piece of bread, popping it into his mouth, "Pelias was sore that I was a faster runner than him. Which, let the record show, I still am," he paused and held up another piece of bread for Hecate, this time with cheese, "and he said if I was really that fast, I should run through the temple of Dionysus and steal some wine."

"No!" Hecate giggled as she chewed, her body relaxing a little more. "Tell me you didn't agree to that?"

"I most certainly did." Aeëtes winked at her, preparing more bites for them both. "Luckily, I'm pretty sure that Dionysus considered it a form of worship."

"I'm almost positive he did!" Hecate was fully relaxed now, cuddling into Aeëtes's chest and melting into the sturdiness of it. She accepted bites of food from his hand and once their breakfast was gone, he began stroking her arm gently. Each touch made Hecate's soul feel like it was going to burst; she was nervous she was going to get addicted to this feeling. Aeëtes was so warm and strong, yet she felt safe in his presence. Her eyelids fluttered, and she wondered if she was going to fall asleep on him.

"I was serious." Aeëtes looked at her with a gentle expression. "Tell me more about the Underworld."

And so, Hecate did. She told him stories about Nyx and her dogs, tall tales of how many times she had to get Hermes out of trouble. Hecate even told him about the time that she had walked in on one of the Fates and Hades. The entire time that she talked, Aeëtes kept his hands moving over her with caressing touches. It never got overly sexual although they could only be so close to each other without thinking about it, but it was soothing.

They traded story after story, until Hecate was relaxed and laughing, and they were covered in crumbs. She was telling him about an evening where Circe turned Hermes into a hare. Aeëtes was scratching her scalp, and she had an arm tossed around his neck. He listened to every word, hanging off her sentences and always having the perfect thing to say in response.

Hecate finished her story and let out a soft sigh, nuzzling into Aeëtes's neck. A strong sense of pride went through him, knowing that she was relaxed and accepting. It broke his heart to see how much she seemed shocked by each caress, how every touch almost seemed to make her cry—like she had been dying of thirst and didn't know it until someone gave her a cup of water.

He didn't know how much longer they sat there, but he didn't care. There was nothing that could pull him from the feeling of Hecate in his arms, the smell of cinnamon in her hair. He rested his head on top of hers, giving her a squeeze. She murmured a gentle sound, a lazy smile crossing her face. Aeëtes felt like magic underneath her, his arms feeling stronger than spell work.

"I think you've got a little bit of witchcraft of your own," Hecate scoffed playfully as she balanced her chin on his chest and looked up at him.

"Why?" He kissed her forehead softly, his lips lingering there as he spoke against her skin. "I'd say I'm more of a…lion tamer," Aeëtes teased her, his hands going to her sides and tickling her ribs.

"Aeëtes!" Hecate shrieked, squirming to get away from him as laughter poured out from her. It was a delicious, unhindered sound, that didn't have a stitch of restraint in it. This wasn't Hecate, the terrifying goddess of the Underworld. This was Hecate, the woman.

"Little witch." Aeëtes grinned, tightening his grip on her and hauling her back into his lap as she stopped squirming. She was straddling his waist, and when she looked into his eyes, the carefree attitude evaporated. The tension between them returned, and Aeëtes felt her body stiffen.

No, no, no, no... Aeëtes sighed deeply, his brow furrowing. He felt like he was chasing the wind.

"Aeëtes..." Hecate started slowly, chewing on her lip. He didn't like it when she looked nervous, especially around him. He leaned forward and pressed soft kisses to her hairline, running his hand over her head. Her eyes closed again, and she sighed, leaning into the embrace.

"Yes?" he whispered gently, his arm tightening around her waist. She looked up and he readjusted, leaning down until their foreheads were touching. She could swear that he was looking directly inside of her heart. It felt like there was no one else in the world when he stared at her like that.

"I'm going to need time." Hecate's voice was barely above a whisper. "This... It feels so good. It feels *too* good. I can't get used to this if I feel like it's going to go away."

Aeëtes sighed, hugging her softly. "I'll give you everything, Hecate. I mean that." Hecate let out a long sigh, her voice sounding shaky.

"I'll need everything. I cannot imagine having you for anything less than the rest of my life. That is what terrifies me. I... I just need time." She choked on the last words out and burst into tears, Aeëtes immediately cradling the back of her head and pushing her to his chest.

"Sssh, ssh," he crooned softly, rocking her back and forth. "That's okay. Let it out." He encouraged her, whispering in her ear and pausing every so often to kiss her cheeks. She sniffled, and Aeëtes nodded, as if he was goading her to go on, to release all of the pent-up feelings inside her body. Hecate felt boneless, slumped over Aeëtes's chest but too comfortable to care. "There we go," he murmured into her hair. "Relax into me, little witch. It's alright. This is good."

"I'm a mess." Hecate's voice was muffled, but Aeëtes only

laughed; she felt his chest vibrate with it. He slipped a finger under her chin and lifted it up until she was staring at him.

"Sometimes a mess is a good thing, Hecate. You can be the strong, dangerous, terrifying Goddess of the Underworld. You *are* that," he chuckled warmly, "but I think you'll come to find that it might be nice if every once in a while, just here, where it's us…you don't have to."

Hecate felt her heart expanding in her chest until she thought it would kill her. She opened her mouth to answer him, and all she saw in her mind's eye was the face of a mortal man from centuries ago. The last person who had been this tender with her, who inevitably preferred to be dead than speak to her. She let out a long, controlled breath and closed her eyes.

"I just need time, Aeëtes. I need time." He nodded slowly and cupped her chin, kissing her softly.

"We're both immortal. I've got all the time in the world."

PART III

27

Two days later, Hecate was up early as they prepared to land in Colchis. After their breakfast together, Aeëtes and Hecate had been inseparable. He shared with her his love for sailing, attempting to teach her a variety of knots and tricks for navigation. Hecate proved comically unskilled at both, but whenever he teased her, she waved her hand and used magic. Aeëtes would cry foul through his laughter but never stopped smiling.

Hecate couldn't remember the last time she had so much *fun*. They had temporarily pushed aside all of their worries about Hera or breaking the curse and spent their last full days at sea enjoying each other's company. When the sun set, they would trade more stories with Pelias over wine. Last night, Aeëtes had smiled when Hecate fell asleep on his shoulder, growing more comfortable with him. He carried her to her cabin, and hesitated slightly, not sure if he should stay. She woke up long enough to ask him to stay, and they didn't fall asleep for another few more hours.

Now, as she looked out over the water and watched as they sailed effortlessly into the harbor, she felt like a spell was about to break. Hecate could never imagine that she would be so

comfortable on a ship, away from the Underworld, but now
she didn't want to disembark.

She didn't want this to be over.

Once they sorted out how to break Aeëtes's curse, they
would have to have a conversation. Hecate would be due to go
back to the Underworld, and she had heard of the ultimatum
from Aeëtes's adoptive parents. He had a year to take over the
throne. It was a conversation that she wasn't ready for, but as
the deck began to fill with the crew and they prepared to dock,
she knew that she didn't have a choice.

She was pulled from her thoughts as the noise from shore
became audible. The harbors of Colchis were full of activity
like none of the port cities that they had seen on their journey
so far. Once they had been in sight of the city, Pelias had flown
the royal family's flag to announce their arrival. The king and
queen of Colchis had been made aware that a ship was arriv-
ing, and a greeting party had been assembled.

There were no less than fifteen servants and thirty guards
in gleaming armor and holding spears and banners with the
family crest. There was a litter in the center of it, shining gold
in the daylight, with long, purple curtains that reached the
ground. A massive crowd had gathered around them, eager to
get a glimpse of the royal arrival. Once the ship came to a halt,
the crew was launched into action. Ropes were tossed overboard to secure the boat, and the ramp was descended. Pelias
had bid them goodbye earlier that morning, wanting to turn
around and head back to Greece as soon as he could.

Aeëtes and Hecate stood on deck, waiting to be the first to
walk off the ship. There was a gentle thud when they were
secure, and the crowd let out a shout at the sight of the crown
prince.

Hecate listened to the noise but kept her eyes on Aeëtes.
She wasn't surprised to hear the joyful reaction of the crowd;
he was a well-loved prince, even for all the time that he had
spent abroad. She watched as his face morphed, turning into

something foreign to her. Aeëtes looked like the sun on a cloudy day, impossible to ignore completely, but obscured and camouflaged. Hecate swallowed thickly, gathering her own courage, and slipping her hand into Aeëtes's.

He turned to look at her in shock. His eyes widened slightly, but he managed to keep most of the surprise off his face.

"That's a very public gesture," he whispered the words to her, raising an eyebrow playfully. Hecate felt her mouth go dry, and her stomach was churning, but she smiled.

"I know."

"These are my parents," Aeëtes reminded her, wanting her to be sure. If they stepped off this ship holding hands, it would be as good as a formal declaration that they were engaged. Aeëtes was a crown prince, and she was a goddess. That meant that only trysts or engagements were permitted. It wasn't an option to say that they were doing something *casual*.

"I know." Hecate's smile got wider, her nerves evaporating under the warm look in Aeëtes's eyes. His entire face lit up with excitement like a child with sweets, and she chuckled at him.

She believed him when he told her that it was real. It wouldn't be perfect, and they had a lot of things to discuss, but she trusted him.

"Let's go meet Mom and Dad," Aeëtes's said with a devilish expression, squeezing her hand tighter and leading her off the ship. Hecate was used to crowds as a goddess, but they were always acolytes. Worshippers typically kept a fair distance from their gods out of respect, and likely, a healthy dose of fear. This was a mortal crowd that was excited to see their favored prince. Hecate found herself moving closer to Aeëtes as they walked down the ramp, the masses reaching out to them from all directions.

Hecate bristled slightly, not caring for crowds or people, and found herself stepping closer to Aeëtes. His face had changed again to the face of a prince, waving to his citizens and staying delightfully impassive. He could sense Hecate's agitation, and he quietly placed a hand on her back, guiding her way. She leaned back into the touch as they stepped onto the dock, keeping her face stoic as they approached the litter.

"Father?" Aeëtes scowled, taking a step forward and looking around the crowd of palace staff.

"Aeëtes! My boy."

The king emerged from behind some of his soldiers, giving Hecate her first look of Aeëtes's adoptive father. He was a tall man, but his shoulders drooped slightly, the top of his head balding. For a king, he was dressed simply. His long peplos was well-tailored but lacking any additional refinements. It was clear that he had been well into middle age when Helios had granted his immortality. Hecate studied him, noting that he had opted to travel on foot instead of in the litter. She liked that about him.

He stepped forward and wrapped Aeëtes up in a hug, clapping him on the back soundly, which made Aeëtes's eyes pop open a bit. Hecate bit her lip to keep from smirking at the exchange.

"Hi, Dad," Aeëtes murmured sheepishly, running his hair through his hair as if he was now nervous about the situation. The king pulled back, squeezing Aeëtes's shoulders as he looked him over.

"Tell me! What are you doing back so soon? Have you finally decided to take over for your old man?" Aeëtes opened his mouth to answer, but the king waved it off and kept speaking. "Ah, never mind. We can get into all of those details later." He turned to Hecate, stopping suddenly as he realized that he was standing in front of an immortal. He bowed low at the waist, giving her a warm smile. "The gods be blessed! There must be some good news if Aeëtes has managed to come back with a goddess."

Hecate gave him a warm smile, nodding her head in return

but saying nothing. She had a sneaking suspicion that he didn't know who she was, based on his ambiguous use of the word *goddess*. She filed it away, a blank yet polite expression covering her face. If Aeëtes noticed, he said nothing.

"Well," the king clapped his hands together, which he seemed to do a lot, "Let's get back to the palace. Ah! I'm being thick." He turned to the litter, signaling for the attendants to pull the curtains back. "Goddess, I'd also be inclined to introduce my wife, the queen of Colchis, and Faidra, Aeëtes's fiancée."

Hecate's world stopped.

Aeëtes felt his blood run cold.

No one breathed, except for the mass of people around them, reaching for them.

For a few seconds, he hoped that it wasn't happening.

Then, everything happened too fast. An attendant had stepped forward and pulled back the curtains as instructed, revealing the bodies of his mother and fiancée. They had matching, exuberant smiles as they waved—which felt grotesque to Aeëtes, given the circumstances, but they couldn't have known that. He felt like he was going to be sick. Aeëtes spun around and looked at his father, fury slowly etching on his face.

"What the hell?" he growled, low enough that only his father could hear him. "Why did you bring her here?" The king rolled his eyes, as if this was an argument that he was tired of hearing.

"I brought her here because she is your fiancée, and you've returned to Colchis. I'm not entirely sure which part of that equation surprises you."

Aeëtes felt the cold sinking feeling in his gut turn to anger —a hot, heady frustration that sunk into his bones. He made a sound that was somewhat in between a growl and a shout, pivoting to Hecate.

"Hecate—" He turned to her, holding out a hand in her

direction, but she wouldn't look at him. Her eyes were glued straight ahead, waving gently in a polite manner to his mother and Faidra.

"*Please*," he hissed, trying to get closer to her. She acted as though he didn't exist, stepping forward as the litter was lowered to the ground. The women stood and embraced Hecate, obviously knowing who she was, and she settled down on the litter beside them. Aeëtes couldn't breathe. The curtains were drawn, and the attendants stood, turning and beginning the walk back to the palace. He watched, slack-jawed, his entire body feeling a rush of anxiety and shame.

"How dare you!" Aeëtes snapped at his father. The attendants and soldiers began going back towards the palace, but he put his hand on his father's arm, stopping him. "Father." His voice was sharp, tinged with a cold, piercing tone. "What were you thinking? I told you I wasn't going to marry Faidra!" Aeëtes's chest was heaving as he tried to get enough air in his lungs. His entire universe was collapsing around him, and his nervous system was being unraveled inch by painstaking inch.

The king looked confused before he let out a soft, scoffing noise and began walking. "It's not up to you, Aeëtes. You may be immortal, but you have no place in the pantheon. You are a crown prince, first." He stopped, turning to look at Aeëtes with a dead look in his eyes. "And princes marry whoever they're told to."

Aeëtes didn't move, his father leaving him behind. He promptly turned and walked over to the bushes alongside the side of the road and vomited.

✛ ✛ ✛

HECATE'S entire field of vision had been reduced to a pinprick. She could only hear the king's voice and those two words.

Aeëte's fiancée.

Aeëte's fiancée.

Aeëte's fiancée.

She stopped breathing, and the only thing that saved her was the fact that she was frozen in place. That placated, friendly smile was stuck on her face. She couldn't move. She couldn't emote. Everything in her body was a mix of contradictions—hot and cold, dry and sweaty, gasping for air and taking deep breaths. It was like her entire system had shut down and was restarting from the inside out. The earth trembled underneath her feet, her power stirring within her. It would bend to her will, and she debated letting it open up and swallow her whole, pulling her right back down into the Underworld. The tremor of magic must have been stronger than she thought because there was a soft voice in her head a moment later.

"Do you want to come home, Hecate?" It was Hades.

Hecate's face was flushed red with heat and embarrassment while a sick, cold feeling began building at the base of her spine. It was a dread feeling of shame and anxiety that began escalating, slowly creeping up her spine. She fought the urge to claw at her back to get it to stop. It felt like death. Someone beside her was trying to get her attention. It might have been Aeëtes.

"No." She tried to swallow but couldn't get a single muscle to move. Her hands were trembling, and once she was able to stop hearing the word *fiancée* in her mind, it was replaced with one word.

Foolish. Foolish. Foolish.

Hecate could feel her hands shaking. Thousands of years and she hadn't learned a single lesson. How would she ever face herself ever again? How would she look at a single acolyte without being embarrassed?

You're a fraud. Her thoughts began ripping her apart.

"Hecate." It was Hades again. *"I can feel your distress."* Hecate realized that she must still be sending wave after wave of panicked power into the earth below her. The pebbles trembled around her, but luckily, none of the mortals seemed to notice.

"I can handle it, Hades." Her voice was as sharp as a blade. Her eyes flashed red for a split second, and a cool, indifferent mask slid over her face. If there was anything that Hecate knew without fail, it was that she wouldn't cast a single evil eye at Faidra. She had nothing to do with this.

Hecate widened her smile, waved, and went to join the women.

❦ 28 ❦

The palace of Colchis was beautiful as the small parade approached. They were on a winding dirt road, flanked with lemon trees, the din of the harbor far below them. The structure sat on the highest hill in Colchis, with the bright, red banners of the royal family blowing in the wind. It was a sprawling structure on large grounds, and Hecate could see stables, a private temple, and servant's quarters just from their limited vantage point. The main entrance to the palace was massive, with at least twelve stone columns spanning a wide porch and a series of mosaicked steps leading up to the door. There were great basins lit with fire that she assumed were stoked constantly, with wisps of incense smoke winding up to the roof. Hecate could only imagine that the inside was just as opulent.

The beauty of the home wasn't a surprise, but something about it only managed to twist the knife further in Hecate's stomach. She now existed in two places: her internal world and her external world. Her mind and heart were splintering, but she kept a diplomatic smile on her face.

Everything around her felt like an affront. The breeze, the sweet smell of incense in the air, the sun—the *sun*. She was still fighting the temptation to rip open the ground beneath her and fall into it. On some level, Hecate knew that she was nodding and smiling. She was listening to Aeëtes's adoptive mother and Faidra tell stories and make small talk, inquiring after Hecate's presence in Colchis. She politely waved them off, knowing that they would have to have a larger conversation about their plan once they were inside. The women were slightly skittish around a goddess. Her aloof answers appeased them, and they soon turned to their own conversation.

Hecate couldn't help but notice that Faidra was beautiful. She looked nothing like Hecate. Faidra had long, brunette hair that fell around her face in ringlets. She had the face of aristocracy, with a gently sloping nose and elegant features. She was slim and delicate to Hecate's curves and strong features. Hecate hadn't been self-conscious in thousands of years, but everything about her suddenly felt like...too much.

How dare you let another man make you feel this way? Hecate's inner critic roared back to life, raking her over the coals for her comparisons. *She's a lovely woman. You're a lovely woman. He's an asshole.*

The litter came to a stop. Hecate felt it lowering to the ground, but she was in a fog. She accepted the hand of a servant, who helped her to her feet, and the touch made her feel sick.

She didn't want to be touched.

She wanted everything around her to burn.

She was hardly paying attention. Hecate knew that she wasn't going to be able to keep up her charade much longer, so she applied a glamour to her face and let her smile drop. Everyone around her would only see a polite, apolitical expression on her face, and her voice wouldn't sound too loud or rude. Hecate could scream, rant, and rage, and the glamour would hide it from those standing right next to her. It was a useful spell, but she hated that she felt weak when she used it. She was hiding.

The procession walked inside the palace, and she blindly followed the queen and Faidra. They made their way to the center of a great hall with two huge thrones on one end. Part of the ceiling was open to the sky, and Hecate could smell the sea all the way up the hill. There were more basins full of fire with statues of the gods that lined the walls. Hecate couldn't help a smirk at some of their exaggeratedly likenesses—the image of Zeus, in particular, seemed to take a lot of artistic license. Hecate straightened her shoulders and stood tall while a serving girl came up and offered her a glass of wine. Hecate accepted it and made herself at home on a small bench. There were some musicians playing a gentle tune in the corner, creating what would have normally been a lovely, regal reception.

She watched carefully and studied everyone in the room, turning herself over to her instincts. She wasn't the Hecate from yesterday or even from that morning; she was the Goddess of witchcraft now. The vulnerable, aching pieces of her heart were being hardened again, slowly turning to stone in her chest.

When Aeëtes walked into the room, she felt it. Everything in her soul called out to turn her head, to make the slightest of movements, to seek out his warmth in the cold presence of her wounds.

He caused those wounds, Hecate hissed at herself.

A flicker of red magic danced over her skin, and one of her snakes appeared wrapped around her arm. The glamour wouldn't hide it, but she didn't care. She was a goddess, after all. That's all she was to these people. For some reason, that wasn't enough for her anymore.

Aeëtes was anxious as he felt Hecate's magic spark. He had nearly brawled with his father on the way back to the palace. His eyes scanned the room, landing on her immediately, looking relaxed and sipping from a cup of wine. She appeared so casual that it startled him, making him break out in a sweat.

His mother had seated herself in her throne, his father walking past to join her. The lead pit in his stomach grew as his eyes finally settled on Faidra, sitting on a bench opposite Hecate. Faidra gave him a soft smile and patted the seat next to her, and Aeëtes almost got sick again. He knew that Hecate was watching them. He turned to look at her, but she was as still as marble. The entire scene was so normal, so mind-blowingly casual, that Aeëtes thought he was going to drop to his knees and start screaming.

His parents on their thrones, chatting. *Aren't you concerned why I showed up here with a goddess?*

Hecate sitting in the great hall, drinking. *Don't you understand I'm in love with you?*

Faidra lounging opposite the goddess, beckoning. *We're not engaged!*

Aeëtes was about to break when his father sat down with a massive sigh. The king held up his hands to get everyone's attention, and the small conversations around the room stopped. Aeëtes was standing in the very center of the hall and felt like he was in trouble.

"Now, son," his father held a hand out and pointed towards Aeëtes as if he was exalting him. "Please, tell us the good news. Tell this old man that you have come home to take over the throne." Aeëtes had to fight to keep from groaning exasperatedly, shaking his head as he looked up at the ceiling.

"That's not why I'm here—"

"Aeëtes." The king cut him off, his voice angry. "You know, we have had enough of your gallivanting around Greece, without any concern for your mother and I..." Aeëtes grit his teeth and began to grind his jaw, fists forming at his sides. He started speaking, but his father cut him off, and pretty soon, both Aeëtes and the king were yelling at one another from across the hall.

"I know, we can discuss that later..."

"We will discuss this *now*..."

"That's not why I'm here—"

"There are greater matters at hand."

Hecate stood, straightening her shoulders and putting her cup down. She spoke clearly, cutting through the cacophony of the two men. "Aeëtes was cursed by Hera."

Silence fell over the room as every face turned to Hecate. Aeëtes let out a long sigh, burying his head in his hands. He had wanted to approach that subject delicately with his parents, especially since they were here to contact Helios. It was a conversation that he was hoping to have with cooler heads, but as always, this proved difficult with his adoptive father. At this rate, he wasn't looking forward to conversing with his birth father, either. Hecate didn't elaborate, letting the silence go on. It was finally the queen who broke the tension, standing and taking a step towards her son.

"Aeëtes, is this true?" Her voice was full of concern, her face twisted in fear. Hecate's heart went out to her, and she felt a twinge of guilt at springing that news on a mother. She kept her eyes purposefully off Faidra.

"Yes," Aeëtes sighed, and his mother ran to him. She threw her arms around her son and held him close, Aeëtes bending his shoulders so she could manage it. For a brief moment, even in a crowded room, Aeëtes let himself be held by his mother.

Something about it rotated the knife in Hecate's stomach. She didn't let herself think on it.

"What do we do?" The queen's voice was anxious when she finally pulled away from her son, her hands cupping his face. "Is this why Hecate is with you?" She turned to look at the goddess, her face imploring. "Are you able to help us?"

Hecate nodded once, giving the queen what she hoped was an encouraging smile. Even if she couldn't manage it, she knew that her glamour would be effective enough. "I know something that might work..." Hecate started before she stopped and got the attention of one of the servants. "Bring out some food and wine for the room. This is going to take a while."

They disappeared to do her bidding, and Hecate stepped into the center of the room and told the entire story. No one uttered a word as she went through Hera's curse on Aeëtes, the temporary stay that Circe managed, or how Hera had sent the Scylla after them. Finally, after she had dictated all of their adventures, Hecate paused. Aeëtes managed to only look sheepish, keeping his eyes on the floor. The king and queen were stunned; the queen had been reacting quietly the whole time, but the king was stoic. Hecate couldn't help herself as she stole a glance at Faidra, who was chewing on her lip with a puzzled expression.

"Is what she says true, Aeëtes?" The king stood and looked at his son, who took a step back in surprise.

"You would doubt a goddess?" Aeëtes's voice was sharp. "You insult her by asking me this." Hecate felt her heart flutter, but she stamped it down, her gaze going directly to the king.

"I know that you have done something to garner great favor from Helios. At least, you have some camaraderie since he decides to drop off his children in Colchis." Hecate moved closer to the king, and the flames that lit the hall flickered. Coils of red power pooled around her feet and left footprints on the tile as she walked; the second snake appeared on her other arm, hissing dreadfully. The queen and Faidra were wide-eyed but said nothing; Aeëtes had the same, moon-eyed expression that he always did when Hecate's magic flared.

The king was wise enough to sit down, his lips pulling into a tight line. "I misspoke, Goddess."

"You did," Hecate snapped, her power refusing to recede. "There's a spell that I know, and it will reverse the curse. However, we need the blood of Aeëtes's mother." Hecate softened her tone, pulling some of that dark magic back into her, speaking respectfully. "His birth mother. We need Helios to tell us who that is. You are going to call on Helios for us."

"Surely, it would be easier for a god to call on one of their own?" the queen asked quietly with no disrespect in her tone. Hecate shook her head.

"Gods are fickle. Helios is on the fringes of Olympus, on a good day. He would just as soon ignore me than purposefully decide to not help us. You and your husband have a better relationship with Helios. It's as simple as that."

"It's politics." The queen gave Hecate a small nod. "I can understand that."

Hecate scoffed, "You have no idea."

"You'll do this." The queen turned to the king and demanded it. There was no space for debate in her demand, and Hecate decided that she liked Aeëtes's adoptive mother.

"I'll do this," the king agreed, standing and bowing in Hecate's direction. "We have a temple to Helios on the palace grounds. If you all will excuse me, I will put forth your request immediately."

Hecate nodded once, making it clear that the king had been dismissed from his own home. No one said anything else as he left the room, but not without tossing a disappointed look at Aeëtes. Hecate watched as he seemed to crumple under the stare. The once-confident and always-smiling Aeëtes seemed to shrink in Colchis, ricocheting between trying to get approval from his adoptive father and not wanting the life that had been chosen for him. Hecate couldn't even imagine what was going through his head, now that they were—hopefully—going to summon Helios.

It doesn't matter what's going through his head. She growled, pulling the last of her power back into her body and strengthening her glamour. *You are here to defeat Hera, defend your honor, respect a life debt, and go home.*

Faidra quietly stood up and slipped out a side door, disappearing down a hallway without saying a word. As soon as she was gone, Aeëtes nearly ran towards Hecate, his face looked equally terrified and upset. As soon as he opened his mouth to say something, Hecate turned to the queen, who was halfway out the door.

"Do you have a place where I can freshen up?"

His mother turned around, and it stopped Aeëtes in his tracks. He didn't want to have an audience to this conversation. The pain on his face was nearly palpable.

"Of course. I can show you to your rooms where you will be staying if you like." The queen held an arm out for Hecate in invitation. Hecate picked up her skirt in one hand, walked out of the room, and didn't spare a single look at Aeëtes as she went.

𓎟 29 𓂀

Hecate followed the queen through the winding halls of the palace, taking note of how many effigies to Helios dotted the passageways.

"Have you always worshipped Helios so...devoutly?" Hecate asked the queen, keeping stride with her. She let out a long sigh, and her steps faltered for a second, but she recovered quickly.

"No," she admitted quietly as if it were a great secret. "It was reactionary. After Helios brought us Aeëtes, my husband began covering the palace in homage to the Sun God. The temple was rededicated to be solely for his use, too." Hecate knew it was actually Circe's arrival that caused the change, but they no longer remembered her. They walked in comfortable silence for the rest of the way, before the queen pushed open a door to an expansive set of chambers.

"If there's anything else that I can get for you, please don't hesitate to find me directly." Hecate turned and looked at her with a warm smile in acceptance, genuinely appreciating the woman's soft countenance. There was an arrogance to the king that she didn't like, but the queen seemed different, gentler.

Hecate stepped inside, turning at the last minute to get the queen's attention.

"I can see why Helios brought you his son," she murmured, her eyes nearly downcast. "You have a very kind heart." The queen seemed almost taken aback, and she froze where she was standing. Hecate continued, "Trust me, I know what lies in a woman's heart."

The queen was pulled out of her reverie, dipping into a bow towards the immortal.

"I'm honored, Goddess." Her smile reached her eyes. "There is no finer compliment from no greater judge of character."

Hecate tilted her head in acquiescence, and the queen backed away a few paces before turning and disappearing down the hall.

Hecate watched until the woman's fleeting figure was gone and took a deep breath, shutting the door to the room. It was expansive and finely decorated, and she knew that it was likely kept for other members of visiting royalty. She waited for a few beats to ensure that there were no servants in the wings... and once she was sure, she sank down to her feet and let her glamour dissolve.

Hecate cried.

And cried.

And cried.

Until the sun had set, and the only comfort she could find was in Nyx's presence in the night sky.

✞ ✞ ✞

WHEN HECATE BLINKED her eyes open, she knew that something was wrong. At some point the night before, she had pulled herself into bed and fallen asleep. The sky outside was an unnatural color, parts of it were spotted with dark clouds of navy, while the horizon was decorated in swaths of green and orange. Hecate could sense the powers in the heavens and knew that Nyx had retreated to the Underworld. Eos and Astraeus were still in the sky, pulling and pushing against one another in a way that was ripping the horizon in pieces.

What in the gods' name is happening? Hecate got out of bed, kicking away the sheets, and stepped towards her open windows. She could hear the shocked cries of people within the city walls, screaming and shouting in peril that the sun hadn't risen.

Oh, Helios... Hecate was barely able to contain her nearly instantaneous rage. *What the hell have you done now?* Her opinion of the god had deteriorated swiftly over the past few weeks, but if he was now holding back the sun in retribution... She wouldn't hesitate to finally call the entire pantheon into settling this skirmish. Hecate let out a low growl and started heading for the door, preparing for a fight; she tightened the belt around her waist and pulled her hair back, twisting it into a braided crown around her head.

"*Fucking* Helios."

"That's quite a welcome," a deep, baritone voice called out to Hecate from the corner of the room. As soon as it spoke, she felt the umber power of Helios's magic, and she knew that he had arrived seconds before—otherwise, she would've felt his power.

Hecate spun on her heel and nearly hissed at him. He held up his hands in mock defeat, a blank look on his face. "Don't you normally have snakes that do that for you?"

"Tread lightly, Sun God." Hecate put the emphasis on his title like it was an insult. "You've created quite the mess here."

"I thought you needed me to help you clean up *your* mess." He smirked, leaning against the wall. He had one foot propped up against it, and his arms crossed over his chest, every inch of him emanating a light glow. Hecate shook her head, those tell-tale red sparks dancing over her skin again.

"You've already given away immortality to this family as a reward for making them raise your children," she sneered, looking down her nose at him as she stepped closer. "Then you made them forget Circe. Aeëtes wonders why he wasn't good enough to be raised as a god..."

"He doesn't have any power," Helios shrugged, "I could tell." Hecate's face nearly short-circuited with anger.

"He doesn't have any *power?*" The words came tumbling out of her like a vortex. "You gave away your son because you didn't think that he would be *powerful* enough for you?"

"He would never last in Olympus, Hecate." Helios rolled his eyes, and Hecate felt another wave of righteous power roll of off her. Helios answered in kind, the bright aura around him increasing, and they heard the stones of the palace begin to creak in response.

"How dare you?" She gritted her teeth. "I cannot believe that you'd give up a child because you didn't think that they would serve you enough as a pawn!"

Helios seemed unbothered. "I've heard his father's prayers. He doesn't even want to take over the crown here. He has no ambition."

"Thank the gods for that!" Hecate spat, her power pooling around her feet. "Aeëtes is nothing like the other gods, you selfish bastards. He is *good* and kind and..." Hecate stopped, her words trailing off as the hurt that he had inflicted on her came rushing back. Helios raised an eyebrow as he watched her countenance change and the color drain from her face.

"Interesting." Helios shrugged again. "I suppose you have always been interested in rather macabre and boring things." The last of Hecate's control went out the window, and she snapped her fingers, tossing her hand in Helios's direction. Her two large dogs emerged from the cloud of magic at her feet, both of them lunging for Helios. He let out a sharp yell as they bit his wrists and pinned them against the wall. Helios's light flared brighter still around him, but it had no effect.

"Listen to me." Hecate crossed the rest of the space between him, getting in his face. She squared her shoulders and stared at him, both of her dogs refusing to let go. "You will tell me the name of Aeëtes's and Circe's mother. You will then walk out of this room and put the *fucking* sun in the sky. You will restore Circe's memory to her adoptive parent's minds to at least give her a semblance of a family." She pulled a small, black parazonium dagger from thin air, ironically gleaming in the light of Helios's power. Hecate pressed it up against his neck until a thin line of ichor shone on the blade. "Do we have an understanding?"

There was a sudden obliterating blast of heat, knocking Hecate backward, so she fell on the floor. The dogs flickered with another wave of magic, their grip strengthening and managing to keep Helios in place as he struggled.

"I don't have to agree to a single thing you say, you witch!" Helios cursed her, spitting on the floor at her feet. Hecate jumped back up, tossing the blade to the side. She rolled her neck and slowly started laughing. The sound made Helios's stomach begin to twist as the heads of the virgin and the crone manifested. Her eyes rolled back into her head until they shone red, and tendrils of magic erupted from her fingers. The air around them was filled with the thick smell of cinnamon and death, the sky going red outside with the expanse of Hecate's rage.

Helios's eyes got wide, and he started nodding, the scent of his panic only making the dogs bite down harder. He yelped in response, trying to shake them off but to no avail.

"Alright, alright!" He yelped like a child. "I'll do it!" Hecate kept laughing, making no effort to rein in her power.

"I'll *do* it!" Helios yelled again, the sky flickering like a flame outside the windows. Hecate could hear the increasing screams of the mortals, terrified that the world was ending in the cosmos above them. Cracks had appeared in the walls of the room as rubble and stones fell from the ceiling. The palace was caving under the impacts of two gods, pushing their power at one another. It was a fight that was normally saved for the skies—man-made structure could never withstand it.

"Give me a *name*, Helios!" Hecate screamed, her voice echoing throughout the heavens in a shockingly deep echo. Helios opened his mouth to speak, but suddenly, the floor gave way beneath their feet, and the gods began to fall.

For a few minutes, there was nothing. There were only stones and wood and thatch in the air around them.

But there was noise.

So much noise.

Hecate couldn't see anything, the world around her was in shades of black and obscured with dust. She felt a sudden impact and realized that they must have hit the ground. It took a few more seconds for her to blink the dirt from her eyes. They were standing in the rubble of the palace's northeast wing. The building still stood tall behind them with a corner carved out from it, the gods' power bringing it down around them.

"Helios!" She turned around and began searching for him, the dogs already sniffing and turning through rubble.

"Easy, witch," Helios's voice called out from behind her, stepping out from underneath a pile of bent wooden beams. "It seems that you've already shown your beloved's family a very...interesting brand of attitude. I guess that's what they get for bringing a necromancer in their home."

Hecate's upper lip curled as she stepped over a stone and walked towards him, conjuring the black blade once more. Helios eyed it, and she watched him shiver.

"I'd be very careful if I were you." She nearly twitched with anger. "We all know that Apollo could do your job." It was Helios's turn to go red, flames appearing on his feet and light surging from inside of him.

"Don't you mention that lyre-playing fraud to me!" he growled, stepping towards the goddess like they were getting ready to go to blows.

Hecate laughed gaily, her voice becoming a light trill. "Who? Apollo? From where I'm standing, you're so irrelevant that Zeus *forgot* there was a Sun God, and he handed it off to that *fraud*. So you tell me, who's more of a phony?"

Helios was in her face immediately, both of their powers pushing against each other in the atmosphere.

"He doesn't do anything!"

"He'll be remembered," Hecate growled, pushing the dagger against Helios's side. "You will be lost to time, mark my words. The only ones who will speak your name will be the dead spirits that this *necromancer,*" she growled the word back to him, "speaks to!"

Helios sneered but said nothing, both of them staring at one another for a few more perilous moments. Hecate heard a series of voices behind them, and she realized that the palace had been evacuated, and everyone was now watching. She bristled, pulling back some of her magic and letting her faces condense back into one.

"Tell me," she snapped, exhaling sharply. "And be sure to follow through on the rest of my demands." She cautioned him, and he knew that she was referring to restoring the memory of Circe to the king and queen.

"That will take time," he begrudgingly admitted. "If you want the sun to rise today, I'll have to come back another time."

"I'll know if you don't," Hecate warned him, applying more pressure to the dagger. Helios winced and nodded, sweat now beading on his brow.

"I'll do it."

"And the name?" Helios's eyes flickered away, looking down at his feet. "The *name.*" Hecate repeated herself, jabbing the dagger at him again. Helios let out a coughing sound and twisted away from her. The noise of the crowd was growing louder behind them, and Hecate wanted Helios out of Colchis before Aeëtes saw him. "Now, Helios!"

"Clymene," he snapped, his eyes flicking back up to Hecate as his face twisted, as if saying it out loud brought him physical pain.

"Where can I find her?"

"You didn't ask me to tell you that," Helios growled out and shook his head. Hecate hissed, dropping the knife to his groin.

"I'm asking you now."

"Hecate—"

"Now, Helios."

"She's dead!" Helios yelled, and Hecate released her grip on him in shock. He stepped away from her, cursing as he did so. He let out an angry yelp and kicked at a piece of stone, sending it flying off the hill. Helios spun around and snarled at Hecate. "Are you happy? She's dead. She gave me Circe and Aeëtes, and we could never be together, and now she's *dead*."

Hecate shook her head, staring at him with a detached indifference. "She lived long enough after she bore you Circe to bring you Aeëtes. Why did you abandon them here?"

Helios sighed, rubbing a hand over his face as he resigned himself to telling the story. "We couldn't be together. I was in the sky, and she was always in the sea. We brought Circe here, in the East where the sun meets the sea, so we could both watch her grow up. We did the same with Aeëtes years later."

Hecate felt the agony coming off him, but she couldn't find it in her heart to have any empathy for Helios.

"When did you wipe the king and queen's memories of Circe? Did she know about that?"

Helios shook his head, tears in his eyes. "No. She asked too many questions about Clymene, who was already gone. I couldn't take it anymore."

"You're not fit to be a parent." Hecate looked at him with disdain. "She would be furious with you."

"I know." Helios's voice was quiet. "I know." Hecate let out a long sigh, the crushing realization of Aeëtes's parentage rolling over her. The spell wouldn't work without the blood of his mother, and Circe's patchwork spell wasn't going to last forever. They needed to think of another solution, and fast.

"Be gone, Helios," Hecate muttered, her voice tired. She had nothing else to say to him as the light around Helios began to increase in strength, and he vanished in a blinding flash. Not even a full second later, the mottled colors of the sky cleared, and the sun had risen. Hecate heard the echoing screams of humanity in surprise, followed closely by their cheers of relief as they realized the sun had returned.

Hecate rolled her eyes at the fickle nature of mortals, taking a closer look at the rubble around her. She waved her hands over the stones and stepped over the debris. It only took a few flicks of her fingers, and the corner of the palace that had fallen was restored. She stood back to admire her handiwork when Aeëtes's voice reached her.

"My gods! Hecate! Oh, are you okay? What happened? We heard—" He stopped talking as she turned to him and held up a hand, silencing him. The king and queen were right behind him, stunned looks on their faces.

"I summoned Helios." The king looked sick. "I did what was asked. I don't know why…"

"He came." Hecate nodded in the king's direction. "We've spoken."

"He was here?" The king looked like he was going to pass out. "I didn't see him. I went to the temple, and I made sure…" He was babbling, and Hecate pressed a finger to her temple, annoyed.

"Stop talking." She waved her hand from Aeëtes's direction towards the king. "Please. Both of you. Yes, that was Helios. He came directly to me." She looked at Aeëtes, but her gaze was detached, as if she was looking straight through him. "We need a new plan. Your mother is…unreachable."

She settled on her word choice carefully, not ready to have a discussion with him about Clymene. Aeëtes's eyes got wide, and his complexion blanched, panic consuming his features as he tried to rationalize her words. Hecate felt a deep twinge in her gut and an urge to go towards him to comfort him...but then she saw Faidra standing a few paces behind him.

There is someone else who is here to catch his tears. Hecate reminded herself harshly and put some effort into glamouring her expression again. The queen sensed the tension in the air and, ever the politician, gracefully stepped forward and offered Hecate her arm.

"Shall I escort you inside, Goddess? It looks like you have done a lovely job of remodeling your quarters already," she said in jest, with genuine warmth, looking up at the restored rooms. In that moment, Hecate had never been more grateful for the woman's soft presence. She accepted the queen's arm, grinning sweetly at her.

"You have no idea how many times I've had to redo my own kitchen."

The women walked in silence back to the guest chambers. Hecate felt a weight settling into her bones; too much had happened, and her heart felt like it was spiraling into a million different pieces. She didn't know how to break the news about Clymene to Aeëtes, but she knew that she had to be the one to do it.

As Hecate opened the door to disappear back into the solace of her rooms for a few hours, the queen placed a hand on her shoulder. "Would you like to join us for breakfast? Or...lunch? I'll be honest, I'm not quite sure what time it is now." She chuckled, and a small smile crossed Hecate's face, both women looking back out the windows as if to ensure that the sun was still in the sky.

"While I'm sure dining in your home is a lovely experience," Hecate shook her head, "I need a few hours to myself."

"Shall I send food to your rooms?"

"That would be lovely," Hecate murmured while departing, the queen slipping away as the door was shut between them. Hecate slid down the door, sinking to the tile, until she leaned over entirely and pressed her cheek to its cool surface.

She felt like she was overheating with the weight of the

world on her shoulders. Her mind wasn't working in a straight line, it felt like it was spiraling, and she couldn't channel her focus long enough to think about alternative solutions to Hera's curse. She let out a quiet sob against the floor and pushed herself up to a sitting position. There was a glimmer of magic that generated in front of her, one of her dogs pulling itself out of thin air. Hecate leaned forward and wrapped her arms around its neck, burying her face in its black fur. Her tears mixed with the red magic on its skin, and Hecate let herself go for the second time in as many days. She managed to get to the bedroom and threw herself on the mattress, several more dogs stepping out of the air and joining her. She fell asleep in the center of them, barricading herself from her emotions.

Someone brought food up to the room and ended up leaving it outside of the door. Hecate eventually pulled herself together and began pacing, nearly wearing a groove into the new flooring. Her brain whirled as she thought of any other way to reverse one of Hera's curses. It was easy enough to outdo them, but removing curses was a different matter entirely. Plus, Aeëtes was immortal but only a demi-god. She was nervous that anything too extreme would kill him.

A sharp knock at the door brought Hecate back from her reverie, and she blinked rapidly and looked around the room. It was dusk now, the sun finally setting behind the horizon. Whoever was at the door knocked again, bringing Hecate's attention fully back to the present.

She walked over and threw it open without thinking, and her heart stopped. Aeëtes stood in front of her, his eyes were red with tears, and his face was anxious.

"What do you—" Hecate started, but Aeëtes stormed in past her. Hecate slammed the door shut and turned to face him, feeling her ire rise.

"Faidra isn't my fiancée," Aeëtes blurted it out, looking utterly miserable. He hadn't changed since they got off the ship, and his hair was messy; even one of his sandals was untied. The words were a shock to Hecate's system, but she couldn't manage any response. She started searching her soul, trying to find some semblance of relief at his words, but there was nothing. Hecate could hardly bear to look at him and how distraught he seemed, but no matter how genuine, there was no balm to her bleeding heart in those words. The tension between them now was wholly unnatural, all the ease of their previous banter and budding intimacy was now gone. They stared at one another, and it might as well have been from miles apart instead of across the room.

"I don't want to play this game," Hecate finally sighed, sliding down into a nearby chair. "We need to focus on how to break Hera's curse."

"I don't care about that!" Aeëtes snapped, crossing the short distance between them, and kneeling down in front of Hecate. She jerked back from him in surprise, studying his face as her mind whirled with how panicked he was. "Please, you have to believe me. My parents have set up the arrangement. I told them I didn't want it, but they haven't listened."

Hecate's eyes screwed shut, and she tried to keep the tears at bay. She shook her head, but when she spoke, her voice was thick with tears. "I don't want to hear this. I can't, Aeëtes. If she cares for you and believes that you've been promised to one another... It's too much."

"It can't be. You have to understand, this isn't..."

"We. Need. To. Focus," Hecate spit the words out, standing up and striding away from Aeëtes. She needed to put some space between them before she caved. Aeëtes dropped his head to the chair where she had been sitting, letting his tears fall freely, as opposed to Hecate. She heard it and bit down on her cheek so harshly, it bled, keeping her eyes fixed out the window.

"Helios told me about your mother," she said softly, hoping to ease the blow. Aeëtes's head snapped up, and his mouth gaped, unable to find words but imploring her to go on. When she didn't after a minute, the atmosphere between them changed once more. The air got thick. Somehow, he knew what she was going to say. He straightened up, letting out a long, slow breath as if he was attempting to calm himself down.

Aeëtes stopped crying and looked down at his feet, both of them now unable to speak freely or even look at each other.

"She's gone, isn't she?" Aeëtes's voice was hoarse. Hecate nodded slowly and Aeëtes said nothing in response. He felt like he could see the barrier between them that Hecate was building, and it was only adding to his distress.

"Yes," Hecate confirmed, her tone soft. "Her name was Clymene. It sounded like your father really loved her."

"Not enough to have a family with her," Aeëtes snapped, his sadness morphing into frustration. "Sure, they had children, but abandoning Circe and me is hardly something to honor her memory." He was growling. Hecate agreed with him, making a soft noise of assent and picking up her head to finally look at him. She had buried her heart, but at the sight of his torn expression, it tried to crawl its way up from the depths.

"He's a jealous, flighty god, Aeëtes. You're nothing like him."

He didn't respond right away. Aeëtes finally met her gaze, his eyes pleading.

"Why are you still even here, Hecate?"

The question shocked her, and she found herself nearly running from the room. Aeëtes straightened until he was standing at his full height, something changing in his features. Aeëtes had never known his mother, and now he was confident that he didn't care to know his father. He had his real parents, no matter how tumultuous that relationship was. Now, he had Circe.

But he wanted Hecate.

He felt a final piece of his resolve come to him, settling into place. Hecate was still staring at him, full of surprise, and he repeated the question. "Why are you still here?"

"You know why!" The words tumbled out of her, almost defensively. "Without your mother, the spell that I had in mind won't work. I need to come up with something else."

"To defeat Hera."

"Yes!" Hecate scoffed, throwing her hands up in the air. "To defeat Hera." Aeëtes shook his head and took a step towards her.

"I'm serious. Yes, she's the worst, but I'm one person. You're doing all of this to defeat Hera? You're going to stay here now, for an indeterminate amount of time, to find a different spell—living outside of the Underworld, no less—just to defeat Hera?"

Hecate's expression grew tense, "My honor is on the line, Aeëtes." The words sounded hollow in her mouth. She sounded like an Olympian, and she hated it. It was a deceitful and prideful thing to say, to insist that the reason she remained now was one of principle and not because of the man in front of her.

"Your honor," he scoffed, turning away. "Of course."

There were a few more terse moments of silence, and Hecate watched as his hands flexed into fists and released several times.

"It's too much, Aeëtes. Faidra, Clymene... You need time to figure all of these things out," Hecate sighed, her traitorous tone turning wistful. "It doesn't matter what you think you feel for me. You're going to need more time."

"Time, time, time! Do you need more time or do I?" Aeëtes snapped, and everything around the couple started to cave-in on itself. There were tears in his eyes when he spoke, abandoning any rational principle left in his body and tossing the last of his care to the winds. "I was understanding when you said you needed time, Hecate. I got that. But it's been what, a thousand years? More?"

Hecate took a step forward, moving from the defensive to the offensive, nearly snarling at him. "Don't you tell me how long I need—"

"That's what you're trying to do to me, isn't it?" Aeëtes crossed his arms over his chest, and Hecate's mouth dropped open. She knew that she had been caught. Aeëtes had given her all the space that she needed to come around to the idea of them together, and he hadn't given her a single deadline or ultimatum. Now, here she stood, trying to force time on him.

"I meant it, Hecate. I don't know what else I need to do to convince you, but I meant it when I said that I wasn't going anywhere." Hecate felt a fresh wave of panic rising in her chest; this wasn't a conversation that she was ready to have. Regardless of the situation concerning Faidra, if Faidra had feelings for him or was expecting to marry him, she wasn't going to get in the way of things. She refused to be the other woman, no matter how many times Aeëtes tried to convince her that it wasn't the case. He had also just learned about Clymene. Now, here he was, refusing yet again to leave.

"Aeëtes…"

"No. I've never known my mother. I didn't think that she was living a happy, peaceful life somewhere. Despite what you may think, I'm not that naïve."

"I don't think that you're…"

"Stop." Aeëtes held up a hand and quieted her. "I'm not saying that you're wrong. It's a lot to process, but that's life. Things happen, especially when you're fucking immortal, if you haven't noticed. I know how I feel about you, and some bullshit engagement or family drama isn't going to change that. I'm not going to lose you, too."

"I won't be some pawn for your emotional regulation, Aeëtes." Hecate tried to put some anger in her voice, but there was none left. It came out pleading, and she hated herself for it. He only shook his head, throwing up his hands and seemingly praying for someone to listen to him.

"You're the only person I know who sees yourself as a pawn." He frowned when he spoke, rubbing his eyes like he was tired. "I'm not doing this now." Aeëtes started heading towards the door as Hecate stared at him, dumbstruck. He paused at the threshold, looking over his shoulder at her with an expression that was equal parts exhausted and hopeful. "I'm not going anywhere."

"You're standing at the door right now."

Aeëtes shrugged. "I'll try again tomorrow." He was gone. Yet, Hecate realized that she knew he would be back. She *trusted* that he would be back.

She didn't like how it made her feel.

✟ ✟ ✟

HECATE KNEW that she was hiding. She didn't leave her room for the rest of the day, even once the sun finally set on what had been a very long, emotionally overwhelming day. The moonlight was coming in through the open window, and she leaned herself against the wall, breathing in the night air and listening to the sea down in the harbor. There was something calming about Colchis, and she could see how a younger Clymene and Helios would've found some solace in this place. All it held for her now was heartbreak.

The breeze picked up outside her window, suddenly smelling overwhelmingly of myrrh, and she quickly took a few steps back. She would know the scent of that magic anywhere. The air in her room began to circulate, as if it were moving in a vortex around the corners, until there was another sharp gust of wind, which caused Hermes to come tumbling in through the window.

The god could barely fit and nearly got stuck in the frame,

pushing himself through with a grunt and landing on the floor in a rather undignified tangle. Hermes was all golden limbs and blonde curls, even his winged sandals causing yellow sparks when they scraped on the floor. It brought a smile to Hecate's face in the darkness, even when she felt like she was slowly carving pieces of her heart up.

"Hermes, have you ever made a normal entrance?" she chided him, sliding a hand to her hip. Hermes made a rather undignified squawking sound as he stood, shaking himself and adjusting his shoe.

"My vixen." He grinned, holding out both of his arms and presenting himself to her like a present. "Where would the fun in that be? Besides, no one suspects anything when you make as obnoxious of an entrance as I do." He winked at her, his eyes full of trickery.

"Trickster," Hecate quipped at him, unable to keep a little mirth out of her voice whenever she spoke to him. Hermes only smiled, giving her an exaggerated bow and plopping down into a chair, remarkably ungracefully.

"You say that like it's a bad thing. Now, O Fearful One, why did you need me so terribly?"

"Need you?" Hecate's eyebrows rose as she eyed him carefully. "Where did you get that idea from?"

Hermes shrugged, rubbing his fingers together until a trickle of golden magic appeared, solidifying itself into a cup of nectar. He sipped it slowly, keeping his eyes on the goddess, and his lips shone with gold as he set the cup back down. "Everyone seems to forget I'm the messenger god, too." He was calculating now, his voice taking on a harder edge. Hecate knew this side of him, too, but it was rare to see both the devious trickster and calculating messenger at once. He shrugged, running a finger around the lip of his cup. "I spoke to Helios. Rather, Helios was venting about his day, rather loudly, I might add, and I heard about it. I came straight here to see you, obviously."

"Obviously," Hecate deadpanned, eyeing him with scrutiny. She trusted Hermes, for the most part, but she knew that he could be bought and paid for, like any Olympian. He played both sides during the titan war to his advantage, something that she would be wise to never forget. Hermes made a big show of looking around the room.

"I don't see Aeëtes here. I was so hoping that you two would be looking for a third this evening." His tone was conspiratorial, but Hecate knew that he also wasn't joking in the slightest. She bristled slightly at the thought of Aeëtes.

"Ah," he said slowly, "So we're both going to be disappointed tonight then."

"I don't know what you mean."

Hermes snapped his fingers and his cup disappeared, and he motioned for Hecate to sit in the chair opposite him. She did so, but not without taking her eyes off him.

"Level with me, Goddess." Hermes's eyes were open and expressive, and she sensed a bit of his devilish demeanor trickle away. "You haven't been in the Underworld for a few weeks now. I know that your trip was open-ended, but here you are in Colchis. What's happening?"

Hecate chewed on her lip, her silence more telling than almost anything she would've said out loud.

"Ah." Hermes nodded, and he snapped his fingers again, two more cups of nectar appearing in his hands. He handed one to her with a dramatic grimace. "It seems I took the drinks away too early. Drink up, tell your best friend Hermes what's happening with the very pretty prince boy."

Hecate let out a sharp burst of laughter. Hermes's ability to shift from calculating mischief to outlandish companion never ceased to make her smile. She accepted the cup from him and took a long sip, letting it refresh her tired bones.

"I learned about Clymene today."

"Ah." Hermes nodded, taking a sip of his own. "A sad story, that one."

"You knew?" She looked at him in shock, but Hermes only shrugged.

"I know a lot of things. Let's assume when it comes to the gods and their affairs," he haggled his eyebrows, "I know *everything.*"

Hecate scoffed playfully but continued. "Then you know we can't use his mother for the spell that I need to break Hera's curse on him. Circe's remedy continues to hold, but we don't know for how long. He also learned about Clymene today, too, so…"

"Let me guess," Hermes crossed his legs at the knee, "you think that by removing yourself from the equation, you're going to give him some space to work out his mommy issues, and he'll realize he doesn't love you?"

Hecate blushed a furious shade of crimson and sat up straighter, stuttering. "N-no!"

"That's a yes." Hermes shrugged, taking another sip. "You're making excuses for Faidra, too, I imagine?" Hecate nearly fell out of her chair.

"You know about her, too?"

Hermes looked bored. "I told you, it would be so much easier if you just acted like I knew everything."

Hecate stared at him warily for a second before she visibly slumped in her chair.

"Yes. Fine. It's the news of his mother *and* an engagement though, Hermes. Surely he needs—"

"Hecate, stop talking," Hermes quipped, sitting up a little straighter and pointing a finger at her. Hecate's eyes got wide. "Yes, I know, someone just told the mighty and terrifying Underworld goddess to shut up." He rolled his eyes. "Moving on. Darling, having mommy issues and some bizarre engagement his parents decided on doesn't make Aeëtes a bad person. Hell, it just makes him an Olympian." Hermes laughed at his own joke, snapping his fingers and refilling their cups. Hecate floundered slightly, trying to come up with a response but Hermes kept talking.

"He's a good man." His voice was gentle, and he leaned forward, grabbing hold of Hecate's hand and giving it a squeeze. "I know that you didn't expect to hear that from me, but it's true. You can see it in his eyes, Hecate, my *gods*." Hermes shook his head. "That man *loves* you."

Hecate suddenly choked back a sob, a few tears falling down her face. She knew that Hermes was right, but hearing it come out of his mouth—the last place that she expected it—sent a million more cracks into the empty place in her chest.

"Oh, my veracious night terror," Hermes crooned, standing up and pulling Hecate to her feet. He wrapped her up in a tight hug, kissing her forehead. "Look at you, with *feelings*. It's adorable. You're suffering like the rest of us."

"I hate you," Hecate muttered, the words sounding muffled in his chest.

"I know." He patted her hair a few times. "This is scary. You're very scary, though, so you'll figure it out." He pulled away from her and cupped her cheek, swiping away the last of her tears with his thumb. His smirk was back as he looked at her with a glint in his eyes. "Doesn't mean you can't make him work for it a little."

"Hermes!" Hecate chided him, giving him a playful shove. The scent of myrrh picked up around them again, and Hecate knew he was getting ready to depart.

"Just a thought!" He clapped his hands together. "Everyone loves a hot man on his knees."

"You—" Hecate picked up her cup to throw it at him, but he was already gone, his laugh disappearing on the wind.

❧ 31 ❧

Hecate waited until first light before nearly bolting from the palace. She was feeling more resolved after her conversation with Hermes, but there were fragments of fear that were hanging around in her mind. She wanted to make it into the center of town and visit her temple; there was nothing that calmed her racing mind more, her ability to connect with women and help them ease their woes. The air was thick with the smell of smoke and the sea, and she couldn't help but think of Aeëtes somewhere in the palace behind her. He wasn't lying when he said that his parents put together the engagement—that much she trusted at this point —but she had reservations without knowing Faidra.

Have they ever been close? Does she feel for him? What does that even look like, if I'm *the one getting in the way?* Hecate looked at the lemon trees as she wound her way to the marketplace, making sure that her glamour was in place. She had a tendency to scowl when deep in thought and she knew she was doing it now. *You could just ask Aeëtes, you fool.* Her thoughts argued with one another, one side of her brain wanting to just return home to the Underworld and the other side demanding she go speak to Aeëtes. *Go to the temple first.* A third part of her brain, a mediator of sorts, chimed in. *I'm going insane.*

One thing that always surprised Hecate was how the mortal cities almost all felt the same. She knew that there were rich differences, and she enjoyed them all, but there was a comforting homecoming of sorts for her at every temple. Marketplaces were crowded; people yelled and laughed in the streets, and the prayers of the devoted and the desperate tickled her skin like whispers. She weaved through the crowds effortlessly, catching the tail end of haggling conversations and early morning meetings. Her temple was hidden behind a few of the market stalls, the smell of cinnamon incense making its way up to the heavens. Hecate always thought that was ironic —the smoke of her offerings always went up, up, up when she so often was in rest beneath their feet.

It was crowded as she moved towards the entrance, her glamour so well intact that none of the devotees around her recognized their goddess. She felt her magic ebb and flow in response to them, the power to soothe and seek revenge, when necessary, came flooding out of her. The inside of the temple was similar to any one that she had seen before, simple, but she appreciated how well cared for it was.

Hecate was glad to see that there was no statue of her in the center of the long hall. It always made her a little embarrassed to come face to face with the likeliness of herself. Instead, there were two great growling marble statues of two dogs that flanked the entrance to the altar room. She grinned as she ducked in between them, commending their accuracy. Once she was inside, she sucked in a deep breath, mingling with the women around her. They were of all ages and class, some dripping in jewelry and others in simply spun robes. Women lounged on cushions on the floor or knelt in prayer at the apex of the room, lightning candles and additional sticks of incense and clumps of scented resin to amplify their requests.

Hecate always debated whether to tell them she heard them all, incense or not, but she did so love the way it smelled. Her heart was eased in the familiarity of a setting that she knew, leaving her concerns outside.

She had admitted to Aeëtes that it was a self-imposed fear that her acolytes wouldn't support her having a partner. Yet, the thought crossed her mind as she sat amongst them.

Let's limit our excuses to maybe one or two at a time. It was Hermes's voice that she heard chastising her in her head, as if he was there. Hecate was content to push the matter aside for the rest of the day until she stumbled into a woman on her left and everything within her ceased up.

She grabbed the woman's waist to keep them both from falling, and as soon as she initiated the touch, a long stream of the woman's prayers began flooding Hecate's mind.

He is a wonderful man. A very kind man.

He's never here.

He is a blessing.

I do not want to marry him.

Goddess, please. I cannot bear this; both of our hearts will break. I do not want to marry him. If he only looked at me long enough to talk to me, I could tell him.

I do not want to marry him.

Hecate's heart seized as Aeëtes's face flashed in her mind. She blinked rapidly and came back to the present, the voice dying out in her conscience. The woman that Hecate was still holding onto, was Faidra.

"Excuse me?" she said softly, not recognizing Hecate under her glamour. "Are you alright?"

It took Hecate a second to compose herself before she nodded.

You're all out of excuses, my terrifying one. Hecate fought the urge to roll her eyes as her internal monologue sounded a lot like Hermes.

"Can I speak to you outside for a second?" Hecate asked her gently, removing her hands from Faidra's waist. She nodded, a look of concern crossing her face, as she let Hecate lead them outside. They took a few steps away from the entrance to the temple, ducking into an alley, where Faidra paused, only looking slightly dubious that she had now followed a woman she didn't know into an alley outside. Hecate looked around, and once she was sure that no one could see them, she let her glamour drop.

As soon as it fell, Faidra gasped, her hand coming up and covering her face. "I'm so sorry," she started speaking quickly, shaking her head, "I had no idea. I did not recognize you..."

"You couldn't have." Hecate stepped closer to her and put a hand on Faidra's arm. "Please do not chastise yourself for this, for not recognizing me on the spot." Hecate let out a small laugh, as if this was a joke between the two of them, and it eased Faidra's worries. She looked up at Hecate with imploring eyes, and Hecate could see the tears that were building there.

"I wanted to ask you ever since you got here if you... if you had maybe heard my prayers." Faidra made a sniffling sound and wiped at her nose with the back of her hand. "But you were always with the queen. I didn't want to misspeak in front of her or speak poorly of my situation."

Hecate gave her a soft smile in encouragement and knew that she was telling the truth.

"You are kind to be so considerate of others, Faidra." Hecate tilted her head to one side. "I have heard your prayers. It is true that you do not want to marry Aeëtes, then?"

"Yes, oh to the gods, yes. Neither of us wants this. I don't think he even realizes that I don't want this, but I can't get him alone to tell him."

"He is a very good match, you know." Hecate struggled to keep her voice impassive, curious to see what Faidra's reaction would be. The woman flushed, pushing some of the ringlet curls out of her face.

"Aeëtes is a fine match but..." There was a gleam in her eyes that Hecate identified immediately, a look that she had been trained over the centuries to identify. A look that every woman knew.

"There is another." Hecate winked at Faidra, wanting to make sure that the woman felt encouraged and not threatened. She only blushed further and nodded, her curls bouncing around her open face.

"He's back home."

"Where is home for you, child?" There was a commotion outside of the alley as a heavy wagon passed, and Hecate pulled them a little further into the shadows to ensure that they weren't overheard.

"Near Athens," Faidra replied, looking wistfully up at the sky. "My father is a tradesman, a rather wealthy one, but this was his opportunity to get into the echelons of royalty. I have other sisters. If I agreed to this, then it would mean better matches for them, too."

"You are kindhearted to think of them. You would sacrifice your own happiness?" Hecate implored her, her mind already beginning to tick.

"For my sisters? Absolutely. I couldn't refuse the match without it being a huge blow to our family. My sister's matches would suffer, if I ever got another proposal at all."

"And your beloved? He did not come to propose to you or contest the match?"

Faidra flushed a little brighter at that, her cheeks turning red.

"He works for my father." Faidra swallowed thickly. "My father would have never approved the match with someone who makes so little. He would've seen it as a breach of loyalty, too, and he would have lost his job."

"I see." Hecate was fully attuned to Faidra's story, her own thoughts of Aeëtes taking a backseat for a moment. These were the moments when women cried out to her for help, and she would damn herself for the rest of her immortal life if she did not answer the call. "What if he were to fall into prosperity?"

Faidra's eyes got wide before she sighed and let out a long sigh. "I don't think it would be enough. What's better than a crown prince when it comes to a marriage proposal?"

"Your father sounds like he is certainly...entrepreneurial." Hecate rolled her eyes, which got a laugh from Faidra. She was quiet for a moment as Hecate began thinking before she bit her lip and spoke again.

"Goddess? Perhaps if, well, if Aeëtes was the one who had an even better match, then the engagement would be broken. If he had an even better option, then no one would fault me or his family for taking it."

Hecate was confused as she looked at the woman, her face pensive. "If Aeëtes was the one who had a better match?"

Faidra looked downright sheepish as she nodded her head. "If Aeëtes were to become, say...a king consort...of an immortal variety."

It was Hecate's turn to blush as she ran her mind through what Faidra was saying. Certainly, something couldn't be falling together right in front of her? Of course she had known since Hermes visited her the night before what she was going to do about Aeëtes. Her heart left her no choice. If this were an opportunity to help Faidra reunite with her love, effectively dissolving the engagement, then it would remove one of the last blockages in their way.

Don't forget that you still have a curse to break. Hecate made a mental list of all the things that were standing in between her and Aeëtes, and she was surprised to find that once she got out of her own way, there were very few things left. If any at all.

"If I have misspoken, Goddess, please do forgive me." Faidra's voice was pleading, and Hecate realized that she hadn't spoken for a few minutes, making Faidra nervous that she had offended the goddess.

"Oh!" Hecate grabbed Faidra's hands and gave them a comforting squeeze. "Oh, no, you're fine, Faidra. I was thinking through what you have said. I should know by now not to deal with mortal politics before my breakfast." She grinned widely, dropping Faidra's hands and giving her a wink. "I do think that you might be onto something, however. Finish your prayers and your errands, and do not seek me out at the palace. I will see you the next time I summon the king and queen for an audience. Everything will be handled, Faidra."

"Oh, Hecate! Bless you." Faidra started crying tears of joy, throwing her arms around Hecate's middle. Hecate hugged the woman back, placing her chin on Faidra's head and letting her gather her composure for a few minutes longer.

"It will be sorted. I will orchestrate it so the king is the one to break the engagement between you and Aeëtes, freeing you from any repercussions. You will send a letter to your father and alert him that you are coming home, and under what conditions. Perhaps you shall find that by the time you make it back to Athens, your very enterprising father has already secured a match for you with a member of his household that he trusts, who has recently fallen into a miraculous fortune."

Faidra pulled back from Hecate, fresh, ecstatic tears still dampening her cheeks, while she wiped at her eyes and smiled. "Goddess, I will worship you for all the days of my life. Truly, every woman is indebted to you."

Hecate gave her another sly wink and let her glamour slowly pour back over her face until she appeared just like any other mortal woman in front of Faidra.

Faidra smiled, reaching out and giving Hecate's hand a squeeze before she slipped out of the alley and disappeared, honoring Hecate's request to not seek her out anymore until the time was right.

Hecate watched Faidra go, and in the deepest recesses of her chest, felt the scattered, tiny parts of her heart begin to beat again as they assembled themselves once more.

The sun was almost at midday now, and there was only one thing that Hecate needed to do next.

I need to tell Aeëtes I love him.

❧ 32 ❧

H ecate travelled on human legs, but she had never felt
so free. She bid farewell to Faidra and began
walking towards the palace, slowly at first, but as
soon as she was out of sight from the temple, she began to run.
There was something gloriously unhinged about it, hidden
from her immortal identity, the hem of her peplos whipping
around her ankles. She dodged in and out of the marketplace,
ducking underneath a stall and not stopping when her hair fell
out of her braid. She hadn't run like this since she was a child.
One of those carefree, exuberant sprints, where nothing
mattered except getting where you were going as *fast* as you
could, with no regard to how you looked or who saw you.

It was wholly undignified, and she knew if anyone recognized her, they would be shocked, but nothing else mattered
except getting to the palace and finding Aeëtes.

I love him. I love him. I love *him!* It was the only thought that
rang through her head and her heart, pushing her on even
when her side started to split. Not even a mortal body could
get her to slow her pace. She wound up through the lemon
trees and inhaled great, greedy gulps of air, nearly leaping up
the palace steps and ignoring the guards. Hecate let her

glamour drop but didn't slow down, narrowly missing crashing into a servant holding a basket of food. The servant swerved at the last second and managed to avoid spilling the contents but took a few shaky steps backward.

"I'm so sorry!" Hecate called over her shoulder, but she didn't stop.

The serving girl looked like she had seen a ghost, although Hecate did look a little half wild. Her face felt like it might crack in two with the strength of her smile, and she felt her stomach twisting. She raced through the halls, popping her head in and out various antechambers and storerooms, until she had almost made a full circle. The doors to the great hall were there to greet her, and Hecate finally slowed down slightly, wondering where she could find Aeëtes.

He hasn't gone somewhere, has he?

No sooner did she think it than she managed to conjure him. The doors swung open, and Aeëtes walked out, his father next to him. He looked muted, dressed in a shorter chiton that matched his father's, his features drawn in tight, and his hair pulled back. The king's expression was no friendlier, and whatever they had been discussing hadn't put either of them in good moods.

"Aeëtes!" Hecate called out from down the hall, and his entire body responded. Aeëtes whipped around to find the source of her voice, his face lighting up and his entire countenance brightening when he saw her.

"Hecate." He started laughing when he saw her appearance. "Is there a fire somewhere? What has gotten into you?" He had no idea what had happened to her, but even from a distance he could see the joy in her eyes.

Hecate had run through this scenario a million different times in her head, even in moments of doubt when she was certain there was no future for them. In some versions, it was a quiet moment between the two of them. There were other renditions that involved loud declarations of undying passions.

None of those made-up stories in her head proved to be nearly
as exhilarating as this moment where Hecate stood, a stone's
throw from Aeëtes and the king of Colchis, and yelled down
the hallway at the top of her lungs.

"I love you, Aeëtes!"

Her voice echoed throughout the palace, sounding abun-
dant and practically effervescent. Hecate clapped her hands
over her mouth immediately, and starting giggling like a
schoolgirl, but she couldn't help herself. The change in Aeëtes
was instantaneous. Without warning, the entire hallway was
full of a shining light that was so intense, it threatened to block
out the sun. It pulsed like a beacon for a few seconds before
disappearing, revealing Aeëtes, smiling like a fool and running
at full speed toward her.

Hecate grabbed her peplos and held it up as she took off in
a run, both of them colliding into each other with a force that
rivaled gravity. That was what they were—two celestial bodies
that had contained multitudes, hurt and death and everything
in between, but had finally found a way to choose life. Hecate
jumped up into Aeëtes's arms and wrapped her legs around his
waist as he caught her without hesitation.

Aeëtes cupped her face as he looked at her, both of them
nearly panting with the exertion and excitement. He laughed,
loud and unencumbered, and looked at her with the most open
expression that she had ever seen.

"I love you too, little witch," he whispered the words like
they were sacraments, closing the rest of the gap between them
and capturing her mouth with his. There was finally nothing
that was keeping them apart, not a wound or a wall, and the
embrace reflected that for the first time. Hecate gave herself
entirely over to Aeëtes, relaxing all her weight onto him as he
held her. The kiss... Nothing else mattered but that kiss.
Aeëtes kissed her like she was water in a drought, and Hecate
felt every last splinter and crack in her heart shatter until she
was wide open to him. She felt his hands cupping her jaw and

holding onto her waist, every part of him seemed to fit against her perfectly. Every solid inch of him was met with soft curve, and they both thought that they were going to incinerate themselves on the spot.

It set their souls on fire and burned their fears to ash, fortifying everything that they had ever felt for one another. Hecate wound her hands up into Aeëtes's hair and pulled, breaking his lips from hers as they both tried to breathe like they'd forgotten how.

Hecate dropped her head to his shoulder as he held her, refusing to put her down. Aeëtes leaned his cheek to hers, chuckling softly until it got louder and louder, and both of them collapsed into delirious bouts of laughter right there in the middle of the hall. It had cleared out quickly after Hecate's arrival. Aeëtes leaned against the stone and slowly slid down it, until he was sitting on the floor with Hecate straddling his lap. Neither of them said anything else; they just laughed, running their hands over each other's faces and bodies to prove that it was real.

Aeëtes leaned in to kiss her again, his lips grazing hers as he tightened his grip on her. "Am I dreaming?" He murmured against her skin, leaving goosebumps in his wake. Hecate shivered, her whole body feeling like it was pure electricity, and she shook her head.

"I am so very, very alive right now." She let her head fall back, and Aeëtes's lips traced down, nipping along her jaw, down her neck, so, so close to her chest...

"Say it again." His voice was raspy as he sat up a little straighter, kissing behind her ear and nipping at her sweet spot. "I have to hear it."

"I love you, Aeëtes." Hecate smiled, and there was no hesitation in her voice. Her chest was rising and falling with each breath, her thoughts a delicious, scattered mess that she never wanted to clean up.

"Oh gods," Aeëtes cursed, keeping an arm around Hecate's

waist. He effortlessly lifted them both up in an impressive bout of strength that made Hecate's insides clench. She made a little squeak at the sudden movement, tightening her legs around him, but he didn't drop her. She knew that he never would. He started moving, and she had no idea where to, but she didn't care. Her arms were haphazardly tossed around his neck as she stared at him, both of them smiling like children, who only had eyes for each other.

"Take me upstairs," Hecate whispered, leaning forward and pressing kisses of her own to Aeëtes's chest.

"Anything. Anything you fucking want," Aeëtes grunted with a huff, and she could tell that neither of them was going to last long once they got behind closed doors.

It took a disturbingly long time for them to make it to the door to Aeëtes's chambers. Hecate unhooked her legs from around him and stood gracefully, but as soon as her legs touched the ground, the entire palace shook. There were a myriad of sharp, breaking sounds and shouts from the servants, and the couple watched as a statue toppled over a few feet away.

The mood vanished instantly, both Hecate and Aeëtes spinning around and evaluating the hallway as if they could identify the source of the threat. It stopped as soon as it started, but they held on through the aftershocks as tremors shook the stone walls.

"As much as I would want to take credit for that," Aeëtes grunted, "I don't think we literally made the ground shake."

"Not yet, anyway," Hecate whined, both of them now feeling the edges of their madness slip away as they focused on the chaos surrounding them. Aeëtes made a frustrated noise and a not-so-subtle move to adjust himself.

"What do you think that was?" Aeëtes assessed some of the damage in the hall, but the shaking had stopped as if it had never happened. Hecate felt her power bubbling to the surface, evaluating everything from the sunlight to the breeze. No sooner did she step away from Aeëtes than a thick, cloying scent came in on the wind. It was one that they both recognized, full of rotting flowers and sickly-sweet fruit.

"Fuck," Aeëtes growled, shivering once.

Hecate felt her blood beginning to boil, her face contorting into a mask of rage. She started to surrender her mortal body, red sparks jumping from her fingers and her hair beginning to stick up at the ends. The heads of the maiden and the crone began flickering on her shoulders like fire, and great columns of black smoke appeared on her right and her left. Aeëtes hardly reacted, but he did step away from the smoke just in time, and two dogs emerged from it. Hecate bit her lip and made a sharp whistle, snapping her fingers and sending the dogs in opposite directions. They went off down the hall, baying like hounds, thick on the scent of Hera and trying to detect her presence in the palace.

Aeëtes turned to Hecate, looking nervous for the first time. "My mother... Hecate, I don't want anything to happen to her."

She nodded in agreement, neither of them commenting on the fact that he only mentioned his mother. There was another tremor that rocked the palace, and Hecate sent a wave of power out through the foundations to meet it. The walls and floorboards were covered in a sheen of red magic, fortifying the building and fighting off the ricochets of Hera's threats on the palace.

"Follow me," Hecate demanded, but she held her hand out behind herself as she walked. Aeëtes grabbed it and pulled her closer to him, intertwining their fingers as they ran outside. "That conniving—" Hecate fought to keep herself from cursing as they hit the tiled steps.

They walked out into chaos. The entire sky had turned a disgusting shade of pink, covered in green and blueish clouds like a decomposing bruise. Even in the distance, the sea seemed rough and choppy. The air was thick and humid, the scent of rotting flowers on the breeze. There were people running in every direction, guards shouting orders and servants running for their lives. Aeëtes grabbed the sleeve of a passing man, stopping him as he tried to run past.

"Have you seen the queen?" he barked, his voice full of concern.

The man shook his head, prying Aeëtes's hands off him and disappearing. There was a shrieking sound that echoed on the wind, getting Hecate and Aeëtes's attention as they stepped off the palace steps. A vortex was taking shape in the heavens above them, the beginnings of a whirlwind making its way down to the earth.

"Hecate," Aeëtes cautioned.

She barely heard him as her eyes glazed over, glowing red, the faces of the maiden and the crone staring out at the crowd around them. She left red footprints as she walked away from the palace and into the chaos, Aeëtes trailing after her. Smoke gathered around her ankles, spinning in a circle that killed the grass where she was standing. She was muttering words under her breath that Aeëtes didn't catch, and he didn't know if he would understand them if he did hear them. Scrolling, red text appeared written all over her arms and legs, and a glowing triple moon was emblazoned on her forehead.

"Hecate!" Aeëtes called out to her again, the wind escalating around them.

The trees were nearly bent to the crowd, leaves and pieces of rubble whipping around their heads. Most of the people around them had run for cover, leaving Hecate and Aeëtes standing alone as they waited to face Hera as she descended from the sky.

"Grab a hold of me!" Hecate screamed, her voice barely carrying over the wind. She dug her heels into the ground, and Aeëtes leapt forward, holding onto her elbow tightly and gluing himself to her side. He watched as the dead grass beneath them withered away to dust before his eyes, the earth cracking in a nearly perfect, concentric circle.

"What's happening?!" Aeëtes was shouting, squinting as he tried to see through the storm unleashing around them. Hecate turned to him, her mouth twisted up into a grim smile.

"We're dragging this bitch down to hell."

❧ 33 ❧

As soon as Hecate said it, everything went black. Aeëtes felt the ground give out from underneath him, and they were falling. The air was knocked from his lungs as he tumbled through the air, no longer able to see Hecate or even the light above him. It seemed to go on forever, as if time and space had been pulled and twisted into another dimension. He spun aimlessly, clawing at anything that he could find purchase on, but came up with nothing. Aeëtes yelled out for Hecate's name in the darkness, feeling tension building behind his eyes as he cried out into the abyss.

No response.

He did it again, screaming with everything that he had left, the disillusioning feeling of falling head over foot nearly wiping him out. He didn't know how long he had been falling when he resolved himself to some sort of inevitable end, not even entirely sure what that would be. He had only one thought as he tossed over his control to the darkness.

I wish we had more time.

The darkness responded.

"I should've known that your faith would be shaken with

just a little free fall." It was Hecate's voice, deeper, but full of jest.

"Hecate!" Aeëtes cried out for her, still falling, but trying to situate himself in midair as he did so. He desperately looked around for her, trying to catch even the smallest glimpse of her hair or eyes to right him. There was a great, blinding flash, and everything around him was illuminated, as if the sun had suddenly rose to its midpoint.

Before Aeëtes could process a single sight around him, the soft earth rose up to greet him, and he landed on it gently, as if he had only tripped over a stone. Aeëtes was on his back, and he blinked rapidly, shaking his head to try and make sense of his surroundings. He pushed himself up to his elbows, taking in the landscape around him. They were in a field of some sort, with a forest tree line not far off, and a river running through it.

A bright light, like a shooting star, appeared in the hazy sky and began falling down to the earth where Aeëtes sat. He watched it, transfixed, and as it got closer, he realized that it was Hecate. Her entire body was encapsulated in a red flame, and her skin was crawling with red snakes, emblazoned on her skin like living tattoos. She was dropping from the same height that he had fallen from, albeit, doing it much more gracefully. When she landed, she did so on her feet and sent a massive tremor through the earth beneath him. Aeëtes jumped up to his feet and ran to her, completely unfazed by her appearance, sticking his hands through the flame to cup her face and pull her to him.

He could feel Hecate smile into their embrace, but Aeëtes couldn't stop; he kissed her until he needed to breathe. When he finally pulled away, Hecate was laughing, but she stroked his cheek gently.

"I should have warned you," she smiled, "but it was a little fun to watch." She winked and Aeëtes could only shake his head in wonderment. He had a feeling he knew where they were, solely based on the fact that Hecate seemed more *alive*. Her eyes were brighter, and her countenance seemed lighter. There were also the manifestations of her power, which were all-encompassing and written all over her skin, surrounding her in flame.

"Where are we?" Aeëtes asked, finally sounding a little bit more like himself, now that he caught his breath. He looked around again. It could have been anywhere in Greece, but there was something...different about it.

"This is the Underworld, my love," Hecate nodded towards the forest and the river. "We're on the edge of Asphodel and Elysium. That's Lethe."

"Why are we here?" Aeëtes was only slightly overwhelmed, which was a rather impressive response when you suddenly dropped through the earth and into the Underworld.

Hecate rolled her shoulders once and took a few steps away from him, peering up into the sky as if she was looking straight through the hole that they had fallen through. "I had to draw Hera away from Colchis. Fights between gods don't end well if they happen in the mortal realm."

"They end up fine for the gods," Aeëtes shrugged, but Hecate only turned to look at him.

"Exactly," she chided. "It wouldn't have gone well for anyone else. Your mother included."

"Do you think she...?"

"She's fine," Hecate affirmed, stepping back towards Aeëtes and grabbing his hand. "I sensed her before I pulled us down here. Now, look, Hera will be pulling through any moment. It takes her a little bit longer to get down here than me. Do not interfere, do you understand me, Aeëtes?"

His brow furrowed as he angled his body towards her, wrapping an arm around her waist and tugging her to him. "I don't like it, Hecate. It's too simple. After all this time, you're just going to drop Hera into the Underworld and fight it out? Why not do this before?"

Hecate chewed on her lip, a flicker of insecurity appearing on her face. She let out a long sigh, "It was about honor. I didn't want to fight Hera head-on. She is sneaky and underhanded, and this isn't going to end in a way that brings about a simple resolution. And... I was worried about you." She said the last part in a rush, looking away from Aeëtes as if she didn't want to see his face. He lit up. "I still don't know what's going to happen to your curse. We'll have to cross that bridge when we come to it, but before, I wanted to try and find every possible way to break it. Curses, witchcraft, spells, they have a life of their own, Aeëtes. Taking out Hera won't necessarily break the curse, even though she created it. Now that we know about Clymene, I don't know how I'll break it but...we have to stop Hera first. It has to take precedence, she—"

"She'll destroy the mortal world in pursuit."

"Yes." Hecate let out another long sigh. "There's more."

"Go on," Aeëtes said gently, reaching his hand through the flames once more to tuck a piece of hair behind her ear.

Hecate seemed pained, leaning her head into his embrace. She paused for a moment, letting her eyes fall closed, before she continued. "Like I said, curses have a life of their own. Defeating Hera doesn't mean that it'll break the curse, but it also means..."

"Tell me."

"It also means that it could kill you." Aeëtes sucked in a sharp breath but didn't respond, imploring her to go on. "It's why I wanted to break the curse, first. I... I don't know if I loved you, but I cared about you from the moment I saw you." Hecate let out a small hiccup, and a few tears appeared on her cheeks. "I had to try and break the curse before engaging with Hera in a fight to the end. Which this will be. She's too petty to let it be anything else. That curse ties you to her in some way, which means fighting her could break the curse, not affect it, or kill you." She flinched when she said the last part, as if it physically pained her. Aeëtes said nothing for a few minutes, his arms keeping Hecate close to his body. There was a soft breeze that moved through the fields, as if it was pushing them together. They stayed there for a moment, witch and demi-god, a creature of the Underworld and a child of the sun.

When Aeëtes spoke, it was full of charm. "Who cares if it kills me?"

"What?" Hecate pulled away from him in shock, fear blanketing her features. "How could you say that?"

Aeëtes shrugged, his smile now stretching from ear to ear. "I'm already in the Underworld, aren't I?"

"Y-yes, but..."

"And you're the necromancer, aren't you?" Aeëtes slid a finger under her chin and tilted Hecate's face up to his. Her expression was bewildered, tears flowing freely now. She could only nod in response. Aeëtes's smile softened as he leaned down and pressed a chaste kiss to her forehead.

"Then what does it matter if I'm dead? I'll still have you."

Hecate felt like her body was going to explode into a million pieces, her joy and relief rushing over her in a palpable sensation. The last of her fear ebbed away as Aeëtes managed to close the wound that had been bleeding for a thousand years. His lips trailed over her skin as he moved down her nose, gently kissing her lips once.

"Not even death will keep me from you, little witch."

Hecate threw her arms around his shoulders and kissed him back, the flames leaping from her body to his, encompassing both in the rich, ebbing tide of her power.

Aeëtes's arms slid down her back and gripped her thighs, getting ready to pick her up and take them both to the ground, but a massive screeching sound pierced through the air. Hecate ripped herself from Aeëtes and stood a few feet away, her arms ready at her sides as she started scanning the heavens for the threat.

Aeëtes looked up and saw it, that same dreadful vortex appearing in the skies above them. It was tinged in the cantan-

kerous shades of pink and green, the smell of rotting flowers
putrefying on the wind. There was another deadly screech, and
he watched on as out dropped Hera, hurtling towards the
ground. Her long, signature brunette hair was whipping
around her face, her eyes tinged with a sick glow. She landed
on the ground with the same impact as Hecate, sending
another shockwave through the Underworld, and Aeëtes got a
good look at the queen of the gods enraged.

He had seen her mad before, but never like this. She
looked more like a demon or a deranged siren than a goddess.
Her skin had taken on the appearance of a bruise, and the hem
of her tunic was strewn with rotting flowers. Even her hands
had long, broken nails, nearly filed to the shape of claws. She
stalked towards Hecate, and every step she took, the grass died
beneath her feet. Hera was everything that was supposed to be
divine — flowers, light, and growth — but she was filled with rot
from the inside.

Hecate turned to look at Aeëtes, tossing her chin in his
direction. "Stand back, Aeëtes, and get out of the way."

He did what she said without question; he was no fool to
think that he would be able to help in a fight between the
goddesses. Aeëtes found a large boulder a stone's throw away,
and ran to it, standing at its side to keep an eye on the feud.

Hecate had turned her attention to Hera, the tri-head
appearing, and the snakes on her skin began moving. They
writhed until they slowly became three-dimensional then
pulled themselves off her skin and dropped to the ground.
Whenever one fell, a new one would take its place around her
arms, until it, too, fell off. They followed Hecate as she walked,
almost like a living, undulating train of her skirt.

Hera and Hecate stalked towards one another until they
were barely forty feet apart.

"All I have ever asked is that you give me what's mine,"
Hera hissed, and Aeëtes could hear her voice echoing
throughout the Underworld. Hecate shook her head once, not

even honoring Hera with a verbal response. Hera shrieked and spat in anger.

"Then I guess there's no point in pleasantries," Hera roared and crouched, leaping up in the air. Hecate did the same, both of the goddesses kicking off the ground in a fury of power. They went soaring towards one another, nearly obscured in clouds of pink and red magic, rotting flowers falling from Hera as snakes littered the ground underneath Hecate.

The goddesses crashed into one another in midair, causing a crash like a thunderclap to shake the very foundations of hell. The sky above them went dark, as if a storm were rolling in, and even lightning began flashing amongst them. Aeëtes could only see the goddesses now, illuminated by their own power, as they went falling to the earth amidst a storming sky. Waves of power rolled off them like shockwaves, and Aeëtes found himself sliding down to the ground and gripping the boulder to not get blown away.

Hera and Hecate were tangled together as they fell, Hecate with her hands wrapped tightly around Hera's throat. Hera clawed for purchase, streaking her nails across the crone's face, but nothing broke Hecate's concentration. She was murmuring, beginning to wind together a spell that Hera could feel, the trickles of Hecate's magic feeling like spiderwebs on her skin.

Before she could try to retaliate, they crashed into the ground. The goddesses jumped to their feet and climbed out of the pit that their impact had made, smoke now rising up from all around them. The atmosphere was responding to the threat of the gods, and it was throwing the entire Underworld into a storm. Hecate stood with her arms held out, her lips ever moving, and Hera began to shriek. The spell felt like it was crawling all over her arms and legs, and then it began to tighten. It was a binding spell, one that would keep Hera bound to the land that she was on.

"You're going to have to try harder than that!" she yelled at Hecate, reaching down and pulling the magic off of her like she was pulling weeds off her skirt. Hecate felt a sharp sting at a spell broken, and both of the goddesses were launching themselves at one another.

Aeëtes was transfixed, gripping the stone tightly and finding himself desperately thinking of a way to help. A calm voice appeared next to him, causing him to fall over in surprise.

"Hecate has to be careful." Aeëtes looked up to see Thanatos, now perched on the boulder next to him. His dark hair was nearly covering his eyes, and his armor gleamed in the dark light of the storm.

"What does that mean?" Aeëtes urged him, standing up and staring at the god. "What do you mean she has to be careful?"

Thanatos turned to look at Aeëtes, studying him. "You don't know much about witchcraft, do you?"

"I missed that subject when I was younger," Aeëtes deadpanned, flinching when there was another explosion and a wave of power that poured out from the battle behind him.

"Witchcraft is powerful," Thanatos warned him. "There has to be some sort of balancing act in the universe to keep it from running wild. Whatever you send out comes back to you." He waited until Aeëtes processed that information, realization dawning on him. There was another shriek, and Aeëtes couldn't bear to look to see who it had come from.

"Hecate can only do so much because if she ends Hera outright…"

"She's eventually doomed herself," Thanatos finished for him, both of them turning to look at the brawl. The goddesses were entangled, and Aeëtes was pained to see that Hecate was the one who was beginning to look tired.

"What do we do?" Aeëtes hissed as he turned back to Thanatos with rage in his eyes. "Why are you here?"

Thanatos shrugged, looking utterly unbothered. "*Someone* here is on my list. I don't know who."

"You don't *know?*" Aeëtes suppressed the desire to punch him in the jaw. "How do you not know?" Thanatos had a dazed look on his face, as if he were looking at something none of them could see.

"It's changing too quickly. Every other second, I'm here for Hera, or Hecate, or...you." He turned to look at Aeëtes with cold, blue eyes. Then something changed in the air around them. It happened quickly, like a flash of lightning, and the atmosphere dropped twenty degrees. Aeëtes almost screamed as all the color drained from his vision, the entire world had gone black and white. A small, serpentine smile appeared on Thanatos's face, his pupils dilating. His countenance flickered and Aeëtes felt a chill go down his spine as he looked at the God of death, who seemed to be coming alive.

"Never fear, Aeëtes." His voice sounded like oil, "When will you remember that witchcraft is not the only power that Hecate possesses?" Aeëtes tumbled back from the boulder and fell backwards, his eyes going wide as he stared on in shock. Thanatos stood up, stretching until he stood over ten feet tall. His body began to emanate a blue light, his eyes going entirely black. He licked his lips, and Aeëtes could see that his teeth had grown out into fangs. A wicked looking blade appeared at his waist, which Aeëtes knew hadn't been there before.

Thanatos often got a bad reputation as the God of Death. He was kind and gentle, appearing as rest, peace, and eternal sleep. This was *not* that god. This was the God of death as retribution, vengeance, and finality. Thanatos looked positively hungry as he stared at the goddesses, who were entrenched with each other once again, their clothes ripped and bleeding ichor from various scratches on their skin. They seemed to be catching their breath, a few feet apart from one another, finding a small reprieve.

Aeëtes watched on and Hecate began to change. She also started to expand, standing taller and taller as her eyes rolled back into her head, and the faces of the maiden and the crone vanished. Every bone in her body emerged through her skin, like breaking the surface of water, settling there. It happened slowly, first her fingers, then her arms and legs, until the bones fortified, and Hecate was wearing armor made of her own skeleton.

Her hair turned white, and her cheekbones became more pronounced, her brow changing until Aeëtes realized that she was wearing a death mask of her own face. The triple moon circlet that she wore around her forehead twisted, morphing into finger bones that were so translucent, they looked like they were made of moonlight. They stood straight up towards the sky, making a crown of death and stardust. Hecate let her head fall back and she let out a massive wail, a deep, baritone sound that shook the Underworld. The incantations and snakes that were inked on her skin turned black, falling off her like dust. A cloud of ashes encompassed her, cold fire burning in her eyes. She began to weep, and when each tear hit the earth beneath her, a shade sprung up in its place.

Aeëtes couldn't pull his eyes off her, not even to see what Hera or Thanatos were doing. Hecate's feet lifted off the ground until she was writhing in midair. Cold winds began blowing over the fields around them, shades and ghosts appearing beneath her as she continued to weep. In that moment, she was nothing—she was not alive, not dead; she was balanced somewhere on the precipice between total destruction and rebirth. Aeëtes watched on as the souls of the dead began amassing around her, none of them moving, all of them waiting for the command of one creature—the necromancer.

The goddess who could speak with the dead.

Hecate's body twisted. She was standing up, gently lowering herself down until her feet touched the ground. Her clothes had vanished, but her skin was obscured with rows and rows of black script. The words kept moving and changing so quickly that Aeëtes didn't know what they were...until somehow, he knew. They were the names of the dead. Every one. Every name since the dawn of time, inked onto her skin as if waiting to be chosen and called upon.

Hecate was staring at Hera, who Aeëtes now realized was screaming. She had fallen to her knees and was crawling away from Hecate as best as she could, pulling herself along the ground. Hecate took one step towards Hera, and she threw her hands up in fear, covering her eyes.

"Ah, there it is." Thanatos made a tsk sound, getting Aeëtes's attention. His eyes gleamed as he looked down at Aeëtes, winking. "I was so hoping that this would be how I'd get to spend my day."

Aeëtes was dumbfounded. Thanatos leaned down, and Aeëtes felt himself shrinking back subconsciously.

"Do you want to know what happened to the shade that broke Hecate's heart after Hades gave me permission?" Thanatos was grinning maniacally, but his voice was cool as metal. Aeëtes found himself nodding, even though he wasn't entirely sure that he wanted to know.

"I ate it," Thanatos whispered, but then a glimpse of his previous demeanor showed through. "Whoever breaks the necromancer's heart," he warned Aeëtes again, "surely gets eaten by the God of death."

Aeëtes felt a chill shake his whole body; there was no ending more finite. Everyone met Thanatos once. To meet him twice, was to die again and never return. Aeëtes could only nod, and then Thanatos disappeared in a cloud of black smoke. He watched on as those black clouds raced over the fields towards Hera and Hecate, suddenly enveloping Hera's body entirely. There was another massive clap of thunder as light-ning struck the field. The earth shook as the storm raged, the ghosts of a thousand souls still standing around them, waiting for their command.

The smoke was gone—along with any trace of Hera and Thanatos. Aeëtes stood on shaky legs, his eyes solely focused on Hecate. Slowly, she turned to look at him. He knew that she could see him, even from a distance, and he met her gaze head-on.

He didn't recognize the goddess in front of him, but he didn't care. He knew it was Hecate, and that was enough.

Aeëtes took one step towards her, but for the second time that day, everything went black.

❧ 34 ❧

When Aeëtes blinked his eyes open, the first thing he noticed was that the air didn't smell like rotting flowers anymore. The second thing that he noticed was the soft, soothing sensations of fingers running through his hair. He was warm, so, so *warm*, and he leaned into the touch. After everything that he had witnessed, how he had felt the temperature drop around him and the chills that had taken over his body, nothing felt better.

If this is death, I don't care if I ever breathe again. Aeëtes's vision slowly came into focus, and he realized he was still in the fields, closer to the riverbank now. He was unmistakably in Hecate's lap, and those were her fingers moving across his scalp, in the sweetest touch that he had ever known. His mind short-circuited for a second, and everything came rushing back to him.

"Hecate!" He tried to sit up, but she placed a hand on his shoulder. Aeëtes twisted in her lap until he could look up at her face, seeing that she had returned to her mortal body. His brow furrowed in concern. There was something in her eyes that he didn't understand. She seemed almost…resigned, sad.

"What happened?" Aeëtes was confused, but she kept

stroking him like she never wanted to let go. Hecate was sitting up straight, one hand running over his hair and down his jaw, the other holding onto a small, earthen clay cup. Her hair was the same auburn shade that he had grown accustomed to, a few braids running through it. His eyes ran over her as he tried to evaluate her for any injury, but he saw nothing, even her peplos was tied neatly.

"Everything's fine," she said with a small smile that didn't reach her eyes. Aeëtes was immediately skeptical of it. He didn't like it. Hecate had never lied to him. She had struggled to be vulnerable with him, but she had never lied to him—and this wasn't her. Something was terribly wrong.

"I know you haven't spent a lot of time in the mortal world, but are you aware that that is what humans say when everything is absolutely *not* fine?"

Hecate chuckled, but it still managed to be a sad sound, and Aeëtes watched a tear fall down her cheek.

"What happened—" He tried to sit up, but Hecate kept him in her lap, her immortal strength overpowering him. He wasn't complaining, but he stared at her face, trying to understand what was wrong.

"Please tell me," he tried again, his voice growing a little more frantic. "Whatever it is, I promise, we can figure it out."

Hecate nodded, and it briefly eased the tension in Aeëtes's chest. She tilted his head up and brought the cup closer to him.

"Have some water, and then we can talk about it." Hecate's tone was encouraging as she brought it closer to his lips, and Aeëtes leaned forward, ready to accept it. It seemed a normal enough request until a million things came rushing back to him just as he felt the cool clay against his skin. His hand flew up and grabbed Hecate's wrists, pulling it away from his face. She was stunned by the sudden movement, allowing Aeëtes to sit up and move out of her lap. He stared at her, his eyes going wide and feeling his body begin to tense. Aeëtes was still holding onto her wrist, both of them staring at the incriminating cup in Hecate's hand.

"Hecate..." Aeëtes's voice was gravelly. "Tell me that's not water from Lethe."

She looked away from him, her tears falling freely now as she couldn't meet his eyes. Aeëtes dropped her wrist and stood up, the cup falling to the ground and spilling at his feet. He forced himself to breathe, feeling betrayal and heartbreak all wrapped up in one sickening sensation. Aeëtes started to pace, unable to keep his hands still, flexing them into fists and releasing repeatedly.

After everything that we've been through, after finally admitting that she loved me... How could she do this?

He looked over at Hecate and was ready to demand answers, and he saw her on the ground. She had remained there, with her knees pulled up to her chest, sobbing softly. No matter how angry he was, it was a sight that he couldn't get over, and he got on his knees before her again.

"Please," he grabbed her hands, "Please, why would you do this, Hecate? Just tell me. Talk to me." Aeëtes gave her hands a soft squeeze, his own eyes wet, and his tone was full of longing. "I don't care what's happened. Is this about Hera? I'll fight the rest of the gods with you, my little witch. I don't care!"

Hecate lifted her head from her knees, staring at him as she shook her head back and forth. "You need to forget me, Aeëtes. You need to forget *this*. You need to forget."

"Never!" Aeëtes growled at her. It was the harshest tone that he had ever taken with her, and she shivered. "How could you ask that of me?" Hecate stood to her feet and grabbed Aeëtes's chiton, her face twisting in one of shame and anger, and she pulled him a few feet to the river's shore. She tossed him towards the water, the movement surprising Aeëtes enough that he stumbled and fell into its shallows. He sat there for a minute on his hands and knees in the shallow water, listening as Hecate buried her head in her hands and sobbed.

"Drink it!" she snapped. "Forget me, forget this, forget that it ever happened!"

Aeëtes pushed up to his knees and slapped at the water's surface, splashing both of them. He stood up and looked at Hecate, shaking his head as he gritted his teeth.

"Do you know what you would condemn me to if I drank?" His tone was deadly quiet. Hecate had never heard him speak this way. She shook her head, sniffling with the tears that she was trying to contain from him. He had seen her cry too often.

"I would forget your face," Aeëtes growled at her. "I would forget your name and my own. I wouldn't know you if you called out to me in the street and my own memories would cease to exist. But I would never forget *you*." Hecate sucked in a sharp gasp, and Aeëtes stepped closer to her. "I would spend the rest of my days as a ghost of a man, as a shade, with an ache in my heart that would never be filled. They would tell stories of the man who ate without fulfilling his hunger and drank but always felt thirst. I would go mad with longing for you, not knowing who you were, and you would condemn me to a life of madness and suffering that no immortal man could fathom!" Aeëtes's hand was ripping through his hair as he tore at his own clothes. "I would forget your face but not even the waters of Lethe would make me forget how I feel about you, Hecate! I would search forever for you, not knowing what I was looking for." He shouted at her, his breath ragged. His shoulders shook as his face changed from rage to a cruel laugh, bewildered. "You would condemn me to this?"

Hecate couldn't breathe. She stared at him, trying to process everything that he was offering. The strength of his love and the passion in his admission—she had never expected it from anyone, not even when he said he loved her. Aeëtes laughed, a crazed, sardonic sound, and shrugged.

"Then I'll drink." He turned around and fell to his knees in the water, preparing to dip his head beneath the surface and surrender himself to madness. As soon as he bent down,

Hecate crashed into his side, knocking them both onto the shore.

"No!" she screamed at him. Aeëtes was lying on the sand with his legs in the water, and Hecate found herself scrambling to get on top of him. Their wet clothes were weighing them down, a tangle of soaking cotton and limbs. She managed to straddle his waist, cupping his face and shaking her head back and forth as she tried to choke out the words. Aeëtes was panting, trying to catch his breath, but he put a hand on her hip to steady her.

"Why?" he almost whimpered.

Hecate closed her eyes and wiped at them, her face full of shame. "You saw me." Her voice was weak. "You saw me. I couldn't bear to see the look of disgust in your eyes when you remembered."

"What?" Aeëtes sat up a little bit more until they were face to face, sitting on the banks of Lethe. "You thought I would be disgusted when I saw you as...the necromancer?" He filled in the gaps. Hecate nodded.

"Only Thanatos can look upon me when I'm like that. Not even Nyx has seen it. It serves its purpose, but it is a heavy weight to bear."

"You were magnificent!" Aeëtes nearly shouted it, looking stunned, as though he was shocked that anyone could see her like that and not think the same thing. "It was glorious, terrifying, and stunning, my love."

Hecate hiccupped and fought to keep another sob from clawing free from her chest. She had never, ever known this kind of acceptance in her life, and she felt like her body might rip in half to let her spirit out in joy. Aeëtes kissed her softly and continued. "If the other gods knew what it meant..." Aeëtes eyes got wider when he thought about the implications, but Hecate only shrugged.

"They know. They haven't seen it, but they know. It's similar to Nyx. She could gobble up the world tomorrow, but she doesn't."

"Like how you could command an army of every person, immortal, and monster that has ever lived and died, but you don't?" Aeëtes poked her cheek gently in jest, and a small smile cracked through Hecate's distraught features.

"Yes, like that. We don't do it because..."

"Because you care." Aeëtes kissed her forehead. "You keep the balance, and you don't want the world to end." Hecate nodded. "Did you kill Hera?" Aeëtes asked her gently, needing to know. Hecate said nothing, and that was enough of a confirmation for Aeëtes. They would figure all of that out later.

"At least we know that killing Hera didn't mean her curse would kill me." Aeëtes paused for a second, his thumb making soothing circles on Hecate's thigh. "Do you think I am still cursed?"

"You are," Hecate sighed, looking tired. "I can sense it on you and Circe's magic. We'll have to see, once we get you out of the Underworld, how the curse reacts. Magic works a little bit different down here."

Aeëtes was quiet for a moment, and he looked up at Hecate. "Tell me we're done with this. Please tell me that you're done with the doubts and the evasions. If you don't want to be with me, then I'll accept that, but if you love me...love me, Hecate." His tone was pleading, and his hands tightened their grip on her ever so slightly. Hecate's eyes found his as she stared at him, overcome with her own emotions.

She closed the gap between them and kissed him, her hands tangling up in his hair. Aeëtes left his eyes fall shut as he groaned into her mouth, Hecate taking the opportunity to deepen the embrace between them. Her hand moved and tore at the fastening at his shoulder, letting his chiton fall until he was bare-chested underneath her. She ran her hands across his chest, feeling his strong body beneath hers, and felt intoxicated after a few simple touches. Everything in her body was singing for him now, wanting to drive away the last of their separation with touches.

Hecate undulated her hips on top of Aeëtes, feeling his growing hardness beneath her. It sent a fresh wave of arousal through her, the ache between her legs intensifying.

"Oh gods," Aeëtes moaned, his head falling back as his hands gripped her thighs. "You do that too much, and this is going to be over before it's started."

Hecate giggled, a breathless sound, and shook her head as she rocked her hips against him.

"You love me too much to let that happen." Her tone was full of mischief now, and Aeëtes opened his eyes, arching a brow at her.

"Is that so?"

"Mmhmm," Hecate replied smugly, working herself up as she kept up her pacing, driving Aeëtes insane with the pressure and friction of her hips against him. His hand reached up and pulled her peplos down, exposing her breasts to him. Aeëtes leaned forward and sucked one into his mouth, pressing a sharp bite to her nipple that made Hecate gasp. He lapped his tongue over it to soothe the sting, and Hecate felt her eyes nearly roll back into her head at the sensation. He knew how to mix the right amount of pain with her pleasure, and it made her body go wild. She was nearly working herself into a frenzy by practically dry-humping him, and she yelped as his free hand slid underneath the bunched-up fabric at her waist.

Hecate may have been straddling Aeëtes, but he was working her like a toy. That mouth was alternating between her breasts, one hand around her waist, and the other slowly exploring her sex. His fingers ran through her wetness, and he made a guttural noise, pulling his mouth off of her only long enough to curse. His thumb found her clit and started making slow, intense circles, adding the right amount of pressure every time he would bite her playfully. It didn't take long until she was putty in his hands, the water still lapping up around their legs, adding to the frenzy of the moment. Hecate knew that it would affect them if they drank it, but there was something a little terrifying and utterly debauched about fucking in the shallows of Lethe. And she *loved* it.

"Please," Hecate was panting, "Aeëtes, I need to feel you inside of me." She clawed at his shoulders for purchase. He shook his head, a wicked grin coming over his face.

"No." His tone was playful. "Not yet, little witch. You've put me through my paces to get here, haven't you?" Hecate flushed even further, her cheeks turning pink, but she said nothing while she squirmed. "Haven't you?" Aeëtes asked again, rubbing faster circles around her clit. Hecate bit her tongue, refusing to answer him, even though she felt her whole body aching to answer. Aeëtes only chuckled, a dark and wicked sound that added to her arousal. He kept his merciless pace and knew that she was close.

"Answer me when you come, Hecate," he demanded, his tone leaving no room for argument. "Scream it out so the whole Underworld can hear you, and then I'll fuck you." Hecate made a sharp whimpering sound as she felt herself getting even closer to the edge. "But I'll be nice and change the question." He bit her breast again and made her body twitch. "Do you love me, Hecate?" He pressed against her clit and didn't stop rubbing the same, wicked circles, never letting up the pressure until Hecate's entire body spasmed, and he felt her release flood over his fingers.

Her back bent nearly in half as she screamed, nothing but white-hot pleasure turning her blood into fire. "Y-Yes!" she finally managed to gasp the word out as her thighs shook around Aeëtes for what felt like a blissful eternity. He stroked her gently as she came down, his expression full of a devilish and satisfied smirk. "Please," Hecate gasped, her body shining with sweat, "Please, Aeëtes…"

He knew what she was asking for, and he couldn't hold back a moment longer. Their clothes were bunched around

their waists, and he ripped hers off, flipping Hecate on her
back. She landed in the wet sand, the impact somehow only
magnifying the intensity of her desire. In a second, Aeëtes was
on top of her, completely blocking out her senses with nothing
but sweat and arousal. She let out a wanton moan at the sensation, being utterly caged in between his arms and under his
body. Aeëtes hand fumbled around his waist as he finally
managed to tear the rest of his chiton off, grabbing a hold of
Hecate's leg and wrapping it around his waist.

She felt him at her entrance and opened her mouth to
demand that he move. "Aeët— *ahh!*"

Hecate was cut off as he drove inside of her with one movement, and Aeëtes let out an animalistic moan at the feeling. She
was gripping him like a vice, soft and hot, her previous release
still coating her thighs. He felt the water licking at their feet
and the entire picture was almost wrong; he felt mad but one
look at Hecate's blissed out face, and he realized that he didn't
care.

He pulled out, and Hecate made a whimper at the loss
before Aeëtes shifted his hips and began fucking her into the
ground. Hecate was overwhelmed as every thought was simply
pushed from her head. All she could sense was the thick burn
of Aeëtes, stretching her in such a delicious burn, she thought
that she would never get enough of it. Her body was cushioned
by the soft earth, naked against the sand—which she knew she
would regret later—but in that moment, it all seemed to add to
her stimulation, pushing her higher and higher.

She didn't know how long they stayed like that, Aeëtes
rolling his hips into her like he would never stop. She didn't
want him to. Suddenly, Aeëtes mouth was at her ear, coaxing
her in a gentle tone that didn't fit the merciless way he fucked
her. The duality made her body shake.

"Come for me, Hecate," he whispered, the words feeling
like they were carved in her skin. "Come for me, nice and loud.
I want the whole world to know how I make your body sing.

How much I love you." It sent Hecate over the edge, and her whole body shook in ways that she didn't know it could. He talked her through her orgasm, which seemed never-ending, and he didn't stop thrusting his hips. "So good, little witch. That's it. You sound utterly debauched," he bit her earlobe. "The dignified, stoic Hecate…" Aeëtes made a playful tsk sound. "Do you think everyone knows how pretty you scream for me now?"

She clenched around him, and it sent Aeëtes over the edge, spilling into her for what felt like an eternity. When his strength finally gave out, he landed on the sand next to Hecate. Both of them barely had the strength to open their eyes, panting against the sand. It was a few moments before Aeëtes managed to reach over and pull Hecate closer.

"Do you think we should get out of here and get dressed?" His voice was wrecked when he said it, barely above a whisper. Hecate managed a small laugh and shook her head.

"I don't think anyone who heard that is going to come bother us now."

That was enough of an answer for Aeëtes, so they slept. Curled up on the banks of the river of oblivion, letting it wash away their sweat and their fears as an act of defiance.

A eëtes and Hecate eventually pulled themselves from the banks of Lethe, Hecate whisking them away to her Underworld home. She found herself nervous to show it to Aeëtes; she had never brought a lover there before, and she knew that once she had memories of him in this space, it would never entirely be just hers ever again.

When Aeëtes walked through the courtyard and into the kitchen, his face lit up so brightly that Hecate found the rest of her nerves falling away. He listened with rapt attention as she gave him a tour through the space, showing him the fireplace, rows and rows of jars stuffed with herbs, and even her dogs. At least, the two dogs in her home that weren't made of magic. It had been a few weeks since she had been back, and there were a litany of unanswered prayers and requests scrawled all over the magical hearth. Aeëtes watched as she looked at it nervously, and he simply kissed her forehead and sat down at her kitchen table, content to watch her work.

Aeëtes watched in utter fascination as Hecate moved through her kitchen with grace, seeing what she looked like at work in the Underworld for the first time. Hecate, on the other hand, was alive with the knowledge that having Aeëtes in her home, having a partner in her life, didn't get in her way. He added to it, with his warm presence and soft smiles in the corner.

A few hours later, they were nestled together in the kitchen, sharing a simple meal when the fire in Hecate's hearth flared up. The light from the window flickered, as if it were alternating between light and day. Aeëtes looked at Hecate, his nerves amping up, but she only smiled.

"That's Nyx, beloved," she crooned, standing up to meet her friend. Aeëtes nearly tripped over himself to do the same, finding himself a little nervous to meet the primordial. Even on good terms. There was a rush of black smoke through the kitchen that left stardust on the walls in its wake, and then appearing out of it, was the goddess herself. Aeëtes's eyes got wide as Hecate rushed over and hugged her friend tightly, the gesture seeming a little out of place for such an ancient being. Nyx stood a little taller than Hecate, with long, gleaming black hair the color of midnight. Her peplos was black, a strong contrast to Hecate's typical shades of red, and she had piercing eyes that seemed to look right through him.

"Let me see him then," Nyx announced, gently pushing Hecate to the side as she stalked towards Aeëtes. He swallowed thickly, bowing his head out of deference as he felt Nyx's eyes roam over him in evaluation. She was silent for a second, the bottom half of her not having materialized into a mortal body, the smoke intertwining with Aeëtes's legs. Nyx's placed a pale finger under Aeëtes's chin and made him look up at her, staring directly into his eyes. He couldn't help it and gasped, seeing the multitudes of the nighttime skies in her eyes. It was glorious, but he found himself seeking out for the familiar cinnamon and rosemary scent of Hecate's power. Nyx seemed to sense this, and she smiled.

"I like him." She grinned, and Aeëtes nearly collapsed back onto the kitchen bench in relief. Nyx turned to Hecate, and her smile spread wider. "He certainly is a bit opposite of you, though."

"It works," Hecate blushed and began busying herself with something in the kitchen to keep her hands occupied. "Now, I'm sure you're here to talk about Hera."

"I can't be here simply to pass judgement on the first man you've fucked more than once in a century?" The casual way that Nyx said it made Aeëtes want to laugh, but he stamped it down and turned his focus to Hecate's dogs.

Hecate rolled her eyes. "You've done that now." She stopped, biting her lip, showing a rare sign of nerves. "Have I caused you a lot of trouble?"

Neither Aeëtes nor Hecate had really spoken about the fact that she had killed Hera.

The queen of the gods.

She didn't exactly fill out that title in the way that one would think, but she was still technically the queen. Nyx dropped down fully into a human form and sat down at the table, still facing Hecate.

"I've just come from Olympus." Her tone was impossible to discern. "And it wasn't the most pleasant of conversations." She paused there, and Aeëtes felt like he was going to burst with anticipation.

"And?" he nearly shrieked, turning to look at Nyx. He immediately clapped a hand over his mouth, having the decency to look sheepish after trying to command a primordial. Nyx furrowed her brow as she stared at him for a second, causing his blood to turn cold with fear, before she burst out into laughter.

"He'll be fine amongst the gods." Nyx waved her hand as if dismissing any other notion, "He's just precocious enough."

Hecate smiled, but also urged her friend to go on. "What about Hera?"

"Well, I'm sure that no one is surprised to learn that Zeus wasn't all that upset." This time, Aeëtes bit his lip to keep from laughing. "Most of the gods weren't really sad about it, actually. The only concern is…"

"Perception." Hecate rolled her eyes, and Nyx nodded. Even after the titan wars, they had struck a deal that the pantheon would go on ruling Greece—effectively making Nyx and Erebus behind-the-scenes puppet masters since the gods only cared about the mortals' perceptions to thrive off their worship.

"Exactly. They're worried that this will cause a lot of undue attention to be focused on you."

"Undue?" Aeëtes's voice was angry. "How dare they! She's worthier of worship than any of those selfish…"

"I know," Nyx said softly, her face amused as she watched how quickly Aeëtes sprung to Hecate's defense. "Which is why there will be no retribution towards Hecate. Hera broke the law first by cursing an immortal, a son of Helios. Anything that came after that, they're willing to decree was fair game. But they have decided to keep the news of Hera's demise from the mortal realm."

Hecate only rolled her eyes at that. "Like how Zeus defeated Kronos?"

Nyx chuckled darkly. "Exactly like that—"

There was a large crash that came from the courtyard, which made Aeëtes startle but only got groans from Nyx and Hecate. A few seconds later, a golden shag of curls poked its head through the door, and Hermes surveyed the scene with a smile.

"Your deviousness!" he crowed in Hecate's direction before giving Nyx a solemn nod. "Nyx."

Aeëtes laughed at the drastic difference in which he greeted each goddess. Hermes set his sights on Aeëtes and stepped entirely into the kitchen.

"Aeëtes!" He threw his arms out and leaned over, wrapping up Aeëtes in a tight hug and rocking him back and forth comically. "You made it! Welcome to Hecate's kitchen. Everyone's welcome."

"They are not!" Hecate snapped from the kitchen, holding out a sprig of fennel like it was a weapon. Hermes giggled and sat down next to Aeëtes.

"She's lying. She loves it when we all show up here, especially at all hours and unannounced."

Aeëtes shook his head in joyful disbelief, looking up at Hecate, who was staring at him with a murderous glare in her eyes. Nyx rolled her eyes and started to dissipate, giving Hecate a warm smile.

"Good to see you doing so well, darling. This kitchen is getting a little bit too full for me now." She rolled her eyes at Hermes, who only quaked slightly, and disappeared from the kitchen.

"Does she always do that?" Aeëtes looked in surprise at where Nyx had been standing. Hecate and Hermes both nodded, neither of them seeming bothered by it. Even Hecate's dogs didn't blink. Aeëtes took a deep breath and settled back down where he was sitting, realizing that it was going to take him a while to get used to being around immortals.

"I had to follow Nyx here from Olympus. The gossip is just too good." Hermes grinned, kicking his feet up on the table. "Have you found a way to break his curse yet?" Hermes made a big show of sniffing Aeëtes. "He still smells like Hera."

Hecate's face wrinkled up in disgust. "I know. And no, I haven't. I'm a little worried to see what happens to that curse when we go back to the mortal world."

"It might tear him into pieces," Hermes said nonchalantly, even though they both could sense the joke in his voice. "You also could slip through the realms and then realize you're stuck as a sheep forever."

Aeëtes bristled nervously. "Well. It was a ram, at least."

Hermes ruffled his hair. "Of course it was." Hermes looked

up to Hecate. "You both don't want to just stay in the Under-world? Provided that you could overlook that stench."

Aeëtes was in constant wonderment at Hermes's attitude, but he couldn't avoid smiling every time he said something foolish. Hecate seemed to bristle at the thought.

"No." She stepped out from behind the kitchen counter, looking at Aeëtes. "That wouldn't be fair to him or to me, in the end. Besides," her smile was warm, "I know that he wants to check in with his parents in Colchis."

"Ah, yes," Hermes sighed dramatically, giving a fake yawn and wrapping his hand around Aeëtes's shoulder when he did. Aeëtes looked confused, but Hecate just gave him a little nod, mouthing *'He does this.'*

"Does your mother approve of your woman, Aeëtes?" Hermes looked at him, speaking with mock sincerity. Hecate sucked in a sharp breath, her hands flying up to her face.

"Hermes." Hecate sounded shocked. "You're brilliant."

"Oh, I know," he smirked, "but why this time?"

"His mother," Hecate said, but slower this time. "His mother!" Both Hermes and Aeëtes looked at her in confusion. Hecate ran over and grabbed hold of Aeëtes's face, kissing him soundly. Hermes made a catcalling sound and applauded, Hecate grinning wildly when she stepped back.

"Your *mother*, Aeëtes," Hecate was ecstatic. "I was worried that the spell to break Hera's curse wouldn't work without Clymene. It'll work with your adoptive mother."

Aeëtes's eyes got wide as he stared at her, his mouth slowly splitting into a wide grin.

"The gods," he swore. "I think you're right."

"Why didn't I think of this before?" Hecate shook her head as she looked around the room. "I guess I hadn't seen the two of you together, I didn't understand that you were close. Blood ties don't matter. Of course. She's your mother. She raised you, and she loves you. It'll work."

"Once again, I'm glad to see that I am truly the answer to

everyone's problems." Hermes smiled, standing up from the
table and moving towards the door. "Don't forget what I said,
Hecate, if you need a third—"

"We'll ask who you recommend!" Aeëtes hollered in
response, making Hecate snort with laughter and an outraged
Hermes squawk as he disappeared on the wind.

✛ ✛ ✛

HECATE AND AEËTES made it back to Colchis, happy to find
that there had been no lasting damage to the palace. Aeëtes
learned that they had been gone a week and that time moved a
little bit differently in the Underworld. The queen was more
than happy to assist Hecate, who with a finger prick of blood
and some dirt from the palace grounds, was easily able to
reverse Hera's spell. Aeëtes had been picked up on the wind
with a burst of bright, golden light—for a moment, Hecate was
worried that he had been turned into a ram again. Luckily, he
landed on only two strong feet, with the Golden Fleece
wrapped around his waist.

The king was more than happy to keep it in Colchis
although they were sure that the tale would end up on the
wind soon enough. Hecate even had the king formally break
Faidra and Aeëtes's engagement, and Faidra made it back to
Athens and straight into the arms of her beloved.

The tension between the king and Aeëtes came to a head
over dinner one evening as he continued to argue that Aeëtes
should take over, even if just to protect the fleece from people
who would inevitably come to find it. To Hecate's surprise, he
had agreed—on one condition. His parents had to stay on as
regents for all the time he planned on spending in the Underworld. The portal to Asphodel that Hecate had opened up in

their battle with Hera had remained, making it easy enough for them to commute between the two places. Of course, Aeëtes couldn't be sure how much time passed when they were gone, and he often found himself a little… distracted, once they were alone. The king learned quickly not to demand too many answers about what they'd gotten up to when he complained they were gone for too long.

A few months later, Hecate and Aeëtes were on the banks of Lethe, which had become a rather macabre, romantic spot for the two of them.

"It's fitting for the necromancer," Aeëtes had grinned, pressing another kiss to Hecate's brow.

She snuggled into his side, her hand making small patterns on his chest. There was nothing between them anymore, and he was overjoyed each day to find her continuously growing ever comfortable with him. She managed to surprise him in the best of ways, pushing him when they needed it and knowing when they needed space. Sometimes, they still quarreled, although now they made up in ways that had become rather annoying to anyone within earshot.

They had seemingly overcome the insurmountable — ending with broken curses, one dead queen of the gods, and a new title for Aeëtes. He had gone from an immortal crown prince to an immortal king and consort to a goddess.

Hecate, one could wager, broke the greatest curse of all — the one that ages ago, she had placed around her own heart.

Aeëtes watched as she fell asleep next to him, neither of them willing to move just yet. No part of him yearned for his freedom anymore. In fact, he knew now that the best things in life sometimes happened when you were standing still.

I ended up with the greatest adventure of all.

EPILOGUE

Thanatos was spending a few, precious moments in the Underworld — the God of Death's services were always in demand and breaks were few and far between — when a sudden sense of drowsiness threatened to overtake him. He blinked rapidly, sitting up straighter on the throne he kept in his receiving hall. A throne he hardly ever sat on, in a home that hardly ever got used. He had protested its creation at the start.

"Why do I even need a residence, mother?" Thanatos rolled his eyes at Nyx, the Goddess of Night. He was one of the few creatures in existence who was able to do so and live. She scoffed in return.

"It sends a message and it's nice to have some place to come home to."

"Not when it's empty."

It had been a thousand years. The house was still empty. It was tucked into the mouth of a cave, next to the source of Lethe. Thanatos had never gotten around to decorating it, or letting Hecate do it, much to her chagrin. Although, the throne had been a nice touch. It was a gift from his twin brother, Hypnos, and while Thanatos had scoffed at its obvious macabre — he had come to appreciate the chair carved from bone. He ran his finger across a skull embedded in the arm, trying to will away the onset dreariness. Gods didn't get tired. The God of Death never got tired. That was a job for...

"Hypnos!" Thanatos barked, his deep voice echoing out through the spacious rafters. "Don't sneak up on me like that or I'll —"

"You'll do what? Kill me?" Hypnos's laughter mixed with the echoes of his brother's booming commands until they both faded away. White smoke poured down from the ceiling, spiraling towards the ground in a vortex. The smoke suddenly dissipated in a burst of poppies, and standing in the middle of the fray, was Hypnos.

"You know that killing isn't technically part of my job description. And do you *have* to show up like that every time? Are the flowers really necessary?" Thanatos groaned and leaned further back. He was sitting on the throne haphazardly, with his legs bent over one arm and his head over the other. He rubbed his brow as if he had a headache.

Hypnos only smiled, a soft, lazy grin, as one might expect. Even though they were twins, there were very few physical similarities between the brothers. Thanatos stood nearly a head taller than almost every other god in their mortal forms. Hypnos only came up to his brother's shoulder. Thanatos had black hair that was so dark, it was almost blue, like his eyes; Hypnos's hair was white and his eyes were a golden yellow. It fit them. The God of Death, tall and immovable, made for violence, and the God of Sleep, peaceful and almost sunny in his disposition, despite his work by moonlight.

"They're not just flowers," Hypnos hissed, "They're poppies. Don't be insulting." He took a few steps up the dais where Thanatos had been trying to enjoy a few moments of solitude.

"If you insist on showing up here in a cloud of flowers,

you're subjecting yourself to my mockery." Thanatos growled, his eyes still closed.

"Yes, yes, you're very cruel and full of quips," Hypnos poked his brother's cheek, "The world would implode if they ever learned how romantic you are." Thanatos's eyes flung open at the accusation, nearly snapping his teeth at Hypnos, who burst into laughter.

"Oh, defensive are we?" He took a few steps backward, putting his hands on his hips. "What did you do with the other throne?" He cocked his head to one side, letting out a yawn. "I gave you two."

"Is there a reason you're here?" Thanatos narrowed his eyes and sat up straighter, staring at Hypnos.

"I wanted to be the one to tell you." Hypnos looked nearly giddy, which was an impressive feat for him. He was more often prone to falling asleep in the middle of a conversation. If anything was holding his attention this devoutly... Thanatos groaned.

"Tell me what?" There was a beat of silence and Thanatos leveled his stare at Hypnos, who now looked like he was about to nod off where he stood. "Damn it, brother! We already have one Hermes, we don't need two." Thanatos couldn't help but chuckle slightly under his breath, knowing that it was hardly Hypnos's fault that he was the God of Sleep. Hypnos startled and shook his head rapidly to clear it, a sleepy smile crossing his face again.

"It seems like Mom and Dad have decided you need some help." Hypnos's joy was short-lived. Thanatos didn't say a word as he stood up slowly. A cold, sharp wind suddenly blew through the receiving hall, making Hypnos shiver.

"They think I need *help?*" Thanatos's eyes were now shining, a chilled, almost dead look to them. Even Hypnos quivered a little at the sight and he knew that he was probably the safest person in existence from Thanatos. Probably.

"Well, you know," Hypnos shrugged, taking another step

back, "You're hardly ever in the Underworld. Look at you now, trying to catch a break."

"I *was* trying to take a break," Thanatos hissed, stepping closer to his brother. "What do you mean 'they think I need some help'?"

Hypnos started to turn into poppies, staring with his feet, then his legs as white smoke filled the room.

"Tell me!" Thanatos barked at his dissipating brother. There was a sleepy little laugh in response, Hypnos's voice quiet and hypnotic as he floated away.

"You're getting a partner..." The words echoed in the hall, ringing out with Hypnos's singsong tone, and Thanatos clenched his fists. He felt a cold rush of anger go flooding through him, and it took all of his control to avoid his deity form. All of the flames went out in the room, coating Thanatos in darkness, as he tried to keep his rage contained at the threat of his brother's words.

There was not a chance in hell — and he knew the Underworld and all of its chances very well — that he would allow himself to be saddled with another god. Who would even *want* to work with him? Everyone feared the God of Death, he wasn't welcome in the mortal world or on Mt. Olympus. No one would understand the intricacies that the job required him... there wasn't a soul alive, or dead, that knew how terribly Thanatos's heart beat for the dying. For the wounded. For the sick. He cared more for the mortal world than any god or primordial in existence.

You couldn't care about your reputation when you were the God of the Dead, you had to ignore what *everyone* said about you. Thanatos never cared. He cared about the dying and the dead, and easing their transition into the cradle of the Underworld. Every immortal that he had ever met worried about their reputation, they used it like currency. Hardly a year ago, his own parents had been nearly torn apart on the issue of reputation. He'd heard rumors about how even Hecate

had worried about her relationship with her acolytes when she
had taken a consort.

*No, no, this will not do. Whoever they are, they won't last very long.
I'll see to it.* A cold, calculating smile spread across his face in
the blackness, as he sat back down in his throne.

Everyone falls to their knees in front of Death eventually.

ALSO BY MOLLY TULLIS

The Asphodel Series

Consort of Darkness

Don't miss the first story in the Asphodel series: the story of Nyx and Erebus.

———

The Romanov Oracle

A fantasy stand-alone based on the story of Anastasia Romanova.

ABOUT THE AUTHOR

Molly Tullis would have picked the Phantom of the Opera over Raoul and named her French bulldog Jean Valjean. She only believes in black clothing, red lipstick, and never turns down an iced coffee or tequila. She enjoys writing fantasy, romance, or any genre with an opportunity to insert a dark-haired, morally grey man. Her debut novel, *The Romanov Oracle*, was inspired by a love of history and a simultaneous desire to rewrite it with more magic.

When not identifying as an author, she identifies as a woman with bangs, finger tattoos, and a nose ring, who can tell you what planets are making you sad.

Her DMs are always open on Instagram and Patreon (@thebibliophileblonde), and you can get information on all upcoming projects at www.thebibliophileblonde.com.

Printed in Great Britain
by Amazon

82446573R00193